Praise for Victor McGlothin

"McGlothin weaves convincing historical elements into a fast-moving caper, and Baltimore Floyd is a delightful scoundrel."
—*Publishers Weekly* on *Ms. Etta's Fast House*

"A talented storyteller with a knack for telling a convincing story, McGlothin manages to weave an entertaining story that may indeed ring true to many readers . . . *What's a Woman to Do* will introduce readers to yet another new and refreshing voice in the world of contemporary African-American fiction."
—QBR

"4 Stars . . . Victor McGlothin has written a superb, true-to-life book. With a masterfully created plot, it explores the turbulent lives of three courageous women. This book offers a gripping, emotional glimpse into the dark world of the unknown."
—*Romantic Times* on *What's a Woman to Do*

"A fast-paced, soulful, dramatic story."
—*The Sunday Oklahoman* on *What's a Woman to Do*

"The pacing of the story and the storyline itself ought to keep the reader interested until the last page is turned since there's plenty of drama and secrets to keep you wondering and guessing until the end. Victor McGlothin has told a story that is sure to satisfy fans of his first novel, AUTUMN LEAVES, as well as new readers."
—Book-remarks.com

"McGlothin's tale is sophisticated and sexy, with the plotting and pacing of first-rate noir."
—*Publishers Weekly* on *Borrow Trouble*

"*Ms. Etta's Fast House* is a captivating and enjoyable read that takes you on a unique journey into the past."
—Urban-Reviews.net

"An absolute page-turner . . . intriguing and thought-provoking."
—Kimberla Lawson Roby, *New York Times* bestselling author on *Autumn Leaves*

Also by Victor McGlothin

Sleep Don't Come Easy

Ms. Etta's Fast House

Borrow Trouble (with Mary Monroe)

Sinful

DOWN ON MY KNEES

VICTOR McGLOTHIN

KENSINGTON PUBLISHING CORP.
http://www.kensingtonbooks.com

DAFINA BOOKS are published by

Kensington Publishing Corp.
850 Third Avenue
New York, NY 10022

All Kensington Titles, Imprints, and Distributed Lines are available at special quantity discounts for bulk purchases for sales promotions, premiums, fund-raising, and educational or institutional use. Special book excerpts or customized printings can also be created to fit specific needs. For details, write or phone the office of the Kensington special sales manager: Kensington Publishing Corp., 850 Third Avenue, New York, NY 10022, attn: Special Sales Department, Phone: 1-800-221-2647.

ISBN-13: 978-0-7582-1347-1
ISBN-10: 0-7582-1347-6

First trade paperback printing: May 2006
First mass market printing: December 2008

10 9 8 7 6 5 4 3 2 1

Printed in the United States of America

ACKNOWLEDGMENTS

To God, I am thankful for all that You have blessed me with.

Terre—my lovely wife, thank you for being a witness to my journey and making it all worthwhile.

Sara Camilli—my agent, for recognizing the possibilities and revealing them to me.

Karen Thomas—my editor, for always demanding my best and then some. You'll never know just how much I owe you.

Three writers who've opened the doors and welcomed me in: Kim Lawson Roby, you've been there since before day one. Where would I be without you? Victoria Christopher Murray, your kindness and generosity is always abundantly clear. Jacqueline Thomas, you simply *get it* and we are the better for it.

A special thanks to the many book clubs and reading groups who've hosted me in the past, along with the fans, who consistently support me, time after time. You all make my literary world go 'round every single day of the year.

God. It's me again—Grace. I sure hope you're listening because I really need You to hear me tonight. I know that You're well versed on my shortcomings concerning sins of the flesh, so I'll get right to it. Lately, my desires have gotten the best of me. This celibacy thing we've talked about isn't working out quite like I'd hoped. It seems that the harder I try to do right, the more I want to do wrong. Not that it's an excuse, it's just that I get so lonely sometimes. I've even fooled myself into thinking that sharing a man's warm embrace could somehow satisfy those urges, but it's never enough. Eventually, I find myself wanting more and more, until, well, You know the rest. I guess what I'm praying for is some extra consideration this evening because that old feeling has me wanting to do the kinds of things I promised I wouldn't. You know my weakness, so I'm asking for the strength to make it through the night. Thank You, God, for hearing me out. In Jesus' name. Amen.

1

Flextime with Tyson

Grace Hilliard sauntered into the lobby of the Hotel Carlyle just as she had done once a month for the past year. Her canary yellow skirt swayed in step with her confident strut. An impish grin danced on her full lips when the doorman stopped dead in his tracks to inventory the most attractive curves he'd seen all day. Upon stepping inside the elevator, Grace turned around slowly, wearing a self-assured smirk befitting a woman who was quite accustomed to drawing attention. She wasn't in the least bit surprised when she noticed that the doorman hadn't moved an inch from the very spot where his curiosity had rendered him defenseless. He had seen Grace on several occasions, gliding past with a patented, carefree ease that accompanied her like a silken shadow. Regardless of how often he'd viewed that perfectly framed picture, the way she moved captivated him every time.

Although Grace was attractive in her own right, including being blessed with radiant skin, the deepest shade of chocolate conceivable, she would have been categorized as overqualified in the assets department compared to America's flawed idea of beauty. Fortunately, she wasn't the kind of woman who wasted her time trying to live up to fashion-industry standards. She was way too busy working her shapely size twelve like a part-time job to give it much thought at all. Grace wore self-confidence as if it were a badge of honor. In fact, she was honored to be a proud black woman, although she'd discovered wearing that particular designer label was at times as much a blessing as it was a curse after having to deal with male business associates, who rarely knew how to manage a working relationship to benefit both parties involved. She had discovered for herself some time ago that manipulating circumstances as a means to an end offered better results when it wasn't personal, but rather for the sake of business. Because of her strong work ethic, Grace didn't allow anyone to confuse one with the other under any circumstances.

Likewise, Grace wasn't the type to become disillusioned immediately following casual, albeit mind-blowing, sexual acrobatics. After experiencing her share of disappointment, she understood the high cost associated with permitting her emotions to climb into the same bed she shared with a man that wasn't hers. "Check your emotions at the door, girl," Grace whispered softly, to remind herself, whenever tempted by the silly notion that casual sex, no matter how physically rewarding, ever resulted in anything other than what it actually was, fun and games.

That's exactly what Grace had in mind with Tyson Sharp, the epitome of fun and games, sensual bliss, and good times, when suddenly, her purse began to vibrate. She slid her hand inside the brown leather tote bag dangling from her manicured fingertips. While fishing around inside it, her heart rate quickened. "Oops, that is not a cell phone," she chuckled quietly, after discovering that it was another battery-operated device vying for her attention instead. She flipped the "off" switch and then wrestled it back to the bottom of the bag. "Got to be more careful. Ain't that right, Big Mike?" she said jokingly. No sooner had she stepped off the elevator onto the ninth floor, than her bag started up again with another chorus of "Good Vibrations." This time, it was the flip phone summoning her.

"Hey you," Grace cooed seductively into the tiny handheld. "I'm running a bit late, so I knew you'd be calling. How did I know? Because you always get impatient when you want some. Yes, I do like that about you. Huh? What else? Oh, don't trip; isn't being my sex slave good enough?" Grace strolled down the long corridor leading to room 921, their favorite pleasure nest, where Tyson was undoubtedly undressed, cocked and ready for her arrival.

"Hey, I'm here. Yeah, right outside," Grace confirmed, anxious and aroused. "What, you want me to knock? All right then, get your naked self out of that bed and open up."

When the door swung slowly from the inside, Grace tilted her head to catch a glimpse of what wasn't concealed behind it. "Ooh, is all that for me?" she asked, knowing that it was.

Tyson's smile widened. "Every inch. Just tell me how you want it," he answered cunningly, with the same dose of spirited verbal foreplay that Grace had initiated. As he hung a DO NOT DISTURB sign outside and locked the door, she leaned against the mahogany armoire to watch him. Tyson's muscles seemed to gather together in all the right places when her eyes traveled his entire body. She studied his dark skin, deep set dark brown eyes, sculptured arms and thighs, washboard abs beneath a developed chest, broad shoulders, and the tightest butt she'd ever seen. And as usual, Grace blushed seductively with her gaze trained on the talent.

Imagining what the opening act would be when the talent show began, Grace became giddy with anticipation, knowing that sooner or later Tyson Sharp always got around to doing what she liked best of all. Today, however, Grace was hardly in the mood for appetizers. She slipped out of the skirt and let it hit the floor, noting how Tyson's eyes narrowed when they landed on her thighs. "What you looking at?" she teased as he took two measured steps toward her.

"Everything I see," he told her convincingly.

"Tyson," Grace whispered urgently, her white silk blouse falling onto the cloth-covered chair near the thick drapery. She fell back on the bed, pulling Tyson down with her. "Mmm, what are you going to do to me?"

"That thing you like," he answered softly, tracing her body with his soft lips and fingertips. "That thing that keeps you running back to me."

Grace caressed his bald head gently until the irresistible urge to guide it between her legs refused to be denied. "Ooh, yeah, that's it," she moaned passionately. "That's it. That's what I want."

Of course, Tyson knew exactly what Grace wanted, as well as how she wanted it. He'd made time in his busy schedule to get away from a thriving financial services business to do just that, before she returned the favor with unrivaled proficiency. While Tyson was a brilliant money manager, drop-dead gorgeous, and generous to a fault, at age thirty-five, he had yet to grow into the kind of man who possessed the maturity required to look past his own accomplishments in order to applaud someone else's. He wore shallowness like the impeccable designer suit tailored to perfection that hung in the hotel-room closet. Other than that, Tyson Sharp was a single woman's dream, and a married woman's fantasy.

Hours after receiving more of what she wanted, Grace was staring at her own reflection in the large rectangular bathroom mirror, once she'd wiped the steam away with a bath towel. She opened the miniature makeup kit she'd brought along, then paused to get a glimpse at what a single and satisfied woman looked like after an afternoon rendezvous with one of Dallas's finest bachelors. Grace ran her fingers along the ridges on her supple breasts, admiring how they were still holding their shape and fullness after thirty-six years. Then she giggled quietly when she noticed her hair sticking up in a hideous telltale just-got-laid fashion. She quickly made herself presentable, collected her clothing, and exited the lavish den of sin, with Tyson sleeping off the after-effects of Grace's naughty nimbleness. The thought of snuggling up next to him zigzagged through her mind, but she chased it away before it caused her to do something stupid, something emotional, something she would have regretted. Grace had to remember that flextime with Tyson was simply an exercise in futility, nothing more. Besides, she was already up against Friday evening traffic. She was forced to hurry to make it home in time for dinner with the one true love of her life, her thirteen-year-old son, André.

It was half past five when Grace zoomed out of the hotel parking garage. During the thirty-five-minute drive home, she grew increasingly uneasy. Having feelings of culpability and exhilaration, an edgy twinge gnawed in the pit of her stomach. As she pulled into the driveway of her two-story buff-colored brick home in a well-to-do subdivision, it occurred to her that she had forgotten to pack a spare pair of panties. In such a hurry to make her scheduled appointment, it didn't cross her mind until then.

Grace parked her Volvo SUV in the garage and entered through the laundry room, with intentions of slinking past André undetected. She tiptoed around the cherrywood dinner table and eased into the mouth of the hallway leading to the master bedroom. When it appeared the coast was clear, Grace quickly realized that the jig was up.

"Hey, Ma," André said loudly, with his hands fastened to the controls of a PlayStation video game, his elbows resting on his bony knees.

Grace smiled awkwardly as she entered into the den. Deliberately, she moved directly behind the evenly brown-hued teenager when she answered his standard salutation. "Hey, yourself," she replied pleasantly to the gangly boy evolving into a young man before her eyes. "And what did I tell you about that 'Hey, Ma' stuff?"

André continued wrestling with the video-game controls until he realized what she'd said. After placing the joystick on the coffee table, he climbed off the walnut-colored sofa. Grace panicked when he approached her from the opposite side of the broad sectional. "Where are you going?" she stammered, fearing the inevitable.

"To say hello proper, like my mother taught me."

Grace wanted to back away as he reached out for her, but she couldn't think of an acceptable excuse for doing so. "You didn't have to get up," she said, in an exasperated tone. "All I expected was a sensible acknowledgment."

"I know. That's what I got up to do," André told her, with a warm embrace. "How's that?"

"Uhh, very refreshing actually," she answered, then immediately changed the subject before her peculiar behavior was called into question. "So would you like to go out later, or should I whip up something for dinner?" Suddenly, André leaned away from his mother, wrinkled his nose, then sniffed the air.

Oh my Lord, Grace thought to herself, hoping to high heaven that her child didn't recognize the remnants of grown folks' business or have a clue what she'd been up to on the other side of town.

"Mom, you smell kinda funny," he said as he continued sniffing around her. "Kinda like those stinky little soap bars from that hotel on the San Antonio Riverwalk that gave me a rash."

Frozen in her humiliation, Grace played it off as best she could. "Don't be silly, Dré. I haven't been anywhere near San Antonio." She was thoroughly relieved that he hadn't learned enough about life to ask whether she'd been anywhere near a hotel. Immediately following a narrow escape, Grace snatched up the telephone and hit "2" on the speed dial to order a pizza. Then she slid into the shower again to rinse away the incriminating evidence. While languishing in her solitude, a single tear streaked down her cheek. It occurred to her that André was no longer the boy she'd said good-bye to that morning before heading off to work. His senses were sharpening, and there wouldn't be many years left to offer motherly advice or see to it that his homework was completed to her strict specifications. She wasn't prepared for André's ascension into manhood or having to increase her level of cleverness to get around his impending understanding regarding her indiscretions with men. Grace remained in the shower for quite some time to conceal her sadness and troubled soul with undeniable traces of gratuitous sex hiding just beneath it.

2

Beautiful Words

Saturday morning at eleven sharp, Grace scurried around inside the ladies' powder room just off the main chapel of church as she mixed in Golden Glimmer eye shadow with a delicate brushstroke of Mocha Madness foundation to even out the hue. Chandelle was a blushing bride-to-be, but her skin tone was much too rich to apply the makeup directly from the small container, as intended by the manufacturer.

"I don't know what that cosmetics company was thinking when they marketed this precious-metal line to sistahs without adding a touch of bronze," Grace grumbled while dabbling her own mixture of ingenuity and good old-fashioned know-how underneath Chandelle's eyebrows. "Someone ought to crash their next sales meeting with some of this here to set them straight."

"I know you're going to make me so beautiful, Grace," Chandelle whispered, holding her eyes closed. "I saw the photos from Maryland's wedding, when she was shoving them in everybody's face at the job. The way you put her face together like a movie star sent me running to your office. I wasn't too proud to beg, either."

Grace tilted her head to the side as she thought back to the memorable scene that had happened two years earlier. "Yeah, I do recall a skinny little college grad fresh off the bus traipsing into my office and interrupting my conference call." She laughed when the memory came back crystal clear, as if it had happened yesterday. *"Miss Hilliard, Miss Hilliard!"* Grace mocked, while trying to imitate Chandelle's excited voice. *"I know you don't know me, but I just peeped Maryland's wedding album, and her makeup was so tight that no one even noticed her ugly dress."* Other women in the busy room snickered.

Chandelle chuckled lightly herself as she reminisced. "How was I to know you were a corporate big shot? All I knew was that you had a rep for being nice to everyone, and that you'd worked magic on Maryland. You probably won't admit it, but that chick needed it more than most. That's when I figured there was hope for me. After you said yes, all I needed then was a man."

"Be nice, now," Grace warned. "Maryland has already taken the plunge, and now has an adorable set of twins and a backyard. You still need the minister to ink your deal, so lighten up. Not everyone is a natural beauty like you, Chandelle, with a line of men beating her door down for the honor of sharing their last name."

Chandelle blushed, casting her eyes away. Grace had helped her to realize how insensitive she had been to Maryland and other women who couldn't pass for a Fashion Fair model with a shake dancer's behind. Suddenly Chandelle reached across the small vanity to hug Grace. "You're right, but then, you always are," she said. "I had no business putting anybody down that way. I should be happy that Maryland's happy. There are way too many black women who never get the chance to wear these white satin shoes or sit here and have friends and family fussing over their special day. My bad."

"Uh-huh, now close your eyes again so I can finish what I showed up early for," Grace advised, "to help you look your very best on your special day. Besides, I'm sure there's a young man waiting to get all this fluff out of the way so he can get on with the honeymoon."

"Who you telling?" Chandelle huffed. "We've put all that on hold a few months ago, so I'm praying that I don't pop when the preacher says, now he can kiss the bride." She took a deep breath, opened her eyes, and then stared at herself in the mirror. "Ohhh, Grace. It's, I'm so . . ."

"Get a hold of yourself, girl," Grace demanded. "If you cry on me and have my masterpiece running down your face before all those people get to be blown away, you'll be assigned to the copying machine for a month."

"I won't cry," Chandelle whimpered. "I won't. I'm just so nervous and so glad that I have a friend like you."

"Good, then straighten up and get ready for the biggest event of your life next to pushing your way into this world." Grace brushed a few renegade strands of hair away from the younger woman's face. "Now, that's more like it. There's nothing to be nervous about. Just think of all the joys to come after the ceremony, and you'll be fine. I've seen enough wedding ceremonies, up close too, so I know what I'm talking about. Been a bridesmaid nearly twenty times." Without giving it much thought, Grace smiled brilliantly as she gave her work a final once-over. "Chandelle, all these people came to see your blessing, live and in Technicolor, so enjoy it."

"Thanks so much, for everything," Chandelle replied, before her curious gaze and statement spun Grace's world in a whole other direction. "All those times, Grace, leading someone else down the aisle, you've never once thought about jumping the broom yourself?" If Grace had seen it coming, she might've ducked. "Well I'm sure that you'll settle down when you get tired of running men, on your terms," Chandelle concluded. "Not many women get the chance to walk in Grace Hilliard's shoes, either."

Before Grace had the opportunity to dissect or debate what her younger associate had presumed about her personal life and the men in it, the stern wedding planner knocked on the door to announce the time had come for the ceremony to begin. "I know Chandelle didn't just try to tell me about my business," Grace said to herself. "If she wasn't getting married today, I'd strangle her."

Little did Grace know that her private life wasn't all that private. Over the years, several of Grace's coworkers had caught wind of her fun-and-games arrangements with no strings attached; so it was speculated that she hadn't married because she already had a great career, a gorgeous home, an expensive car, and a wonderful son with his head in the books instead of on some gang-related most-wanted poster. In reality, Grace had been too busy building her reputation as a savvy marketing executive in a male-dominated environment and raising the kind of son any mother would be proud of to realize she had never been asked to become some man's wife, at least not by one who was serious and sober at the same time. Chandelle's assumptions forced Grace to challenge each decision she'd ever made regarding the men she allowed to rent space in her head, or those she'd rationalized to be worthy enough to jump in her bed.

Although reasonably disturbed, Grace tried to convince herself that Chandelle was too young to comprehend life on her level and was grossly incorrect about her personal affairs, but the truth was irrefutable. Now, Grace remembered something she'd read in the Bible, regarding the validity of truth and consequence emanating from the simple minds of children. She was standing outside the wedding chapel before it hit her like a ton of bricks. *Out of the mouth of babes*, Grace thought to herself. Chandelle was born in the early 80s and was already getting married. Suddenly, Grace was deflated when it occurred to her that she was enrolled in college before the bride realized that ponytails and pink dresses weren't the only things differentiating girls from boys. Where had all the time gone?

The chapel was buzzing with anticipation. Three hundred guests became animated once the procession march began and the entrance doors opened. Just as she had many times before, Grace accepted the arm of a willing groomsman and followed the parade of bridesmaids, adorned in elegant gold and cream gowns, into the presence of excited onlookers, but this wedding was different from the others. Instead of merely witnessing the happy couple agree to have and to hold, in sickness and in health, so on and so forth, she observed every single detail from beginning to end.

Well-wishers, family, friends, and those who attended out of curiosity, envy or worse glanced expectedly down the aisle. The bossy wedding planner reprimanded Grace when she failed to smile during the procession. "This is a joyous occasion, so act like you would if it were yours," the woman insisted, through clenched teeth, as she marched by. After cursing under her breath, Grace agreed that, although the wedding planner's delivery lacked tact, she was absolutely correct. The guests had received costly invitations, marked this particular date on their calendars, wrapped thoughtful gifts, gotten dressed, and arrived on time to witness two people in love confess it before God and everyone else.

Ribbons and bows matching the bridesmaids' dresses were fastened to the ends of each pew. The lights were brightly illuminated. "Pomp and Circumstance" rang throughout the hall while two professional photographers and an imposing video-camera crew captured each millisecond for posterity's sake. Grace looked on, thoroughly impressed by the grand spectacle. She tried to remember an instance where she was more absorbed by an event that didn't directly benefit her. When nothing came to mind, the thought of only going through the motions during all of the previous ceremonies caused her to feel somewhat disappointed. There had been numerous occasions to celebrate, holy unions of friends and loved ones, but she'd merely managed to watch while neglecting to actually see the significance of a heavenly communion that God himself had ordained. Out of nowhere, Grace found herself looking forward to her own special day.

She stood with the other two attendants, gushing and wonderfully arrayed in designer taffeta gowns, but neither of them shared Grace's mixed emotions when the officiating minister appeared with a handsome groom and entourage in close step behind him.

The small ring bearer, wearing a dashing miniature tuxedo, held onto a white satin pillow for dear life. As he tiptoed toward the taped X marking his spot in the well-choreographed production, Grace winked at the child's mother, who was hand signaling further directives from the second pew. A darling flower girl followed his path while flinging red and yellow rose petals to and fro, like she'd been shown during the rehearsal. Her dress was a scaled-down replica of the bridesmaids'.

After the little girl reached her position, she stuck out her tongue in reply to a heckling sibling who was making funny faces at her from the safe confines of the crowd. It was difficult for Grace to concede that she missed out on all of this before, but she had.

The groom sighed deeply, with a stream of tight breaths as the pianist dove into the wedding march. "Here comes the bride," the minister said, to notify the groom that his life was about to change. The audience rose to its feet. Despite having chatted with the woman of the hour moments before, Grace stretched her neck, along with the audience, to catch an early peek of Chandelle. Her friend glided down the aisle effortlessly as if she'd practiced endlessly, graciously accepting a chorus of oohs and ahhs. It appeared as if Chandelle's fiancé was going to faint after laying eyes on her exquisite strapless wedding gown. When she exchanged initial glances with him, the poor man was visibly awestruck by her appearance. Afterwards she mouthed "thank you" to Grace, whose eyes had begun misting uncontrollably.

"You're welcome," Grace mouthed in return, yet to realize that she had the most to be thankful for. Within hours, Chandelle's makeup would be washed away, but the gift she'd given Grace would last for the remaining days of her life. For that, she would be forever grateful.

After Chandelle's brand-new husband promised to love her, come hell or high water, he held her around the waist like she was made of glass, then he kissed her so eagerly that it bordered on obscenity. The minister turned his eyes away, thoroughly uncomfortable with the sensual tongue dancing exhibition that took place on the very spot where deacons served Holy Communion every Sunday morning. The audience cheered when Chandelle was announced as "Mrs." with a new last name. They laughed heartily when they saw the smeared lipstick ring circling her husband's mouth. Chandelle's special day was a true blessing, and one that the Lord had fashioned just for her.

Grace continued taking it all in, posing with the wedding party for one photo after the next, wondering why she hadn't taken the same interest in the one thing most women have longed for since they were little girls refining their mudpie skills or improving on their Easy Bake Oven metal-sheet-cake technique.

During the reception, Grace felt out of place, so she raised her glass to the happy couple, sipped a flute of champagne, then left the festivities shaken and stirred. She decided that an entire world existed on the outer fringes of hers. From that point forward, she was intent on paying attention to other positive things she hadn't given any thought to but should have. Although Grace had no plans of racing frantically through the streets with expectations of landing a husband, she was inclined to examine her current relationships, just in case there was a diamond in the rough she might have overlooked.

3

I Said to Myself

"André," Grace hollered as her son dashed from her silver sport-utility vehicle. "Don't forget your Bible and make sure you stop by the office to tell Sister Jones what I said about the women's retreat. I'll attend, but I'm not going to present this year."

André reached into the backseat, grabbed a black book bag, then turned toward the church activity center, on his way to Bible class, when his mother called his name again. "Dré!"

"Yes, ma'am," he sighed. "I'll give Sister Jones the message, but she likes to hug too much."

"She's getting old, baby, so let her squeeze on a fine young man if that makes her day." After André considered the compliment within his mother's orders, he stuck his chest out and grinned.

"All right, Mama," he said, appraising the situation differently than before. "But no kisses. Her mustache itches."

Grace shook her head, holding in the laughter fighting to get out as she pulled away from the curb to search for a parking space. She slammed on the brakes when an old woman whipped a 1975 model Lincoln Continental in front of her car. The boat-sized deathtrap rambled nimbly into an available spot. "Ooh, somebody's gonna make me cuss this morning," Grace said under her breath, seething. By the time she'd circled the lot and lucked out on another open parking space, Grace was running later than she planned. She reasoned that her favorite pew, seven rows from the back, would be full, so she decided to relax and take her sweet time for once. It actually felt good to have three male ushers stumbling over themselves to find her an alternate seat.

"Good morning, Sister Hilliard," one of the ushers welcomed, with opened arms of course.

"You sure do look nice, Grace," another of them complimented, reserving his sly appraisal until she was a few paces ahead of him.

"Thank you, brothers, praise God," she replied, to shift their minds back on the Lord's business, instead of locked on her fitted coral designer suit.

After taking a seat and adjusting her long skirt, Grace collected a songbook, attendance card, and a tithing envelope. Since she was sitting on the opposite side of the auditorium the church's edifice seemed a bit unfamiliar, different somehow. There were several more families with younger children around her, and various young couples who appeared to be participating in the time-honored Southern tradition of *church dating,* the nonthreatening getting-to-know-you date allowing interested parties to be seen in public together without committing to anything more serious than that. Now, that took Grace back to a time when showing up to worship without a man on her arm caused other men to wonder why such an attractive woman arrived unescorted. When they learned that she had a child, they stopped wondering. It was peculiar to Grace how single men with illegitimate children found it in their hearts to cast stones or reclassify her for being in the exact same situation. That level of hypocrisy convinced her to blow every one of them off once they came to their senses years later. Growth and maturity taught them how much of a woman a single mother had to be, taking care of finances, keeping house, preparing meals, staying fit, and raising the children, but Grace thought it better to keep her bedroom affairs out of the Lord's house, and fellow Christians from the church out of hers. That way, she didn't have to be concerned about a brother spending Saturday night with her, then cozying up to his next victim on Sunday morning. She'd seen it all before, and it turned out just as ugly every time. Inevitably, Grace felt better about doing her dirt outside the confines of the church, as if God wouldn't be so apt to notice the sins she committed elsewhere. Unfortunately, the same couldn't be said for Albert Jenkins, the congregation Casanova. When he slithered by with a stack of programs, Grace avoided eye contact while accepting the handout.

Albert was the nice-looking, fair-skinned, smooth-operator type. He anxiously waited for church service to begin so he could start putting in his bid for baby-mama number five. Even though the elders had pulled his coat, reprimanding him for his lascivious behavior, the preacher's son was determined to maneuver his way through the church on a bullet train to hell. As Albert caught three of his child-support-check recipients eyeballing him, he moved farther away from Grace before being forced to lie about his lewd intentions, to all three of them, after the final prayer. Every church had at least one skirt-chasing menace. Albert Jenkins was the shameless scourge of Fellowship Union.

Once the church's chicken hawk moved on, Grace thanked God for His speedy answer to her silent prayer, but she hadn't anticipated the little extra He'd thrown in just for grins. Suddenly, everything appeared more pleasant than before. The song leader started in with "Mansion, Robe and Crown," young fathers wrangled in their little ones, and dutiful mothers doted over infants and tussling toddlers not yet ready to settle in for the next three hours of songs and soul-stirring sermons. Observing those families in bloom was blissful for Grace. Listening to proud fathers giving instructions to their children about do's and don'ts during worship service was priceless. Sure, Grace loved André more than life itself, and showered him with as much kindness and understanding as one parent could, but she recognized at that instant that he'd been missing out on a slice of life she could never provide, a father-son relationship with a caring role model.

Throughout the remainder of the service, Grace thanked God for giving her the strength and presence of mind to have done right by her son, at least the best she could by herself. After blotting her eyes with a folded Kleenex tissue, she was certain that her household was in order and her son had received the best of everything she knew how to give him. But what had previously surpassed being adequate, now appeared to be sorely lacking. She daydreamed throughout the sermon, with her mind wavering over providing more of a family unit for André and being true to her own passions. She'd seen several marriages falter within the first year because, contrary to the common belief, not every one of them was a match made in heaven. Some of the couples had no business signing the license or pretending love had anything to do with their "I do's."

As Grace filed out of the sanctuary, she made a mental note to pray for discernment, fearing that she had become her own worst critic. André had been sitting in his usual place, at the very back of the auditorium, among other teenagers who had earned the trust of their parents to camp out without chaperones. This was André's first month of freedom, a freedom Grace thought seriously of rescinding. "Hey, Ma," the boy called out when she puttered by, her head lowered in deep reflection. "Mama!" his voice rose.

Grace's eyes fluttered when she heard her child above the chatter. "Yes, Dré," she answered from the throes of careful contemplation.

"I'll meet you by the car," he shouted, then disappeared into the maze of parishioners before his mother had the chance to ask why. André cruised through the outside doors, then over to the west side of the building, where the high schoolers met to engage in fellowship in a manner that suited them. They were clueless to the fact that so many marriages had begun in the west wing of the activity center, cultivated over time under the watchful eyes of God. When André sensed that his brief stint of adolescent exchange had grown to a close, he doubled-timed it to the Volvo before Grace showed up to embarrass him with his peers looking on.

"Did you get to say everything you needed to say?" she asked him, while backing her vehicle out of a tight spot. Of course, André wanted to avoid the question altogether, but he knew Grace was merely letting him know that she knew what he'd been up to.

"There wasn't much to say," André responded softly, with a hint of reluctance. "At least not yet," he added as an honest afterthought. "I've got time."

Merely the thought of her child preparing his lines to spring on someone's daughter stayed with Grace long after she'd dropped him off at Skyler Barnes's house, André's friend and high-school basketball superstar. *Since when did Silly String and chasing spiders morph into macking to young girls and looking for the right time to make a move on one he'd developed feelings for?* Grace asked herself.

Linda Allen was seated at a booth and sipping from a tall glass of peach-flavored iced tea when Grace arrived for their once-a-month Sunday brunch at Ursula's Chicken and Waffles. Linda, pleasantly plump, high yellow with a cropped hairstyle and big brown eyes, was decked out in a casual denim outfit that suggested she'd passed on yet another worship service, but Grace had her own issues to contend with, so she didn't bring it up. Shelia Chatham, the most scandalously carefree member of the trio, entered just behind Grace. Shelia, cinnamon brown and conceited, was dressed in her Sunday best and yapping into her cell phone a mile a minute. "Yeah, that was kinda nice. Can we do it again? Oooh, especially that," she crooned seductively into the small telephone. Shelia placed an index finger up to her thin lips to quiet her girlfriends. Grace and Linda looked at each other with matching shame-on-her expressions. "Uh-huh, baby, you know just how to set me off. What? Yeah, baby, I'm naked right now," Shelia added, rolling her eyes whatever-style. She was annoyed by the male caller but thought it necessary to put in work for a payoff on the back end. All of her male friends, as she commonly referred to them, were instructed to show up at her place with little trinkets of appreciation for her time, or not show up at all. "I'm about to step into a hot bubble bath right now. No, you can't. Richard, I need some me time," she said. "Just cause I'm about to get wet doesn't mean I want to get you wet, too." Shelia glared at Linda when it appeared she might bust out laughing and ruin her fantasy chat with the man she'd met the week before. "I let you paint my toenails Friday night, so they don't need any attention right now. I gotta go. Don't make me hang up on you. Find something else to do until I can call you back. Bye!" As soon as she clicked the flip phone closed and shut Richard out of her mind, Grace struggled to hold her tongue. "What?" Shelia hissed. "Don't be looking at me like that."

"Like what, Shelia?" Grace challenged, knowingly.

"Like you're the kinkiest heffa this side of the projects," Linda chimed in.

"Uh-uh, Linda!" Shelia objected, throwing her hand up to accentuate her point. She shook her finger to warn against their mad dash into her affairs. "I know how y'all get down, so it would behoove the two of you to do what? Let it go and leave it alone," Shelia suggested with her patented get-your-nose-out-of-mine smirk. She opened an oval-shaped silverplated compact case, one of her many gifts from a married admirer. After eyeing her reflection in the mirror, she snickered heartily. "Y'all are just mad because I'm getting paid to have my toes sucked and polished, and you're not."

"Ewwh, that's nothing to be bragging about," Linda countered. "Now, if you were getting somcthing else sucked by that fine specimen of a black man, Tyson Sharp, like my girl Grace does, then I'd be sipping on some hater-ade instead of this peach tea." Linda paused long enough to perform a self-appraisal before fanning herself with an open hand. "See, all this is what keeps my stock up. Men fall for these adorable bedroom eyes, this rich butterscotch complexion, this bountiful booty I got from my mama's side of the family, or the way I moan when a brotha's got his tongue gliding up and down it."

"Tell her, Linda," Grace said jokingly. "Would you tell her."

"Ain't got to, Grace, she already knows I can make the tail wag the dog, and then some. It's honey sweet and deep," Linda added, in the event that anyone missed her act of self-aggrandizement. The ladies always shared a laugh over silly sniping sessions which reminded them that secrets rarely survived in their midst. Grace's monthly tryst with Tyson and her infrequent encounters with his fill-in, Greg Anderson, were common knowledge among the tightly knit circle. Shelia's personal business was worthy of two bestselling novels, and Linda couldn't play the prude after following a musician from gig to gig, up and down the New Jersey Turnpike, sixteen months ago. She blamed it on missing her exit, when the truth involved her burning up the highway for the private and uninterrupted encores he laid on her deep into the night. Regardless of how ridiculous the situations they found themselves in, the trio was always there for one another to help sort out the dramatic details and pick up the pieces when it was all over but the crying. Shelia, Linda, and Grace were simply a small faction of black women trying to get their kicks without allowing random emotions get in the way of having a good time.

When the waiter appeared, he introduced himself, then announced the brunch specials. Shelia rolled her eyes when the young, muscle-bound man stared past Linda's outstanding attributes and seemed rather intrigued by her short, wavy hairstyle. "Uh, is there something you want?" Shelia snapped rudely, as the others peered up from their menus.

"Uh-huh, but not from you," the waiter retorted rudely, smacking his lips. "I would kill for my hair to behave like girlfriend's over there. I am sick with envy over those waves. Who does your hair?" The young man's flamboyant personality caught Grace by surprise. She turned away, covering her mouth with her manicured fingertips. At first glance she would not have guessed that he was gay, but his keenly arched eyebrows, pouty lips poking out like a disgruntled five-year-old's, and his wishing that his hair would behave like Linda's removed any doubt that he was openly out and about. Grace had heard more than her share of tragic stories about women getting involved with men on the down-low and then later discovering they'd been paying rent on closet space. However, the waiter wasn't even thinking of making a pass at one of them.

"Linda, could you hook him up with your stylist, then maybe he can get back to his job and get us something to eat?" Shelia recommended hastily. The waiter rolled his neck in opposition to her crass comment, smacked his lips again, then scribbled down their orders before walking away. "And your hands better be clean," Shelia yelled after him.

"What's wrong, Grace?" Linda asked, as she studied her friend's sour expression. "Is the thought of that brotha getting with another brotha bothering you?"

"Please, you know that's not my type of hype regardless," Grace answered, still obviously perturbed about something. "No, I've come to grips with men who don't want to be men, who'd rather be with men, and who'd give anything to be women. No matter how hard you try, there's no way to make sense out of nonsense."

"Okay, then, what's got you looking like you just lost your good thing?" Shelia prodded, also really wanting to know.

After Grace deliberated awhile, she cleared her throat and cast a labored smile that didn't fool either of the other women. "I went to a beautiful wedding yesterday, you know, Chandelle from the office? I agreed to serve as a maid of honor, put her makeup together. The thanks I got was her hitting me with a statement that left a mark." Grace glanced down at the table, not certain how her discussion with a younger woman would play out in present company. "It was innocent enough, but it stung a little when Chandelle asked me if I had ever thought about finding someone to get serious with, married-serious with," she added for clarification. "Actually I hadn't, but it doesn't seem that far-fetched now that I've actually let the idea play around in my head."

"Shoot, I've let it move furniture into mine," Linda sighed. Shelia wanted to add her two cents but had nothing positive to offer so she kept quiet, for now. She had been thoroughly jaded against married-serious relationships after experiencing a terrible heartbreak several years ago.

"I don't believe it," Linda offered, clasping her hands together underneath her chin. "Chandelle opened your eyes, and ripped off your superwoman cape at the same time?" Linda had known Grace for years and had never once heard her express love or pain about a man she'd spent time with. This was new and uncharted territory.

"It would seem so, girl." Grace's gaze drifted off into

space like that sneaky idea Chandelle planted was more than just an idea. "Maybe it was a good thing, me getting a wake-up call to start thinking about long-term situations. It put a jacked-up spell on me all right, and I want my cape back."

"There's something to be said for sharing a black woman's woes," Shelia contributed finally. "I was starting to think that you weren't human, Grace. And I hope you don't take this wrong, but I'm kinda glad you've become one of us." Shelia smiled awkwardly for no particular reason. "If you keep moving, that spell won't get the chance to put a hold on you."

"What's that?" questioned Grace, when she noticed the vulnerable expression hanging on Shelia's face.

"Plight of the black woman. More of us are single than married, with more heartbreaks than dreams."

Linda's eyes sparkled as she sought to climb out of the funk encompassing their intimate circle. "But Grace's blues aren't exactly like ours, Shelia. See, Grace already has the big house, the fancy car, and the movie-star clothes. She just needs to decide which of her flextimers gets to share all of that with her." There was a hint of jealously in Linda's tone, although she didn't mean any harm to Grace. Her loneliness just happened to get in the way while she assessed the situation. As far as she could see, a man would have to be crazy not to fall all over himself if Grace wanted him to. And if she offered forever as an option, he'd certainly vie for the platinum package with all the trimmings. Linda had no idea how wrong she was about the men in Grace's life, or the way they'd respond to exercising long-term options on love.

If it wasn't for Shelia's easygoing attitude, their Sunday brunch would have been hijacked. "Well, I know one thing, Linda. I'm willing to go out of my way to get Grace's cape back 'cause y'all done killed my groove. No, don't try to cheer me up. My groove don't even work no mo'. It just up and quit."

When Grace laughed out loud, Linda followed suit. "Grace,

hurry up and handle your business, find that super-cape, and I'll get my groove back. That's right. Me and Shelia."

When the waiter returned with their entrées, Shelia heckled him. "What you come back for? You're the competition. Go on now, before you steal another black woman's man. Go on! Git!"

4

All That Man!

A bustling herd of storm clouds rolled past the large plate-glass windows of Grace's corner office at Pinnacle Marketing. Monday mornings and gray skies seemed to go together like lyrics of a sad song played over a slow musical beat. Trying not to think about the conversation she'd had with Shelia and Linda, Grace felt better about getting her cape back. The cape was her force field shielding her from the various agonies caused by serious relationships with men. By not getting too close, she wouldn't get exposed, hurt, or heartbroken. The cape was pliable, impenetrable, and machine washable. The cape came fully accessorized and coordinated perfectly with any ensemble. The drawback was how it also covered Grace's eyes to reality like a lead veil. She dealt with the misconception that her cape had been the solution, when in actuality it kept her wrapped in a cocoon of false security, daring her to consider the possibilities outside of it. The worst thing that could have happened to Grace was getting her cape back.

Grace was thumbing through a fashion magazine when

Marcia, her trusty executive assistant, poked her head in. "Miss Hilliard, aren't you meeting with All-Jams to oversee their TV spot?"

Confused by the question, Grace shook the cobwebs from her mind. She laid the magazine on her broad mahogany desk and then glanced at her expensive Movado timepiece. "Yes, but that's not until next week. Is there something wrong with Allen Foray's schedule?"

The short brunette who never wore makeup under any circumstances flashed the same confused look back at her boss. "No, there's no problem with Mr. Foray. He showed up at the shoot an hour ago, right on schedule." Marcia watched Grace's mind warm up to the thought of missing out on a very important matter for her biggest account.

Grace panicked. "They're not shooting the spot on the twenty-second?"

"I'm afraid not," Marcia informed her reluctantly.

"They're filming my million-dollar commercial today?"

"I'm afraid so."

"I have to get over there before something gets broken that I can't fix."

After the elevator doors opened in the underground parking garage, Grace found her car and climbed in. She called ahead to the studio, had the director paged, then issued an immediate order to stop filming. Much to her chagrin, the director was quick to complain how his time had already been wasted trying to convince the superstar basketball player that his Captain Dream Creams costume didn't make him look like a Village People reject. Grace informed him that she would be there momentarily. Then she prayed all the way up the tollway that the professional basketball icon wouldn't remind her of the waiter from yesterday's outing at Ursula's. There'd be no faking it if he did.

"Miss Hilliard! Miss Hilliard!" shouted an oversensitive foreign director wearing faded black jeans and a thirty-dollar department store T-shirt. "Miss Hilliard, this Allen Foray is impossible to work with. He tells me to go away for street credit. I can not shop for something I do not understand where to buy." Patrik was ultraprofessional, Italian, and came highly recommended. The lofty recommendation also included several reservations outlining his inability to work with amateurs. Rich amateurs were out of the question because they were not known to be readily accepting of his constructive criticisms.

"Patrik! Patrik! Slow down," Grace demanded with a firm tone. "I told you I'd handle it, and I will. Take a deep breath, have a latté, and then get your crew ready. I'll be out in a jiff with the hundred-million-dollar man." She leaned in closer to the director, who was still fuming. "I know where to whip up some street credit and how to serve it up too." She left Patrik standing in the middle of the hall pulling his hair out.

"I'm out!" the six-foot eight-inch athlete barked from the comforts of a plush mole-hair love seat. His publicist was in full agreement when Grace walked into his private dressing room unannounced. She'd seen photos of Allen Foray in magazines. She'd watched him score fifty points against the Lakers, too. But, the reason she'd selected him for the All-Jams co-op with Dream Creams' national marketing campaign had everything to do with her son André believing that Allen was the end-all, be-all in basketball.

"Excuse me," the young female yuppie type shrieked as she marched in Grace's direction. "This is a private room, and Allen Foray doesn't want to be disturbed." The publicist, attired in a flattering Aztec print Missoni belted dress, couldn't have been out of college more than two weeks. Grace considered complimenting her taste but didn't have the time to waste gratifying words on her.

Grace stopped the willowy blonde in midstride. "Miss, you might want to get somewhere, sit down, and be still!" Now that Grace had captured the star's attention, she lit in and didn't let up until she had mastered the situation, demanded his respect and exacted a change of heart. "Allen Foray, my name is Grace Hilliard. That may not mean anything to you yet, but suggesting that you're going to walk out on my production is unacceptable." When Allen stood up, he towered over Grace but underestimated her range. "Oh, you think by stretching your legs, I'm supposed to let you breach a contract after you've cashed my check. Oh yes, I've confirmed it. My money belongs to you, and for the remainder of this campaign your time belongs to me." The publicist was stunned but smart enough to do as she was told while taking it all in.

"Who is she supposed to be?" the arrogant athlete asked, expecting his publicist to jump in and save him.

"Grace Hilliard," the publicist reminded him, so that he wouldn't forget again.

"Grace. Look. I've done all kinds of commercials, from cars to cattle, but I'm not putting on that Captain Cream Puff costume. I've got a rep, and I'm not strapping on some tricked-out Batman tights."

"You'll do exactly as I say," Grace argued, "because you're a man of your word, my son's hardwood hero, and I know you don't want to be sued by the number-one snack company in the southwest. Otherwise, you will be required to return the half-million-dollar advance. You will also be dragged through the courts and branded as a thief."

"Thief?" Allen questioned in disbelief.

"That's right, Mr. Foray, so you can close your mouth. Let me tell you something serious. If you disappoint me, I'll have no other course of action but to forbid my son from idolizing the egotistical, money-grubbing, simpleminded jerk that he's convinced you're not."

"What? Simpleminded?" he objected.

"Furthermore, it might be tolerated when you come up short on the basketball court, but there is one thing I will not stand for and that's another black man being less than what his mother intended, a stand-up and stand-by-your-word role model she could be proud of," Grace huffed. Without awaiting a response, she called Patrik on her cell phone. "Mr. Foray will be ready in twenty minutes." After ending the call, Grace stared up at Allen in his splendidly tailored Hugo Boss suit and size-fifteen leather Gucci lace-ups. "Well what are you waiting for, lotion?" Grace snapped curtly.

Wide eyed and intrigued, Allen began pacing back and forth while contemplating this scary woman's threats. "Okay, hold on!" he grunted. "You might be used to getting your way wherever you come from, but let's not forget who the star is around here."

Grace crossed her arms defiantly and then pursed her lips before replying to Allen's idea of swaggering while on her turf. "I'll concede that if you keep in mind who is willing and able to haul *the star* into a long and drawn out mud bath in the press," she growled smartly.

Allen grimaced, groping for a witty comeback that eluded him. "All right, Grace, I'll admit you got me with the things you said about my mother, and I know you're going off on me because that's what they sent you in here to do. I can see how serious you're taking this, and I'm not trying to let nobody down, but come on now, I can't do the tights." Allen was searching desperately for a way out, or at least a way to save face.

"First thing, there is no *they*, I'm it. And on second thought, about the tights, you don't have to wear them," Grace said, compromising to meet Allen halfway. "Wardrobe!" she summoned. "We're burning daylight!" Before Allen or the publicist knew what was going on, two seamstresses appeared with a selection of basketball shorts to complete the costume. Grace continued, "Please find something that Mr. Foray agrees to, and put five identical pieces together. We're a go in fifteen minutes." Grace exited the dressing room after walking on water, leading a stubborn horse to it, and subsequently getting him to lap it up.

"Why do they always have to take the 'make your mama

proud' route?" Allen remarked just above a whisper as he slid out of his dress slacks. Suddenly, a warm smile creased his lips. "Grace Hilliard, huh? She's different. I'll give her that." After looking at his rusty knees, his frown chased that smile away. "And she was right, I do need some lotion."

Patrik was excited once the taping concluded. He had had no problems getting Allen to rehearse his lines, or shoot additional four-second promos and voice-overs for upcoming radio drops. Working with Allen Foray was an enjoyable experience, and working for Grace Hilliard was a pleasure. "Thank you, Miss Hilliard," Patrik beamed with delight. "This was stupendous, and only because of you."

"Don't mention it," she replied, with a sly wink. "Manipulating a man's ego is often the cost of doing business."

"Oh yeah, is that all it was?" Allen asked from the shadows of a darkened studio. He'd been watching Grace, listening and waiting. "I was thinking how nice it was to click with a grown woman for a change. I'd hate to imagine that I was wrong."

"You think we clicked?" Grace blushed. "I'd categorize it as more of a clank, but I'm flattered nonetheless, so let's just leave it at that." She pretended not to notice his youthful charm and creamy smooth everything else.

"Since you're holding all the cards, I have no choice but to roll with that for now." Allen passed Grace a business card with his home phone number handwritten on the back of it. "Here are the digits at the house. If you change your mind, call me." He looked Grace over, slowly, from head to toe. "Call me up for anything at all, even if you just want someone to talk to."

"Thank you, Allen, but don't hold your breath. I wouldn't waste a call on a good-looking man like you for the sake of conversation. However, I will have Patrik's people contact your people when the early edits are finished." Grace tossed a harmless leer at the tower of late night motivation and held her breath. Allen was simply too young and too rough around the edges for her taste. "You did a great job today, Mister All-World Allen," she offered, praising his work and his work ethic. Grace hushed the naughty thoughts suggesting that she treat herself to a long night with the wealthy millionaire and his fat-free physique. Allen may have been young, but Grace knew he'd be ready, willing, and able if she ever decided to use the private number written on the flipside of that business card. In the meantime, she placed it inside her purse for safekeeping.

The following morning, Grace was still pleased with herself, and excited over the potential revenues she hoped would result from the commercial shoot the day before. Since there weren't any pressing issues to be handled at the office, she decided to work from home part of the day and spend the morning reflecting on a chance to steal a major account from a competitor.

Later, Grace wandered into the office after a lengthy shopping expedition to the mall proved unsuccessful. She was kicking herself for neglecting to stop by Nordstrom's on her way in. Since scuffing the heel on her favorite pair of eggshell white slingbacks, she'd made random visits to various department stores looking for suitable replacements. Marcia stopped her at the reception area as soon as she entered the suite.

"Miss Hilliard, some packages came for you earlier today." Marcia glanced at her manager from the corner of her eye. "Any luck?" Marcia assumed that Grace's leisurely morning had included a trip to at least one shoe store.

"Nope, but I won't give up without a fight."

"Neither will Allen Foray, if you ask me," Marcia predicted, as if she'd given it a considerable amount of thought.

Grace followed Marcia's finger, which pointed to a beautiful flower arrangement resting on the opposite side of the reception area. Squinting at the small envelope taped to the glass vase, Grace turned her gaze back to Marcia. "What's this?" she asked, clueless that a particular millionaire had his sites set on getting next to her.

"Probably just what it looks like," the assistant answered amiably. "I'm not sure what happened at that shoot yesterday, but if I had to guess, you made a lasting impression when you put Allen in his place. Rich pretty boys like him often come preassembled with an Oedipus complex. Don't be surprised if he's the type who doesn't mind being spanked."

"And you gathered all that from him sending me one dozen yellow roses? Shows how much you know, junior psychologist, yellow roses are for friendship," Grace replied.

Marcia giggled, with her eyes on the computer screen. "Maybe so but there's more. The persistent Mr. Foray had a courier deliver two big boxes of goodies after that."

Grace began to take more stock in Marcia's attempt at psychoanalyzing people she hardly even knew. Funny thing was she often hit the nail right on the head, although this time she had help. Patrik had called earlier to shower additional praise on Grace's efforts with Allen. Marcia had put two and two together, and oddly enough, it equaled twelve long-stemmed roses and a new admirer.

On the way to her office, the scent of fresh flowers caused Grace to think of a simpler time, when she had worked summers helping in her mother's floral shop. Her quiet moment reminiscing was interrupted by Marcia, who popped in with the vase Grace had purposely left behind. "In case you're wondering, Allen is twenty-six, a North Carolina grad, a lifetime card-carrying member of the NAACP, and unattached at the moment, although his last relationship ended with a battery of arrests for stalking."

"Arrests?" Grace shrieked.

"Oh, her, not him," Marcia clarified, handing Grace a stack of articles about Allen she'd downloaded from the Internet. "I guess you could say that the one-hundred-million-dollar media darling cash-cow, aka Captain Dream Creams, is young, single, and free."

Tapping her finger against the collection of stories written about Allen, Grace winced. "I'm crazy for even entertaining the idea of seeing that boy. We have nothing in common."

"That multimillion-dollar baby seems to be looking for a new mama to kiss him on his boo-boo," Marcia joked.

"Oh, is that what you young people are calling it these days?" Grace smirked, "gotcha" style, but Marcia had done her homework.

"I've read several accounts of where a younger man clings to a slightly older woman when facing adverse circumstances, pain, or injury. You'll note on page six there, at the bottom, that Allen's contract is up at the end of this season, and the Mavericks might not be able to provide the best offer because of the league's luxury tax." When Grace failed to see the importance in Marcia's inferences, she raised her brow, guessing that a conclusion was close at hand. "Miss Hilliard, that superstar is a southern boy. He loves Dallas, as noted on page two, and he doesn't want to be traded to New Jersey. I think that's highlighted on page four, if not on page five."

Grace didn't like the fact that her assistant was playing matchmaker on the clock, instead of working on Pinnacle's business, but she had to give her assistant major props for the extensive research she'd amassed in short order. "Marcia, I'm going to pretend that we've never had this discussion but if we did I'd have to end it like this. I'm sure that your intensions were good, but I'm not accustomed to discussing my personal affairs with employees, not even my favorite one. Since there's nothing between me and Allen, it's all hypothetical. I'll say this and be done with it. Everything you've said about him may be true, but I don't mix business with pleasure, no matter how enticing. More importantly, I already have one son, and I'm not in the practice of raising some other woman's for her. Thank you, and do close the door on your way out."

Grace held the stack of Internet articles above the wastepaper basket, working up the strength to chuck them. When she felt Marcia standing outside her door peeking through the blinds, the strength she needed prevailed. As the pages of Allen's exploits hit the bottom of the trash pail, so did his chances of having Grace play the Big-Sister-Mama-Lover-Friend role in his or any other man's true-to-life after-dinner theater. She was becoming more determined to land the starring role as The Only Woman in a deserving man's production of *Happily Ever After.* Anything else was unacceptable.

5

Boys to Men

It was six-thirty when Grace arrived at John Quinn High School. Rain was falling like sifted flour. She collected a handful of reports from the leather satchel lying on the front passenger seat. When it didn't appear the storm would subside anytime soon, she winced at the thought of getting drenched before making it to the back door of the gymnasium. While searching frantically for her umbrella, Grace ran across a plastic poncho stuffed under the backseat. She'd purchased it months before for just such an occasion, hoping that she'd never actually have to use it. But there it was, still folded neatly in its clear package. After wrestling the poncho over her head, she opened the car door and set out to brave the elements. She felt like a wet dog striding over puddles in the uneven parking lot. If she hadn't clutched the reports tightly against her chest, they would have taken flight in the gusting wind. Turning back never crossed her mind because her child was inside, preparing for his first high-school basketball game. Getting caught in a downpour wasn't enough to deter her from being there, for it would have been catastrophic had she missed his shining moment.

Once inside, Grace shed her plastic shawl, then shook droplets of water from her hands and hair. A short jaunt to the ladies' room served as a rest haven, as she patted herself dry as best she could with a pile of paper towels. Since no one really attended freshmen ball games, she took comfort in knowing the crowd would be sparse. Parents who dared to fight the traffic and flash flooding wouldn't give a rat's behind about her tattered appearance, she reasoned, while exiting the gloomy little room where graffiti detailed the names and sexual prowess of boys who rated far too experienced for their age, according to the girls eager to share it. Grace smiled when she didn't see André's name scribbled among others. There were far too many Kwans and Shuns mixed in to tell them apart.

A heftily built white man with oily skin and thick, dark hair smiled cordially at Grace as she passed through the gym doors. "That'll be three dollars, ma'am," he informed her. "Gotta charge something if the refs are gonna get paid." His full belly pressed against the open cash box, which rested on a rickety card table, and his breath smelled like a pack of menthol cigarettes.

"Can't have a sporting event without officials," Grace agreed, digging through her purse for small bills. "Can you break a twenty?"

"Yep, but I'll have to wait until halftime when the snack bar opens," the man huffed, nearly out of breath.

"Tell you what, keep the whole thing. My son's playing tonight, and it'll be worth every penny." The stubby doorkeeper didn't respond to Grace's comment. Instead, he nodded his thick head back and forth like nothing she would ever say or do mattered to him, then he went back to drooling over the group of cheerleaders jogging off from center court. "You're welcome," Grace mumbled softly, knowing that it fell on deaf ears. *Pervert!*

Grace's previous speculations proved correct. The stands were littered with slightly more fans than players, so it wasn't difficult finding a seat. She spotted André in the team's huddle just before the game started. Her chest swelled with pride. She couldn't have been more delighted if the bleachers were filled with people chanting her child's name. With the stack of damp reports sitting next to her, Grace decided to review them during intermittent breaks in the action and make the most of her time.

"Hey, Miss Hilliard, I thought that was you," Skyler Barnes yelled as he climbed down two rows to greet her. Despite being a senior, a celebrated talent, and touted as one of the top recruits in the country, he always found time to talk hoops with André and map out maneuvers explaining how to break down an opposing team's defense with a deadly crossover.

"Skyler, I'm surprised to see you," Grace said evenly. "I know you've got to be very busy, with college scouts beating down your grandmother's door."

"Yes, ma'am, that's why I'm here," he confessed. "The phone won't stop ringing. Plus it's Dré's first time to shine. Wouldn't miss that for the world, Miss Hilliard. He's gonna be good before long, you'll see. The boy's got heart." Grace smiled at the baby-faced man-child, with his six-five frame and basketball sneakers long enough to cross the Atlantic. Skyler was a thoughtful young man and thought a lot of his protégé. It was obvious his grandmother had raised him right.

As soon as the game began, André streaked down the court. He sprinted faster than Grace knew he could, and then he caught a deep pass and laid the ball in for the first basket. "Yeah!" Skyler cheered. "I told you he got game, Miss H, told you." Grace blushed over the next three quarters until the coach pulled André out for the remainder of the game. His players were ahead by twenty-five points, and there was no sense in embarrassing the visiting team. When Dré pulled on his sweats, Skyler nodded his head approvingly. "Eighteen points, seven assists, and five rebounds," he rattled off, from memory. "He'll be fight'n them off with a stick."

Before Grace opened her mouth to question the young man's idea of a compliment, he'd picked up and made it halfway to the snack bar. *Fighting them off,* she thought, not sure how to take it. *Fighting who off? I know he wasn't talking about those fast-tail little girls writing their business on the restroom walls. André isn't ready to deal with these overexposed, overdeveloped high school hoochies. Better not be anything on his mind but hitting the books.* No sooner than the game ended, two of the cheerleaders were all up in André's face, batting their eyes and shaking their pom-poms at him.

"Oh God," Grace huffed. "I know she didn't just slide him her phone number on the sneak tip. That used to be one of my best moves." Before her very eyes, her baby was growing up, too fast for her taste, and those young hussies were acting too grown for their own good.

"Hey Ma," André hailed gleefully, walking up in a cool, slow, bobbing manner. "I'm glad you made it."

"Uh-huh, I made it all right." She was looking at him sideways.

"What? I hit eighteen."

"I saw, and the seven assists with five rebounds."

"Dang, you caught all that?" André was noticeably impressed that she'd paid attention. "I didn't know you'd be keeping stats, or I would have gone for thirty."

"I was enjoying the game too much to keep up," she admitted, "but Skyler didn't miss a single thing."

"He never does, Ma."

Grace contemplated telling André that she'd peeped the cheerleader's well-devised sleight-of-hand phone-number pass, but thought better of it. Perhaps it was more prudent to let him enjoy the moment and think he'd put one over on her. Lord knows, she'd gotten away with her share of mischief when she was his age. Besides, there wasn't much Grace could do but watch him spread his wings and pray that several years passed before he became consumed with girls in short skirts and getting at what was underneath them.

Skyler spotted André in the parking lot from the confines of an old rusted-out Chevrolet Impala. The skies were so clear that it seemed improbable a storm had blown through a couple of hours before, except for the pools of puddles here and there. "Dré," Skyler yelled out, approaching with long, nimble strides. "Hey man, good game today. Next time, keep the ball a little closer to your hip. A better guard would have locked down and come away with a few gimmies."

"Thanks Sky, I'll watch that. It's too bad Central didn't bring a better guard with them." The boys slapped high-fives as Grace fiddled in her purse for car keys. André peered through the windows of the SUV to see if she'd locked them inside, but two large boxes caught his attention instead. "Ma, what are those?"

Grace glanced up with her keyless remote in hand. "Oh, just a little something for a hotshot freshman point guard and his personal statistician." She unlocked the rear doors with a steady eye on the fellows, noting their curiosity. "It appears that a very famous Dallas Maverick wanted to say thanks to a couple of deserving fans."

André's eyes grew wide as he tore into the first box. "Ahh, Ma, basketballs signed by All-World Allen Foray!" He shoved the second box into Skyler's waiting arms, then dove back into the other goodies at the bottom of the one he'd claimed for his own. Grace stood back, out of the way, as both boys rifled through professional basketball marketing apparel and NBA-approved knickknacks.

"Miss H!" Skyler cheered. "Ah, man, this is old-school hype. Can I keep the throwback jersey?"

"Yes, of course," Grace shrugged, feeling like a mother with two sons. She understood the marketing ploy behind old-school nostalgic jerseys, but failed to understand why it was so fashionable to wear something brand new that was carefully manufactured to look twenty years old. "I met with Allen yesterday for a bit of business and told him how much of a role model he was," she recounted. "Then he had this stuff sent over afterward. No big deal."

"No big deal!" the boys chuckled in unison. "Women just don't know."

Allen had scored major points with Grace's son, so his conning strategy to get in through the back door was in full tilt. She figured he'd show up again, merely by chance of course, and then lay on the charm with her the best way he knew how. The sad thing was, at Allen's age, he didn't know nearly enough about grown women to pull it off.

"You're the greatest, Miss Hilliard," Skyler thanked her with big, round, adoring eyes.

"Yeah Ma, the greatest," added André, without taking his eyes off his new toys. *He was still a boy after all,* she thought, like a small child on Christmas morning after she had been taken to the cleaners by department store advertisements promoting good tidings and bad credit.

Suddenly Grace remembered another thing: she'd forgotten her marketing reports in the bleachers. "Hey guys, I'll be right back. Keep an eye on the car."

Without hesitation, she marched back toward the metal gymnasium doors, where the sweaty pervert was turning the locks. "Could you wait a second? I need to get something!" she yelled, when it was obvious he'd seen Grace approaching but couldn't have cared less. "I know you're not trying to close that door while I'm standing here!" She couldn't believe his utter disregard and rudeness.

"Too late," the stumpy cash-box handler fired back. "I'm locking up."

"How long do you think they'll lock you up when I tell the school board about your high-school-girls-gone-wild cheerleader fantasies?" The sweaty doorkeeper smirked sheer displeasure at being called out. "Uh-huh, I saw you looking real hard at those underaged girls, and I'm sure their parents would take offense to that," Grace added, stepping past him while his mouth hung open. *Freak!*

Relieved that her important files were still where she'd left them, Grace sorted through the stack to ensure none had fallen through to the floor beneath the stands. Her smile dissolved as she descended the bleacher steps. There was a man, a fine one, discussing the game with André's coach. Grace assumed he was one of the other player's parents, a married parent at that, so she tried not to stare too hard.

"Oh my goodness," someone whispered. Grace was mortified when both men turned toward her after hearing the whispers as well, indicating that those words had not only come out of her mouth, but also had come out much louder than she'd thought.

"Excuse me," said the handsome gentleman with caramel-colored skin and flawless features.

"Nothing, just almost slipped," she lied, avoiding eye contact. *Don't look back*, she thought to herself. *Grace, don't you dare look back at him.* And wouldn't you know, when she did glance over her shoulder, he was still there wearing the same curious expression and gazing in her direction. She thought, *Some sistah is a very lucky woman, Grace, just keep right on moving.* She assumed that Mr. Oh-My-Goodness had to be attached because he was so well groomed and looked too adorable in his navy sports coat and khaki slacks to be unattached.

"You want to unlock that chain!" Grace barked at the doorkeeper standing too close for comfort. He glared at her briefly and then unlocked the chains he'd placed around the door handles. "Like you didn't know I'd be coming back the same way," she hissed. The man stepped aside as she strutted down the steps to the parking lot, and out of his life.

As Grace approached the boys, still ogling the sportswear she'd given them, she opened her car door, then stole a glance back at the gym, wondering if the well-dressed man inside was thinking about her, too. She shrugged and shook it off when it occurred to her that it probably didn't matter. He *had* to belong to someone. He had to.

"Good night, Skyler. Take care. André, let's roll," Grace announced hurriedly after noticing that neither of the boys were eager to relinquish their moment of enjoyment. "We've got to get home," she added when her son frowned. Grace rolled her eyes in return and sentenced him to silence. "Don't ask, Dré. Don't ask." She didn't know exactly what she was running from, but something about that man had made her nervous, nervous and foolish. That's why she couldn't wait to see him again, even if it was for just a hot minute to investigate those striking features of his one more time. There was no harm in just looking at another woman's man, Grace reasoned all the way home, unless he was the kind of man who made her feel nervous and foolish.

Speaking of foolish, Greg Anderson called on Grace's cell phone during her trip to her side of town. She fished the phone out of her purse and read the name on her caller display. Without giving it a second thought, she tossed the tiny flip phone back into her purse and let it stay there until she reached her house and took her sweet time settling in. Greg was her other "just-a-friend," as she put it when André asked who the man was that sent over a bucket of chocolate-covered raisins on her birthday. If there was ever a man who made Grace laugh harder than any well-written sitcom, it was Greg. His comical look at life was refreshing in the beginning, but as the saying goes, the one thing she most admired about him was the same thing that irked her to no end after she'd gotten to know him. It was Greg's humorous disposition, bordering on adolescent behavior, that had Grace asking herself why she was considering driving clear across town to play house.

She discovered that Greg had left two additional messages. Feeling unsure about whether to make the trip to his place or not, Grace sat on her bed and contemplated. She returned his calls, and prepared herself to take a pass on his offer until Greg picked up on the first ring and made her laugh until her sides hurt. Grace smiled ear to ear when Greg sang into the phone, "Anderson's Mortuary. You tag 'em, we bag 'em, two wings and a gizzard basket while you wait."

"You are too silly for words, Greg," she chuckled. "I know you checked your caller ID, so you know who this is."

"It'd better be Amazing Grace, because that's who's got me taking cold showers."

"Humph. If I know you, it's probably crowded in there," she answered back, closing the bedroom door before locking it. She walked over to her chaise longue, covered in a majestic cream fabric, matching the special-ordered comforter on her king-size bed. Since no one, under any circumstances, was allowed in her boudoir without being invited, Grace felt enough at ease to strip down to nothing if she were so inclined to talk dirty until verbal stimulation wasn't enough to get her through the night.

"Grace. Grace! You still there?" Greg asked, his voice rising to get her attention. "I was telling you about the three-ring circus act in town from Senegal. I had the Triplets on the Trapeze over to the house last week and I got all three of 'em drunk on a six pack of Malt Duck, but they didn't allow for audience participation, so all I got to do was watch." His shtick was wasted on Grace. She was busy recalling her last flextime episode with Tyson, and getting more of what she wanted on a more frequent basis.

"Hmmm, I'm sorry, Greg. My mind wandered. It was a very long day." With the telephone propped on her shoulder, Grace slid on a silk three-quarter robe with a pastel Asian print detailed in mauve and teal.

"Good, then you should wander on over here and let me put your mind at ease with something from the freak sack. Forget what happened the last time, when I forgot to take my ginseng," he apologized. "I even lifted some powered rhinoceros tusk off that circus troop to make up for it, and you know that's hard to get."

Grace's thighs had begun brushing softly against one another, and before she knew it, she'd drifted away again. "Greg, did you say something about a rhinoceros?"

"Yeah, they say Viagra ain't got nothing on rhinoceros tusks. It's the aphrodisiac from the motherland." Although he was joking about Senegalese Circus Troupes and Triplet Trapeze acts, Greg had been known to come by very peculiar sexual stimulants every now and then. Some of them even worked. Greg sensed that Grace was nibbling at his bait. If he could get her to bite, he'd be that much closer to nibbling at hers.

Imagining him trying out something new from his bag of tricks, Grace felt warm inside as both of her eyes opened wide. She laughed just thinking about how ridiculous Greg looked, crossing his fingers on the other end. "So this tusk business, where do you put it?" she asked finally.

"I don't know. I didn't think to steal the directions too," he chuckled in a carefree manner. "I can't think of everything."

"Okay. All right, Greg. You got me." Grace figured she was due some authentic tribal experimentation, or else she'd stay up all night tossing, turning, and wishing she had. "I'll be there shortly."

"How shortly?" he begged to know.

"We'll both know when I get there, won't we? Just make sure you have that motherland aphrodisiac ready."

"It's ready now, baby, oh . . . You mean that powered stuff," he cackled. "'Cause you know, I'm always packing that Urban Root. I don't leave home without it."

"I'll be there within the hour to see if you're making promises again that you can't keep," Grace sniped quickly, then hung up the phone.

6

Bag O' Tricks

Grace slipped on an orange tank top and the first jogging suit she came across in her spacious walk-in closet. By the time she put on a neatly folded navy blue velour two-piece from the top shelf, André had already showered, completed his homework, and parked himself in front of the television. He never missed the *SportCenter* highlights. "Dré," Grace called out with an empty gym bag tossed over her shoulder, "I'm going to get in a quick workout. I'll be back before ten." She hated lying to him, but it wasn't a lie, entirely. It just wasn't the whole truth. When she saw his head nodding, although he neglected to turn away from the tube, she knew he'd heard her just fine.

The subdivision Greg lived in was thirty-five minutes away if Grace hurried. That left her an hour to get in a good horizontal cardio workout and return home before André headed off to bed. Although he was old enough to tuck himself in and was very responsible for his age, she felt there was something maternally wrong about letting him sleep in that big house of their's alone. There was no time to get caught up in Greg's shenanigans or his idea of extended foreplay. She was determined to get in, get what she came for, and get out.

When Grace turned into his driveway, the garage door elevated on cue. Greg patiently awaited her arrival, not leaving anything to chance. His neighbors had gotten an earful the last time a woman showed up and preceded to go slap off while he was in the middle of satisfying another one. Ever since that night, Greg made it a point to conceal any appearance of adult entertainment from passersby.

"There she is," he sang, wrapped in a thick cloth robe dyed in deep purple. "Come over here so I can do some thangs to you."

"You cut your hair," Grace noticed after imagining what sort of thangs he had in mind.

"Yeah, I did. All of it," he answered with a goofy grin. The belt holding his robe closed loosened even further when he extended his arms to embrace her. His rippled stomach and skinny legs reminded Grace of a much younger man's body, despite his being four years older than she. Greg was considered more cute than handsome. His fair complexion was smooth, with freckles sprinkled here and there, and he was sporting the scrawniest goatee imaginable. His decision to dispense with pubic hair altogether was an obvious mistake, but Grace didn't have time to inquire about his reasoning behind the bald and bold look.

Eventually, Grace lowered her workout bag to the floor, studied her sports watch, and then she did as instructed so that Greg could get busy doing some of those thangs to her. The citrus scent of his shower gel tickled her nose. "That's nice," she cooed, over both his fresh fragrance and the way he gently fondled her breasts. Her nipples stiffened before she'd had the chance to push Greg away. "I need a shower. The long day and all."

"Good, I'll come in and keep you company."

"No, that won't be necessary. I'll be right out," Grace declined.

"I'll be watching," he informed her, with his hands cupping her behind.

"I know you will."

As promised, Greg spied on Grace through a thin opening in the shower curtain. He stroked himself aggressively while eying every square inch of her soapy skin. Climbing in to join her occurred to Greg more than once, but it was more erotic from his vantage point. He was turned on, just as he always had been whenever observing Grace from the confines of his own private peep show. When she stepped out, soaking wet and glistening, Greg gulped and licked his lips. His heart rate quickened as the thought of meeting his desires head-on became overwhelming. "C'mon now, I'm about to burst," he murmured, wrestling on a condom.

"Slow down, Greg," she advised as he whisked her towel away. "What about that African powder you were talking about?"

Greg pulled her toward the bedroom. "I got it right here, baby. Ooh, lay down."

Grace pulled back the indigo-hued linen sheets, then sat on the bed. "Blue, I like blue," she moaned. "You know what else I like?"

Sprinkling a fine white powder between Grace's legs, Greg gestured that he understood without a doubt what she liked, but had other ideas. "Yeah, but I want to try this out first." He flicked on the antique lamp resting on the nightstand so he could see the powder taking effect. "Let me know when it starts to tingle."

"Oh, it's tingling already," Grace confessed, with heated breath. "I want to feel you inside. Give it to me." Grace felt a prevailing sensation between her thighs. She ached, panting louder and louder. Greg maneuvered his way into her, looking on with his typical wide-eyed gaze as she began to gyrate in ecstasy. "It's hot, Greg. Ooh, it's hot. Give it to me.

Give. Give. Give. Oh, that's it. Harder! Harder!" She writhed beneath his best efforts to keep up, but he wasn't capable of creating the satisfaction she begged for. "Get the bag, honey," Grace ordered. Her mouth was as dry as desert sand, but she hadn't noticed. She could think of nothing but having him to quench her raging fire. "Hurry, Greg! Please!"

He leapt from the bed to search his top drawer. When he returned, with a black sackcloth bag, Grace swallowed hard. Greg reached inside and came out with a small handheld battery-operated manipulator. The soft rubber toy was fashioned in the shape of a miniature dolphin, with a vibrating head and tail. When it met Grace's skin, she screamed, "Ahhh! That's it. Ahhh!" Grace caught glimpses of Greg's sinister grin while his head bobbed up and down. She screamed, "Okay, I want you. Come on, honey, I want you!" Always willing to close the show, Greg tossed the manipulator aside and then assumed its place.

There was such a chorus of moaning and bodies smacking violently together, it would have been difficult to distinguish which belonged to whom. Grace wrapped her legs around Greg's neck as he placed a pillow under her behind to heighten the impact of penetration. Grace was enthralled in the throes of passion when her eyes rolled back in her head. "Oh, it's coming baby! Give it to me! Oh, God, it's good! Oh, Godddd!"

Suddenly, Greg slammed on the brakes. His body stiffened. "Grace, I've told you about that," he reprimanded her.

"Don't stop!" she pleaded loudly.

"Don't call God's or nobody else's name who ain't already naked and in this bed. You want Him to see what you're doing? Well, I don't."

"Greg, I'm begging you. I was almost there. Don't go getting all righteous on me now."

He tried to unlock her legs from around his neck, but she wouldn't allow it. "Grace, I had my immorality in check, but no, you had to go calling His name and bringing attention to us."

"So what, you're just going to leave me all hot and bothered like this?" Grace was visibly upset to the point of becoming hostile.

Greg considered the alternative, which would have left them both high and dry. "Nah, I didn't necessarily say that." Obviously, his ethics were not beyond reproach. "It's just hard to concentrate on pleasing you and trying to dodge thunderbolts at the same time. When you scream out His name like that, it gives me the creeps." Greg's eyes floated up toward the ceiling. She scowled angrily and pushed him away with the balls of her feet.

"Hey, what was that for?" he bellowed sorrowfully.

"Now you've ruined it for me too," Grace huffed. When he attempted to mount her again, she stifled his aim. "Quit it, Greg! Move!"

"Whoa, you're serious?"

"That's the problem here, we're not serious, neither of us." Grace pulled the bedsheets up to her neck.

Greg propped up two pillows directly behind her. "Here, lay your head on this." Saddled with a deflated erection to match his deflated ego, Greg sat up with his back against the headboard. "Are you going to tell me what's really going on with you, or do I have to guess?"

"Whew, it's nothing and everything," she answered, staring into the semidarkness.

"Oh, I see, it's a riddle."

"No Greg, it's a shame. It's a shame that we've been hooking up for years on and off between other lovers who've passed through our lives. I think we continue to hold part-time spaces for each other only because of a comfort level we share."

Taking the time to consider Grace's heartfelt interpretation of their long-term commitment-free arrangement, Greg scratched at the stubble on his chin and then said the first thing that came to mind. "Are you pregnant?"

"Are you kidding?"

"Okay, cool. So we can get back to butt-naked business, then?"

"Negro, you must be insane!" Insulted, Grace punched him in the chest.

"Ouch, that hurt!"

"So does what I've allowed to happen for far too long. I'm in my prime, and wasting my best years getting down with you, no strings attached."

"It's been good, though," Greg argued. "You have to admit that."

"Yeah, I guess, but it hasn't been fulfilling." Grace sat up on her elbows and looked Greg in the eye so that she could detect whether his next statement would be a lie. "Greg, I want you to be honest, even if you think it'll hurt my feelings." When it appeared that Greg was trying to decide whether to lie or not, Grace popped him again.

"Hey! If you don't stop hitting me, I'ma call the po-po. I'm not above calling the law." He rubbed the sore spot vigorously. "Okay, the truth."

"What do you think about getting married?"

"Who, with you?" he squealed, panic making his eyes as big as saucers.

"Not necessarily with me, stupid, but now that you're getting all indignant about it, why not me? Tell me why, after all this time, you've not once asked me to get involved in a more substantial relationship than just getting together like this."

"Well, there was that one time I tried to introduce you to this white girl at my office, but nooo, you weren't into a ménage à trois." After joking his way through a tense situation, Greg offered the most sincere answer he could. "Grace, I'll say this, but I don't need you hitting me. Us beige brothas bruise easy." When she smirked at Greg, he almost laughed.

"Okay, then. You must know that I care about you and I think you're a great catch, just not the right one for me."

"Oh, you'll need to elaborate, because I don't understand how such a great catch can't be right for you."

"Look. I'll explain it the best way I know how. You have a nice body, a pretty face, and you even do that thing with your tongue, but you can also be moody at times. Besides, I can't deal with a woman who already has everything she needs. In case you've missed it, a man likes to feel needed even if he isn't. Like it or not, that's the way it is."

"Me, moody?" That was all that Grace heard. "Forget you, then. Get out of my bed," she ranted, kicking at him. "Get out!"

Greg threw up his hands to defend himself. "Hold on, Grace! Hold on, now."

"Why should I?"

"Because this is *my* bed!" he answered wildly, stating the obvious.

"Cool, be that way," Grace spat, snatching the sheets from his clutches. "Then I'll get out and never ever let you put your grubby hands anywhere near 'sweet precious' again."

Laughing under his breath, Greg shook his head. "That might bother me if I thought you could actually pull it off. Grace, don't be hasty. You enjoy sex as much as I do. You're a freak, just like me. That's why we've gotten along like two freaky peas in a pod for so long."

Grace leaned in closely toward the assured expression plastered on Greg's face. She said, "Maybe you'd like to think I'm wilder than most, but you haven't even seen my best tricks, and now you never will." She made her tongue dance just the way he liked, then put it away and smacked her lips closed.

"You've been holding out on me?" Greg asked excitedly. He was even more stimulated than before, wanting to experience what she'd kept from him.

"Uh-huh, and holding back, too." Grace went around the bedroom, gathering her things to get dressed. When Greg eased up behind her, she felt admittedly weak in the knees but found the strength to hold firm when she saw his reflection in the dresser's mirror along with hers. "See, that's what I'm talking about. I want a man who can hold me like this *every day,* not just when he's trying to jump up and down on me *today.*"

"Aren't you taking this a bit too far?" Greg protested. "I mean, we've seen each other through some tough times. Doesn't that count for anything? Doesn't that matter?"

"No, it doesn't. Not enough, anyway," Grace replied. "If it weren't so trifling of me, it'd be kinda funny, the way I've been fooling myself into thinking that it did matter, and that's my fault." Grace quickly wrestled on her running shorts and workout top before tossing her sweats into the gym bag she'd brought along for appearances. She turned around to face Greg and then placed her arms around his neck affectionately. "Greg, at times you have been a dear friend to me, and for that I'm eternally thankful, but from now on the only fool I'll be is for my husband. Oh, and by the way, I'm taking the freak sack with me."

"Uh, that's not a good idea, Grace," he objected, with both hands raised in a pleading position. "You gotta leave the bag o' tricks."

"And why would I want to do that?" she questioned, holding the bag behind her back.

"See, 'cause some of those tricks in that bag were donated by some uh . . . other sistahs." Greg gulped like he had before and braced himself for another quick jab to the chest.

Grace was repulsed by the revelation. "You mean you've been using these same toys on other women? That's so nasty, Greg. Yuck!" She held the cloth bag at arm's length for him to reclaim it. "At least you had the decency to wash them."

"Huh? You can wash them?" he mumbled awkwardly.

"Now I've got to rush home, disinfect myself, and pray I didn't catch anything. Stupid!"

As she strutted away from his side door, Greg followed in close step behind her with the bedsheet gathered around his waist. "Grace! Grace!" he hollered after her. "If you do this, you live with it, but don't walk away acting like you're Halle Berry fine, because you're not!"

"And you're no Denzel, so that makes us about even," Grace sniped evenly through clenched teeth.

"See . . . See here, Grace. That's just like a woman, always wanting what they can't have. Denzel's already gotta wife!" With Greg standing in the doorway of his home, the wind kicked up, exposing Greg's freshly shaven pubic region.

Grace frowned at it disapprovingly. "And somewhere out there is a Denzel for me too, baldy!"

Halfway back down the tollway, Grace turned the radio off. She devoted the long ride home to deep contemplation over the roads she'd traveled down, ultimately leading her to this place, the place that had her sneaking out of the house for a late-evening rendezvous and lying about it. That was the same place that convinced her to schedule monthly flex-time romps around Tyson Sharp's availability. Loneliness was that place. She despised it, but often found herself trapped there, in another compromising position, before recognizing her surroundings. Once again, it had lured Grace into its clutches, and afterwards sent her home with the radio off, devoting the long ride to deep contemplation, sadness and regret.

7

Shakespeare in the Hood

The morning after, Grace pulled up in front of the high school to drop off André. For some strange reason, she felt it necessary to hug him as if he were heading off for his first day of kindergarten, instead of just another day in ninth grade. "Mama, are you all right?" André asked when Grace held firmly onto the sleeve of his thin jacket. "Ma, I'll be late." Eventually she released him, wanting to say how sorry she was for leaving him alone to slip by and hook up with Greg, but she immediately reconsidered when realizing it would have served no purpose. Lamenting her affair could have also opened a disastrous line of questioning she wasn't prepared for, so she waved good-bye with a faltering smile.

"Have a good day, son," Grace said in parting.

"Yeah, thanks," André responded awkwardly, wondering if there was something else to be said. "That it?"

"Just that I'll pick you up at Skyler's after the parent-teacher conference tonight. Don't forget to send my thanks to his grandmother."

"Yes, ma'am. I'll tell Miss Pearl." André darted off toward the school building with his book bag bobbing up and down over his left shoulder. Before Grace dragged herself from the curb, she observed how her child had grown so independent and self-assured without having a man around to emulate. So many other fatherless boys had become involved with gangs, or drugs, and subsequently the law, by his age. But André wasn't actually fatherless. His father was thoughtless and selfish, although Grace was too proud to demand active participation from him in their child's life. She wouldn't have known for certain if he were still alive had it not been for the thirteen years of steady child support sitting in a trust fund with André's name on it. Grace hadn't seen "the sperm donor," as she called him, in almost as long as she'd been depositing the full extent of his parental assistance. Honestly, she gave up imagining how life would have been for her if she had married Edward in college, like other young expectant mothers nearing college graduation. Since André stopped mentioning his father a few years before, Grace followed his lead. Other than those monthly deposits, it was as if he never really existed at all. On the other hand, Grace was constantly reminded to the contrary each time she viewed Edward's image when looking at André's.

When Grace snapped out of her daze, she was startled by a host of anxious parents in the drop-off lane, leaning on their car horns. She got the message that the time had come for her to move on. André already had.

André strolled into the classroom along with twenty-three other chattering teenagers. His teacher, Wallace Peters, was smartly dressed in a dark plaid sports coat, white button-down shirt, and khaki slacks. He wrote two words on the blackboard in bold print, DESTINY and AMBITION. Mr. Peters had the distinction of being known as a teacher extraordinaire, talented and adored by his students. So much so, that the kids rarely missed his English literature class, which was a required course, when ditching other subjects was commonplace in the urban high school. After Grace had moved to the suburbs, she promised to keep André around more people who looked like him so she rented out their older home and wisely retained ownership for André to continue playing basketball in that district.

"Good morning, Mr. Wallace," saluted several students as they entered his classroom. The young girls flirted behind his back, knowing he wouldn't have tolerated that sort of foolishness had he been aware of it.

"Don't let him catch you checking him out like that," whispered the same cheerleader who had offered her phone number to André.

"Shoot, Mr. Wallace knows he fine. All the lady teachers peep him every chance they get," her girlfriend replied discreetly. "And they don't care who see 'em. Humph, you can't make my momma miss a parent-teacher meeting with him, when you can't drag her butt down here for nothing else." The young girl was right on several fronts. Her mother had it bad for the attractive teacher with thick eyebrows, flawless skin, and what some might have thought of as great hair. Additionally, several female teachers structured their breaks around his, looking for the chance to discuss poetry, current affairs, or the most popular question, Why he was so fine and still single.

"Mr. Wallace, is the test gonna be this Friday?" one of the young men asked.

"Not if it's a pop test," he answered cleverly. "Those are given when you least expect it."

"Since I'm expecting one on Friday, it won't be given then, huh?" the boy answered, undoubtedly unprepared for the exam.

"One can always hope, Tariq," Mr. Peters remarked, with a cordial grin. "One can always hope."

"Keep hope alive," André joked, in his best Jesse Jackson impersonation. The classroom lit up in unbridled laughter. Skyler, seated across from his little buddy, was an honored guest in freshman lit for the duration of the semester. Although he was passing a senior-level English course, he'd asked for a special concession to brush up on the basics before graduating in the spring. Within the first week of class, Mr. Peters discovered the real reason Skyler wanted to be in the class with André.

"It would serve Tariq better to keep his book opened," countered the witty instructor. After a clamorous chorus of "Oohs" sounded off the walls, the teacher turned toward the words he'd written on the board. Mr. Wallace pointed at them emphatically, and then he pointed at the students likewise. "Destiny and ambition, young people, those are the two most determining factors in your becoming what you are meant to be, or not."

"Is that the question?" a young man quipped, after having studied *Hamlet* the month before.

"No, Marcus," answered Mr. Peters. "It's the answer, that we're looking for today. The answer," he added, scanning their faces. Now that he had their full attention, their minds were also opened to new, unforeseen possibilities for their futures. Mr. Peters began pacing in front of his desk. The children's eyes followed him back and forth. "We are currently studying another of Shakespeare's masterpieces, *Macbeth*. I have been trying to come up with a practical example to illustrate what Macbeth was going through and how his experiences apply to you." Skyler tossed a glance at André from the corner of his eye, suggesting that all of them were about to get hit with some heavy philosophizing. Skyler's assumption was correct, and many of his classmates' lives would be permanently altered after the discussion had time to sink in.

"Take Macbeth, a smart, rugged soldier," noted Mr. Peters. "He was given all that he needed while serving King Duncan during battle, and he was also rewarded with great wealth and power. One night, three witches came to him and shared a prophecy that he would some day be king himself. Now, that was good news, and Macbeth believed it to be true. Upon arriving home, he told his wife what the witches prophesized. Lady Macbeth decided that the quickest way to fulfill the prophecy was to assassinate the current king post-haste . . . That means right away. Understand this, class, how Macbeth's ambitious wife persuaded him to go against his best thought of waiting it out. After Macbeth had the king killed and took his seat on the throne, he also had to kill the star witnesses to cover it up. Eventually, his conscience wouldn't allow him to sleep because his dreams became filled with disturbing visions of ghosts. Listening to Lady Macbeth had influenced him to seek something very valuable through dishonest means." The students were locked on to the teacher's every word. When he began pacing again, their gazes grew even more intense. "Ultimately, Macbeth's blind ambition changed his life, and later caused him to be murdered in the end. Of course, his wife and children met the same fate, as you have read for yourselves, I'm sure." André's mind was racing, as if viewing a fascinating trailer to an upcoming movie he hadn't seen. "I know that some of you are thinking that kind of stuff happened a long time ago, so let's apply those circumstances to modern occurrences."

There were so many blank faces staring back at him, because very few students understood his intent. "We'll tackle it one incident at a time. First, the witches coming to Macbeth could have been nothing more than his own desires of being king manifesting themselves into his personal thoughts."

"Was there anything wrong with that?" someone asked from the back row. "I mean, people have been telling me all my life that I could be anything I wanted to be, even the president if I believed it. That's kinda like the king, right?"

"Yes it is, and you are correct. There was nothing wrong with Macbeth wanting to be rich and powerful, but he let someone else get inside his head and convince him to do wrong."

"Ooh, that's right!" the cheerleader shouted. "Macbeth's

wife kept picking at him until she punked him to snuff out King Duncan. That was wrong."

"Yeah, that Lady Macbeth was a trip," Tariq chimed. "I know too many brothas on lockdown now because of triflin' females."

"Whut-ever," the cheerleader snapped back.

"That may very well be true, Tariq," Mr. Peters agreed. "But I'm sure there are many more brothas responsible for sending their friends to prison because of—"

"Peer pressure," offered Skyler. "I thought that was something new, but I guess it's been getting people twisted for centuries."

"Exactly!" Mr. Peters slapped his hands together when he felt the discussion moving in the direction he'd counted on. "Once Macbeth decided he would take the crown, he devised a plan to jack it, as you young people like to say."

"But once he jacked the crown, he had to pop, I mean kill, all the witnesses," said the boy sitting next to Tariq. "Mr. Peters, Macbeth should have divorced ole girl before she got him jammed up. Didn't they already have a big crib?"

"They did, at that, but ole girl wanted more, and she wanted it fast," the teacher explained.

"Mr. Peters, I can see why someone might get talked into doing something they figure they can get away with, but it never seems to work out that way," the cheerleader's cohort reasoned. "Or else there wouldn't be more black men in prison than there are in college. Didn't the Macbeths know that all they had to do was wait on the king to die on his own? I mean, he was real old."

"Let me ask the class this." Mr. Peters was really cooking. He had arrived at the point he'd dreamt of when he agreed to teach young inner-city students. "If you all knew that a nice home, a nice car, and a good life were waiting for you on the other side of that door and around the corner, would you allow your destiny to unfold and work toward meeting it, or let your ambitions and other people lead you down the wrong path? And before you answer, remember that Macbeth couldn't enjoy his kingdom because the nightmares and ghosts of the men he'd killed continued haunting him."

"Like a conscience, when you're about to get caught up with the wrong crowd, in the wrong place, at the wrong time," asserted another male student from the back row. "My cousin is doing a ten-year bid 'cause he swiped a Benz but was way too nervous to roll in it. He didn't get no sleep neither. Got busted trying to take the whip back. After being awake for three days, po-po snatched him up. He sent me a letter all about it. Said he slept in the back of the squad car all the way downtown. Said that was the best sleep he ever had."

Mr. Peters nodded assuredly. "Once a person decides to take something that doesn't belong to him, it's very likely that he'll lose a part of himself in the process. Macbeth lost the good life he'd worked hard for. He lost his wife and children, all taken away by going against what he knew to be right in his own mind. This is a very tragic story that didn't have to turn out the way it did. And neither do any of yours."

"Mr. Peters," André said, barely audible as his classmates pondered over their own stories, still yet to be written, "do you think that Shakespeare wrote this story as a message to young kids dealing with the problems of growing up?"

"That's a good question, André. Actually, he wrote it as a reflection of his times, hoping that the adults would recognize all the bad things that came out of doing wrong, when doing right is always the best option. Here's the thing I want you all to get from this extremely powerful look at human nature," Wallace Peters continued. "Destiny is the where and how each of us will end up in life, or in the next life for that matter, and ambition is the fuel that will get us there."

When the school bell rang, no one moved. Somber expressions covered the young adults' faces until their teacher reminded them that his class was over. Silence ushered them to their next destinations, with Wallace praying that his discussions made enough positive inroads to enact a difference in the next phase of their lives. As far as he was concerned, he owed them at least that much.

Later that evening, Grace wheeled in and out of traffic en route to the parent-teacher meeting. She had been held up by a late call from a corporate partner at All-Jams Sports Management. After sitting still for all the praise she could take, once the client had viewed the rough cuts of Allen Foray's Captain Dream Creams commercial, Grace had to excuse herself and race through the building in the interest of her most important client of all, André. When she finally made it to the school, the visitors' parking lot was packed. Some of the parents had definite reasons to camp out with educators who held the keys to their children's college educations. For Grace, it was merely going through the motions so that she could cross the meeting off of her good-parenting list. André's grades were superb so there was no apparent cause for concern. Although Grace was curious because he had been going on about some superteacher who had a waiting list of students who wanted to take his English literature class.

Grace entered the building, thinking how much things had changed since her school days, when there would have been a waiting list to get out of freshman English. A helpful school staffer pointed out the direction to the Language Arts wing. Grace followed them to the tee until she ran smack dab into a line formed outside of room 222. It seemed odd standing idly by for over five minutes. There had to be some peculiar circumstance, she imagined, to explain how parents met with other teachers on the same hall with the greatest of ease, and yet she hadn't bettered her position in the endless chain of women. Women? That was the most peculiar detail, one that's she'd overlooked until now. Why were there only women, patient and primping women, on line to speak with this Mr. Peters?

"Excuse me," Grace said, getting the attention of a white

lady standing in front of her. "Uh, is this the line to see Mr. Peters?"

"Yeah, girl," she answered with a thick southern drawl, her flat white cheeks turning flush. "I wouldn't mind standing here all night to get in a good conversation with that dreamboat." *Dreamboat?*

"We are talking about a teacher, right?" Grace wanted to be sure that the dreamboat comment was awarded to a man who spent the better part of his day quoting the standard old-English fables while trying to keep the boys and girls from planning a mutiny to overthrow boredom. "So, what gives? I must have missed the memo. Are there always so many single women here to get in a good conversation with the dreamboat?"

"Chile, yes, and I'm here every time, only some of us aren't single." Mr. Peters's admirer held her dainty hand out to flash a multicarat diamond ring. By the size of that rock, Grace knew that the woman wasn't single by a long shot. "I'd rather leave my husband at home busying himself with other, less pressing things, if you know what I mean. He has no idea that Wallace Peters is so good looking or he'd be standing right where you are and watching my every move." The way she tossed her long blond hair to the side, Grace imagined what moves she intended on making when it was her turn to bat those baby blues at Wallace.

Uh-uh-uh, Wallace Peters, Grace thought. "I don't have time for this. Maybe I'll call the principal's office to reschedule."

"You'd be the only one, if you did, sugar." They inched up along the wall as a busty black woman exited the room wearing too much makeup and too little clothing. "See, now that's what I was talking about. That sister knows she didn't have to spruce up like that. Hell, now I feel overdressed." *Did she say that sister?*

This is crazy, Grace thought. *Has propositioning teachers for better grades come to this?* Perhaps high school had gotten more competitive than she remembered. "Thanks for the information, but I'm going to pass on the meet-and-greet, good-looking dreamboats considered," Grace commented as she stepped out of line.

The blonde held out both hands and studied her French manicured tips. "I can see that you're new here. Tell you what. Why'ont you tippy-toe by the door and sneak a peek before you go? I'll hold your place for you."

Grace camouflaged her you've-got-to-be-kidding-me smirk with a lighthearted chuckle. "Okay, I'll do that, but just for grins."

"I would if I's you. Believe me, you won't regret it one itsy-bitsy bit."

As Grace stepped out of her place in line, the woman behind her shuffled into the vacant space and smiled heartily as if she'd just found the perfect purse on sale. Grace couldn't believe some of the dirty looks she received while sauntering to the head of the chain-o-chicks dressed in their nightclub clothes. They sneered at her as if she were also auditioning for the part in a major movie they coveted. Harboring reservations, Grace walked by the open doorway and glanced inside without breaking stride. Her heart skipped a beat when she saw him, Mr. Oh-My-Goodness he's the incredibly handsome him from the basketball game. Now she understood why Wallace Peters commanded a standing-room-only audience. He'd earned those rave reviews from the blonde, and probably had scores of silly single mothers, and some not so single, marking their calendars with the next conference date. Only Grace wasn't going out like that. It wasn't that she didn't want to, her pride wouldn't stand for it. But, oh, how she wished it did. Turning an about-face to reclaim her link in the chain was out of the question. However, she felt duty-bound to give the leggy blonde her props on making a very astute assessment regarding ole dreamboat's lofty credentials. He was all that, and a hat to match.

Receiving the same shady leers from the other mothers as

before, Grace slowed to whisper a few words to blondie. "I'm going to run along, but I've gotta hand it to you. If I had a man, I'd have left him at home too."

"Who you telling?" remarked the woman who had taken Grace's place.

The blonde held out her hand for some soul-sister dap. "I was born at night, honey, but it wasn't last night." Grace slapped the woman's hand and laughed about her encounter with the cool white chick all the way to her car.

8

A Change 'Gone Come

On Friday morning, Grace stared out of her window behind closed office doors. She'd neglected the mounting stack of marketing reports and an assortment of things to do in her day planner. The one issue refusing to be shelved on the back burner was a necessary discussion with Tyson Sharp. Grace had blown off the annoying thought, but it continued to hang around at her door, pounding adamantly. She needed to exhale, and a calming retreat to assist her in doing so.

Within minutes, gentle winds were speaking to Grace while she sat on a park bench two blocks from her office building. She listened attentively to the quiet words surrounding her as a family of mallard ducks swam by in perfect formation, with the mother leading the expedition. The proud father duck brought up the rear, providing security for six of the cutest ducklings on the planet. Grace observed them floating downstream, effortlessly it seemed, although she suspected their little feet motored rapidly to keep pace. All families were like that, she reasoned. Despite how easily it appeared to sustain harmony, a lot of work was actually required to hold it together and remain closely knit. She was prepared to put in the work, but didn't have anyone bringing up the rear to share the load with. That's when she concentrated on the wind's oration, which she'd heard so many times before. It was constant when she sat still long enough to listen. "*Grace*," it called out to her, *"there are so many opportunities you've missed, so many plans you've neglected to make. Enjoy life as it was intended, to the fullest. Live life long and wide, long and wide."*

I hear you, she thought silently. *I always do. It's just that I've grown accustomed to making the best of a glass half full. All of my life, I've felt like a kid in a candy store, sampling handfuls of chocolate-covered raisins. Much like the men in my past, and present too, I guess. I've been fortunate enough to sample more than my fair share of treats, one bite at a time. Funny how long it's taken me to understand what it is that I've been missing. I know what pleases me, and I also know what I need. The joke's on me though, because the two of them are hardly the same thing at the same time, so I often find myself sacrificing one for the other.* She said out loud, "Somehow, that's got to change." As the winds brushed against the back of Grace's neck, she realized that it wasn't the winds she'd visited the park bench in order to receive a kind word. It hadn't been nature calling out to her, but The Comforter instead speaking to her all along.

"Something's gotta change, huh?" Tyson asked, standing behind her.

"Yes it does," Grace replied, after hearing him characterize her entire life in one simple sentence. When he stepped around the park bench, Grace managed a labored smile. Tyson's expensive cologne tickled her nose. "You smell good, like the first days of spring," she told him. "But then you always do." Her eyes glanced up at his broad shoulders and his tailored dress shirt with gold-and-diamond-studded cuff links.

Beyond all that glitz, Tyson's expression couldn't conceal

the curiosity hiding behind it. "Thanks, thanks a lot," he offered while studying her face for telltale clues. He sat down alongside her, careful not to rush into whatever it was that she'd insisted he meet her there to discuss. He decided to let it come out slow and easy, and then deal with it accordingly. "It's peaceful here," he said, observing the tranquil setting. "Is this where you come to think?"

"No, it's where I come to listen." Her answer was far above Tyson's realm of understanding, but he nodded as if fully comprehending what she meant. After sharing a lengthy bout of silence, Grace addressed the reason she wanted to see him, in private and away from anyone who could potentially interrupt her once she started to ease her troubled mind. "Tyson, I want to thank you for coming here. I know you're very busy. I also want to thank you for being a dear friend over the past couple of years."

Tyson smiled awkwardly. "It's been my pleasure. You know how I feel, about you."

"That's just it. I don't know how you feel, not about us," Grace admitted sadly. "Of course, I know how you make me feel, but that's beside the point. I've enjoyed every second we've spent together, and I do mean every single one, but I can't say that it has amounted to much. If I never saw you again, I'd miss our special times, but that's as far as it goes. That's what we've been to each other, a collection of special times."

"I think I know what this is about," Tyson sighed, clasping his hands together underneath his chin. "You've finally come around to wanting more than what I've given."

"Finally?" Grace repeated in a way that confused Tyson. He assumed that she had a better grasp of eventual expectations in part-time affairs of the heart. After being involved in so many of them, he certainly did.

"Yeah, every woman develops expectations of some kind, eventually," he informed her. "Actually, I'm surprised it's taken you this long."

"So does this mean you're interested in taking our situation to the next level?"

"I'm sorry, but no," Tyson answered softly, not willing to relinquish his freedom or entertain anything other than their current arrangement, a physical association and, up until now, the superficial conversation that usually accompanied it. "Look, Grace, I'm not the marrying kind or the kind to settle down. Whether you were willing to acknowledge it or not, you knew that about me, or else you wouldn't have waited all this time to bring it up." Tyson glanced at his shiny Rolex. "Sweetheart, I need to know something." Grace gazed at him with sorrowful eyes, not sure what to expect now. "Are you in love with me?" he asked, more serious than she'd ever seen him. She shook her head despite wanting to be, and wishing she was, but she failed to come up with the answer she knew didn't exist. "Grace, are you having our baby?" Tyson questioned as a solemn afterthought.

Grace shook her head again and told him, "No."

Oddly, Tyson's expression softened to the point that it was very difficult to read. His stoic gaze fostered a hint of disappointment when he learned that she wasn't pregnant; that was the odd part. Grace decided to forget about trying to understand a man who'd just told her that she didn't stand a ghost of a chance with him, so she drew her eyes away and lowered her head.

"It appears that you've asked me here to do one of two things, then," Tyson suggested after making a few assumptions from the other side of that odd expression of his. "Either you plan on letting me go, or you plan on demanding a more substantial turn of events. Since neither of those appeal to me, I'll make it easy for you." Grace wanted to stop him, turn back the clock, and rethink her position before inviting him there, but she couldn't move. For some reason, unclear to her at that particular moment, she needed to hear him say it. "I'm not what you need, and I doubt you can continue on like we have been, so I guess this means good-bye." Tyson leaned toward Grace. He kissed her on the forehead and wrapped his strong arms around her shoulders. "I knew this day would come, our thing running its course, I mean. You're a beautiful woman with so much to offer. Any man would be lucky to have such a wonderful wife. I'm just not ready to be anyone's husband. Besides, you can do a whole lot better than me. You'll see."

"What if I don't want to do a whole lot better than you?" she said, more rhetorically than as a real question.

"Grace, don't do this. You ever wonder why I've kept you at arm's length? I'm smart enough to recognize my shortcomings, and there are a lot of them. But by my limiting your view, it's harder for you to see the flaws and chips in any diamond. I'd have to work overtime if I let you get too close. No expectations, no long-term relationship goals, no hopes and dreams of growing old together. That's me, Grace, nothing but smoke and mirrors."

Within the blink of an eye, Grace felt as if she was grasping at straws. Partly she wanted Tyson to fight for her, argue violently to retain the smallest thread of companionship, but he didn't. That's when Grace realized their flextime together had been more important to her than she was previously ready to admit. She'd valued Tyson's friendship, intimate generosity, and company more than she should have. Now that he was walking out of her life, there was no one to blame but herself. Tyson certainly refused to accept any portion of it. He laid his excuse at Grace's feet after insinuating that she should have known better. Well, she *should* have.

Tyson continued holding her until his cell phone chimed. He explained that he had to catch a flight. He kissed her again and promised to keep in touch, but she knew as soon as he breathed those words, their association would forever be relegated to a love she used to know. Grace appreciated his honesty, the kind way in which he let her down easily while pretending that it was him who'd lost out. Two days later she was still trying to convince herself of the same thing.

Sunday afternoon, after church service concluded, Grace attempted to dodge that bothersome church fly, Albert Jenkins. She could sense that he was working his way up to a conversation because he kept circling the conversation she had going on with Sister Jones about the upcoming women's retreat. "Sistah Grace," he said, all low and sneaky like, "lemme holler at you for a moment."

"No, I'm all hollered out, Albert. And even if I weren't tired of men who are afraid of making a commitment worth having, you'd be the last brotha I'm willing to give that opportunity," Grace fussed. "Now, don't make me get ugly and loud talk you up in the Lord's house, or we'll both be sorry." Albert was in the wind before she said something she'd have to repent for afterward.

When Grace noticed Sister Wynovia Kolislaw's grape-colored wide-brimmed hat floating down the hallway, cluttered with fellow worshippers, she made her way through the pack to ask a special favor. "Sistah Kolislaw, can I please speak with you a minute?" The deacon's wife narrowed those tired eyes of hers at Grace, and then she flashed her a spirited wink.

"Sure thing, sugar," agreed the elderly matriarch. "Meet me in Brotha Deacon's office in a few minutes. This girdle is riding up a might, and I can't stand it another second." The older woman wiggled her hips uncomfortably, and tugged at her purple dress as she headed into the ladies' restroom. Grace went in the other direction, having second thoughts about telling her business to a church member. She'd seen it go bad too many times to count when someone's personal issues had become common knowledge by the end of service after confiding in the wrong somebody. Hopefully for Grace, that wouldn't be the case.

"Whew! That's a lot better," Sister Kolislaw huffed, while taking a seat behind her husband's desk. "Grace, keep your weight down, cause if you don't, you'll be carrying around a lot more than that long face. Take it from a woman who knows."

"Yes, ma'am," replied Grace, holding in a giggle. "I wanted to get your advice on something personal." She thought about dancing around the truth, but suspected that a cagey old Bible thumper like Sister Kolislaw would see right through it. "I've been, uh . . . wondering—"

"Why you ain't married yet?" the older woman predicted.

Shock spread throughout Grace's body, but showed mostly on her face. "Uh, yes and no," she stammered.

"Mostly yes, I'd bet?"

"Yes, ma'am, mostly yes, but how'd you know?"

The seventy-year-old whipped off her big hat and laid it on the desk. She narrowed her eyes again while digging out an ancient pair of bifocals from the top drawer. "Let me tell you something. A woman who prances around without a care in the world the way you do has either got herself one good man, or she's keeping company with several stand-ins to pass the time until a good one comes along. When you've seen so many people's whole lives play out from the cradle to the grave like I have, some things are as clear as day. I figured you'd ask for a sit-down last week, but you didn't. Chile, I'm just glad that you decided to get some help with your problem before making a terrible mistake. Most young people would rather ask advice from folks who don't know any better than they do, like silly girlfriends with too many problems of their own to figure a way out of a wet paper bag."

"Oh, I don't have a problem," Grace said, before staring

into a set of squinted eyes again. "Okay, who am I fooling? I wouldn't be here if I didn't."

Sister Kolislaw smiled heartily at Grace. "Now that we got that out the way, let's get down to business. First of all, I think you've done a fine job raising André. He's a delightful boy and growing taller than a Mississippi pine. I know you proud of him, too, the way he's turning out without a man to guide him. Uh-huh, I see the way you dote on him. He's blessed to have you care for him the way you do."

"Yes, ma'am, I'm blessed as well. He is a good son."

After pulling a thick file out of the rickety bottom drawer, Sister Kolislaw hummed a spiritual as her fingers flipped from one page to the next. "Uh-huh, Jesus is on my mind. Oh, here we go!" She took out a single sheet of paper and slid it underneath her hat. "Before we get this show on the road, I want to hear what you think the matter is."

"Well, I've had my fill of stand-ins like the ones you were talking about, but until lately, I've not been interested in getting serious. I've been focused on providing for André and climbing the corporate ladder."

"The which?" Sistah Kolislaw asked.

"You know, the corporate ladder to success," Grace explained. "A single mother has to play the game to get ahead in a man's world." After Grace's short dissertation regarding the workplace, she felt ridiculous.

"Uh-huh, just what I suspected. You've been focusing on the wrong things, Grace. The Lord will provide for you and your child if you diligently seek Him. That's straight from the Good Book. Spending all that time playing games has got you on the losing end of life. True, it is a man's world, and it always will be. That there's God's design, so ain't no use arguing the point, but I will tell you a couple o' things you can fix, if you had the right mind to."

"Of course, I'm open to suggestions." Grace was all ears.

"Good, then we can move in the right direction for a change." Sister Kolislaw scratched at her gray wig as she leaned back in the chair. "Just listen and don't say nothing until I'm through, or else you might miss something." Grace agreed, so she continued. "You're too strong, Grace, too self-sufficient, never looking to lean on a strong shoulder. It's not healthy for a woman to be alone in this world, especially if she can help it. A man who finds a wife finds a good thing. The problem is some women don't know how to look lost. Other ones outsmart themselves into thinking they don't need no man at all unless it's for carnal gain. And too many women done forgot their home training. Just flouncing around, ready to throw their legs open the first time a fellow calls 'em cutie-pie or treats 'em to a hot meal. Grace, try keeping the treasure to your earthly kingdom under lock and key until a man's ready to purchase a castle and make you his queen." When it appeared as if Grace was going to comment, she received a stern warning. "And before you open your mouth to defend yourself, let me finish. The only woman who doesn't need a man is the one who doesn't care about living life to the fullest, long and wide, while enjoying the best life has to offer." That was the second time in as many days Grace was told to live life long and wide. "God designed it that way, and that's the way it ought to be, praise His holy name. I got book, chapter, and verse for everything I've told you, but seeing is believing, so here you go. See for yourself." She raised her hat from the desk, picking up the single sheet of paper she handed to Grace. There were several scriptural references typed on it, with book, chapter, and verse to be studied. "If you do have your heart set on arguing with the Word, you go ahead on, then, but you'll come out on the wrong end every time."

"Sistah Kolislaw?"

"Yes, Grace?"

"No disrespect, but times have changed a bit since you were single and out here by yourself."

"You don't think we had the same concerns about sleeping around when I was in my prime? The stories I could tell you. Look here, a man has to feel like he's earning the goodies, even if he ain't, or else he won't place no value on it. That's how I hooked Brotha Deacon years ago. Lord knows he sulked outside my bedroom window for months until I said, 'I do' instead of 'I will.'" The old woman chuckled so hard that her wig shook. "Believe you me, he couldn't get me down that aisle fast enough. Ask Sistah Lana Washington, Sistah Sylvia Everhart, Sistah Tonetta Johnson, and a whole slew of others how they managed to get hitched within a year of having this same talk I'm having with you. The Lord says, 'Seek and ye shall find, that's the Kingdom of God.' In the meantime, work on keeping your legs closed, your options open and your head in the Good Book. Sex is one of the most powerful things you have. Don't be so quick to give your power away. Just wait and see what blessings abound once you harness that power by storing it up. Study to show yourself approved, and the Word will convict you."

"Yes, ma'am," was all Grace could say. She politely thanked Sister Kolislaw but couldn't help turning against the thought of vowing celibacy. *That kind old lady meant well, but she has to be off her rocker if she expects me to deny the very desires that God himself planted deep down inside me. There has to be another way. There has to be.*

9

Sum of the Whole Matter

On the ride home from church, Grace was uncharacteristically quiet. André listened to the radio turned down low. He read two articles from the latest issue of *Sports Illustrated* magazine before stumbling over Skyler's name in a section mentioning high school basketball All-American candidates. "Ma!" he yelled. Grace jerked the steering wheel when she was startled by his tone.

"Dré! What's wrong?"

"It's Skyler, he's in this magazine. They're listing him with the best prep ballplayers in the country." André was amazed, but Grace was working hard at calming her nerves.

"That's good for Skyler, honey. But next time, take it easy. I could have hit someone when you yelled out like that."

"I'm sorry," he apologized without taking his eyes away from his best friend's name and photo on the page. "It says here that Sky's thinking about going pro after graduating this year."

"Well, it's a big step from schooling teenage boys to

holding his own against grown men who've dedicated themselves to being the top basketball players in the world. I'm sure that he and his grandmother will discuss it and do what's best for him and his future."

André smiled even harder than before when he imagined how an NBA contract would help with the ailing woman's medical bills. "They sure could use the money. Skyler says they might have to move if Miss Pearl can't find another job that lets her sit down more. She still works for the cleaning company, but I've heard her talking about how much harder it's been to get around lately."

Grace smiled at André after he exhibited more concern for the welfare of his friend's family than joy at Skyler's potential to jump straight into the glamour and glitz that accompanies the professional ranks. Sister Kolislaw was correct in her astute observations about André. He was a good kid, with his heart in the right place. Grace had done an awesome job raising him to that point, and it was reflected in the fine young man he'd become. André's growth caused Grace to take a fair appraisal of how well she had matured as a Christian, or not. The single sheet of paper Sister Kolislaw gave her was burning a hole in her purse. She couldn't wait to get home, settle in, and review the Scriptures that assisted other single women's ascension to the next phase of their lives, the just-married phase.

The next hour was torture. Grace prepared smothered steaks, mashed potatoes, and snow peas. André finished dinner so fast that the meal she'd fussed over disappeared in one blazing woof. He stretched out on the sofa to catch the second half of the Dallas Cowboys vs. Green Bay Packers football game while Grace shuttled peas from one side of her plate to the other. So many things had changed in the past couple of weeks. Her world had been rocked off its axis after Chandelle questioned her voluntarily single status. Not that it caused her concern, but rather, it forced a self-assessment that resulted in an unfavorable evaluation. Grace wondered how one comment could transform her life, distort her self-worth, and reveal a fractured view of who she thought she was, which until then, had suited her just fine. After it was all said and done, there was no denying that the single-by-design lifestyle Grace had engineered had been motoring along at one hundred miles an hour despite a host of errors in judgment lurking just beneath the hood. The time had come to appraise the damage she'd sustained along her journey.

Grace opened her Bible, hoping she could afford the demand for payment when the bill was due. She made herself comfortable on the chaise longue, then covered her bare legs with a multicolored throw. With the list of Scriptures propped against her legs, and a copy of an NIV Bible settled against her lap, she took a deep breath and dove in. The first passage was found in the book of Genesis, which made perfect sense. That's where man and woman began, after all. Genesis 2:18, 21 and 22. Grace read to herself, "And the Lord God said, 'It is not good that man should be alone, I will make him a helper comparable to him.'" She'd read that particular verse several times throughout her studies, but it didn't carry the same weight that it did now. "It's not so good for woman to be alone either, if she can help it," Grace commented to herself, thinking back on Sister Kolislaw's words regarding that very topic. "Verses 21 and 22" she reminded herself, reading further. "And the Lord God caused a deep sleep to fall on Adam, and he slept; and He took one of his ribs, and closed up the flesh in its place. And the rib which the Lord God had taken from man, He made into a woman, and He brought her to the man." Grace sighed tenderly. "Now that's a perfect love if ever there was one. 'And He brought her to the man,'" she repeated for emphasis' sake. *That must have been something to see, a man who didn't have any doubts that his woman was made just for him.* Grace hadn't considered herself a hopeless romantic before then, but she had to give God His props for hooking up Adam and Eve the way He did. So far, Sister Kolislaw's contribution was all right with Grace, so she had no problems continuing on. The next passage was found in Proverbs 18:22. Grace thumbed through the Bible with rapid vigor. "He who finds a wife finds a good thing, and obtains favor from the Lord," she read, smiling at the lost art of looking lost and being found like the older woman had suggested earlier. Eagerly moving on to the following scriptural reference, Grace felt good about her decision to visit with a seasoned veteran instead of taking her concerns to Linda and Shelia for a dose of beauty-shop psychobabble.

Proverbs 31:10–12 was the third passage listed, with "The Virtuous Wife" as the subtext. Grace perked up when she began following the words discussing what a virtuous wife was. "Who can find a virtuous wife? For her worth is far above rubies. The heart of her husband safely trusts her; so that he will have no lack of gain. She does him good and not evil all the days of her life." That definition sounded so good that Grace agreed with it while searching for the next verse written on the sheet. "That's all a sistah wants to be, a good woman for a lucky man who appreciates what she has to offer. Maybe I am too good for Tyson. After all, he should know better than anybody."

Matthew 6:30–34 rang a bell, but Grace couldn't remember why until she read it for herself. It had been used to make a point by her own minister the month before while reprimanding the congregation for a record low in tithing. "Now if God so clothes the grass of the field, which is alive today, and tomorrow is thrown into the oven, will He not much more clothe you, O you of little faith? Therefore do not worry, saying, 'What shall we eat?' or 'What shall we drink?' or 'What shall we wear?' For after all these things the Gentiles seek. For your Heavenly Father knows that you need all these things. But seek first the kingdom of God and His righteousness, and all these things shall be added to you. Therefore do not worry about tomorrow, for tomorrow will worry about its own things. Sufficient for the day is its own trouble." Nodding her head, Grace chuckled. "Uh-uh-uh, Sister Kolislaw is three for three. She's slick, too, putting me on the spot with that talk about playing corporate games and losing my focus. Bless her heart." Grace's prescribed Bible study was moving along swimmingly. Her spirits were uplifted and all was made well with her soul, until she read the following Scripture, which poured salt on an open wound.

I Corinthians 6:18–20. "Flee from sexual immorality," she read, slowing to watch the train wreck that was her own conscience slamming into the truth. "Every sin that a man does is outside the body, but he who commits sexual immorality sins against his own body. Or do you not know that your body is the temple of the Holy Spirit who is in you, whom you have from God, and you are not your own? For you were bought at a price; therefore glorify God in your body and in your spirit, which is God's." After the last word rolled off her tongue, Grace turned away from her lesson but she couldn't escape the thought of having placed little to no stock in the way she allowed too many undeserving men come and go as they pleased in and out of her temple. She wanted to say how much of a mistake it had been scheduling flex-time with Tyson and running her behind clear across town to share a freaky bag of tricks with Greg, tricks that he neglected to sanitize after episodes with other freaks.

Grace sat there for a moment before she gathered the nerve to resume. She hadn't adequately prepared herself for a mind-bending, soul-stirring epiphany, but the process had already begun. There was no derailing it now that she'd caught a glimpse of the big picture, the one she'd neglected to see while living merely for the moment.

Grace was trembling. Her hurried pace slowed to a deliberate crawl. She read the remaining passages silently because she lacked the words to justify her actions or the sins she'd actively participated in while disregarding their repercussions. For Grace, this served as a wake-up call arranged without her prior knowledge but answered with the gravest sincerity. As she forged ahead, tears trickled down her face. She contemplated wiping them away immediately, then deemed them proper evidence of her repentance.

After the following Scripture, Grace penciled personal notes in the margins of the "Course on Conviction," which is what she'd come to refer to the sheet of paper presented by the caring church member. I Corinthians 6: 9–10 read, "Do you not know that the unrighteous will not inherit the kingdom of God? Do not be deceived. Neither fornicators, nor idolaters, nor adulterers, nor homosexuals, nor sodomites. Nor thieves, nor covetous, nor drunkards, nor revilers, nor extortioners will enter the kingdom of God." Sighing again, much deeper this time, Grace felt as though an anvil had been placed on her chest. *I guess it's true what I learned as a little girl in Sunday school,* she thought to herself. *No sinner is any better or worse than any other one. Wrong is wrong, like it or not, and we're all doing wrong together.* Eventually Grace reached in her purse, resting beside the chaise, and pulled out a handful of tissues. She dabbed her eyes before braving the remaining Scriptures listed on the sheet.

I Corinthians 11:11–12 said, "Nevertheless, neither is man independent of woman, nor woman independent of man, in the Lord. For as woman came from man, even so man comes through woman; but all things are from God."

I Corinthians 7:1-2 read, "Now concerning the things of which you wrote to me: It is good for a man not to touch a woman. Nevertheless, because of sexual immorality, let each man have his own wife, and let each woman have her own husband. Let the husband render to his wife the affection due her, and likewise also the wife to her husband."

Romans 12:1–2 stated, "I beseech you therefore, brethren, by the mercies of God, that you present your bodies a living sacrifice, holy, acceptable to God, which is your reasonable service. And do not be conformed to this world, but be transformed by the renewing of your mind, that you may prove what is good and acceptable and the perfect will of God."

I Peter 1:13–15 read, "Beloved, I beg you as sojourners and pilgrims, abstain from fleshly lusts which war against the soul."

I Thessalonians 4:3–5 said, "For this is the will of God, your sanctification that you should abstain from sexual immorality; that each of you should know how to possess his own vessel in sanctification and honor, not in passion or lust, like the Gentiles who do not know God."

James 4:7 stated, "Therefore submit to God. Resist the Devil and he will flee from you. Draw near to God and He will draw near you. Cleanse your hands, you sinners; and purify your hearts, you double-minded."

Matthew 26:41 read, "Watch and pray, least you enter into temptation. The spirit indeed is willing, but the flesh is weak."

II Peter 1:5–7 said, "But also for this reason, given all diligence, add to your faith virtue, to virtue knowledge, to knowledge self-control, to self-control perseverance, to perseverance godliness, to godliness brotherly kindness, and to brotherly kindness love." Semblances of a smile found its way onto Grace's face when an abundant light appeared at the end of a very dark tunnel. She thought, *It stands to reason that a sistah would have to go through a long stretch of self-control, perseverance and tossin' and turnin' in order to get her hands on some brotherly kindness and love.* When it seemed that the Word had drowned her in a sea of despair, the sun made a remarkable comeback, and Grace had begun to bask in its radiance.

There was a light tap at Grace's bedroom door. "Yes," she answered. André opened it cautiously and stuck his head in.

"Ma, you all right?" he asked when his curious eyes discovered her disheveled in a manner he had never seen before.

"Yes, I'm a whole lot better now, thank you."

"I almost forgot to tell you that my English teacher, Mr. Peters, wants you to call him. He said you left before he could talk to you at parents' night."

"I'll take care of it. And André," she paused to collect herself, "I love you so much."

"I know Ma. I know," he replied, knowing full well that she did with all her heart.

Grace turned the page on her Bible study as André closed her bedroom door. She was mentally drained and spiritually uplifted all at once. The appreciation she owed Sister Kolislaw could wait, but the overdue gratitude fit for a king could not. She eased off the longue and planted herself against it. Grace felt a swell of emotion come over her as she cleared her mind of all earthly woes and opened it to heavenly matters long since neglected. She prayed, *Father, God. I hope you still recognize my voice. This is Grace. It's been a while since I've made the time to come to you like this. I know I should have done better, and I'm sorry. Please accept my humble apologies as I submit myself to you the best way I know how. God, I can see your presence around me every day. You've allowed me to enjoy a wonderful job, a beautiful home, and a loving child. Although there's no possible way for me to give you back a fraction of what you've blessed me with, I'd like to try. There hasn't been a great deal of honor in the way I've shared my body with men, but I see that now. I see it clearly, and it hurts. Please help me to honor you and your many blessings. Father, I want to be a better Christian than I have been. I want you to be proud of me, all of me. If you haven't already, I beg of you not to turn your face away from me and the rising tides of life. I do believe that you have a plan for me. Hopefully, I can live up to it and your expectations. We both know that I've fallen short up 'til now.*

I'm repenting from sexual immorality and lusts of the flesh, but I need you to stand by me. Please don't give up on me in spite of how I've failed you. I need you, Father. I need you. It's in your son's name, Jesus Christ, I submit myself to you. Amen.

10

Convictions and Contradictions

Sitting around the conference table were seven of the top executives from 100 Grand sports drink, all anxiously awaiting what Grace had taken it upon herself to produce at her own expense. She'd met with Patrik, the temperamental director, and the budding superstar Allen Foray, and then scripted a twenty-second television commercial with serious intentions of commandeering the beverage company's thirty-million-dollar marketing campaign. Grace's boss, Ted Lansford, sat nervously and fidgeted because he'd not been given the privilege of previewing the strategy which could double profits for Pinnacle Marketing, the firm he'd built from the ground up. Furthermore, Grace made Ted promise her a partnership if 100 Grand bought in on her idea.

With all eyes on Grace, she composed herself to hit the ground running. She wore her best-fitting business suit, a Donna Karan gray flannel ensemble tailored in the European tradition and cut high in the waist. She stood, smiled assuredly at Ted, and then started in with her idea of acquiring a sizable piece of a growing industry.

"Gentlemen and lady," Grace began, with a wink to the only other female in attendance, "I'm glad that you've agreed to take this meeting with us, and I'm certain that it will be time well spent. As you all know, the sports-beverage industry has enjoyed tremendous growth in the past decade, with no apparent reason for that trend to decline. When I learned that you were looking for a firm to usher your new product into the competitive arena, I lay awake at night thinking about the perfect pitch. I came up with a gem." Grace felt a little sorry for Ted, still antsy beyond belief as she pressed the remote control to close the thick-panel window blinds. "Hold on to your seats, because the next twenty seconds will forge a lasting business relationship and make all of us a bunch of money." Everyone but Ted laughed when Grace's lighthearted humor alleviated the escalating tension. "Lights, camera, action," she said, pressing the control again to darken the room. The wall-sized viewing screen remained black with flickers of white mixed in, reminiscent of an old silent movie.

Suddenly Allen Foray's familiar voice started in while the screen came to life with a shot of him moving in slow motion, bare chested but wearing workout shorts and running shoes. "Growing up, there was this kid who lived on my block," his deep voice began. "He was a better dancer, more athletic, and a whole lot stronger than me." The frame shifted to Allen in the weight room, dark shadows as his only companions. As his muscles flexed with each powerful bench press, the solemn voice-over started in again. "I gave up dancing . . . But I never stopped training. That other kid, he's all grown up, too, but now he has to buy a ticket to watch me play." Several frames of Allen's highlights dashed across the screen. The beverage execs were oohing and ahhing over the impressive, lightning-quick, full-court acrobatics. The last scene showed Allen hitting a winning shot as the buzzer sounded in a packed arena. While the crowd cheered, Allen looked directly into the camera and flashed a brilliant set of perfect teeth. "Oh, yeah, dancing is way overrated. Ain't life grand?" Before the screen faded to black again, thunderous applause rang throughout the conference room.

When the lights came up, Ted was standing to applaud Grace's genius. "Bravo!" he shouted "Bravo!

"Well done, Grace," hailed 100 Grand's chief marketing executive, Healy Wilcox. "Using a term I know you'll appreciate, it's a slam dunk. I'm sure that I speak for everyone in saying, where do we sign?" Grace's boss couldn't control himself. He was so elated that he hugged Grace too hard and took her breath away. "You're a lucky man to have talent like Grace on your team, Ted," Mr. Wilcox beamed.

"I'm smart enough to know what to do about it as well," Ted replied. "It's not every day a man gets to see his partner shine like this. Right, Grace?"

"I'd have it no other way, Ted," she answered in her best business voice. Now that Pinnacle, Allen Foray, and 100 Grand were all in bed together, save the paperwork, Grace had time to breathe. She declined Ted's offer to crack open a case of champagne and throw a party to celebrate the biggest deal he could imagine, and instead retreated behind a closed office door and hid there. Her hands shook as she dialed Patrik's phone number to share the good news. "Yes, that's right," she confirmed. "They loved it. Yes, especially the director's keen eye for detail." Grace laughed when Patrik began spouting high-pitched jubilations in his native Italian. "English, Patrik. English!" she pleaded joyously. Actually, it didn't matter which language he reveled in, Grace understood all the way down to her toes how it felt to be validated because of his work. She shared the same feelings about hers. When Grace hung up the phone, Patrik was still going at it and patting himself on the back. He probably didn't notice that he'd been talking to a dial tone for quite some time, and likely didn't care.

Grace offered a few kind words of thanks to God for revealing His promise to her. Then she turned her leather chair toward the window and stared out. Even with all the hoopla in the building, she couldn't help feeling that something was missing but she couldn't put her finger on it. As she searched her purse for Allen's business card, it hit her like a stiff winter breeze. Her victory was eerily hollow when she realized that her recent success paled in comparison to the thought of being loved by the right man, the one man whom God had created for her to spend the rest of her life with. Meeting that man would have been Grace's idea of a heaven on earth. In the meantime, she planned on keeping the promise she'd made while down on her knees. There was no way she'd let Him down, not if she could help it.

"Come in," Grace yelled to whoever it was knocking at her office door.

"Congratulations," Chandelle squealed, barreling toward Grace's desk. "I heard the good news. Shoot, everybody's so proud of you. Mr. Lansford is breaking his neck ordering your blinged-out business cards with 'partner' added behind your name."

"Oh, Ted is just covering his bases so I don't go getting any more ideas that don't include him," Grace suggested playfully. "Forget about that. Let's talk about something really important. I want to hear about your news."

"You're so sweet to care about little ole me." Chandelle blushed at Grace's thoughtfulness, knowing that she had more pressing business to attend to instead of sitting still and listening to a newlywed gushing over a honeymoon set in a tropical paradise. However, that didn't stop Chandelle from whipping out the bulky photo album she'd been hiding behind her back. "Okay, okay, look. These pictures were taken inside our hotel room. You know I had to remove the spicy ones of my Marvin before I came in."

"Ooh, Chandelle!" Grace howled.

"Can't be too careful these days. Let a sistah find out what you got going on at home, and she starts wantin' it for herself."

"I know that's right," Grace agreed. "But it's not just the sistahs you have to watch nowadays."

"I'm saying. That's why I was looking real hard at the redhead from the Photomart when I noticed my envelope came up a little light. Humph, some of my best action shots were missing. But, don't worry. I've still got the negatives." Grace laughed harder than she wanted to, although it felt real good to see a newlywed recounting her wedding-night bliss.

After sitting through explanations over what inspired each photo in the album, Grace thanked Chandelle for sharing her private moments. Then she strongly suggested that any additional such girlfriend chats take place after business hours or during lunch. The younger woman understood and headed for the door with the bundle of Mediterranean memories tucked safely beneath her arms. Suddenly, she spun on her heels. "Grace, I know that you've already given me more company time than you should have, but I wanted to ask you one more thing."

"Sure, what is it?"

"I was kinda wondering about you and the stuff we discussed at church."

"Yes, I remember." Grace felt an ounce of apprehension wash over her because it was Chandelle's prodding that forced the changes in her life and the way she'd viewed it in the first place.

"Well, not that it's any of my business," Chandelle stated before second-guessing her place in the office of the new partner. Grace looked at her as if to say, "And I'm sure that it won't be," before Chandelle continued. "But I'm having so much fun getting to know Marvin, as man and wife, I mean. My mother never had a husband, and she died alone without one loving her like a woman is supposed to be loved. Please think about tomorrow while you're conquering the world today." Grace considered the advice Chandelle offered, and realized she did have an occasion to smile, if for no other reason than the possibilities she hadn't given much deliberation. She was content in knowing that God was working on her man while doing a number on her too. Eventually, there would be the perfect someone to witness her life, while she did her best to improve it on God's terms, Grace hoped. All she had to do was keep right on living until he arrived.

Later, as she grabbed her purse and floated out of the office to meet Linda and Shelia for lunch, a warm smile was still evident on Grace's lips. "That Chandelle's got an old soul," she heard herself say as she pulled into midday traffic on the expressway.

While answering the summons of a vibrating cell phone, and feeling no less than perfect herself Grace stepped out of her car to valet park at Bijoux's. The fair-haired attendant flirted with Grace, but she didn't acknowledge his subtle proposition. Besides, the girls had arrived ahead of her and needed to get back to their respective jobs before too long. "Hello, this is Grace. Yes, Allen," she smacked pleasantly, "I was going to call you. No, we haven't agreed on a firm figure yet, but I'd have to guess that Wilcox and his people will present a nice round number you can't pass up. Remember, this deal is unusual because you and I shot it on the chance that it would pay off, so don't worry. It will. Just be sure to put your accountant on notice and put me in touch with your agent."

Shelia flagged Grace down as she scanned the busy restaurant. When she approached the spacious booth in the back, Linda was rocking steadily to piped-in music streaming from an overhead speaker. Something by The Supremes had her singing along Motown style while perusing the lunch menu.

Grace waved back then pointed at the phone and held up her index finger, suggesting that she was wrapping up the call. "See, Allen, I knew it was gold, and because you believed in me, every other player will be wishing they were in your shoes. Not bad for one sweaty afternoon, huh?" That comment sent chills through Shelia because it sounded like something she could sink her teeth into. "All right, we'll talk, but I have two VIPs waiting on me. Gotta go, bye." Grace flipped her tiny phone closed, then dropped it into her handbag. "Ladies, my deepest apologies," she offered in earnest. "I know your time is important, but some men can be very persistent."

"With sweaty afternoons and whatnot, I'll bet every other player would want to be in his shoes," Shelia said, hoping to kick-start the spur-of-the-moment meeting Grace had convened without explaining why.

"There you go, running through the gutter and getting all excited over nothing," Graced commented, trying to minimize Shelia's query, but Linda jumped on the bandwagon and took the wheel.

"I'm all excited over nothing, too, if that's the case." Linda was chomping at the bit to be thoroughly informed on what Grace saw fit to regard as nothing. "Tell us who that was on the phone, and we'll work backward to what stunts he pulled to get you all sweaty. Sound like a plan, Shelia?"

"That'll work for me," Shelia chimed in on cue.

"Speaking of work," Grace asserted, to scratch their itchy noses. "that's why I've asked you two to meet me here. I've been doing a lot of thinking lately and the first part of my lifestyle modification has come to fruition. I was just speaking to Allen Foray."

"All-World, All-Women-Want-Him Allen Foray?" Shelia asked, with her eyes about to fall out of her head.

"Whatever, Shelia," Grace answered, not at all interested in her opinion of a man much too young for either of them.

"Whatever? Uh-uh. See, you've got it all wrong. He can have it whenever, wherever and however he pleases. All he'd have to do was let a sistah know when to stop, and go for ice water and warm towels. You hear me?"

Trying not to laugh along with her two closest friends, Grace shook her head disapprovingly. "No, it's strictly business between us. I convinced him to shoot a commercial on my dime, and then I pitched it to a sports-drink company this morning. They ate it up, like I knew they would."

"I don't know, Grace. Shelia's got a point," Linda debated, offering her unsolicited two cents. "You might want to rethink your strictly business philosophy. I heard that Allen is *real tall*, especially when he's lying down."

"You know what they say about opinions, Linda? Everybody's got one." Grace had the hardest time getting out what she'd been wrestling with because of their overzealous carnal inclinations.

"Yeah, and I also know what they say about one basketball player in particular." Linda tossed a wicked glance across the table at Shelia.

"Uh-huh, he's *real tall*," Shelia answered, fanning herself with an open hand.

"Okay, since neither of you are willing to hear me out," Grace huffed, "I'll just pay for lunch and keep my business to myself."

"Whoa, hold on now!" Shelia objected.

"Yeah, we didn't say all that," Linda agreed, opening the menu to the more expensive dinner items. "Since you're feeding us, I, for one, am willing to hear you out and hold you up if I have to. Watch this." Linda placed her hand up to her mouth. "This is me shutting up." When Shelia nodded that she was prepared to shut up too, Grace settled in to contribute what she'd gone there to converse about.

"Good, now this has been very difficult for me, and I have no idea how you'll take it, but here goes. Due to some blessed, albeit strange occurrences, I've decided to take my life in another direction."

Linda eyed her suspiciously. "Grace, you're not about to tell us that you've gone gay or anything, are you?"

"I hope not," Shelia added, smirking her displeasure. "Because I'm not trying to imagine you looking at my booty."

"Ain't nobody said nothing about getting with women.

Actually I'm not trying to get with men, either," Grace said explicitly. "I've decided to take a vow of celibacy."

"Uh-uh, girl, take it back!" That was Shelia, shaking her head frantically. "Grace, I'd rather deal with you looking at my booty. Tell her, Linda!"

"Tell her what? I'm not trying to be all that concerned about your booty either!"

"No, silly. Tell her about that time I tried the celibacy thing, and how it blew up in my face. I can't even talk about it."

"Oh, yeah, I can tell her that. Grace, girl? You know I love you like a play-cousin, so I'll give it to you straight, no chaser. Shelia tried to go without two years ago, and she ain't never had the Devil chasing her like he did then. Within a few weeks, Shelia was giving the good stuff to every Tom, Dick, and Harry—"

"And James," Shelia hissed reluctantly.

"Ooh, I forgot about him," Linda remembered. "Your girl over there was serving it up to the kinds of dudes she don't even like."

"Broke ones, them's the kind I don't like, but all I wanted to do was screw," Shelia whispered, almost embarrassed over what she'd done and who she'd done it with. "There was this dude at the car wash who couldn't even afford to detail my car, and there I was, letting him drive it on weekends."

"Whaaaat?" Grace said, completely astonished.

"That's not the worst of it," Linda added. "She was out of control, constantly on patrol and blazin', that's why her car kept conveniently overheating in front of firehouses all over town. She almost ran halfway through the Dallas firemen's calendar before she came to her senses."

"Some of those firemen really know how to handle a hose," Shelia explained while fanning herself again.

"I wouldn't have any idea, cause you know I'm a virgin," Linda said, straight faced.

"Yeah, and you're a liar too," teased Shelia. "You were working the other half of the beefcake calendar, if memory serves me correctly. I distinctly remember bumping into you somewhere in the middle and both of us fighting over June and July, the identical twins from the south side. They tried to play us stupid, had me coming in the front, and sneaking Linda in the back." Grace was doubled over then. She couldn't fight it off any longer.

"Listen, Grace, I know it sounds funny, but seriously, when the Devil's chasing you, it's almost worth it to let him catch you every now and then," Shelia reasoned, after thinking back.

"Sounds like you let him catch you every chance you got," Grace presumed.

"Sure did," Linda chuckled. "She even let him tie her up a few times, too."

"Hold on, y'all." Shelia answered her cell phone as the waiter approached cautiously. "I want the shrimp and pasta. Uh-uh, not from you," she said into the telephone. "I'm ordering lunch. Nah, baby, I'm not with no other dude! What? You already know what you can do for me. Yes, at nine o'clock, and don't think o' showing up empty-handed like you did the last time, or my front door won't be the only thing you can't get in. Are we clear on that? Cool." Shelia perked up as if she hadn't just set some man straight on her demands. "See you at nine then, bye baby."

"Shelia might be too trifling for words at times, Grace, but she's straight up about this. Going without is hard when you're used to having it on the regular. We're beautiful desert flowers, each of us, craving as much rain as we can get. I know that casual sex is wrong, but if it makes us happy, it can't be all bad. Celibacy ain't nothing but a double-cross waiting to happen. If you ask me, it's a dirty trick. God made us sexual creatures, then He expects us to act like it's not the best thing since sliced bread. Besides that, it's free."

Shelia was diametrically opposed to that line of thinking. "Speak for yourself Linda, mine ain't free. I charge whatever the market will bear. Trips, trinkets, and treasures—my good stuff costs. I'll take it up with God when I see Him. Until then, I'm chargin'!" Shelia worked as a part-time comedienne and traveled on the weekends when her nine-to-five wasn't covering her credit-card bills. "I'm an entertainer. I get paid to entertain, don't matter if I'm making a man laugh 'til he can't stop or if he's getting his while I'm on top. Mama's gonna get hers. Baldwin in Baltimore, Carlton in Cali, they all got to pay to get on this ride."

Grace was at odds with their opinions but she wasn't any less of a sinner than either of them, and she knew it. Fortunately, she had seen the error of her ways and didn't plan on backsliding. She had to choose her words carefully to not offend dear friends, but she had to say something to stand up for righteousness' sake. "Shelia, I hope you take this in the spirit it's given, but I would be remiss if I held my tongue. Sin isn't free, and charging for it only adds insult to injury. I'm not pretending that I haven't done my share of dirt, too, but with God looking over me, I'm on my way to being a better person and a better Christian. My vow of celibacy is the cross I've decided to bear. I appreciate you telling me to be on guard for the pitfalls, I really do. I'm sure that it's going to take everything I have to walk the straight and narrow, but broad is the way that leads to destruction, and many take it. Anyway, I'm ready for love, and I can't wait for the right somebody to love me back."

Shelia and Linda both turned their faces away, undoubtedly avoiding the blinding light Grace shone on their shared but faulty philosophy. As luck would have it, Shelia took her enlightenment with a receiving spirit. "I hear you, Grace, and I applaud your decision to seek the kingdom and all that, but love hasn't been anything for me but fool's gold. Even if you do find it, there's no guarantee it'll be real, or that it'll last. I'll take my chances with jewelry and department-store baubles. I can have those appraised, and diamonds are forever."

"Don't pay her no mind, Grace." Linda placed her hand over Grace's. "All Shelia's got is a closet full of toasters. I guess the current market isn't bearing nothing but small appliances."

A labored grin traced Shelia's lips. "Who you telling? If another brotha shows up carrying something with Westinghouse stamped on it, I'ma hurt somebody." Grace slid in closer to her two best friends for a befitting group hug. Neither of them had to say it, although it was apparent to the waiter as he delivered their entrées.

"Hold still. If a picture is worth a thousand words," he said, snapping a Polaroid camera, "this one should be worth two thousand. *Friendship Personified.* And, yes, I am pushing for a bigger tip, so this picture is yours to keep."

When Grace climbed into her car at the end of lunch, she was happy and uplifted, happy that she'd made it through her discussion with the girls, and uplifted after voicing her convictions with the people closest to her who knew her darkest secrets. Although neither of her friends was in any position to stand in judgment of the others' transgressions, each of them would be responsible for seeking redemption regarding her own.

11

Heavy on My Mind

During the next two weeks, Grace decided it was more prudent limiting herself to the confines of her home when she wasn't at the office. The promise she'd made in earnest, to God as well as to herself, was harder to keep than she'd initially anticipated. Grace continually reminded herself that a woman's natural urges were nothing more than bumps in the road which had to be smoothed out with constant prayer and positive reflection. Still, warring against the ever present tide of a naughty nuisance attacking her throughout each day presented a new set of problems altogether.

After fighting the temptation to browse through her electronic address book, Grace turned off the television in her bedroom. She glanced at the clock radio on her nightstand and shook her head. At eleven-thirty, an hour past what she considered her bedtime, Grace shed her peach-hued lounging clothes and climbed in a hot bath. Even though the heated pool of satiny bubbles was relaxing, exhilarating, and safe as long as she was alone, memories of Tyson's gentle touch began skirting around in her mind. Before she knew it, the soapy loofa traced her thighs, just as Tyson had done with his tongue to get her juices flowing during a flextime tryst at the hotel. Grace tilted her head back until it rested against the neck pad attached to the sunken Jacuzzi bathtub. "The hotel," she sighed, with her eyes closed. An impish hint of a smile worked its way on her heart-shaped lips when she remembered what kinds of things took place in room number 921. It was her idea to select a room nearest to the ice machine with its boisterous churning and constant clattering. The worst room on each floor was always available and due to its undesirable location, which adequately drowned out her passionate cries, Grace felt uninhibited and free to vocalize her appreciation during Tyson's talent show. "Ooh, I miss that man," Grace groaned over the steamed heat rising from the water. "Oomph, who am I fooling, I miss the talent," was her immediate and honest re-evaluation. She wanted to be held, kissed erotically in several places, and satisfied despite it being in direct opposition to her newfound morality and stance on saving her body for the Lord, unless another man, the right one, was willing to put his name on it for keeps. After the water's temperature began to cool, Grace lifted a stainless steel lever to drain the tub. Unfortunately, the heat between her legs hadn't cooled a single degree. Peering down at her nipples standing at attention, she frowned, wondering how long she would have to confront those irrepressible urges and defer the fevered pitches of lust.

Shaking loose from her dark mood that she'd dodged with the best efforts she could muster, Grace discovered something else waiting in the wings as she massaged her skin with scented lotion. She thought it strange, at first, how her skin seemed to respond eagerly to her own fingertips, the way it had with the men who knew how to go about caressing her. It was as if she'd overlooked the textured ridges, peaks, and valleys that Greg found so inviting. Grace seized the moment to get to know her own body for a change, instead of getting caught up in the strong, hard angles and crests of a man's. Perhaps she could get along without a man, she hoped, if she really put her mind to it. That's exactly what she'd have to do, learn to enjoy self when she was alone by herself. Of course, that was easier said than done.

The cool briskness of her sheets sent an uncomfortable chill up the base of Grace's back to the nape of her neck when she eased her naked frame into bed. "Ooh, it's cold. Cold!" she whooped, while wincing and wiggling. Several moments later, she settled in with designs on alleviating the tightly wound anxiety knotted up inside her. *I never thought I'd be taking matters in my own hands,* she thought while attempting to reconcile her worldly woes. Masturbation, self-gratification, and letting your fingers do the walking were all terms and phrases Grace had attributed to pitiful, lonely women who didn't have a man. She smirked when realizing she had become one of them.

Her considerable lack of practice made that first night out of the blocks an arduous undertaking. Grace labored meticulously to re-create the encounters she'd spent in the hands of a skillful lover by lighting candles, gyrating slowly to soft music humming from the quiet radio program, and stroking everything that mattered. So many times she grew ever so close to experiencing the pleasurable sensations that her men had worked diligently to provide. So many times she came to the brink of ecstasy but failed to maneuver her way through the passages of fulfillment.

Refusing to give in before exhausting every possibility, Grace panted excitedly as she continued, touching herself tenderly and then adding more determination when it came to mind that what she truly craved was penetration. The tension was overwhelming, but her ineptness left much to be desired, too much, in fact, to properly manipulate the situation accurately. "Agghh!" she ranted disappointedly, with the pillow held against her. "Okay, I give up!" Grace flung the pillow against the wall. "Men are so much better at this," she whined. "Why didn't I pay more attention? Finding my G-spot can't be that hard if Greg knows how to do it. I'll even bet that schoolteacher has it figured out."

Grace glared spitefully at the clock radio before slamming her hand down on the top of it. "Shut up!" she yelled, resenting the annoying late-night deejay's mindless chatter. *He must love hearing his own voice,* she thought, because he went on and on about nothing instead of playing the soothing sounds she'd tuned in to be serenaded by. "Know when to shut up!" With another pillow shoved snugly between her thighs, Grace gave in to her whimpering sobs of frustration. "I want some . . . soooo bad. Just one little talent show. Just one," she muttered until falling asleep, mentally exhausted and emotionally drained.

When morning came, Grace was an utter mess. Her head wasn't the only part of her that ached. After tossing and turning as the sun looked on and laughed she dragged herself out of bed and staggered into the restroom. There was an angered scowl staring back at her from the vanity mirror. Grace struggled to find enough strength to make it through the day after the night had failed her so miserably. She took a deep breath, yawned, and then scratched her scalp. "My hair hurts," she pouted to her worrisome reflection. "I'm not going to make it, am I?"

Hardly speaking to André while en route to school, Grace sulked quietly until he mentioned something that had been troubling him. "Ma, did you leave your TV on last night?"

"No, honey," she answered, her voice barely audible. "Why would you think that?"

He furrowed his brow and then shook his head. "I'ont know. Bad dreams, I guess. But I could have sworn I heard a woman who must have been mad about something because she kept screaming, 'Shut up! Know when to shut up!' " he mocked, imitating a high pitched shrill. "It must've been a nightmare, huh?"

"Uh-huh, must've been," Grace replied solemnly. *Yours*

and mine both, she thought, as André opened the car door. "Dré, tell Mr. Peters that I've been thinking about him. I meant, about calling him . . . to reschedule that meeting." Was that a Freudian slip? Did Grace actually mean to say that she had been thinking about Wallace subconsciously? At that precise moment, she was convinced it was going to be a very long day.

Shuffling slowly down the hall with her head hanging low, Grace bumped into Awkward Bob when she turned into the company's sixth-floor break room. Bob was employed as a marketing analyst, and was in his late twenties, bleached blond, and obviously going through something. He'd been awarded the nickname of Awkward Bob because of his in-the-closet-and-out-again personality. When a nosy coworker learned that Bob didn't feel comfortable living as a man or a woman, news quickly circulated that he felt equally awkward about having to choose one over the other. In a word, everything about him was just that, awkward. Typically, he arrived at work in traditional male business attire, but on other occurrences he'd play dress-up while exploring his feminine side, which usually consisted of showing off something straight legged and tailored from a hot female designer line. That particular day, he was sporting a knockoff, similar to the gray Donna Karan ensemble, down to the high-waisted slacks that Grace had worn when she wowed the executives from the sports drink company

"Excuse me, Awk . . . uh, Bob," Grace stuttered, nearly calling him by his dreaded nickname. "I should have watched where I was going."

"It's quite all right, Miss Hilliard. I don't mind rubbing elbows with other corporate divas from time to time," he answered in a hushed but giddy tone, appraising Grace's black and cream houndstooth blazer. "By the way, you are working that blazer, gurl."

Grace was too tired to discuss Bob's keen eye for women's apparel, so she smiled her thanks and walked over to the freshly brewed pot of coffee. She leaned against the counter while searching for the personal mug she'd used for hot tea several months earlier. When it wasn't to be found, Grace settled for a white Styrofoam cup to fill with a morning pick-me-up. As soon as she poured every grain from three separate packs of sugar in and began stirring, her assistant strode in with a very familiar mug.

"Morning, Miss Hilliard," Marcia saluted sharply, returning for her second cup within the hour.

"Marcia," Grace said, eyeing the mug suspiciously, "uh, that mug you're holding looks a lot like the one I tucked way in the back on the second shelf."

"Interesting. That's exactly where I found this one a few months back," Marcia admitted innocently. "Had I known it was yours, I'd have asked first. I've been using it so long, I adopted it." When Marcia noticed how Grace continued staring at the mug as if she was waiting on it to be returned to its rightful owner, she frowned apologetically. "Oh, I'm sorry, you want it back? I just figured since I've had it for a while, and seeing as how you rarely drink coffee . . ." she explained, her comment trailing off at the end to suggest she be allowed to keep it.

"No, it's not that big a deal. I'm just not a fan of Styrofoam." What Grace wanted to say was, *I may as well get used to giving up the things I previously counted on being there when I wanted them.*"See you later, Em," Grace said as she exited the break room, feeling slightly less like Corporate Grace than normal. Marcia suspected that something was bothering her boss because she seldom called her by a single initial, unless she was disenchanted by her associate's actions.

When Grace reached her corner office, there was a large man sitting in the leather chair opposite Grace's desk. Since he was facing the window, she couldn't see his face. "Yes, may I help you?" Grace asked, talking to the back of his head.

"I'm game, but I doubt that you will," he flirted, in a laid-back, sexy tone.

"Allen?" Grace said as her voice elevated with surprise. "I didn't know we had an appointment to meet today."

"We didn't, but I woke up at five A.M. thinking about you," Allen replied casually. Grace was startled. Her hand trembled as she lowered the small cup onto her desk. Allen grinned, recognizing a rattled woman when he saw one. "Maybe you've had enough coffee already."

Grace saw his lips moving, but she hadn't heard a word he said. She was hyper-focused on his silky skin and that emerald green three-thousand dollar custom-made all-weather suede suit. She had a thing for suede, and he was covered in it. "Huh? I mean, excuse me?" was her best attempt at landing on her feet. Instantly, Shelia's comment about Allen being *real tall* sent Grace into a flabbergasted tailspin.

"I was just saying how much I owe you for hooking up that commercial for me with Hundred Grand," Allen confirmed after analyzing how his comment must have come across. "Ahh, now, don't get it twisted. I wouldn't have a problem waking up with you on my mind, or in my bed for that matter, but I got the message the first and the second time we met. Besides, I ain't one for getting my face cracked by the same woman on a regular basis, no matter how fine she is. I've been known to be hardheaded, but that's a stretch even for me. You ever heard of the saying, the bigger the man, the bigger the ego? Well, that fits me down to my size fifteens." Grace thought she'd swoon right there on her desk. *Did he just say something about having me in his bed with fifteen inches of something lying next to me,* she asked herself. *Oh Lawd, those are some mighty long features.*

In a desperate move to save face, Grace tried to snap out of the horny hangover she'd climbed out of the bed with. She shuffled some papers on her desk for no apparent reason, looking away from Allen's steely eyes the entire time. "Okay, let me close this door," she panted, sensing that the situation had taken an unexpected turn. Grace shot out of her chair, straightened her clothes, and then quickly walked past him. Allen's expensive fragrance tickled her nose as she reached for the doorknob. "Father help me," she heard herself say before returning to her desk. "Um, Allen, I was out of line when I assumed that you were insinuating what I, uh . . . assumed," she backpedaled. "But I can't have my clients showing up here without an appointment. Next time, I would appreciate it if you'd call ahead and get with my assistant. She'll make room on my schedule, I assure you."

Allen ran his hands down his muscular thighs, settling deeper into the chair, as well as into the conversation. "That's why I decided to slide by today. Grace, let me get right to it. Even though you're a poor man's heartache and a rich man's checkmate, I'm not used to being told when to come and go. Maybe you've heard how making it on time to scheduled appointments ain't ever been my thing. This morning, I woke up with visions of loveliness. Taking nothing from you, that vision of mine was the seven-digit sports drink contract waiting on my signature."

Still a touch embarrassed, Grace smiled peculiarly. "Talk about getting your face cracked." Since Corporate Grace had always been the one she could count on, that's what she dished out to Allen, as best she could. "Mr. Foray, Allen, hopefully I haven't ruined an extremely profitable business relationship by tripping all over my assumptions. With that said, perhaps you should tell me where I figure in with your hesitance to autograph the contract that you seem to approve of?"

"No doubt, no doubt. I get along fine with the numbers. It's just that I'm used to women coming at me with their hands out, on the take for everything they can get. Other than my moms, you're the only woman who's been looking out for my best interest and expecting nothing in return."

"I take it you don't get along fine with that?" Grace joked, using the same wording he had. When Allen caught it, his bright smile uncovered every one of his pearly whites.

"Oh, you got jokes too? I find a sense of humor very appealing in a woman." He let that comment hang in the air longer than Grace was comfortable with. "But I know when I'm out of my league. I just wanted to say thanks for being the kind of sistah that any man would be proud to have on his arm and build a life with, even if that brotha ain't me." Allen's heartfelt words stunned Grace. She was utterly floored by his honest, albeit sophomorically home-boyish, display of endearment.

Blushing, her face lit up like Times Square. She noticed indications suggesting that in time, he'd mature and become the man she knew he could be, just not now. "Wow, Allen," she said eventually, as Corporate Grace stepped aside long enough for her to accept his gratitude in the sincere spirit with which it was presented. "You're very welcome, although wonders never cease. I'll try to remember those kind words during the next full moon, when I wake up reminded that the world does not revolve around me."

As the multimillionaire stood to leave, he extended his long arm, at the end of it the biggest hand Grace had ever seen. The hardest thing she'd done all day was chasing away her own visions of that hand of his working the magic she fell short of conjuring up for herself the night before. "Allen, just this once, I feel that a warm, nonintimate hug would be more fitting for the occasion." After she walked around her large desk to meet him, Allen smothered her with a gentle embrace, then backed away.

"Maybe things could be different between us further on down the road?" he suggested, in parting.

"I'm afraid that's a million-to-one shot," she answered with utmost sincerity.

"Good, then I still have a chance," Allen jested. "See, I got jokes too."

Grace was actually glad Allen had stopped by unannounced. He was both a pleasant surprise and more than likely the sweetest regret of her life. "See you, Allen. Take care of yourself out there, and sign that contract before I'm forced to drop in on you for a good talking-to."

"No doubt, I'll take care of it today. With you watching my back, it'll be gravy now that I know what the real deal looks like up close. Much respect, Miss Hilliard, much respect."

During the better part of the day even with the conviction in mind that she'd made the right decision, Grace couldn't help but wonder if she'd made a huge mistake. Sure, Allen was unpolished and rough around the edges, but so were diamonds when initially carved out of the earth. Grace was well aware that she'd passed up a good thing, one perfectly crafted for someone else.

12

Pretty Ricky

Grace's Prada pumps hadn't touched the ground since All-World Allen Foray made her day. She was a bouquet of pleasantness throughout the afternoon. When Marcia tapped on her door just before quitting time, with a brand new replacement for the mug she'd copped for herself, Grace apologized if she'd implied that an in-kind gift was warranted. Marcia wouldn't take no for an answer, offering to wash and hide the mug away where it would be available whenever her boss needed a caffeine fix. Since it wasn't worth arguing over, Grace decided not to. She nodded thank you, as Marcia stood across the desk studying Grace's expression. Once feeling comfortable that she had properly made amends, she smiled, then cheerfully bound out of the office like a child whose world was perfect again.

The sun still shone brightly on Grace's world, too, as she harnessed the seatbelt on her way out of the company parking garage. During the drive home, she traveled along the freeway, humming a few bars from one of the hits as India Arie's *Acoustic Soul* CD played on her car stereo. Another man had affectionately told Grace how wonderful she was. It was strange at the time, because those words didn't hurt one bit when Allen said it. Not like the searing sensation she suffered after fooling with Goofy Greg and his African rhino powder, only to be dismissed when she mentioned a serious "let's take it to the next level" relationship. And it was nothing like feeling that her confidence had been chipped away piece by piece as Tyson saw fit to let her down easy at the park. No, this was different. Allen was kind, thoughtful, and well, yes, he was fine. Grace smiled as she passed by a humongous billboard with his picture plastered on the one-hundred-foot sign. It was a broad illustration of him slam-dunking a basketball with one hand while displaying a Dream Cream snack cake in the other. The caption read, MUNCH TIME IS MY KINDA CRUNCH TIME. Grace chuckled at the shiny blue short set she'd convinced him to wear. Admittedly, Allen was a real cutie even when zooming by at sixty miles an hour. Before she'd passed through the busy downtown area, Grace counted thirteen additional billboards, all using sexy men and women to sell products ranging from mobile homes to expensive jewelry. The last one depicted a half-dressed male-model type on the beach, intertwined with a scantily clad beach bunny, her bathing suit too small to adequately cover her breasts and other assets. The tie-in between jewelry and nearly nude suntanned hotties was lost on Grace, but the jewelry company didn't care about making logical connections. They wanted to persuade as many drivers as possible to catch a glimpse of the company's name and trademark, strategically placed just below that skinny chick's behind. Grace found herself laughing out loud right after she'd passed the jewelry store billboard because all she could think about were plump breasts and thighs from KFC.

The next morning, long after Grace had slept off the bucket of extra crispy she shared with André, she was dragging herself out of bed again, stumbling into the restroom again, and doubting her conviction to sustain her vow of celibacy. The sun outside was shining, but her immediate forecast called for scattered showers of the most wicked kind.

For the second consecutive morning, Grace found herself back in the break room with an increasing need for caffeine. Days of riding her natural high, which infused significantly more pep to Grace's step than she would have guessed, were gone now that her frequent gratuitous sexcapades had become relegated to her past. Learning to live without them presented the kinds of challenges that sent her friend Shelia racing back to the car wash for a low-budget buff and shine.

Marcia was delighted when she entered the small room to find Grace adding half-and-half to the Colombian blend in her new mug. "Wow, Miss Hilliard, two days in a row," was her cheerful salutation. "That's got to be a new record for you."

"Morning, Marcia," Grace mumbled, behind her warm concoction. "Don't go calling the Guinness book people to send off my plaque just yet." Grace was in a miserable and lonely place, but it was a necessary stopover if she really wanted to rehabilitate her constitution. And yes, she would eventually come to understand the importance of enduring the storms of life so that she'd truly be grateful when God saw fit to open up the treasures of Heaven and rain down His blessings of sunshine abundant. Until then, she'd have to settle for early A.M. sugar rushes while concentrating her efforts on sweetening herself.

"Hey, Ricardo," Marcia said in the flirtiest voice she could get away with while on the clock, as her daytime daydream passed by the break-room door. Ricardo Diaz, a good-looking Express Supplies delivery-route driver, stopped his dolly and poked his head in to see whose voice begged to be acknowledged. When he strolled into the break room, his hazel eyes darted back and forth between Marcia and the company's newest partner, Grace. By the time he'd blinked twice, there was no doubt who had called him. Marcia often made excuses to meet him at the elevator, and she'd even gone as far as intentionally omitting an order or two until he was ready to leave, and then springing it on him. Ricardo was accustomed to Marcia's antics, harmless as they were, but he didn't know what to make of Grace, *Ms. Wet Paint*, as in do not touch, as her eyes roamed all over his tight navy shorts that stopped at midthigh and his well-developed chest, and the studying of his bad-boy magnetism that went on for days. Grace hadn't bothered paying attention to Ricardo's stunning attributes before then. Despite his chiseled body, thick dark hair slicked back in a ponytail, and the infinite energy of a seventeen-year-old, he was merely the delivery guy, as far as Grace was concerned. Ricardo from the route, the other women called him—those who had noticed their daily dose of Puerto Rican flavor—was built for speed and logging long hours.

The delivery guy fought back a tattling grin when he caught Ms. Wet Paint slipping. "Marcia, my love, how's tricks?" he said suspiciously. "Got any last-minute orders today?"

"Wouldn't you like to know?" Marcia teased, with a lift in her voice and lust in her eye. She continued lusting until Ricardo's gaze drifted back to Grace, who was trying to look away. Marcia cleared her throat. "Huh-hmm. Now that you've mentioned it, I do have an order for you *on my desk*." She didn't try to hide the fact that she was a bit jealous.

"All right then, I can handle that," Ricardo answered her. "Catch you next time," he added with a friendly wink. "Miss," he bid goodbye to Grace as an afterthought on his way out.

Grace straight-faced Ricardo's good-bye as if he was never there. She wasn't interested in him past just looking at an endless supply of Latin machismo, regardless of how easy on the eyes he happened to be. Ricardo was the delivery guy, period. At least that's what Grace kept telling herself as she strolled out onto the floor, thinking that if she timed it right, she could get a bit closer when he waited for an elevator going down.

As soon as Grace made it to her office, she placed an immediate call to the mailroom, urgently requesting a ream of Express Services labels, and then sauntered through the minefield of workstations toward the reception area. She caught the same types of glances she'd received when sneaking a peek at André's teacher that night at the school, sly contemptuous glances that seemed to insinuate she should have waited her turn to schmooze with Ricardo like everyone else.

After Grace engineered her simply-by-chance run-in, she sidled up behind Marcia at the elevator, who was already there to hatch her own scheme to do the same. When Grace's assistant realized who was standing there, she panicked and made herself scarce by bolting for the ladies' room. On cue, Ricardo rounded the corner with an empty cart. Grace began tapping her shoe on the carpet when it appeared her plan was going to work. She had no idea what to do when the opportunity presented itself. However, she was sure of one thing; there was no way she'd do anything scandalous at work, with so many of her employees looking on.

Seconds before Ricardo eased up next to her, the elevator doors opened. An intern from the mailroom stepped off hurriedly with a shrink-wrapped bundle under his arm. "I believe those are for me," Grace informed the freckle-faced college student.

"Miss Hilliard?" he asked, nervous and surprised that she was so attractive. "They said you needed these right away."

"Thank you," she answered, with an expression that screamed, "You can run along now!" The intern recognized that look all too well, and he hastened to comply just as Grace's expression strongly suggested. The young man disappeared like a shot down the side staircase, leaving the bundle of labels with Grace.

Ricardo allowed the elevator doors to close while watching their strained interaction. A thought crossed his mind, but he let it pass so as not to open his mouth only to say the wrong thing. With a woman like Grace, he'd learned the hard way to speak only after being spoken to or risk being subjected to a devastating outcome afterward.

Grace tore at the thin, transparent plastic covering the stack of shipping labels. "Excuse me," she said finally. "Can I use these for next-day delivery?"

"No, ma'am, those are for regular mail only, but I can run down to the van and get plenty of the ones you need if you want." Grace studied the way he smiled, a little too accommodating for her taste. Momentum had shifted to his end of the court, and she didn't like the way it felt. Ricardo was overly cocky, and flexing as if she was a sex-starved secretary. He had the sex-starved part right, but he'd underestimated her ability to turn the tables and walk away.

"No, that won't be necessary," answered Grace as she spun on her heels to demonstrate just how easy it was to do. The Devil was stalking Grace, just like her girlfriends had predicted he would. Previously, she wouldn't have wasted her time chasing a delivery man. Desperate times had pushed her further than she'd intended to go already, so she popped her collar and shook off Ricardo's mojo as best she could, before finding herself in the worst kind of compromising position, one she'd be repenting over.

Chandelle came out of nowhere with a gang of attitude. "Humph, I saw that. It's a shame that a man can't do his job without trying to get his freak on while he's at it."

"Chandelle, what are you talking about?" Grace asked, praying that her ill-advised elevator rendezvous hadn't been detected.

"I saw what was going on, Grace, with Ricardo Diaz. Uh-huh, Pretty Ricky's what they call him. He used to deliver office supplies to the firm I clerked for when I was in college. Good thing you didn't get too close because he'd have been trying to hit that. Yeah, girl, the word is out on him. He's been known to tap a sistah in the back of that van of his. Not that he's your type, Grace, but you have to watch out for playas like him, he's nasty." Chandelle held out her left hand, proudly inspected her wedding ring, then flounced down the hall in the other direction.

Grace stood there, wondering what was really happening, all the way around. She had allowed herself to traipse behind a delivery guy, and if that weren't bad enough, a younger employee was cautioning her against it. Grace was still trying to figure out how she'd fallen so far and so fast. Linda tried to warn her but she wasn't ready to be told anything at the time. Soon enough, Grace had to come to grips with the incontestable truth that the best lessons learned were the ones causing her to get jammed up after having been forewarned in an I-told-you-so fashion. Those always left a mark.

A few hours later, Grace needed to get away from the office, so she took an early lunch and made a beeline to the mall. She exchanged a pair of shoes at Nordstrom's after purchasing them the week before and discovering she already had the same pair when putting them away in her walk-in closet. On her way out of the department store, she passed by an interesting underwear display in the men's department. She caught herself imagining Tyson in a pair of designer boxers, as she studied the male mannequin over the top of her sunglasses, before heading down to the lower level for salad to go. The food court was bustling with noonday traffic, mostly young mothers pushing baby strollers and businessmen scouting out their next ex-wives. Grace was paying the cashier when a familiar voice called out to her.

"Miss Hilliard, I thought that was you." The voiced belonged to the office supply delivery guy, Mr. Rico Suave, the same one who'd inconceivably managed to pitch a temporary tent in her head. "I didn't think you wasted time shopping for yourself. Thought rich chicks had somebody to fetch stuff for you."

"Excuse you?" she sneered. Grace was attracted to him, but refused to be mistaken for a common hoochie.

"I figured, since we're both off the clock, we could speak freely. No titles, no stress."

"Oh, is *that* what you figured?"

"Yeah, and I'm never wrong about these kinds of things," Ricardo answered proudly.

"Humph, there's a first time for everything," she fired back, in a defining manner.

"Oh, it's like that? Tell you what, lemme ask you one question, then I'll bounce." When Grace didn't shoo him away like a bothersome housefly, he grinned eagerly. "Cool, cool. Question, I've been riding this route for three years, and this morning was the first time you ever had two words to say to me. Why is that?"

"I don't understand the question," Grace sighed, annoyed that he dared to ask her such a thing.

"I mean, women like you only talk to men like me when they really need something, and that doesn't include coming up with a ridiculous question about shipping labels that she's too important to paste on herself. I know you think you're too high class to hook up with a low-end working stiff, so what gives?"

"Actually, I don't typically discuss my personal views regarding potentially suitable mates with men I don't know," Grace answered, observing Ricardo's jaw tightening in a way that proved his assessment of women like her correct. Regardless, she was determined to put an end to all of his nonsense. "Look, Pretty Ricky."

"That's what they call me," he quipped arrogantly.

"Yes, I'm sure they do. And since you asked, I'll set the record straight. I have standards, and I won't apologize for that. Putting your vocation aside, a man is not what he does for a living, because we all have to keep the lights on. With that said, I'd have to say no thank you on general principle because of the stunts you're in the habit of pulling in the back of your company van." Grace assumed she'd flattened Ricardo, but she hadn't come close to tearing off the veneer covering his street-tempered bravado.

"Ahhh, I see," he chuckled. "Chandelle probably told you about us testing the shocks back in the day." When Grace's eyes widened, displaying the shock she couldn't conceal, he smacked his lips. "Oops, I guess she only dished out the dirt on me, like I just served up hers. Now what?"

"Sorry Ricardo, but you did say you had one question. 'Now what?' makes two." Grace thanked the cashier for her salad, wrapped in a white to-go bag. "In case you've forgotten, this is where you bounce. Remember? Oh, and by the way, I don't want there to be any more misunderstandings about us hooking up here or anywhere else. Do you feel me?" she added in a manner he fully understood.

"Huh. Yeah, I feel you all right," Ricardo smirked. "But next time you want to be left alone, you might want to keep your eyes to yourself. Where I come from, staring a man down is seen as an open invitation. Don't sweat it, though, I got the message." As Ricardo sulked off slowly, ego slightly bruised, Grace enjoyed the way his tight shorts cupped his butt like a glove. Too bad he was the type of man to have sex with any woman standing still long enough to let him, and besides that, he was nasty. Nasty, she'd overlooked in her past for the sake of cheap thrills, but his other trait was a deal breaker. When Grace told Ricardo that his current position in life didn't have an effect on her decision not to get involved with the likes of him, she almost believed it herself, almost. In all honesty, his résumé did matter. Right, wrong, or indifferent, it mattered. She had worked hard to get where she was and she wanted a man who had managed to ascend in his career field as well. Grace made no bones about that, not then, not ever.

Chandelle met Grace in her office doorway when she returned from the mall. "Who's that man in the conference room?" Chandelle asked, all giddy and bubbling over with excitement.

"What man? I have a one o'clock on the books, but I didn't see anyone come in."

"I'm sure you didn't see him, if you have to ask, but I'll tell you who I think he is . . ." Chandelle crossed her arms, then looked up and down the hallway to see if anyone was in earshot. "That grown man up in the conference room has your name written all over him. There's no wedding ring, I've already scoped that on your behalf. And I know he's straight too. I had Awkward Bob run him through his gaydar, and he came out clean." If Grace hadn't been so embarrassed for Chandelle, she would have been highly upset for the blatant disregard of their previous discussion about staying out of her personal affairs.

"You seemed to be all worked up over a man that isn't yours," Grace said, casting a disapproving eye. "Didn't you recently get married?"

"Uh, yeah, but I didn't recently go blind. I'm jus' tryna look out for my big sistah, on the hook up tip," Chandelle offered with a wide toothy grin.

"Do I look that hard up to you? Wait. On second thought, don't answer that." Grace weighed her options, and this was no time to be prudish and prideful. If there was somebody to see her, a fine somebody, the least Grace could do was give the man a decent shot at impressing her. Surely she owed him that much.

Grace was about to put her salad away, and hadn't intended on saying anything about the brief chat she had at the mall but couldn't help letting Chandelle know what she knew. "Oh, I almost forgot. While I was out to get lunch, I ran into a special acquaintance of yours. Want to guess who? Lemme help you out. I had an interesting conversation in the food court with Pretty Ricky."

"That's what they call him."

"So I've been told. And accordingly, I feel the need to

look out for my lil' sistah. So I'm going to ask you straight up. Are you still letting him hit that, considering your current status?"

"Naw, uh-uh!" Chandelle protested. "That thing we had ended years ago. I was young, but I was ready. Ricardo started throwing some of that broken Spanglish at me, had me living la vida loca and looking for my panties in the dark."

"Ewwh, in the back of that dirty delivery van?" Grace questioned, fearing the answer.

"Told you he was nasty," Chandelle confirmed, overlooking the fact that she was the one searching for her underwear in the rear of a filthy vehicle. "Okay, so him and me had our fling, but I didn't plan on keeping with that Route-Man Madness my whole life. I was single and on my lunch break, Pretty Ricky had a van . . . What can I say? But hey, don't waste your time standing there rehashing my past, when your future could be sitting down the hall waiting to trip all over his tongue when he gets a load of you." When Grace actually envisioned that, her thighs tingled. If the stranger did have a tongue long enough to stumble over, she was liable to jump him on the spot.

13

Batteries Required

Despite Chandelle's ghetto approach at matchmaking, she had been right before and that was good enough for Grace, so she reached in her Coach purse and came out with a small makeup compact. After dabbing touches of foundation here and there, she made a slow stroll down the long hall toward the conference room. Chandelle stood up in her cubicle and gave a thumbs up to spur Grace on.

Caught up in her associate's idea of every man potentially being the right one, Grace entered the room with grossly unrealistic expectations, the kind that usually resulted in someone getting their feelings hurt. This brief encounter would be no exception to the rule. When Grace announced who she was, Kenton Reese, an executive from Dream Creams, stood to offer his hand. "Hello—I'm Grace Hilliard—the marketing director," she said, all in one hurried pitch. Good thing she did, because that fine example of male masculinity took her remaining breath away.

At first sight, Grace could see that Kenton was more than just a man. His brilliant smile was centered within a perfectly manicured goatee, putting what Greg tried to pass off for one to shame. His complexion was the color of Grace's, maple syrup. She was already imagining how difficult it would be to decipher where his body ended and hers began in the candlelight. His firm frame, concealed by a well-tailored gray flannel three-button suit, must have been sculpted over time, because nobody got to be that fine overnight, Grace reasoned.

As the handsome visitor moved his thin lips to introduce himself, Grace held tightly to his hand and nodded as if she comprehended every word, although she hadn't heard a single thing he said. "Miss Hilliard?" the man repeated for the third time before she snapped out of her enchanted haze. "Miss Hilliard, is there something wrong?"

"What? Oh, I'm sorry. It's just that you remind me of someone," she answered, her head spinning. *Someone from my dreams*, she wanted to say without regard to how it may have been received. "Mister . . . ? I apologize," Grace said, gathering herself together.

"Kenton, Kenton Reese," he informed her, despite just having told her who he was.

"That's right, Kenton Reese," she repeated, still taken aback, and more nervous than a long-tailed cat in a room full of rocking chairs.

Kenton placed his other hand on Grace's arm and then suggested she have a seat. He was honestly concerned that she might fall over. It had happened before to Kenton, the long-time playboy who was determined to mend his ways. At age thirty-five, acquiring wealth and beautiful women had inspired him, both equally so, and not necessarily in that order. Since moving to Dallas from the Washington, DC, area, he'd had his choice of women wrapped in chic designer fashions, every one of them willing to satisfy his every whim. Grace, who was still collecting her faculties, clearly understood why. He looked like money, new money, all crisp and clean, sharply packaged to spike a woman's interest and facilitate important business transactions. In a word, he was dangerous.

"Are you sure this is a good time?" he asked politely, staring into her eyes to see if anyone was home behind them. "I could reschedule, you know."

"No, that won't be necessary," Grace blushed like a southern belle. "I should have eaten breakfast."

"It's the most important meal of the day," Kenton said, like an old friend passing the time, "which is why I came by." Still looking Grace over with the intensity of a seasoned physician, Kenton stepped over to the credenza to get her a glass of water from a pitcher placed there. "Uh, why don't I go?" he offered for the second time. "We'll get together again when you're less . . . distracted."

"No, please don't," quickly escaped from her mouth before she could bridle it. "I'll be okay. I'm fine, really." How embarrassing. Corporate Grace had been highjacked by someone who wanted badly to get down and dirty with a man like Kenton Reese, an educated self-assured slice of beautiful black manhood—a slice that Grace wouldn't have minded sampling until there was nothing left but a smattering of crumbs. Instead of heading for the hills due to her uncharacteristic babbling, Kenton displayed genuine concern for her well-being while she fought her way back to a semblance of normalcy. "Can we start over? And, I'd like you to call me—" she paused, having forgotten her own name. "Grace." Kenton tried to stifle his laughter when Grace turned her face away to hide the humiliation. "You have no idea how badly I wish I could disappear," she sighed.

"Okay, Grace, but there's no need for that," he told her, smiling amiably. "Let's just chalk it up to a case of low blood sugar. And I would feel more comfortable if you called me Kenton." Grace nodded, this time truly in tune with the conversation. "I see that I've caught you on a bad day, so I'll cut it short," he suggested sincerely. Grace was still nodding her head, but deep down she really wanted to oppose his proposition of an abbreviated meeting. "On behalf of Dream Creams, we would like to extend Allen Foray's campaign for an additional six months after the current run." Kenton opened a black leather portfolio with his monogram stenciled on the bottom-left corner. "I'll leave the marketing strategies with you to review at your leisure. There's no reason to hurry."

"Okay, so you'll give me a pass this time? Thank you, Kenton. I'll look forward to reviewing your reports, and thanks for extending the contract. Allen's billboards are getting a lot of press around town."

"When we met with Ted several months ago, he promised results, and assured us that you had the magic to bring it all together. I'm glad we decided to do business with Pinnacle. It's a good fit." Kenton smiled, then gathered his things to end the brief office call, but Grace couldn't let him walk away without putting her bid in to do business with him on another, more intimate, level.

"Kenton, before you go, could you indulge me for a minute, off the record of course?"

"This is a private meeting after all," he replied, confirming that their discussion wouldn't go any further than that conference room.

With a bundle of apprehension, Grace closed her eyes and took a deep breath. "Now, I need you to understand that this is totally out of the ordinary, but would it be too forward to ask, for a friend, if you're seeing anyone?"

Kenton's eyes drifted toward the floor, then back up to rest on Grace's. "I believe that women would get a lot more of what they wanted if they'd simply step up and ask the important questions more often. No, Grace, one that important is never too forward. However, it did come a few months too late. I've found the perfect lady for me after auditioning more than my fair share. You'd like her. She's a lot like you, a savvy black female who's accustomed to being on top.

Please tell your friend that I'm flattered and it's nice to be noticed."

"I'll do that," Grace answered. She smiled wearily and extended her hand. "Hopefully, I'll be well nourished and focused the next time we have business to discuss." Grace knew that her light-headed spell had nothing to do with a lack of food. It was a lack of self-control that her whole lower region throbbed for attention. All of that activity had shut down her brain.

As Kenton turned to leave, he tossed a warm smile at Grace. "It was nice to finally meet you, friend. Good luck with that."

"Thanks. Good-bye, Kenton."

Grace was standing by the window, sipping from the glass of water Kenton had poured, when Chandelle eased up beside her. "You were right. He's as smooth as butter," Grace agreed. Despite the obvious, there was something intriguing about Kenton Reese. He was the first man she'd met in quite some time who didn't hesitate to brag about the woman he loved. It was so refreshing that it actually stung. She'd been sharing her bed and body for too long with men who, unlike Kenton, detested commitment. "Yeah," Grace asserted quietly, "Now I know exactly what I want. Just I wish I knew where to find one." What she wanted was a man so sure that he'd found the right woman to build a life with that he'd readily confess it to other interested females trying to get in the mix. That was the kind of man she would be proud of.

By the end of the week, things had certainly changed since the morning Allen swung by and lifted Grace's spirits. Night after night, Grace had dealt with constant aggravation and disappointment. Trying to pleasure herself without having access to the necessary tools to finish the job was driving her crazy. By the end of the week, things had changed so much for Grace that she was no longer thinking of KFC when she passed by the jewelry store billboard. She still had breasts and thighs on her mind, her breasts and thighs in the hands of a capable man with nothing better to do than put a late-night smile on her face until she told him to stop. That's when she maneuvered her Volvo SUV over three lanes, just in the nick of time, to take the Mockingbird Lane exit. It was inevitable. Sooner or later, she was destined to call on the Booty Boutique, a posh novelty store that offered the likes of flavored condoms, tawdry bedroom attire, chains and whips, scented oils, and life-size blow-up dolls. The boutique stocked accessories to heighten foreplay and assorted toys for grown-up girls and boys who were bent on getting things going their way.

Tired of falling asleep with her sights on satisfaction and steamy fantasies only to wake up with migraines and cramped fingers, Grace was determined to find alternative methods of getting what she needed without going back on her word. The Booty Boutique began as a small upscale "Naughty Nightie" way station for working women on their way home from the office or on their way to a hot date. Over time, the boutique had grown in size and stature to service a very diverse clientele. Outside the shop, Grace sat in her automobile staring at the entrance. Fearing that she might run into someone she knew, perhaps someone from church, she almost backed out of her parking space and headed straight for home. After giving it some additional thought, she concluded that those who were there to purchase personal maintenance equipment were in the same boat as her and needed it just as bad. In the time it took to blink, Grace found herself wandering up and down the aisles, browsing over specialty items with labels reading Hot Pockets, Him-sations, and Pocket Rockets. She placed a hand over her mouth after becoming oddly intrigued by signs pointing to vibrator options with differing lengths and widths. Grace skirted past the compact items to camp out under the sign reading MY NEW BEST FRIEND. Her face glowed when she pulled one of the packages down from the rack. "Ahh, it's kinda heavy, too. Every sistah needs a friend like you," she whispered, to the foot-long servicing device. *I should have picked up this Tongue Twister 3000 last week and saved myself the trouble,* she thought to herself. As if she'd stumbled onto a blue lagoon in the midst of the desert sun, Grace sat her basket down and emptied everything out of it except for the TT3000 and an assortment of lubricating lotions. *Yeah, this should work out just fine, me and my new best friend. Uh-huh, nice to meetcha. We've got a lot of getting acquainted to do.*

There were no apparent signs of apprehension, second thoughts, or humiliation accompanying Grace when she stood in line at the checkout counter. A petite cashier who appeared to be bored to death waved Grace over to the middle register. "I can help you here, ma'am," the younger woman hailed. As she rung up the items going home with Grace, she asked if there was anything else before totaling the transaction.

"Oh, yeah, where do you keep the four-packs of D batteries?" was Grace's request. The cashier pointed to several stacks of four-packs stationed on the wall behind her. Grace placed her right hand over her heart as if she were going to cry tears of joy. "Good, I'll take them all."

After enjoying three consecutive blissful nights of getting acquainted with the Tongue Twister 3000 and subsequently three consecutive nights of restful sleep, Grace was yearning for the warmth of a man's body more than ever, and all the other amenities that came along with the standard package as well. Subsequently, she decided to widen her relationship net with a deadly aim on snagging something worth keeping. *A Kenton Reese clone would adequately suffice,* she thought, *an educated mover and shaker with the body of Adonis and a desire to fall head over heels in love with the right woman.* Grace remembered Kenton recounting how he'd held open auditions to select his mate, so she set out to do the same to land hers. While avoiding the typical happy hour haunts, popular watering holes and nightclubs where men were always on the make for a woman whose morals had taken a dive after one too many cocktails, Grace's options became severely limited.

She'd seen what her church congregation had to offer and cringed when that heathen Albert Jenkins came to mind. Against Sister Kolislaw's better judgment, which Grace questioned silently when told, "you must be crazy to go shopping the net, full of world wide weirdos, expecting to find anything other than a mess of fools with more problems than all the Hebrews in the whole Old Testament combined. Heed my advice Grace. I wouldn't steer you wrong. If'n I told you that a flea could pull a train then you'd best to hook it up," she sat in front of her computer.

"I must be crazy," Grace heard herself say while strolling through the web for a singles site that wasn't a front for wild, undercover, butt-naked orgies. After submitting her e-mail address and additional information, she found herself in the midst of private organizations that specialized in everything from slightly disabled escorts to midget oil-wrestling sports bars. When Grace stumbled onto Christian SingleButLooking.com, she felt safe and confident that it fit her situation like a glove, so she laid her apprehensions aside to take a closer look. Within a very interesting week of dating, Grace would come to realize that neglecting Sister Kolislaw's warnings wasn't her only mistake, but merely the beginning of a long trail of them.

"Let's see here. How many choices do I get?" she thought aloud, browsing the list of attributes for the "Prospects and Potentials" search. "Okay, I'll put in Christian, black men over thirty, physically fit, sense of humor, loves to dance, disease free, college educated, height of six feet and above, God fearing, truly believes there is a Hell, seriously seeking a mate, and celibate." Grace wiggled gleefully as she pressed "enter" on her home computer. "That should give me a lot of intriguing Christian men to choose from." Her monitor flashed ten matches. "Darn, only ten in the entire Dallas metropolitan area. Only ten? Well, all I really need is one," she theorized and kept right on moving.

Grace knew going in that this particular site prided itself on a high success rate because it didn't provide photographs, stating that ninety percent of couples get together based solely on physical attraction, but nearly half of the marriages in the country still managed to fail. This was actually unnerving until Grace remembered reading the home page advertisement that said the site based its matches on spiritual compatibility, chemistry, and social consciousness. Before she clicked the first single brotha bio, she sent up a slightly abbreviated prayer for discernment to help her pick out the ones who best suited her taste. However, Grace didn't take into account that not all of her prayers were answered with the response she was looking for, or within the time frame she expected, especially if God expected her to be still and wait on Him instead. Grace also neglected to keep in mind that there was always an outside chance that His answer was an unequivocal, plain old-fashioned, No.

Tommy Franklin's bio read like a feature from *Perfect Male* magazine, so Grace agreed to meet with him first. She stayed up hours past her bedtime trading instant messages with Tommy before agreeing to a date, and a time and place. Then she remained logged on to set up five additional meet-and-greets with other men whose bios read like absolute can't-misses on her computer printout. At two o'clock in the morning, Grace figured that her time had been well spent and worth the lost sleep.

14

Single But Looking

Grace spent half of the day wrapped up in a bundle of nerves. She imagined meeting Tommy and how nicely he'd measure up to the description crafted on his Web page detailing how he was a well-groomed socialite, with an adventurous spirit and energy to spare, who loved cross-state cycling, rocky roads, and mountain climbing. When Grace arrived five minutes late to Souper Soups and More for a chat over light entrées, she scanned the restaurant praying that Tommy hadn't left thinking he'd been stood up. There were two young couples munching on healthy snacks, an elderly woman smuggling pepperoni into her purse from the buffet, and an extremely large man wearing a paper napkin as a catchall bib while he shoveled salad into his mouth with both hands. Grace thought, *Tommy hadn't arrived yet*. Getting stood up by him was her worst concern, that is, before she met him.

Patiently, Grace waited for another ten minutes before checking with the hostess. "Excuse me, this might sound kinda strange, but I was supposed to meet someone here, a man," she added, behind a cloud of second thoughts. "Has anyone named Tommy called or left a message for a Grace? That's me."

The young lady, a thin ratty brunette in a black second-hand cocktail dress and discount-store flats, put her paper-back novel away and smiled cordially after having had her reading interrupted. She searched the hostess stand high and low, then shook her head. "No, ma'am, I'm sorry," she informed Grace, who turned to walk away, chalking it up as a huge error in judgment. "Ma'am, oh, wait," the hostess called out. "There was a man here about thirty minutes ago, excited about a blind date."

"I must have missed him," Grace sighed. "Oh, well, I was late after all. He probably thought I'd changed my mind."

"Uh, let's take a look around," the hostess offered. "If he decided to stick around, he should still be right over there." The young lady pointed to the salad-shoveling dinosaur, with his head still buried in a foot-tall plate of romaine lettuce.

"Uh-uh, there must be some sort of mistake," Grace whispered as the lady waved her over to his table.

"Sir, is this her?" yelled the hostess, like a clueless innocent do-gooder. The soup and salad monger snapped his head upright, almost flipping the table over with his protruding belly. Grace was horrified as she watched his paper bib bounding up and down with each of his monstrous strides toward her. *Perhaps he'd been waiting on someone else,* she imagined, *another blind date that was fortunate enough to catch a glimpse of his double-stuffing routine and then caught the next bullet-train to Anywhere But Here.*

"Sir, didn't you say that her name was Grace?" asked the annoyingly helpful hostess.

The man was nearly out of breath after wiping both hands on his khaki slacks. "Wow!" he marveled. "You're Grace

Hilliard? Wow! Am I glad to meet you! Tommy Franklin's the name, but friends call me Meat." He shoved his meaty paw toward Grace.

Somewhat startled, she recoiled. "Nice to meet you, Meat."

"I'm sorry for getting started on dinner without you, but as you can see, I'm a big fella and need to keep my strength up." *For what, climbing the Empire State Building and swatting at passing airplanes?* Grace thought.

Reluctantly Grace followed him back to the table he had staked out. It resembled a battlefield, where every item on the menu had put up a gruesome fight before being eaten. Grace sat with her purse on her lap. She was understandably disturbed to learn that Tommy didn't come close to resembling the description on the Web page, and she wasted little time calling him on it. "Tommy, uh . . . Meat, I have a slight problem with the way you painted yourself on the singles site as an adventurous socialite who's into cycling in cross-state events over rocky roads, and mountain climbing."

Meat grinned big and wide, with remnants of food poking out of his mouth like an overstuffed garbage disposal. "See, a brotha's got to be creative if he wants to meet a real fly cutie like you, so I jazzed up my credentials a bit."

"A bit?" Grace questioned, refusing to believe that he knew anything about small amounts.

"Oh, but I didn't lie exactly. See, at four hundred and eighty pounds, every time I make it out of bed and leave my house, it's an adventure for me, and I'd like to think of myself as a socialite. I mean, I do like to get my party on . . . when my hip ain't acting up."

"Your hip?" Grace shuddered.

"Yep, got a new one last year, but it stiffens up every now and then."

Grace shook her head slowly, trying to take in all of her date's girth as well as his lies that well surpassed "not exactly." "Okay Meat, I'll give you those, but come on. What about competitive cycling, rocky roads, and mountain climbing?"

Meat swallowed an entire stack of sliced ham and chased it with a glass of lemonade. Then he waggled his thick index finger at Grace until he noticed a dab of mustard on the tip of it. After he sucked the mustard off, out came the granddaddy of all contrived explanations. "Uh-huh, now, that's the truth, every word of it. I love to *watch* competitive cross-state cycling, I love rocky road ice cream, that's my favorite, and whenever I'm forced to take the stairs, I become a mountain . . . climbing 'em." After he'd finished serving it up thick, Grace was so frustrated that she burst out laughing. "That's not quite the response I usually get, but it's way better than getting cussed out," the mountainous eating machine chuckled.

"Meat, I can see why women go off on you after finding that you've grossly misrepresented yourself online, but this is too ridiculous to get hard-pressed over." She thought it was better to see the irony in the way Meat saw himself, than to make a big deal and end up seeing red.

"Cool, Grace. That's a great attitude," Meat complimented. "Does this mean you'll see me again?"

Grace put her hand on her purse. "Meat, don't make me have to cut you," she joked. "But, seriously, unless you enjoy hurting women by building false expectations, I suggest you be more honest from now on." She glanced at her watch to time-stamp the shortest date in history. "Wow, look at that, four minutes. It was nice meeting you, but I have to go."

Meat's expression saddened as if another one had gotten away. "Grace, if I were all those things you thought I was, would you still be rushing off?" he asked, really wanting to know.

"Of course not," she answered honestly, "unless that man was a liar, too." Tommy "Meat" Franklin scooted his chair away from the table to say good-bye. When he reached out to hug Grace, she stiff-armed him in his beefy chest. "Uh-uh, it's not even like that," she objected harshly.

"Grace, can I call you?" he shouted after her, like a jilted lover.

"Bye, Meat," she answered, without breaking stride.

"Okay then, Grace, be that way!" He held up a lengthy dinner bill. "Well, can you help a brotha out, put a lil' something on this? Grace, Grace!" he bellowed, before eyeing the total. "What, how they gonna charge me for three buffets?"

If Grace's first Internet dating encounter hadn't been so utterly preposterous, she would have been beside herself. She had forty-five minutes to kill before her next appointed time to meet and greet. Sylvester Green had convinced her that an open-all-night diner near downtown was a good place to connect because it was near his office. Grace had her heart set on getting to know the financial whiz, who made a comfortable living by trading stocks, and also dabbled in real-estate investments. His online profile had received substantially more hits than any of the others she matched with on the compatibility rating scale, so it appeared that things were already looking up.

Grace sat at the diner counter drinking tea when a nice-looking man entered through the door. He was tall enough to meet her criteria so she eased off the metal bar stool to approach him, but before she could reach him, another woman stepped through the door and placed her hand in his. Grace picked her face up off the floor and quickly returned to the counter. Embarrassed over almost making a complete fool of herself, Grace made a valiant effort to keep a close lookout, when someone shouting from the sidewalk out in front of the diner drew her attention.

"Don't make me have to chase you for my grip next time, Pumpkin!" a white man threatened to a frightened black woman in cheap heels sprinting up the block to elude his wrath. "You better run!" he heckled loudly. "Better run. Got me out here like a bill collector. Huh, I kinda like that . . . a bill collector. I think I'ma keep that one." The man tilted the brim on his lime green felt hat, snatched up his forest green–checkered slacks by the belt loops, and then buttoned up his pea green sports coat.

Suddenly, Grace didn't think it was such a good idea meeting with this Sylvester guy in a seedy industrial park off the boulevard. Sure it was still light out, but pimps and prostitutes were too much to stomach for the suggested get-acquainted session, so she felt compelled to dash. *Her date would surely understand once she'd sent him an e-mail apology explaining her trepidation,* Grace reasoned. Unfortunately, fate had other ideas. Sylvester Green was already on the scene and resting his behind on the trunk of a classic 1975 kitted-out gangster white-walled Cordova.

As Grace jotted a note to be left with the head waitress, the loud-mouthed pimp plopped down at the counter next to her. "Hey Brown Sugar, slow down so's I can say something good to ya," he heralded, as Grace looked up from scribbling on the small notepad. "Ahh, so you just gonna ignore me? Be that way, with yo fine self. I gots business too." The nuisance continued leering over her shoulder to see just what she was up to, figuring to utilize that information to strike up another conversation. Without notice, he let out a loud cackle. "Haah! Uh-uh, fine brown, you ain't got to write another word down. Your Prince Charmin' has arrived, and I'm glad to be alive," he added, sucking on a gold-rimmed decaying tooth.

"I don't know who you think I am, but I'm not one of your girls," Grace spat harshly, trying to appear tougher than she was.

"You could be, though," the pimp offered, with diamonds in his eyes. "I could put you on the stroll, and we could both get paid. If you wanna be a freak and pop it on the weekend, ain't none of my business unless we go fifty-fifty. If needs be, I can get mine on the back end," he suggested with a devilish leer.

Grace grabbed her purse. "Whatever!" she answered, starting toward the wait stand to hand off the note and beat it out of there before the sun went down.

"Come on, brown skin, don't be like that," the hustler insisted, hot on her heels. "I know you're digging me, or you wouldn't have agreed to bump gums together."

"Man, you need to back off me before I call the law," she warned. "I don't dig you. I don't know you, and I don't want to, so step!"

"Whoopty-whoop?" he yelped, as if to question her demeanor. "If it's like that, don't bother to be e-mailing me no more then, Grace."

The fact that he knew Grace's name stopped her dead in her tracks. "Hold on, what do you mean, e-mailing you, and how do you know my name?"

"Ahh, snap, I guess the work clothes threw you? I'm Sly Green, your Christian single ready to mingle."

Frozen, Grace stared into his eyes like a snake being charmed for the first time. "Show me some ID," she demanded immediately. Reluctantly, he slid his hand inside an alligator man-purse, then begrudgingly presented Grace with his driver's license. "Sylvester Greenberg?" she read aloud. "You're a Jewish pimp!"

"Nah, not really," he countered, as if it didn't matter. "Well, only on my father's side, but, hey, that shouldn't stop us from hooking up like a Reese's peanut butter cup. You and me could fit together quite nicely. Chocolate don't break me out, baby."

Grace was so angry that she was shaking all the way down to the floor. "Let me get this straight, Sylvester!"

"Hey, you need to stall all that," he argued. "Don't nobody call me Sylvester no more. I go by Sly when I'm puttin' in work, like Sly Stallone, the Italian Stallion."

"Yeah, you've got rocks in your head if you think I'm not reporting you to the singles Web site. You're dishonest, a thug and . . ." Grace paused to look him over thoroughly. His throwback platform shoes caught her attention. "And you're not black or even six feet."

"Mere technicalities," Sly debated patiently. "Blackness

is only a state of mind. Don't hate on me 'cause I feel like a brotha . . . oppressed, depressed, distressed, with the man's boot against my chest."

"Sylvester, you *are* the man!" Grace informed him, as if he were unaware.

"So says you." Sly turned his nose up in opposition to Grace's low opinion of him. "Regardless of what you might think of me, you can't interfere with my First Amendment right to freedom of speech. I can say what I want on the Internet."

"Free speech? Don't you mean the lies you tell on your Web page? Show me a financial whiz, making a comfortable living in the trading industry. And on top of that, what's up with the part about dabbling in real-estate investments? Huh? What now, playa?" Grace had reverted back to the days when she grew up fending for herself with knuckleheads like Sly Green, both verbally and otherwise.

"It depends on how you view what it is that I do," he said cautiously. "Look, I make a gang of loot by managing my hospitality agents. Money for honey is a big business, and any time I put my girls on the block, it's a real-estate investment. If they don't hit the street, I don't eat. But you wouldn't understand my education from the school of hard knocks, college girl. Yeah, I've bumped into sistahs like you, all uptight and righteous. Go on then. Beat your feet on the hard concrete. I'll catch the next cyberfreak."

"You ought to be ashamed of yourself for tricking women like me," Grace told him. "But you're probably not, Trick!"

Grace and Sly squabbled back and forth before she got fed up, stomped out to her car, and climbed in it. She was very close to committing a felony, and was so far from the confident no-nonsense woman she had been when thinking that all was well with her soul. Not only had Sylvester Green turned out to be a joke, and a joke on her, she had allowed Satan to pull her down to his level. She prayed over it, repented, and, when she got home, informed the Web site of his lies so that no other woman would have to be faced with Sly's fraudulent fellowship. After unsubscribing to the service, Grace continued receiving e-mail from three extremely persistent suitors. Despite having persuaded each of them to submit photos and copies of proper identification before agreeing to accept their advances, not one of them panned out quite like Grace expected.

Feeling like her soul was just about on empty, Grace rushed home for the second night in a row, prepared dinner, and immediately retreated to her bedroom. The Book of James was the place she'd found herself immersed in since studying Hebrews to help renew her spirits, like a lost sinner trying to find the right path leading back to the fold. "Now faith is the substance of things hoped for, the evidence of things not seen," she read from Hebrews 11:1 and smiled, thinking how important it was for Christians to believe that God's plan would yield all those things they longed for. An unwavering and undeniable faith is what she needed, but that wasn't so easily obtained. Determined to strengthen hers, Grace continued on, praying that the Word would convict her like Sistah Kolislaw predicted it would. "My brethren, count it all joy when you fall into various trials, knowing that the testing of your faith produces patience," Grace read, nodding as her finger glided along the Scripture marked as James 1:2–3. Then she sighed heavily when reaching the twelfth through fifteenth verses. "Blessed is the man who endures temptation . . . let no one say when he is tempted, 'I am tempted by God,' for God cannot be tempted by evil, nor does He Himself tempt anyone. But each is tempted when he is drawn away by his own desires and enticed. Then, when desire has conceived, it gives birth to sin; and sin, when it is full-grown, brings forth death."

Saddened at the thought of destroying the one thing she was supposed to cherish most, Grace wondered how close she'd come to doing just that. Now that she'd begun taking seriously decided steps to fortify her soul, hopefully she'd never have reason to question that again. "Wanting to be a better Christian isn't enough," Grace whispered, when reading the last seven verses of the chapter. "Therefore lay aside all filthiness and overflow of wickedness, and receive with meekness the implanted word, which is able to save your souls. But be doers of the word, and not hearers only, deceiving yourselves. For if anyone is a hearer of the word and not doer, he is like a man observing his natural face in a mirror; for he observes himself, goes away and immediately forgets what kind of man he was. But he who looks into the perfect law of liberty and continues in it, and is not a forgetful hearer but a doer of the work, this one will be blessed in what he does. If anyone among you thinks he is religious, and does not bridle his tongue but deceives his own heart, this one's religion is useless. Pure and undefiled religion before God and the Father is this: to visit orphans and widows in their trouble, and to keep oneself unspotted from the world."

Grace placed a bookmark behind the first chapter of James, laid the Bible on her lap, and then tilted her head back. "Believers of the word and doers of the word," she heard herself say, previously considering them to be one and the same. "Yeah, it is a lot easier to call yourself a believer than to stick your neck out and prove it."

After washing her face and preparing for bed, Grace looked in on André. He was finishing up an assignment for Bible class, due the next Sunday. "Hey, it is getting kinda late, Dré," she suggested from his bedroom doorway.

"Yeah, Ma, I know. I'm almost done," he said in a manner suggesting that she allow him to complete it.

"What does Brother Rodgers have y'all studying this month?"

"Faith and obedience," André frowned. "Why, does the Bible teach anything else? 'Cause if it does, Brother Rodgers must not know about it. Faith and obedience, young brothas, those are the cornerstones of Christianity," André mocked, imitating his Bible class instructor's deep scratchy voice. "If you don't like it, take it up with the Lawd. But if I was you, I'd rather spend that time thanking Him instead." It was difficult to tell who was laughing the loudest. Grace held her stomach while André cackled and watched her. "Ma, it wasn't that funny," he chuckled.

"It is when you think about the most soft-spoken man I know, trying to build a fire beneath a room full of teenagers. That's very funny, bless his heart."

"Bless his heart?" André questioned. "He's not the one who has to stand up in front of everybody and explain why faith without works is dead."

"Hmm, I think that's a great assignment. I'll have to thank Brother Rodgers for putting up with y'all and seeing to *the Lawd's* business," Grace told him, with a slight impression of her own. "Don't stay up too late. School's in the morning."

"Night Ma," was André's way of saying, "I hear you, but I'm still working on that obedience thing."

Upon returning to her room, Grace couldn't resist opening her Bible to the bookmark she'd placed there fewer than thirty minutes before. "Faith without works," she murmured, scanning the following pages of her text. "Faith without works . . . here it is. James 2:17. This also, faith by itself, if it does not have works is dead. But some will say, 'You have faith, and I have works.' Show me your faith without your works and I will show you my faith by my works. You believe that there is one God. You do well. Even the demons believe and tremble! But do you want to know, O foolish man, that faith without works is dead?" Grace closed the Bible and smiled until her cheeks hurt. "Yes James, I do know that, and thanks to a kind and concerned little old man down at the church, so does my son."

15

Widows and Orphans

Despite several days having past since her latest wake-up call, Grace continued to kick herself over her Internet dating fiasco. On the following Sunday, Sister Kolislaw called to her from the second pew. She'd seen Grace enter the sanctuary, watched her interaction with others, and couldn't wait to share her observations. "Grace, is there something we need to talk about?" she'd asked, noting Grace's weary expression. "Uh-huh, I know there is, because it's written all over you."

Reluctantly, Grace couldn't do anything but talk about the types of men she'd met and how pitifully sorry she was for going about things her own way. Like the good friend she was, Sister Kolislaw hugged her and laughed until she lost her breath. After she'd had her fun, the older woman invited Grace into a nearby office, sat her down, and shared some extremely valuable knowledge. "Now that we've gotten all that foolishness out of the way, you might be ready to move on." Grace assumed that she was about to be lavished with at least one more heartfelt "there-there, Grace, it'll be okay," from her advisor but the time for that had come and gone. It was time to get past all of the errors in judgment she'd made and set her sites on moving forward.

"Grace, I noticed how you've lost some of your pride. Uh-huh, it's evident in your step, and in the way you took the time to interact with several members of the congregation. One of the best things that can ever happen to a strong, pretty girl like you has; you've been made humble, Grace. Now God can really work with you, while working on you. Stop chasing these silly men, honey. Let a good one chase you for a change. It'll turn out better that way. I want you to know something I learned many years ago, and it still holds true today. Ain't no man gonna do nothing until he gets it in his head that it's likely to kill him if'n he don't. When he's ready to settle down and marry, there's nobody who can stop him, not even his mama. And, if he's got his mind set against sharing his toys and taking a wife, there's nobody who can make him."

Grace took note because every situation and circumstance that Sister Kolislaw had predicted came true. Chandelle had the right idea, but she had also convinced Grace to push, plot and plan instead of relaxing long enough to enjoy her singleness. One of the best things about being Single Grace was the total love she received from her son. Grace had committed the past two weeks to meeting a companion. In the meanwhile, she had neglected to spend much time with André, although he didn't seem to mind because he'd been at Skyler's shooting baskets and palling around with the big brother he never had.

The next day, Grace allowed Sister Kolislaw's words from their Sunday chat to resonate within her. Spending too much time trying to situate her face in front of the right man's was a bad idea. As Grace parked her SUV in the high-school visitors' parking lot, she closed her eyes and meditated on being the best mother possible, one who always made time for her child, no matter what transpired in her grown-up world. Guilt had Grace feeling like she'd temporarily fallen short as a parent. She vowed to remedy that as quickly as possible.

The school receptionist had Grace sign in before granting her a pass that allowed her access to the rest of the building. After Grace thanked the woman and struck out for André's classroom, she had no idea it was English Lit or that she'd be exchanging words with Wallace Peters. Her mind was focused on getting her son to his dental appointment on time. It wasn't until she'd peeked through the small window in the classroom door that she recognized where she was and who it was looking back at her from the inside.

Wallace excused himself from the room immediately. "Yes, may I help you?" he asked softly, so as not to be overheard by a classroom full of maturing students.

Grace looked him over in one effortless glance. Wallace was just as adorable as the first two times she'd come in contact with him. His fashion-model appeal was also just as alluring but Grace had already wasted too much time sizing up men, so she played it straight down the middle. "I'm sorry to interrupt your lesson, Mr. Peters," she apologized earnestly. "André has a dental appointment."

"I see," preceded a long pause. "I'll get him for you, but I've been wondering about something. Is there any particular reason why you haven't made arrangements to reschedule the parent-teacher meeting? It was very busy the other night, so I can understand why you left. One of the other parents confirmed it was you I saw walking by."

So he did see me when I went by his open door, and he also remembered who I was. Interesting. "It's no excuse, I know, but I have been very busy," Grace said in her own defense. She handed Wallace a business card from her small carrying case. "You can reach me here, and I'll make myself available to fit *your* schedule." Her countenance was strictly professional. Wallace seemed slightly disappointed when he accepted the card, but Grace was too focused on being a better Christian to lower her guard and revert back to that man-chasing phase of her life. Besides, it appeared from the parent-teacher night that Mr. Peters had too many women trying to get on his team as it was. Grace couldn't see adding her name to that list of young and single hopefuls.

Noise began brewing inside the classroom as the students grew restless. Wallace stepped away for a minute and then returned with André in tow. Grace thanked the teacher and did an about-face without any special good-byes or slick exchanges. "Heyyy, boy," she cooed like a brand-new mommy, while strolling down the hall with André by her side.

"Hey, Ma, you okay?" he asked suspiciously.

"I'm great. Why, don't I look great?"

"I'ont know. When you start talking to me like that, like I'm three instead of thirteen . . ." He let the end of his sentence dangle, not wanting to overstate the obvious.

"You know what, you're right, Dré. I'm not okay. We have some catching up to do, you and me. That'll make me feel a lot better about us. What do you say?"

André slung the backpack over his shoulder, then shrugged casually. "That's cool with me." *That's cool with me?* He was certainly becoming more of a man and less of a boy with each passing day. On the way to André's checkup, Grace kidded him about some of the cute girls in his class, and that fast-tailed cheerleader in particular. Watching him come of age made Grace reminisce on her own passage into adulthood, the friends she'd left behind when moving to Dallas from St. Louis, and the importance of cataloging memories that would last a lifetime. Then something whispered to her. It whispered Skyler's name as if his and André's relationship warranted an examination. Nothing unusual had occurred to insinuate that the boys weren't getting along, but those whispers wouldn't stop.

"Dré, I just realized that Skyler wasn't in class today. Didn't you tell me how happy you were after he'd gotten special permission to take that course?" Several moments passed with André staring out of the car window, and then he shrugged his shoulders. Grace knew then that a thorough discussion was indeed necessary.

She guided the car into a convenience-store parking lot and put the gear shift in park. Then she said, "Son, don't make me have to ask what's going on with you and Skyler." Before André fessed up, it was her turn to do the staring. While he fidgeted, Grace grew more impatient. "Dré?" she urged insistently.

"I promised I wouldn't say anything about it," André mumbled in a low childlike tone. With his mother's mind racing a mile a minute over what could be so severe that it required the utmost secrecy, the boy continued looking down at the backpack strap he fiddled with. "Sorry, Ma, I promised."

Facing a dilemma, Grace considered pulling rank and forcing him to go back on his word or leaving it alone until she could get at the truth another way. Reluctantly, she went with the latter. During André's visit with the dentist, his first cavity was discovered. Grace believed in proper hygiene, and that included taking care of teeth. While one cavity wasn't a tragedy all by itself, it sent alarms that he'd been having his way with sweets somewhere other than at home. Since he'd spent a lot of time at Skyler's, it gave her the excuse she needed to drop in and check on things, and possibly gather the information that her son was holding out on.

Lecturing André about the importance of having all of his teeth as an adult was the best Grace could do to stop from choking the truth out of him about Skyler. André almost hopped out of the car before she came to a complete stop at the high school. "Ma, it's my first cavity ever. You shouldn't be this mad at me."

"And you don't have the right to tell me what I should get mad about," she reprimanded him strictly. "I pay the bills, buy the clothes, and feed you. So before you start thinking you can tell me what to do—" Grace cut her rant short when she saw a frightened young man looking back at her. "I'll see you at home. Catch the number nineteen bus!" André had opened his mouth in opposition to taking a long ride on the city's idea of rapid public transportation, but then he had a change of heart.

"Yes, ma'am," he said, glad to be walking away without Grace's hands fastened around his neck.

"And from this point forward, the only promises you make are to me," she shouted out of the passenger window. "You got that?"

"Got it," was the last thing she heard him say before she made a beeline over to visit with Skyler's grandmother.

Grace knocked on the front screened-in door of a small, ancient, white wood-framed house with severely chipped paint. Years had gone by since Grace had moved away, but the old neighborhood hadn't changed all that much. She rather enjoyed her occasional stops to pick up André during the better part of a year and making surprise drops by her rental property to see how that investment was holding up. "Miss Pearl, it's me. Grace!" she hollered, after she heard Skyler's grandmother hollering "who is it" from the other side of the door.

"Hold on, I'm coming!" the older woman barked in a short, choppy manner, as if that was all the hollering she was prepared to do. After jiggling on the knob, she managed to pry it open. "Said I was coming," she huffed, overweight and out of breath.

"Miss Pearl, you feel like having company today?" Grace asked, her words coming out in more of a plea than a question.

The gray-haired widow, her skin the color of rich Nigerian soil and her body thick from an everything-fried diet, leaned over with her fists parked on her generous hips. She felt around in the pockets of her housecoat, worn with a faded floral print, until she found her eyeglasses. She hung them around her neck by the long tennis shoe lace attached and wrestled them onto her face. When her tired eyes focused, she exclaimed with delight, "Gracie, that is you."

"Yes, ma'am, it's been a while."

"Come on in with your pretty self before you have every man on the block fighting to get in my house." The smile that ushered Grace inside was as authentic as the iron bars on the windows, and she was happy to sit with the woman she respected above others who had amassed homes with three-car garages and more living space than they knew what to do with.

This old house was tiny even by the most conservative standards, but it was apparent that it encompassed the grandest scale of love there was. Grace picked up on that the first time she ran late and asked if Miss Pearl would look after André until she closed a major deal. There hadn't been any reason for concern for her son's safety or well-being while he was there, not until now.

Miss Pearl fumbled around in the kitchen, brewing hot tea, as Grace made herself comfortable on an eight-inch-thick sheet of plastic covering the entire sofa. It reminded her of the measures her mother had taken to preserve their furniture when she was young. Suddenly Grace felt warm all over, especially where her behind met with the tightly stretched plastic but that was just fine because it added to the homespun ambiance she couldn't get anywhere else.

"So, what brings you this way in the afternoon, Gracie? Shouldn't you be working?" Miss Pearl handed a silver-plated serving tray, with two cups of hot tea and an antique porcelain sugar caddy, to her visitor before plopping down to rest her bones. "Here, set that down on the coffee table." Grace did as she was instructed, appreciating the woman's hospitality.

"Hmm, Earl Grey. You didn't forget." Grace took a cup and spooned in a liberal helping of sugar. "Yes, ma'am, I should be at work, but something told me to come by here instead."

The woman peered over her glasses, then laughed knowingly. "Humph. Something? Chile, that wasn't nothing but the Holy Spirit," she told Grace with a heavy dose of conviction. "Good thing you're still in the business of listening to it."

"Why would you say that? Has André been giving you trouble?"

"Naw, that boy is a blessing to this house and to Skyler. Those two are thick as thieves. Humph, reminds me of Skyler with his older brother when they were small. Friends to the end they were." There was a faraway look in the woman's eyes when she conjured up scenes from years past with sorrow anchored as an unsinkable backdrop.

Grace didn't like to pry, but there was that something again telling her that she should. "I didn't know that Skyler has an older brother."

"Well, he did until he was almost fifteen. It's a shame that he lost his mother five years ago, and then Donnell passed two years after that. Gangs and drugs are gonna kill everything I love before it's all over," Miss Pearl added as an afterthought. Grace was horrified. Gangs and drugs, two deaths and she'd allowed her child to spend countless evenings there. When she noticed that Miss Pearl had traveled back to that faraway place in her mind again, Grace scanned the room for a box of tissues but the room was poorly lit. The only light emanated from rays of sun streaming in between partially parted drapes bordering the front window.

"I didn't mean to upset you," Grace said, setting out to find a light switch.

"Don't pay me no nevermind, Gracie. I'm just an old woman trying to hold on to memories I ain't ready to let go of yet." She saw what Grace was trying to do and stopped her. "Ain't no use in beating up the switch. Me and the electric company done had us a misunderstanding."

"A misunderstanding?" Grace asked, unable to hide her concern. "What misunderstanding?"

"They can't understand why I can't come up with the

money to pay the bill. I missed too many payments, and they cut off the service."

Grace suddenly remembered André mentioning something about Miss Pearl's work hours having been scaled back because of her inability to climb stairs and keep up with her company's cleaning schedule, but she couldn't believe it had gotten this bad. "Miss Pearl, you've been sitting up here in the dark?" Grace asked finally.

"Only when the sun goes down," she jested to ease her embarrassment.

"Miss Pearl," Grace moaned. When the enormity of the woman's woes hit home, she made a slow return to her seat on the sofa. "And what about Skyler? How does he get his studying done?"

"As best he can," the woman answered with unusual resolve. "He's so proud, that boy. I told him things would work out fine, but he got it in his thick head to go out and fix it hisself. Patience ain't wasted on the youth, that's for sure."

Grace felt her heart rate quicken. How she could have allowed this to happen to people she cared about added an extra helping of guilt to her disbelief. As Grace wrung her hands nervously, she asserted adamantly, "Okay, I'll take care of the misunderstanding between you and the electric company." She stuck out her palm to ward off any opposition from a woman determined to make it on her own. "And don't tell me I can't either," Grace warned. "I'm not going to stand by and let this happen and do nothing about it."

"Gracie, I don't accept charity from nobody! I know you have a good heart but—" she started to say before meeting a firm roadblock.

"But nothing!" Grace stated, louder than she intended. "I'm not offering you anything you haven't already done for me and André. You've given my family the best you had, and now I'm going to do the same, with or without your blessing." Her eyes widened as the old lady shook with laughter. "You think I'm going to let you stop me?"

"Heavens, naw, Gracie," Ms. Pearl chuckled heartily. "I doubt that a team of wild horses could do that. Now, I see where that boy of yours gets his gumption. He had the bright idea that he was beholden to me and brought by two-hundred-seventy-five dollars' worth of small bills and loose change. Said he broke into his piggy bank so's he could help out. That's your chile all right. He's as stiff and stern as you."

Grace bit her bottom lip to keep from laughing too. "Dré did that?"

"Sho' he did. I didn't have the heart to turn his gift away, but I didn't have the will to spend it, neither. It's tucked in the back of the top draw' with my unmentionables. You should've seen his face all taut like yours was a minute ago. It was a sight to see him trying to do his best to be a man." Unexplained tears escaped from her eyes before she could hold them back. "Sometimes it's hard to watch a man-chile face troubles bigger than he's ready to take on," she said out of nowhere.

Grace didn't want to ask her next question, but she couldn't resist. "Miss Pearl, the troubles you mentioned, is that what led to Donnell's death?"

"Whooo. It was like yesterday, you know, times being hard like they was. Donnell quit school before I knew it, turned his back on college scholarships for basketball to pick up odd jobs. He joined up with some bad boys and took on a life of crime." The old lady shook her head, finding it difficult to accept how it could have happened to her grandchild. "He was a good boy, Gracie, just like Skyler. Didn't mean no harm to nobody. Those policemen say they were in the right to kill him, though. Might've been the case, he was there to rob that liquor store when the law pulled up, but that still didn't make it all right with me."

Grace thought the lump in her throat was going to choke her to death. Suddenly, she couldn't breathe. Too many things were going through her head at once. "Skyler, where's

Skyler?" she asked with false calm like a woman defusing a time bomb. Lightning was not going to strike twice if she had anything to say about it.

"I believe he's down at the corner market stacking groceries," was Miss Pearl's best guess. "He's been hanging around down there for a few days."

After getting the exact location of the market and a handful of overdue bills from Skyler's grandmother, Grace grabbed her purse and dashed out of the house as if it were on fire. Within five minutes, she'd found the market, but that's not all she found. Skyler was outside of it with a gang of other young men, all of which appeared destined for hell or jail, and more than likely both.

"Skyler Barnes!" Grace shouted from an open car window. "Get over here, now!" His surprise didn't go unnoticed by the other young men there. When uncertainty jammed him up in the middle of a tense situation, he sighed hard, trying to save face with his sidewalk associates. Grace jumped out of the Volvo with the meanest face she could manufacture leading the way. "Don't make me come over there and shame you in front of your friends!" With those so-called friends watching closely while Skyler treaded water, he made one of the toughest decisions a young man his age had to: face a grown woman's wrath, and fallout from his peers after doing so. Time stood still on that sidewalk. No one moved until the apparent leader of the pack nudged him along.

"I'd go if I was you," the head delinquent suggested with a raised brow. He wasn't sure who Grace was, but the look she'd tossed him spelled trouble in the worst way. "She's scaring me," he added, glancing at her polished shoes, "and I don't even know her."

"Me too," another of them muttered under his breath. The lady who'd rolled up on the group of apparent delinquents meant business, that much they did know. Their assumptions were correct. Grace was willing to do whatever it took to save Skyler from meeting his older brother's fate. When he eased closer to her SUV, she pointed her finger at his face.

"Get your behind over here. Open your mouth so I can see your teeth. Wider! Had me driving around looking for you!" Skyler didn't want to comply, but there was no going back now. In for a penny, in for a pound. "Just as I thought," Grace fussed, "a head full of holes."

"Hey, Sky. Who is she, yo' denniss?" one of the young men joked.

"No, I'm his guidance counselor and his probation officer," Grace lashed back. "Do you want me to call yours?"

"Oh, uh-uh," the homeboy answered promptly. "I didn't mean no disrespect, ma'am. I was just leaving." He had taken off in the other direction by the time Grace pulled away from the curb with Skyler sulking in the passenger seat.

They were sitting in the dental office filling out paperwork when Skyler mustered enough nerve to speak his mind. "Excuse me, Miss Hilliard, but you didn't have to handle me like that in front of my boys. I was just chilling in the cut."

"I've made an agreement with Miss Pearl to handle things as I see fit until you graduate in the spring, you hear me?"

By the way Skyler popped up, you'd have thought he'd seen a ghost. "You talked to Grandma Pearl?"

"Sure did, and she told me about Donnell. We're putting an end to whatever you thought you were getting into. We clear on that?" Skyler didn't know what to say, so he remained silent until forced to give in. "I said, are we clear?" Grace hissed so as not to draw any more attention to themselves than she already had.

"Yes, ma'am," was his barely audible response, although it was loud enough to seal the deal.

The dentist examined Skyler's mouth and discovered seven cavities. Grace wrote a check, commissioning for all of them to be filled at the same time. Three hours later, she helped him to the car, then dropped him off at home. He was sedated and sorry that he hadn't taken better care of his teeth. If Grace hadn't rescued him when she did, he'd have been staring at a world of new troubles to be sorry for. She read days later in the morning paper that three of his boys were arrested later that same evening after breaking into a warehouse six blocks from his home. Grace uncovered, by interrogating André, Skyler's intentions to go in on the heist with them. He'd planned on fencing his share of the stolen goods to get the lights turned back on.

Grace thanked God for sending her there, and then she thanked Him for giving her child's best friend back to him. The last seventy-two hours reminded her of what she'd been studying from the Book of James regarding a Christian's responsibility to care for widows and orphans. Although Skyler didn't actually qualify, he came pretty darn close. Sister Kolislaw's words rang true about God working with Grace while working on her. Now, if He would hurry up and work on her behalf in the husband department, that would have been icing on the cake, a wedding cake.

16

What's a Woman to Do?

When Marcia buzzed Grace's phone, she was working out the details for a high-priority special circumstances meeting with Ted, the senior partner. Grace hadn't been able to sleep soundly since learning of Miss Pearl's dire straits and diminishing health, although the "misunderstanding" with the electric company had been settled with a personal check to cover past-due bills and an additional surplus of one thousand dollars for any future and subsequent misunderstandings. Grace couldn't help thinking what might have happened to Skyler's promising basketball career and formal education if something hadn't persuaded her to drop in on the hood for a quick inspection. What she found there may have saved a young man from a life of crime, and his grandmother from blaming herself over the same atrocity a second time.

"Miss Hilliard, there's a Wallace Peters holding for you," Marcia announced through the speaker phone. Grace didn't answer immediately, so Marcia waited before starting in again. "Excuse me, Miss—"

"Yes, I'm here," Grace interrupted. "Sorry, Marcia. My mind was on another call. I'll speak with Mr. Peters." She read over important documents while Wallace introduced himself because she had little time to spare. André was performing above average in Wallace's class, Skyler had returned to school without missing a beat, and there was a plan in the works to help Ms. Pearl along without having to fight her tooth and nail in order to pull it off. Grace's world had evolved into a catch-all community center, with too much on the table to be distracted by a younger man she didn't know well enough to let herself get worked up over. She was too busy, she'd decided, for niceties that wouldn't directly benefit her or the necessary journey she embarked upon to protect her newly adopted family. If Grace hadn't been so preoccupied, she would have been able to see what was staring her in the face: a good man who seemed interested in the same thing she'd been looking for, a relationship worth investigating.

"Miss Hilliard, don't you agree?" Wallace repeated when his initial question went unanswered.

"Uh, I'm sorry. I wasn't really listening. Where were we?" Grace asked nonchalantly. The papers on her desk ruffled without regard to what impression it might have given Wallace. If a person didn't know better, it would have seemed that she was going out of her way to be blasé toward him.

"I was saying how important it was that André put in extra time helping Skyler comprehend reading passages when he was experiencing enormous difficulty beforehand. It has worked out considerably well. Skyler's natural predilection for secondary math helped André to make major strides in his calculus course, don't you agree?" Wallace was perplexed when Grace appeared detached from the conversation. He had assumed she'd facilitated the home-study collaboration between two of his favorite students.

"Yes, I guess that would make sense," she said flatly. Suddenly, Grace began replaying Wallace's report in her mind.

She laid the documents on the desk and leaned back in her leather chair. "Did you say that André is assisting Skyler with his English coursework, and that Skyler is a math whiz who's been tutoring Dré in applied calculus?"

"Well, yes. I thought you'd arranged it, or at least knew about it," Wallace answered. Grace closed her eyes, uncomfortable with the idea that so much had gone on under her nose. Thank God, it was all positive.

"No, I'm ashamed to say that I had no idea. Perhaps we should meet. I'd like to get your spin on another issue that's just come across my plate. Can you do lunch today?" A long pause lingered while Grace waited.

"Yes, I should be able to move around a few things to make that happen. Oh, and Miss Hilliard, thank you for being concerned enough to step in regarding Skyler's absenteeism," Wallace continued. "I heard about his afternoon at the dentist." Grace wondered what else he'd heard about, and if the boys were sharing other important events with him that they probably wouldn't with her.

After canceling all of her afternoon appointments, Grace trekked to the Java Hut, a trendy coffee bar on the outskirts of the neighborhood. Wallace was already there, sitting at a booth near the back. He watched Grace's entrance, like the other men who were glad they had stopped by the Hut at the perfect time to enjoy the view. "Miss Hilliard, thanks again for making the time," Wallace greeted her, standing to offer a cordial handshake. "I hope you didn't mind coming so far, but I do have another class in an hour."

"No, my afternoon opened up after a few appointments canceled," she lied. "This is very important to me." Corporate Grace worked hard at looking past Wallace's striking features, broad shoulders, tailored brown suit, and starched white button-down shirt, but she couldn't overlook how stylishly he dressed on a teacher's salary. In the three times she'd seen him, his wardrobe and taste in clothing were impeccable. Then scenes from the steamy reoccurring dreams she'd been having flashed before her eyes. Intimate encounters with a dark stranger that she couldn't explain vexed her. Grace had previously preferred pretty boys with lighter complexions that varied distinctly from her own, but recently she found herself straddled with visions of a virile, strong backed warrior with dark skin writhing against hers. Short of breath, she checked herself and turned her eyes away. "I'll have hot tea," she told the waiter, who'd appeared out of nowhere. "Earl Grey, if you have it. Yes, sugar as well. Thank you."

Simultaneously, Wallace had been sizing up Grace as well. The way she'd breezed through the door on a mission, it seemed, although elegantly at the same time, had him sweating beneath the collar. Her coral-hued designer skirt suit was Kasper. He recognized that clothing line by the slimming cut of the jacket. Paying attention to women, everything about them, was an old habit that assisted him in analyzing potential candidates for marriage. He couldn't help it, running across his perfect match had plagued him for years, but no one came close to meeting his highly specific expectations. However, the way Grace sashayed into his life at the basketball game, stole glances at him while he conducted his class, and undoubtedly rescheduled her afternoon to share a booth in a faraway café all worked together for one smashing introduction.

Wallace sipped coffee from his cup and cast a subtle leer across the table at Grace. "Tea is good for the soul, they say," he commented to break the ice.

"Then I'll order a second cup," she groaned wearily, placing her sunshades inside a small rectangular case. "God knows I could use it."

"I'm sure He does. God, I mean."

Grace wasn't exactly certain how to take Wallace's reply, so she changed the subject altogether. "Uh, Mr. Peters, the boys," she said, trying desperately to clear her head, "it would appear that they confide in you, or is it common knowledge about them tutoring one another?"

"No, it's quite the contrary, actually. Skyler was falling behind last term, so his counselor suggested that he take time out to catch up on his reading. Then it was discovered that his inability to retain the assignments was directly linked to his poor reading skills."

"Skyler couldn't read?" Grace asked apprehensively, as if he were her own son.

"It wasn't that severe, but he was a very slow reader. Once André noticed it was taking Skyler twice as long to read the same newspaper articles from the sports page that he had, he came to me. We had a closed-door Read Aloud."

"What's that, this Read Aloud?" Grace asked. Wallace saw that she was locked in on this conversation, unlike the one that took place over the phone.

"That's a mechanism I've found extremely beneficial in rating how well students read and comprehend. Of course, those who don't do well, hate it, and the students who've mastered the written word make the best of it. It's my hope that before the semester ends, each of my students gets a chance to see what that feels like, a chance to shine among their peers."

Grace was taken aback. First she'd learned that André had offered his savings to help Miss Pearl, and now this. "Well, I'll be. André brought Skyler's reading deficiency to you."

"Yes, he's a serious young man for his age, but I wouldn't categorize Skyler's problem as a deficiency. He, like so many inner-city kids, received social promotions without being prepared to move ahead. Typically, my students are as intelligent as you'd find on the other side of the tracks, but they've logged far more hours with a TV, DVD, VCR, iPod or video idiot box than with an open book. In that regard, André certainly stands out."

Grace blushed over the compliment, eased out of Corporate Grace mode, and downshifted into Mama Grace. "How do you mean?" she prodded shamelessly, fishing for additional praise.

"My hat's off to you," Wallace obliged. He recognized where she was taking him, and he didn't mind the ride. "Miss Hilliard—" he continued before being cut off again.

"Grace," she insisted. "Please call me Grace. I think we've moved past the parent-teacher formalities."

"I agree, Grace." When Wallace smiled for the first time since she'd arrived, his perfectly aligned teeth, set between two adorable dimples, had Grace seeing double. As she returned his smile with a reasonable facsimile, he began searching for words that wouldn't come easily. "Oh, uh, yes, I was saying that it's obvious to me that André has parents who've shown they care a great deal about his academics."

If there was a good time for Grace to solidify her available status, this was it. She pondered awhile. *What the heck*, she figured. Wallace was nice, charming, and well heeled, but younger she thought, and a teacher to boot. Maybe he could introduce some of his older, more accomplished friends to her. There was an outside chance to get a Grade A hookup by referral. "I've always made sure that my son made appropriate time to study, and I've stayed on top of his schoolwork. He'll be a black man some day; you know better than anyone that his work has to be exceedingly good in order to get in the door. Corporations looking for the best and the brightest generally don't hold it open for our men unless they see a can't-miss rainmaker who'll increase their stock options." When Grace realized that her grandiose explanation of corporate scouting might have slighted Wallace's decision to choose teaching as a profession, she cringed. "Sorry, Wallace, I didn't mean to make light of your trade. I think it's an honorable profession."

Chuckling, Wallace flashed another grin across the table. "No offense taken. Teaching allows me to give back to the community while molding young minds in the process. I've done it for two years, and I must say the rewards have been numerous. Also, I needed to take a break from the hustle and bustle of a nine to five."

"I see," was all that Grace could say. She wondered if Wallace was truly happy molding those young minds, as he aptly put it. Not that it wasn't a noble vocation, it just appeared that there was more to him than he allowed her to see.

"Just think, if I weren't on staff at André's school, I wouldn't have met you or have had the honor of sharing a worthwhile conversation over warm beverages." Wallace's attempt to lighten the mood failed miserably, although it wasn't due to a lack of trying.

"Wallace, can I be candid?" Grace asked hurriedly. "Oh My Goodness Fine" aside, she felt it necessary to keep things in proper perspective, mostly for his sake. "Look, I'm very thankful that you're working to shape your students' futures because our children can use as much of that as possible. They should be thankful for what you bring to the table, and according to the long line of young mothers outside your door on parent-teacher night, their parents are too. I can't speak for you, but I think you're getting close to speaking out of turn and sending this conversation down a very uncomfortable path."

"May I be allowed to try my hand at that being-candid thing, as well?" Wallace asked. Grace raised her brow and nodded in a deliberate, guarded manner. "I'd like to stay on the same page, if at all possible. And, while I appreciate your assessment of my interest in you, I'll remind you that the greatest fall one can take is the short trip over one's ego." Wallace continued staring at Grace and her wide-eyed you-didn't-just-read-me sneer. "You can quote me on that," he told her with a sly wink.

"Okay, you . . . you took it there. This is where I get off," Grace smacked, after feeling that Wallace had sufficiently tugged at her super cape.

"Before you do get off," he stated, "please keep in mind that I haven't asked you for a single thing, yet."

Grace collected her things and placed the sunshades back on her face. "And I strongly suggest that you don't get any ideas to do so. However, I'll check with some of my eligible, slightly junior girlfriends and inquire about their availability for a young educated man such as yourself. Good day, Mr. Peters."

Grace presumed that Wallace was quite a bit younger than she was but he was merely a few months younger than her. At the time it didn't much matter, so he decided not to take issue at the risk of stifling her steam. Besides, he thought that her feisty disposition was sexy as all get-out.

"Afternoon, Miss Hilliard," Wallace bid her reluctantly as she walked away.

There was something different about Grace compared to all the countless other women who had made it a point to put their faces up in Wallace's. Of course, Grace was polished, attractive, smart as a whip, fun, and feisty. He liked those qualities almost as much as he enjoyed observing the way she'd drawn attention from a host of other men in the coffee bar when she broke out in a slow, wickedly manufactured Caribbean saunter as she exited the small coffee shop. Of course he was looking, Grace knew it. She wanted to see him again, he was sure of that. The long conversation over warm beverages had begun with a great deal of uncertainty on both their parts and had ended with even more as a result of it. Wallace was resolved to get another shot at making a lasting first impression. He'd see to it.

Having her first free afternoon since the last Friday she had spent with Tyson, next to the noisy ice machine, Grace stopped by Miss Pearl's to see how her latest project was panning out. When she drove up to the old house, she saw two enormous utility trucks rested against the curb. Construction workers ripped and plastered, while an assortment of handymen primed and painted. Progress was a good thing. The speed in which Ms. Pearl's home had come alive overnight was simply beautiful.

Grace stood on the sidewalk, marveling at how quickly half a dozen handymen revitalized a house that probably should have been demolished years ago. "No, no," Grace instructed a man with two hands full of rosebushes. "They belong on the other side. The shrubs are supposed to be planted over here, near the porch." After hearing recommendations from the woman paying the bill, a seasoned supervisor climbed down from his rusty pickup to appease her.

"Yes, yes. We will do it to your liking, ma'am," the man in charge promised. "This will be *muy bonita* when we finish, maybe as pretty as Señora Graciela. Don't worry."

"I won't, Franco. Your crew does a wonderful job with the office building, so I know it's in good hands, but this project is for a very special friend, so please take care of it." Grace had no doubt that the facelift would ultimately transform the home into a showplace befitting a *Better Homes and Gardens* layout. "Why don't I get out of your way and let you do what you do best?" She shook his hand and stepped through the wrought-iron gate that had been erected the day before.

"Miss Pearl," Grace called out from the porch. "Miss Pearl, are you in there?"

"Hold on!" the old woman shouted back. "Where else would I be with all these foreigners climbing up and down my house?" Miss Pearl unlatched the new screen door and waved her visitor inside. "Hey, chile. That Mr. Franco you sent down here is pleasant as punch, but I can't understand what the rest of them are saying half the time."

"That doesn't matter as long as you're happy about the results," Grace told her, well aware that a storm had been brewing since the team of workers showed up at dawn, unannounced, two days ago. Miss Pearl hadn't called to complain, but Grace knew it was merely the quiet before the storm. "So, how do you think your home improvements are turning out?" Grace queried, bracing herself.

"Humph, I can't rightly say. Ain't been outside since the hammering started on Wednesday," she answered, her head hanging low.

"Is there a problem, Miss Pearl? I could have more men here tomorrow to get it done faster if that's your concern."

Miss Pearl shook her head while refusing to make eye contact. "Naw, Gracie, the only problem is me taking advantage of you. I ain't ever taken a handout from nobody, and it hurts me to my heart to do such a thing now."

"Oh, I get it," Grace said, reaching into her purse. She whipped out a long list, including costs of materials, labor, and additional charges to have the items Franco's crew had replaced hauled away. Grace snapped the paper out and held the list up for the lady of the house to see.

After Miss Pearl understood that it was something important, she patted down her housecoat until she found her reading glasses. "What's that?" she asked, stretching her neck to get a better look.

"This is your bill for the work I ordered," Grace informed her, straight faced and confident.

"The which?"

"The bill. Remember that misunderstanding you had with the electric company? It seems that we're having the same kind of misunderstanding now." Grace could sense that Miss Pearl was stunned, so she let her in on a little secret she'd kept under wraps. "You weren't ready to give up on this house, and I'm not ready to give up on you." Still lost in Grace's implications, Ms. Pearl scratched her head and frowned.

"Let me get this right. You took it on yourself to call all these fellas over here to fix what you thought needed fixing, without even asking me what I thought, and now you're ready to hand me the bill?"

"Uh-huh," Grace answered without hesitation.

Ms. Pearl's eyes narrowed into thin slits. "Yeah, we sho do have us one heck of a predicament," she contended. "Gracie, I can see that you care for Skyler and me, but you sho have a funny way of showing it. I'd like nothing better than to pay you back every cent, but they done cut back again on my hours. I can't eat, can't sleep, and done lost ten pounds in the meantime." When Grace burst out laughing, the woman jerked her head back. "The whole world done gone crazy, and you're leading the pack."

"Please forgive me, Miss Pearl. I haven't filled you in completely. I asked you to let me take care of things, and I meant everything. Hold on, my cell phone is ringing," Grace said when the call she'd been waiting for came through.

"You ask me, your head is ringing too," smarted one very perplexed homeowner.

Rambling out into the backyard to escape the noise, and itching ears, Grace was glad that Ted returned her call when he did. It was the perfect chance to have that high-priority special circumstances meeting she'd been anxious about facilitating with the so-called powers-that-be. "Yes, Ted, the message I sent you was correct," she confirmed calmly.

"I thought I was hearing things, Grace. You're asking me to sign off on company-sponsored home improvements on a home neither of us owns, you've hired an additional employee we don't need, and the company is supposed to take one hundred dollars from each of her paychecks to reimburse us for the work you're having done on her house?"

"That's exactly what I'm asking you to do, Ted. Just think of it as a company-sponsored neighborhood revitalization program." Again, Grace braced herself for an unfavorable outcome.

"You must think I'm insane to present me with such a ridiculous business deal," Ted replied, and then paused to collect his thoughts. "And I'd have to be insane to pass on such a good idea. I hope it works out like you want it to."

"Oh, thank you, Ted. Thank you from the bottom of my heart." Graced danced around in the backyard as Miss Pearl peeped at her from the kitchen curtains.

"That chile really done lost her mind," the old lady reasoned.

"I owe you, Ted," Grace cooed into her cell phone. "You're no crazier than I am, but this deal isn't business, it's personal."

"I'll tell you about personal. Tell me why I have three of my wife's cousins on the payroll, and neither of them have a clue what we actually do for our clients."

"That's not personal, Ted, that's sad," chuckled Grace.

"I gotta go, partner. I think one of my relatives just got his necktie caught in the paper shredder. Now I have another decision to make. Whether to save him or not is going to be a toughie."

As Graced closed her eyes to give thanks for the miracle she'd prayed for, Miss Pearl motored back to her recliner before being discovered. Grace returned and sat down on the plastic-covered sofa with so much exuberance. She said, "Whew! That would have been hysterical if I'd fallen off."

"Oh, I'd have laughed, too. I'd have dusted you off first, then I'd have laughed."

"Okay, back to our predicament. I knew that you could use a pick-me-up but you were much too proud to let someone help you. So I've arranged a partnership like the boys have. It seems that a position has opened up within the custodial crew that services my building. Here's the deal." The woman sat on the edge of her seat while Grace caught her breath. "We've offering you a job to work between ten and three o'clock so you can be here when Skyler gets home from school. We're also offering to withhold one hundred dollars from each paycheck until the improvements on your house are paid for. In addition, you have to accept our employee-fitness package and spend at least one hour a day with our gym staff."

"With Jim, is he good looking?" Miss Pearl whooped, hoping her new deal also included a man to help her pass the time.

"No, Miss Pearl, *at* the gym. That's our workout facility.

You've allowed your weight to get away from you and I'm not going to let hypertension or high blood pressure take you away from us before it's your time to go."

"I ain't stud'n neither one of them," the woman teased. "We's old friends, they been with me for years." She began to rock back and forth, mulling the proposition over in her head. "Hmm, all that sounds like a mess of blessings before God, and I don't want to seem ungrateful, but I do have one question of my own."

"Okay, shoot," Grace replied excitedly.

"Y'all got an elevator over at that office building?"

"Yes, ma'am, we got a whole bunch of elevators," Grace answered her.

"Then you got a deal."

Grace jumped off the slick plastic and onto the elderly woman's lap. "Yea! Miss Pearl, you've made me so happy."

"And you' making my legs hurt! Grace, get off me!" Miss Pearl hollered, with a load of merriment mixed in. "You're gonna fool around and wreck my good knee, and my chances of keeping my new job."

17

Shameless

On Thursday evening, Shelia called Grace from her car. She and Linda were on a shopping excursion on her side of town and were feeling a serious disconnect from the third part of their girlfriend triad. "Grace, are you going to be home for a minute?" Shelia hollered into the phone, over Linda's cackling in the background.

"Tell her she'd better hide all of her nasty videos because we're coming to loot 'em," Linda bellowed. "We know you've been stocking up, Grace. Give up the goods."

"You can tell Linda I'm holding on to my stash for cold and lonely nights, hot-and-bothered afternoons and whenever I get more than five minutes alone." Grace couldn't believe she was showing out right along with them, as if it hadn't been a rough go on the virtuous side of life. "Yeah, girl, come on over. Dré is at a varsity basketball game, and won't be home until around ten. I'll break out some wine."

Grace was still bubbling over when the ladies rang her doorbell like she'd answer it if they kept their fingers on it. "Move, I gotta pee," Linda urged, as she darted through the door. "Don't y'all start gossiping without me!" she shouted from the downstairs powder room.

"Shelia, I swear I smell rum," Grace said, eying her suspiciously. "Have you two been back to that Jamaican spot on lower Greenville?"

Shelia tried to lie, but it didn't hold up. When she shook her head no, the opposite rolled out of her mouth. "Yeah, but I wasn't supposed to say, because that fine Rasta they call Delmar was asking about you and puffing on some ganja. We musta caught a contact high because we haven't stopped giggling since."

"Ooh, you do look lifted!" Grace noticed, leaning in closer to Shelia and sniffing like André had done to her when he smelled hotel soap on her skin. "Shelia, listen to me. Focus. What else weren't you supposed to tell me?"

Standing there with her mouth and eyes shut, Shelia shook her head again. And, for the second consecutive time, out came the truth. "I cannot tell a lie. Linda smoked a fat spliff with Rasta-man and I . . . I did too."

"How are y'all gonna be getting high and showing up over here with a fresh buzz?" Grace's parental stance had Shelia caught in a quandary after having been reprimanded.

Linda returned, wearing a fake frown. "And how is Shelia standing there, ratting us out, when we pinky-swore to keep it secret?"

"For the same reason you're both too old to pinky-swear," Grace fussed. "Linda. Shelia. How irresponsible. I don't know what to say." Grace folded her arms and patted her foot like she was waiting for answers, and for both of them to repent of their wayward transgressions.

"Well, Linda hit the weed first," Shelia pouted. "Then Delmar held that fat thing in my face, and you know I can't resist a man waving anything long and hot anywhere near my mouth."

Linda held her hand over her mouth, when Shelia's best attempt at coming clean made her look considerably more scandalous. "That's why I can't take her anywhere. She hogged the blunt, started flirting with every man in the joint who had most of his teeth, and then couldn't wait to get here so she could tell you all about it."

Shelia tried to defend herself. "Look who's talking. Shoot, if I told Grace everything, you wouldn't have the nerve to show your face at that bar again. What about the restroom, Linda? Bet you won't tell Grace about that."

Linda's face cracked. She was terrified that Shelia just might spill the beans about her most embarrassing calamity. "Shelia, if you say another word, I'll cancel our friendship card right here, right now." Grace looked on, pondering what Shelia was going to do, and what Linda had done that was so repugnant she wanted it kept quiet.

Both of the ladies, admittedly blazed, were at a standoff, and staring each other down like convicts in a prison yard. "You'd better be glad my high is wearing off, or I'd tell," Shelia huffed eventually. She didn't have it in her to tattle that Linda had accidentally ripped the condom machine off the wall when she was about to get busy with a bothersome barfly named Hedley in the filthy men's room. Shelia had walked in on her jiggling the release knob like her life depended on it.

"Maybe both of you need to settle down and have some coffee," Grace recommended sternly. "I'll break out the wine another time." Linda smacked her lips defiantly and then mumbled something about having a moment of weakness and being held in judgment by somebody who wasn't in any position to chastise her. Shelia heard her but let it go because they not only knew, in full detail, about the other's skeletons, they also knew where the bones were buried.

Grace set up the coffeemaker, then poured in three cups of water to get it going. "Now that we've seen why drugs are a bad idea at any age, let's talk about what y'all bought at the mall."

"Macy's had a sale, so I copped two pairs of boots," Linda

said, shaking off the short melee between old friends. Shelia wasn't quite over it, so she continued to stew silently. "What about you, Grace? We haven't heard from you in a while. Anything juicy happen since the last time we talked? Have any new prospects trying to knock the cobwebs off?"

"How did the discussion go from shopping to who might be trying to get me to go astray?" Grace argued.

Suddenly, Shelia cut her eyes at Grace. "You know that's the real reason we stopped by. Usually, when you're hard to catch up with, it's because you've been up to something we can't wait to hear about."

"She's right, Grace," Linda agreed. "You get all reclusive when you've been getting down and dirty, so spill it."

So many things had transpired since their last hen party, but not the kind of sneaky-freaky they lived to talk about. Grace leaned against the cooking island and exhaled deeply. She had mixed emotions about seeing Tyson again, almost jumping back into a retarded relationship with Greg and meeting Wallace on semifriendly terms, but she wasn't ready to talk about any of that yet. Her mind was a jumbled jigsaw puzzle with missing pieces, so she put together the pieces she didn't mind revealing. "I'm in a good place mentally. My faith has been renewed. I'm proud to say that I am still celibate," she shared in a somewhat subdued tone.

When Shelia suspected there was more to the story, she urged Grace on. "And, come out with it, get to the good part."

"And I am fortified with the Holy Spirit, thank you very much," Grace added, casting a shadow on her girlfriend's expectations of sordid sexual confessions.

Now, it was Linda's turn to prime the pump. "Then why are you biting a hole in your bottom lip?" she asked, her interest piquing.

"Because . . . I am so horny it hurts!" Grace blurted out loud. "It's got me all jacked up, testy, and on edge. Just the other day, my boss called me into his office for a closed-door chat. He said that I needed to work on playing well with others."

"Ooh, Grace got herself thrown in detention." Linda laughed because Grace had been the poster girl for appropriate office etiquette.

"That's not all I got," Grace admitted. "I also got sent home to work on my attitude. And if that weren't bad enough, I stomped onto a crowded elevator going down. Awkward Bob was pressed up against my back, and out of the blue I got so hot."

Shelia's eyes popped out of her head. "Awkward Bob—I thought you said he was gonna have a sex change."

"Well, obviously he hasn't had his man region done yet, because it was rubbing up against my behind. I'm not sure who was more confused, him for aiming that thing in my direction, or me for getting so turned on by it. Humph, Awkward Bob has a lot to think about if he's willing to have all of that cut off. He might want to reconsider that gender-reorientation thing. Believe me, he was *meant* to be a man."

Out of sorts, Shelia shook her head. "Uh-uh-uh. What a mess. How the mighty have fallen. You done tripped and fell over your high-minded morals, Grace. Look at you, huffing and twitching like a crackhead the very first time you came too close to an active pleasure zone. It hurts me to see you like this," she added, as if repulsed all the way down to her core. "Linda, didn't we tell her this would happen?"

"We told her," Linda chimed in on cue. "But did she listen? Nahhh."

"Okay, so you told me," Grace fired back at them. "Now tell me what to do about it."

"Who're you asking? Neither of us have made it this far." Linda added a helping of French vanilla creamer to the cup Grace handed her. "When you figure it out, be sure to let us in on it. Until then, we'll be hanging around your office, riding elevators, and waiting for our chance to back that thang up on Awkward Bob."

Grace laughed so hard she spilled coffee on her jeans. "See, look what you made me do. I knew I should have had tea."

"Uh-huh, that's not the only thing you should have had." Shelia cut her eyes at Grace again. "You need to check yourself."

"You don't have to tell me," Grace confessed. I've been so flustered that I went online and subscribed to one of those dating services." Linda choked on her coffee when she heard the shocking news.

"Grace, you didn't?"

"Psshst, the worst mistake I'm willing to cop to was putting my hopes in SingleButLooking.com." Grace talked about her run-in with Tommy, the lying two-ton human garbage disposal; Sly Greenberg, the Jewish pimp, with an identity crisis; her reluctant meeting with an ancient player who showed up at the date dragging an oxygen tank behind him; the hair stylist named Leroy who indicated he had been delivered from his homosexual past; and the last guy she agreed to see before throwing in the towel. "This one brotha wasn't half bad at first. He arrived on time, he was all right in the looks department, the conversation was stimulating, and he managed a successful engineering firm."

Sitting across the wet bar from her was Shelia, deep in thought as if the last guy's credentials struck a familiar chord, but Linda was about to fall off her stool. "Come on, now, so why aren't you willing to see him again?" inquired Linda.

Grace rolled her eyes. "That was the problem, I saw too much of him on the date. It was going fine, and then it happened. I knocked a fork on the floor and went to pick it up. That's when I saw it."

"Saw what?" the girls asked in unison.

"It!" Grace replied emphatically. "He had it out, under the table, and he was playing with it."

Linda's mouth flew open as Shelia pointed her finger at

Grace, still trying to recall something from a distant memory. "That reminds me of an old boyfriend I had in high school. Hollis Williams. That fool couldn't keep his hand out of his pants long enough to put them on me."

Grace stammered while trying to get out what her surprise had stymied. "That's the same guy! Hollis Williams, the mad handler!"

"Uhh-uh!" Linda shrieked, in disbelief.

"How do you like them apples," said Shelia, contemplating the chances of Grace having a date with one of her old flames. "So you say that Hollis is an engineer now?" She skillfully dodged the dishrag Grace tossed at her head. "I'm just saying, you wouldn't trade in a Porsche because it had a dent in the fender."

"But you would if every time you hit the street, the hood kept flying up." That was Linda making it as plain as plain could be.

"That's what I'm talking about," agreed Grace wholeheartedly. "I never would have imagined it, it but the most normal interaction I've had with a man in the past month was a quaint little war of wits with André's schoolteacher."

"A schoolteacher?" Shelia sneered, as if she could talk after pining for an exhibitionist engineer.

Linda was also astounded. She leaned back and cocked her head to the side. "Grace, don't tell me you're pushing up on schoolteachers now?"

"No one said I was pushing up on anybody. I ducked out on a conference because the line of hot mamas waiting to see him was too long. We made arrangements to get together at the Java Hut. It was nothing special, believe me."

"Then why were there so many single moms in the long serving line?" Linda asked suggestively.

"Who said they were all single?" Grace replied before smacking her lips the way Linda had earlier. "That particular teacher is easy on the eyes and a slick dresser, but he's also a *teacher*. Let's not overlook the obvious."

Shelia was thumbing through her little black address book when she looked up. "You got a point, Grace. A single, nice-dressing grown man who spends his days with a bunch of bratty kids is probably a pedophile."

"No, I don't think so," Grace countered. *Was that Grace defending him?* "I could be wrong, but I doubt it. He didn't strike me as the type of man who's interested in children that way."

"Your vote doesn't count," Linda decided. "You've proven, several times tonight might I add, how flawed your decision-making skills are. You're talking about what strikes you. That's part of what's wrong, you haven't been struck in so long, all of your senses are out of whack."

"That is something she could use, a good whacking," Shelia added, while continually studying the "W" section of her black book. "Grace, you didn't happen to get Hollis Williams's home number while you were eye to eye with his Pocket Pal, did you?"

Linda waved off Shelia's ridiculous question. "She's hopeless, but what are you going to do about this teacher dude?"

"Nothing. I set him straight but good." Grace didn't really believe that was the last time she'd be pitted against the quick-witted Wallace Peters.

"Good, then it's settled. We'll go to the Kappa's Annual Casino Night on Saturday and have ourselves a ball."

After having been reminded of the best man feast in town, Grace grimaced. She'd promised to spend more time with André, and had gone out of her way to get courtside tickets to watch Allen Foray and the Mavericks take on the Los Angeles Lakers. "Ooh, I'm going to pass on Saturday. I have a date with Dré, and I'd hate to break it."

"That's on you, girl. Me and Linda will be knee deep in Crimson and Cream. Those Kappas know how to roll out the red carpet. It'll be packed."

"Yeah, I remember last year's event," Grace said quietly. "Let me talk to André about it, and then I'll get back to you."

Shelia went back to slurping on coffee when she'd finally given up on finding her old boyfriend's contact information. "So Grace, you say that Hollis is doing well for himself?" *Hopeless!*

18

All Bets Are Off

By the time André made it home from Skyler's varsity basketball game, Grace had worn a path in the den. She was serious about spending more quality time with him, but she also craved harmless interaction with normal adult males, if she could get it. The local Dallas graduate chapter of Kappa Alpha Psi threw in with their upper-crust brothers from two bordering suburban bedroom communities, combining their efforts to stage an exciting casino-styled extravaganza. The proceeds were given to charity, but hundreds of single women traipsed through the star-studded affair to try their luck in the dating game, which started the minute they walked in the door. Grace loved the people-watching aspect it presented, because that was the only time she could see high-class African-American men and women drink too much and reduce themselves to heat-seeking enthusiasts. She did not want to miss that.

While wringing her hands over the decision to ask André if he wouldn't mind going with Skyler to watch Allen Foray take on Los Angeles from the first row, her son hit the door with a ravenous appetite. “Hey Ma,” he said, dropping his backpack at the door. The look in his eyes, she’d seen before. The poor boy was starving. Within moments, he had his head stuck in the refrigerator and palms resting on his skinny knees. “Mama, do you still have some of that lasagna left over from Tuesday?”

“Yes, honey, it’s in the Tupperware container on the bottom shelf,” she informed him. “Tell you what, why don’t I heat it up for you while you stop by the restroom to wash up? Go on now. I have something important to talk to you about.”

“Thanks, Ma, stack it high. I’ll be right back.” No sooner than André dashed off, Grace felt like a deadbeat parent for even thinking about putting him off on someone else just so she could have a grown-up evening at the Grande Hotel ballroom with three hundred of the most handsome successful men in the area. *Shame on her*.

A steaming plate of lasagna was waiting on the counter when André returned. Grace noted his carefree attitude when he straddled the bar stool to dig in. He closed his eyes and placed both hands in front of his face like Grace had taught him when he was three years old. She took a deep breath and blushed with pride, thinking back on how far both of them had come, on their own.

André shoveled food into his mouth, one forkful right after another. He smiled at Grace, who was continually looking on and still bursting with pride. It had been a number of years since she’d thought about André’s father, who had once loved her like a hammock loves to sway in the wind until he decided that finding himself and making it big as an attorney didn’t include her bearing his child. Grace was in college then, pregnant and on the Dean’s list. When she graduated with honors, André was the newborn in the first row screaming his head off because it was his feeding time and Grace’s mother had forgotten to pack an extra bottle. Grace smiled when she remembered how he could really open his mouth back then, too.

"So, Ma, what did you want to talk about? I mean, if it's about giving Skyler's grandmother my sock-drawer money, I know I should have cleared it with you first."

"Actually, Dré, sharing your personal savings to help out Miss Pearl and Skyler was the right thing to do. I'm not upset about that. But since you asked, I made a commitment to do more things with you, and that's why I got those court-side tickets from Allen Foray."

"Oh, yeah, Mama, that's tight. I wufff tuffing to Sky'nem 'bout . . ." he mumbled with his mouth full before Grace objected to his table manners.

"Uh-uh, Dré, I know that you know better than to talk with half of Italy hanging out of your mouth."

The boy poured a heaping swig of grape juice down his throat, then swallowed hard. "Sorry, but I was telling Sky and them about it. They think I'm the luckiest because you're always doing stuff like this, like the NBA gear you got for me and Skyler, like coming to my games even in the rain." Suddenly, André's expression changed. He'd been grinning gleefully, then it shifted.

"Dré, what's wrong?" Grace asked as she took two steps closer, fearing that he might have been choking.

"Ma, is there any chance we can get another ticket for Skyler? He's never been to a professional game before, and I have several times. Can you call Mr. Foray for one more ticket?"

"Sorry, but the game was sold out weeks ago. Maybe we can take your friend another time. There will be other games." Instantly, an idea popped into Grace's head. "Speaking of that, I have something that just might work. I was just talking to Linda and Shelia. They told me about a stuffy old charity event I wanted to attend but it happens to be on the same night as the game. I was wondering if you wouldn't mind giving my ticket to Skyler, and then I could do the charity thing with the girls. What do you say?"

"Are you kidding me? Mama, you know I love you like a new pair of Air Jordans but I'd really like it if we could start doing more of the mom-son thing *after* me and Skyler come back from the Lakers game . . . and after you've done the girls-gone-wild thing at the Kappa Casino Fund-raiser." When he looked up and saw Grace's surprised expression, he nodded his head slowly like an old mobster making her a deal she couldn't refuse. "Yeah, all the kids talk about it at school. Rich black people getting all Gee'd up so they can check out other rich black people all Gee'd up. I have to go through the same thing on the first day of school, so I know what a trip that is to watch."

Grace was speechless, shocked, and impressed all at once. "Uh, okay, then that's that. I'll call Miss Pearl and discuss it with her. Thank you for your time," she said in a staccato, rhythmic manner. After speaking with Skyler's grandmother and seeing to it that André would catch a ride home with his friend, Grace wasn't completely convinced that he hadn't brokered a better deal for himself than she had, but it worked out swimmingly, just like it needed to, for the both of them.

Friday night came right on schedule. Grace spoke to André at halftime, on her cell phone, as an extensive line of expensive cars inched toward the busy valet stand. She told her son to behave himself and call her once Skyler dropped him off. Then she flipped her phone shut and checked her makeup in the overhead vanity mirror. Red-jacketed valet attendants darted back and forth to accommodate the multitude of high-strung clientele, all extremely eager to get inside the main ballroom. Annually, the distinguished men's fraternal organization held their fun-filled Las Vegas–style mix-and-mingle to help underprivileged neighborhood kids but many of their guests arrived hoping to take home a special gift or two for themselves. That's how Grace had met Tyson. She'd made a striking appearance, wearing a tightly fitted red hot cocktail dress, and had flounced around playing hard to get, when in actuality she was in the mood to give. Tyson shooed away a flock of women, pursued her, and the rest was history. *This time around, it would be different,* Grace thought. It was a good thing she wasn't willing to bet her own salvation against the house or she'd have lost it all.

"Hey, Grace!" Chandelle shouted over the noisy hubbub spilling into the women's restroom. "Nice dress, nice dress, but I'd have gone the I-want-a-man route, instead of the I-got-a-man-but-he-won't-let-me-wear-my-sexy-clothes-in-public route," she added, leering at Grace's basic black spaghetti-strap number.

"Chandelle, I don't have time for this tonight," Grace told her flat out. She stared at her reflection as she dabbed a tissue across her forehead and cheeks. "Uh-uh, not after you had me barging into that conference room like Scarlet O'Hara in *Gone with the Wind.*"

"And what was wrong with being assertive? Grace, the man did leave the conference room smiling like you'd just promised to give him some."

"The man was practically married, and happy as a punk in prison about it, too. From now on, I'd appreciate it if you'd stay out of my business and let me be single, if that's what's meant to be. If I can accept it, you should be able to." Grace gazed past her own reflection in the broad mirror to find Chandelle sulking like a kid sister who'd gotten her feelings hurt. "What?" Grace barked, feeling a tad guilty for putting Chandelle in her place when she meant no harm.

"I'ont have nothing else to say," Chandelle muttered under her breath. "A sistah I happen to care about just told me to shut up. What can I, a loving friend of hers, say after that?"

Grace turned around to face that loving self-proclaimed friend of hers. "Now, don't go getting all gloomy because I asked you to butt out. You did make me realize that I had been shortchanging myself, but just because I want something doesn't mean I'll get it. Let's go out there and have a good time. Suddenly I feel like flirting."

Chandelle made a miraculous recovery. Her bruised ego suddenly healed, and a devious grin replaced the protruding lips poked out like a third-grade Girl Scout down to her last box of cookies. "That's the Grace I'm talking about," she cheered. "Too bad, though. If you're expecting the men out there to flirt back, you wore the wrong dress for it. I'd have put on a dress so tight that it would have taken some wiggling around on the floor to get into it, know what I'm sayin'." Although Chandelle was out of line, as usual, Grace couldn't do anything but laugh.

Linda spotted the two of them exiting the powder room, talking like lifelong pals. "Shelia, there she is, with a pinup Boomshieka Barbie."

"Where? Oh, I see her now." Shelia took one look at Chandelle's long legs packaged in her tiny satin beige dress, then tugged at hers to reveal more breasts than she was previously comfortable with. "You were right. This year's competition is stiff. Good thing she can't compete with the likes of the twins. Breast men love the twins."

Grace hugged Chandelle and said so long when her husband seemed annoyed that she'd been absent from his company for far too long. "Bye, girl. Don't keep that man standing around here all by himself. A woman like me might get him," Grace kidded. When she noticed the girls motioning for her to join them outside the main ballroom, she headed in their direction. *I should have known*, Grace thought to herself while looking at her friend's cleavage o' plenty. *Shelia's showing off the twins*. "Look at y'all," Grace beamed, "all regal and refined. I like it." Both women were adorned in long extravagant gowns tapered at their waists.

"Don't get to liking it too much," Linda suggested. "This

one is going back to the store tomorrow, which reminds me." She spun around to foster a fake pirouette. "Is my tag showing?" Grace snickered. It had been a long time since she'd pulled the same stunt. Having a good time without funking up a pricey dress to be returned immediately after a swanky affair was a difficult feat to accomplish. "Cool, let's get in there so those high-fallutin Negroes get a look at us before I start to sweat." Shelia propped up the twins again and followed behind Linda and Grace.

The Grande Ballroom was arrayed in deep red and cream-colored sashes and streamers. Bright lights and big smiles illuminated it throughout. Portable slot machines aligned the opposing walls. Roulette wheels, craps tables, and other games were placed in the middle of the room. Grace forked over two hundred dollars to the man sitting behind a make-shift teller window. In return, he handed her poker chips redeemable for prizes donated by major corporations.

"How can you tell who the members from the Dallas chapter are?" Shelia asked, appraising the most pleasant gathering of businessmen ever to don tuxedos. "You know I'm always up for a man-fest, but I hate having to drive home the morning after I've spread my wings all night in the suburbs. Passing by all of those big houses, I get an inferiority complex every time."

"I think the ones from Richardson-Plano wear the white dinner jackets, and the others go with the standard black," Grace pointed out to the best of her recollection.

Linda grabbed a complimentary glass of champagne off a serving tray as a white-jacketed host strolled by. "I'ont know Shelia, I'm willing to do the 'burbs if brothas like him are serving champagne out there, too." She sipped from the glass with her pinky finger outstretched. "Uh-huh, I could get used to this."

"A grown man like him is what I'd like to get used to," Shelia confessed softly as she pointed out a very attractive man worth noting. Both Linda and Grace observed who she was talking about. An attentive group of women surrounded a dashingly handsome blackjack dealer who was mesmerizing his audience by reciting Shakespeare as he fleeced them eloquently, all in the name of charity. When the dealer's concentration was interrupted by spotting Grace, he made no qualms about disappointing his loyal fans and asking another dealer to man his station.

He made his way toward Grace, through the crowded room. As he approached the gleesome threesome, his confident swagger caught the attention of several additional females along the way. Linda was prepared to shake what her mama gave her at him, and Shelia was ready to put in her bid likewise by introducing him to her surgically enhanced accessories. Both ladies were immediately thrown for a loop when the blackjack dealer's eyes remained locked on Grace's. Green with envy, Shelia whispered, "I wonder who he is, and could there be more of them?"

Linda agreed. "Wow, if not, I got next on this one."

Grace let out a lengthy sigh as if she was already bored with the event's selection. "Oh, him," she said matter of factly. "That's the guy I was telling y'all about the other night. He's the *schoolteacher*."

"Him?" Shelia whispered as he drew closer. "Oh-oh, Grace, he's still coming this way. You got to get with that. He's what you call grown-man sexy. If they were making teachers like that when I was coming up, I'd still be in the twelfth grade trying to push up on some private after-hours tutoring."

"What about all of that he-must-be-gay stuff you were popping off at the house?" Grace challenged through clenched teeth.

"She could make a living at being wrong about men," Linda said to Grace as she grabbed Shelia by the arm to haul her away.

"All I'm saying is, I've been thinking about taking some extra classes," Shelia was overheard saying just as Wallace finally reached his destination. "Can't I hang around long enough to ask the man what time school lets out? What? Like you don't wanna know too."

19

Sleight of Hand

"Hey Grace, I thought that was you," Wallace sang when he approached her. "Ouch, nice dress," he complimented, surveying her outfit. "Understated but nice," he added with a slight smile.

"Thank you, Wallace, but I specifically went out of my way so I wouldn't have strange men in my face talking about how nicely understated my dress is." Grace was playing hard to get, and harder to figure out.

"Ahhh, so I've been cast into the strange-men category?"

"Well, I hardly know you, and you are in my face. Furthermore, what are you going to do about your flock?" Grace tossed a quick glance at the bevy of beauties he'd left awaiting his return at the blackjack table. "I'd hate to keep you from your adoring entourage. They look heartbroken and so . . . adoring." She almost giggled when she couldn't think of another word to use, but it seemed to fit most appropriately. "Look at them, staring over here with big puppy-dog eyes, salivating. Perhaps you should have fed them before you left."

Wallace slid both hands inside the pockets of his black tuxedo slacks. He lowered his head for a moment, then raised it again. Gazing into Grace's eyes, he attempted to see what she was working so hard at concealing. "If I need a status report, Grace, I'll get one from my stand-in when I relieve him. What I'd like to know is what you're so afraid of." Grace snatched a class of Chardonnay off a passing tray, similar to the way Shelia had earlier.

"Those little girls over there must have you confused." She took a healthy sip, noticing that their standoff in the middle of the walkway had attracted several sets of roving eyes, from both men and women. "There is very little that frightens me, and a smooth card dealer with his own fan club isn't one of them."

Wallace relaxed his stance before debating with her. "I beg to differ. Actually, there is something very different about you, very different from the first time I saw you coming out of the rain at André's basketball game. I can't call it, but it's there."

"Good different, I hope." Grace said nervously as she began to feel the strain of carrying on a conversation with so many others watching her every move.

"Noticeably different," Wallace answered, with a smooth step toward her. "Yes, you look almost vulnerable. It's extremely becoming. A woman who has it all figured out can't fully appreciate what a man has to offer."

Somewhat at a lost for words, Grace avoided eye contact. "Humph, you think you know me? I'm not like those young, fall down, slip and bump my head with my legs wide opened worship-the-ground-a-fine-man-walks-on types, if that's what you think."

"Not at all," Wallace stated in a low, controlled tone that forced Grace to lean closer in order to hear him. "But I'm beginning to gather what you think about me." He saw that Linda and Shelia were standing nearby, posted up and pretending they weren't taking turns scoping out his and Grace's encounter. "We're not finished with this discussion, you and I," he whispered, standing dangerously close to Grace. "By the way, your perfume is delightful. I like that most of all." Without so much as a good-bye, he turned slowly and walked away.

Grace held the glass of wine up to her face as if to inspect it. "Ooh, I'ma need another one of these."

As soon as Wallace disappeared into the horde of party-goers, Linda skirted past Grace. She shot her a follow-me-so-I-don't-have-to-pump-you-for-information-in-front-of-all-these-nosey-people glare. Grace chuckled, managed to get her hands on another glass of Chardonnay, then headed for the powder room behind Linda. Shelia had gone off in another direction when she'd recognized someone from her past, a man who didn't mind using his charge card liberally at Appliance World. That was her kind of man.

Grace recalled her conversation with Wallace while struggling to make sense of it. Linda apprised her of how it appeared from the vantage point she had. They went back and forth, neither of them aware of Wallace's scheme to get Grace's undivided attention again before the night was over.

He'd stepped outside, noted the time on his classic Movado watch, then casually headed for the valet stand. After interrogating the attendants, he located the one who'd parked Grace's car. "Listen, because this is very important," he told the attentive young man about to be debriefed. "The woman driving that Volvo SUV is very dear to me and I'd hate for anything to happen to her. She's had too much to drink and will undoubtedly demand her car keys. Now, this is where you come in. No matter what she says, I'll need you to act as if you're searching for them, but you will not be able to locate them. Do you understand me?"

"Yes sir, I'll pretend to search for the keys, but I won't be able to find them." Suddenly, a wave of concern came over the young man. "What if she sees them in the key box and takes them from me?"

"That'll be impossible because I'll have them," Wallace explained.

The attendant squinted his eyes as he deliberated. "You'll have them? But what if I get into trouble?"

"Mitchie!" Wallace summoned.

The gruff veteran valet supervisor dashed over in a hurry. "Yes, sir, Mr. Peters?"

"Please clarify to this young man, how important it is that we get all of our guests home safely. Insurance premiums tend to go sky high after a terrible accident regarding an inebriated driver."

The older attendant caught on quickly. He nodded, confirming that he fully comprehended the importance of Wallace's demands. "Don't worry, Mr. Peters. I'll see to it that she doesn't get into her car alone. Oh, and sir, might I add that she's quite the looker. I can understand why you're taking such precautions to get her home without a scratch." He held his hand out to be compensated for his part in Wallace's ruse. After two one-hundred-dollar bills landed in his greasy palm, the scheme was under way. It was Wallace's responsibility to hire the valet company for the event, so he had an inside track. Taking the time to get to know Grace motivated this charade over lost car keys. He needed an opportunity to catch her with her guard down, even if he had to manufacture one himself. Grace was worth it, he reasoned, she was well worth it.

"Good," Wallace said to Mitchie and his young associate. "We'll only have one shot at this, so I'm counting on you two to get it right the first time."

Mitchie shoved the money into his pants pocket. "Consider it done," he announced, grinning big and hard. "She must be really something."

"I'm betting that she is, Mitchie. This one is a keeper. She's worth the trouble to catch and the trouble to keep. You know what they say about thoroughbreds?"

"What, that every man wants to ride one?" Mitchie joked heartily.

"Most of them have no idea that a man comes along every now and then who's willing to bet everything he owns hoping she'll pay off," Wallace explained. "This is the one I'm betting on to win. Wish me luck."

Back inside the ballroom, Linda and Grace located Shelia. She was fake-giggling for some man who couldn't keep his eyes off her breasts. Linda had seen this many times—Shelia laughing at every stale joke and lame story to shake the credit card right out of a man's wallet. If he had known that most women decided within the first five minutes of meeting a man whether they were interested in getting undressed, he would have saved the small talk for the morning after. Shelia had already zeroed in and made mental notes to keep something in his mouth later on that night, so she wouldn't have to listen to more of his boring self-aggrandizing fables once they were horizontal. "Excuse me, I'll be right back," Shelia said convincingly while lightly stroking the back of the man's neck with her outstretched fingernails. "Don't you move an inch unless I'm here to watch," she added so that he'd think twice before drifting on to the next overly aggressive woman in a borrowed gown. When the gentleman licked his lips as she brushed her chest against his, Shelia knew he'd be in that exact same spot if it took her three days to come back.

"Can't y'all see I'm working over there?" she jeered at her partners in crime. "I got a live one. He's about three months from getting his freedom papers."

"He's getting a divorce?" Grace asked, spying at him over Shelia's shoulder.

"I didn't ask if he was married," Shelia said, smirking as if she couldn't have cared less about that. "He's only got three more months of child-support payments. Wanna guess who's gonna be getting herself a new refrigerator?"

Grace smirked at her unscrupulous girlfriend. "You need Jesus."

"I *need* a new refrigerator, and Jesus isn't at the end of an eighteen-year, six-hundred-dollar-a-month commitment."

"Grace, you should know by now that Shelia is going to do what she's got to, with Jesus' help or not."

Before Grace had the chance to argue, her cell phone began vibrating at the bottom of her purse. She fished it out and walked to the corner of the room. She didn't recognize the number, but took the call anyway. "Yes, this is Grace. I can hardly hear you. Dré? You're where? Where's that? No, I'm not mad. I'll be there to get you and Skyler in fifteen minutes. Don't accept any rides from strangers. I'll be right there." She flipped the phone shut and marched back to Shelia and Linda's idea of a promising night out on the town. "Listen, I have to go. André and his friend were on their way home after the game and their ride broke down. I have to pick them up. Shelia, if you can't be good, at least be careful. Make him wrap it up, if you're bent on serving it up. Linda, try to talk some sense into her."

"I've got better things to do with my time," Linda declined. "You just be careful out there looking for the boys."

Grace beat a trail to the exit doors. When someone called her name, she stopped on a dime. It was like hearing a voice from a ghost. As far as she was concerned, that particular ghost had died a long time ago. "Grace Hilliard!" he called out again. She closed her eyes, hoping that it wasn't real, but it was, and happening to her when she least expected it. Grace opened her eyes to find that relentless ghost standing in front of her. He'd aged gracefully. His mustache was much thicker than she remembered it being thirteen years ago. His skin, once the shade of fresh apricots, was darker by comparison, and he'd put on a few pounds in all the right places, but nothing else about him seemed out of place. He was still unavoidably debonair as ever.

"Edward Swenson," she said as if he were an old colleague instead of her son's estranged father. "Imagine meeting you here. I didn't know you were back in the city." *Walk with me Lord. Hold my hand and please don't let go.*

"It's good to see you too," he replied, with a hint of sarcasm. "Actually, I moved my family back three years ago. I've been meaning to look you up."

Did he just admit to being around for years, she thought, *and he didn't have the common courtesy to let me know?* Edward and Grace had discussed getting married after college, when she discovered they were going to be parents, although he'd never got around to asking her. Then Edward decided without telling her that he'd rather attend an out-of-state law school instead of going through with the marriage. Afterwards, Grace carried André to term and delivered him alone. All of those thoughts floated through her mind as she looked him over. "Figures," she said eventually. "Some things never change. I would say that it's good seeing you again, but I don't like to lie."

"Gracie, Grace," Edward uttered, grinning charmingly. "Still the hardened Hilliard, just like your mother."

"You don't have any business talking about my mother, or anything else pertaining to me!" she spat, louder than she had intended. When her outburst drew the attention of others loitering nearby, she hushed her voice. "Don't even think you can come around after all this time and act like you've been the consummate friend to me and the quintessential father to *my* son." She was huffing mad and upset with herself because she couldn't fight it. Proving that he could still rattle her was just what he wanted, and she was giving it to him.

"Don't you mean *our* son, Grace? As I recall, I was there when the miracle happened."

"And as I recall, you haven't been there since. I'm the one who taught him how to tie his shoes, read and write, ride a bike, and wipe his behind. So unless you want all these people to hear what I really think about your sorry excuse for being there, then you'd want to back up out of my face and crawl back under your rock."

Edward grinned like he had a viable answer for that one. "Good for you. Now, I'm gonna teach him how to be a man!" he boasted.

"As soon as somebody teaches you how to be one, hurry up and get back to me. Maybe then you can work on making up for lost time since you abandoned us."

"Abandoned? Is that what you call sending money every month without fail? Huh, I've done the best I could under the circumstances."

"If that's your best," she said, chuckling to keep from crying, "I'd hate to see your worst."

After Grace huffed and puffed hard enough to leave her breathless, Edward flashed a phony smile that barely passed for a real one. "I'm not standing here to deliberate what I've done or haven't done. I've come to realize that I want to be a part of our son's life despite missing a huge part of it."

"I've got to go, Edward. My son needs me at this very moment, and I'm not in the habit of letting him down, so step aside before we're both very sorry you didn't."

As Grace pushed past him, he stifled her getaway once again by grabbing her arm. "You telling me that I can't see my son!" Edward hollered, for all to hear. "Have you turned into one of these bitter black women who have no problems cashing the checks but won't let a good man get to know his own child, huh? Is that it?"

Grace felt her knees knocking. Her heart was pounding so hard that she could have sworn she heard it thump inside her chest. Choking back her rage, she took out a tissue and wiped her nose. "Somebody'd better—" was all she'd managed to say before Wallace appeared and wedged himself in the middle of a bad situation about to get a lot worse.

"Grace, let's go," he ordered, staring down Edward like a guard dog prepared to tear him limb from limb.

"You know you're wrong, Grace!" Edward howled from the doorway after Wallace led her outside. "I thought you were better than this!"

"Just keep moving," Wallace insisted, when Grace considered going back to what Edward had started. On second thought, she jerked past Wallace's grasp but he blocked her path. "Believe me, whatever you're thinking, you'll regret it in the morning."

"I can't believe him! I could kill him! He hadn't been around for thirteen years. Thirteen! And now he has the audacity to challenge me about *my* son," she ranted, stomping angrily on the sidewalk in front of the hotel. "I don't believe this." Grace looked at Wallace as if he understood her pain. "It's so ridiculous, it's freaking unbelievable." Out of the blue, Grace ripped off her shoes and started back inside the hotel again. Wallace chased after her, wrangled his arms around her waist and scooped her off the ground. The valet attendants watched as the wild woman kicked and clawed to get free. "You don't get it! Let me go Wallace! Let me go!"

"Grace! Stop it! I don't have to get it. I just have to be here for you. Please calm down," he pleaded. "Let's get you away from here." He whistled for the valet. The young man raced over, undecided about what he should do. "Get this lady her keys," Wallace instructed impatiently then handed him Grace's claim ticket. The attendant winked at Wallace and then bolted in the opposite direction.

Grace turned away from Wallace, folded her arms across her chest, and fought back a river of tears. When the valet returned to announce that he couldn't find her keys, Grace was livid. "What? Ahhh, that's all I need. These fools have lost my keys, and my child is stranded on the wrong side of town. Hey!" she growled, like someone about to come unglued. "Get the manager over here, now!" she demanded with unbridled anger.

"Yes, ma'am, I'm the manager," Mitchie answered, appearing genuinely concerned for her safety, as well as for his. A woman who was kicking, screaming, and smelling of wine would be enough to turn him on if they were alone or at his place, but that wasn't the case. This woman was causing quite a stir, and in public.

"If someone doesn't come up with my keys, I'll have all of you arrested for theft," Grace threatened. "Believe me, I'm the wrong sistah to mess with!" she screamed.

Mitchie scratched his head, dug into his pocket, and pulled Grace's car keys out like an accomplished magician in grand ta-da fashion. He shook his head, then looked at Wallace for affirmation. "You sure?" he asked apprehensively. Wallace held out his hand and took them from Mitchie before Grace had the chance to. Mitchie stated, "Sorry, ma'am, but you look like you've had too much to drink, and I can't be held responsible for letting you get behind the wheel."

"It's not up to you," she barked at the attendant. "Wallace, give me my keys so I can go."

"Sorry, Grace, but I can't do that. You're not in any shape to drive."

Grace charged at him, frantically reaching for what rightfully belonged to her. "Give them to me," she insisted. "André needs me. He's out on the streets somewhere waiting for me."

"Mitchie, toss mine to me," Wallace asserted when he saw his plan couldn't have worked out better. Only now, the crisis was real. Grace did need him, and he was there for her. Wallace held firmly to her waist with one hand as he caught his keys with the other one. "Thanks, Mitch, it'll be okay."

"That's what he thinks, Mitchie!" Grace mocked. "I'm pressing charges on the whole lot of you first thing tomorrow morning."

Wallace shook off her idle threats, suggesting to the valet manager that she didn't mean it. "It's cool, man. Trust me, it's cool. I got this."

After Wallace was forced to throw Grace over his shoulder to transport her to his car, Linda appeared at the stand to retrieve hers. "What happened up here?" she asked, as people gossiped about some drunken woman throwing one whale of a fit.

"Just an ordinary night at the Hotel Grande," Mitchie answered. "A woman who drank too much about to get cozy with a man who needs to get over his love for horses. Yep, two crazy people falling in love," he added, scratching his head. "Tickets please!"

Linda sauntered closer to the curb. She watched as Wallace wrestled Grace into his shiny, gold-colored Jaguar. Shelia wandered out with her big spender in tow. "Linda, I heard there was a big commotion out here."

"Uh-huh, Linda replied plainly.

"They said something about a woman getting ig'nant, pulling off her pumps and everything."

"Uh-huh, that's the story."

"Hey, did you ever see Grace after she was all stank-a-dank-dank with the schoolteacher?"

"Uh-huh," Linda answered once more. "I saw her getting carried off into the night by a real live caveman. That schoolteacher wasn't taking no for an answer."

Shelia stared toward the parking lot along with Linda, trying to see what had her friend so starry eyed. "Guess Grace changed her mind, huh?"

"Uh-uh," Linda corrected her with a warm smile. "Looks like that schoolteacher changed it for her."

20
Twisted

The Jaguar whisked through late-night traffic after Grace told Wallace where to find Skyler's broken-down whoop-die. She sat in the passenger seat, stomping mad with mascara staining her taut cheeks. Grace stared out of the side window and shook her head. *The entire scene was something right out of a movie*, she thought. A very bad movie where the single mother had to deal with her baby-daddy after he hopped on the next plane and ditched her and their son for a promising career, then married the first chick he met as soon as his feet touched down. Grace knew about Edward's other family. Their mutual friends had kept her in the loop throughout the years until she refused to listen any longer. She'd seen it all before, but this time, it was happening to her, although she couldn't understand why or how.

"Now that you've given everyone something to talk about, maybe you're through with the likes of Edward Swenson," Wallace said before pressing his lips tightly to hold in his negative feelings about Grace's ex. She let his words soak in while she gawked at his white dinner jacket, realizing it was like the one Edward wore.

"Don't tell me that you and Edward belong to the same chapter!" she yelled, pulling on her pumps. "Oh no, one messed-up frat rat is enough for me. Let me outta this car." Grace had gotten herself worked up all over again. "Is that why you took me away from there, to save him from me?"

"Don't be ridiculous, Grace. I was thinking only of you," Wallace professed honestly. "I wouldn't have minded seeing you get prehistoric on him, but that's beside the point. You may have had good reason, but you lost it, and that was not cool."

"Like I care what you think is cool! I don't even know why you stuck your nose in my business in the first place. It's not like you have anything to do with me and my lame excuse for a baby-daddy anyway," she ranted. "Uhhhgh, I hate him!" Grace slammed her foot against the dashboard, stubbing her toe. "Ouch, ouch, ouch!" she wailed. "I think I broke it."

"Yeah, my glove box is busted thanks to you."

"What, your glove box? I was talking about my toe, and all you can think about is a piece of plastic?" When Grace looked up at Wallace, after rubbing her right foot, she squinted. He was smiling, actually smiling, while she sat there, utterly pissed. "Did I miss a joke? Huh, Wallace, is this funny to you?"

"Yeah, kinda," he answered, laughing now. "Yep. It's funny that you'd think I cared more about any part of this car than what you've had to go through tonight. You were so mad when you tore off those high heels and tried to run back inside with them, poised to strike. I couldn't let it go any further than it already had."

Without warning, a faint semblance of a smile parted Grace's lips. "I guess it must've been a little funny in a twisted animalistic-mother-protecting-her-young sorta way."

"Yeah, that's . . . what I meant," Wallace mused, laughing harder than before. "You're really something. You know that?"

Grace sighed, still feeling around for broken bones. "Humph, I don't know what happened. I had it all together once, I really did. Nothing bothered me," she said, for the sake of sharing how things used to be. "I didn't let anything get under my skin. I had it all together, then, poof, the hinges came off."

"Good," was Wallace's sole response.

"Good? What's so good about it?"

"It's good that you realize your perfect world isn't so perfect."

Grace adjusted herself in the leather seat before questioning his statement. "Is that supposed to be some Shakespearean philosophizing, or are you playing Dr. Phil now?"

"Neither," he answered, again with a one-word reply.

"Then how do you feel justified sitting there all smug, psychoanalyzing my life and telling me what you think is good about it?"

Wallace exited the interstate near the downtown area. Prostitutes patrolled the boulevard, while degenerates went up and down the block to pick over forbidden fruit. "I'm not saying that I have all the answers, but I know when God is trying to tell me something. Maybe it's your turn to listen."

"So, now you're preaching to me? You just don't stop," Grace ranted. "I-I listen to God plenty, and we get along just fine. I know Jesus. Talking to me like I don't know Jesus. You've got some nerve."

Wallace smiled because Grace was still fuming, and he enjoyed seeing her raw, uninhibited emotions run amuck. He circled the block until he spotted an abandoned car with the hood up. "That might be it up there," he said, pointing up the road.

Grace leaned forward to get a better look at the idle car. "Yeah, that's Skyler's jalopy, but I don't see the boys." She took out her cell phone and called home, but no one answered. "I pray that nothing happened to them. This is not a good place to hitchhike, and I told that boy not to accept any rides from strangers." As she punched in another phone number, she glared at Wallace. "I'll get back to you in a minute. Don't think I'm letting you off the hook." Wallace heard her as he continuously scouted their immediate surroundings for signs of foul play and carjackers. "Miss Pearl, this is Grace. Have you seen the boys since they left for the basketball game?" she asked frantically. "Oh, that's great. Are they okay? Who? Yes, ma'am. I'll be right there. Thanks. Bye." She placed the phone back in her purse and cast a narrow-eyed stare at Wallace. "Since you know so much about everything, tell me, why are you driving an expensive car, single, and probably living with yo' mama?"

"Ooh, that's cold," Wallace chuckled. "Shrewd."

"Well? I may not have it all figured out either, but what about your situation? How can a teacher afford such a nice car, and why did you get involved in the fight between me and Edward back at the hotel? Up at the corner, take a left," she added as an afterthought.

"Not that it's any of your business, and I'm not one to put mine on a hotel sidewalk, but I'll tell you anyway. I have a side hustle, from teaching. I got involved tonight because I've had my share of bad run-ins with Edward too. I'm interested in you, and because coming to your rescue was the right thing to do." Wallace pulled into the parking lot of an open-all-night McDonald's. He looked over at Grace to note her reaction, but she wouldn't return his gaze.

He rescued me, how chivalrous, she thought. *I've never been rescued before. Hmmm . . . now what?* "Why are we here?" Grace asked, as if the lights had just come on.

Wallace stroked his chin while looking her over. "It wouldn't be such a good idea to let André see you like that."

Grace flipped down the sun visor, then opened the flap over the small vanity mirror. She wanted to scream when she saw a pair of raccoon eyes staring back at her. "Ehhhh. You mean I've been looking like this the whole time?"

"Yep, I'm afraid so."

"Shoot, looks like I needed more than rescuing. A washcloth and a makeover would do for starters," Grace complained.

"Uh-huh, that's why we're here," Wallace answered knowingly.

Grace shot another stinging glare at him for being a know-it-all. "Okay, I'll give you this one, but don't think this means anything. I'll be right back."

"And I'll be right here." Wallace fought back a chuckle begging to get out as Grace contemplated making another smart remark to even the score. "Is there something you wanted to say to me?" he baited her.

"You're not what I expected," she mumbled, as if it pained her greatly to admit she was thankful for all of his generosity.

As Wallace watched Grace sashay into the fast-food restaurant, he felt as if he could read her mind. "You're welcome," he said quietly. "You're welcome."

The second Grace entered the restroom she recoiled at the sight of a woman dressed in a tight, short Lycra dress with a leopard print washing herself in the sink. Grace turned to leave, but the woman stopped her. "Uh-uh, you ain't got to go. I'm almost done," she offered kindly. "At least it's still early. They got a lot of soap tonight."

Not certain what to do, Grace leaned up against the door and tried to concentrate on something other than the streetwalker washing herself in the hand basin. Unexpectedly, Grace realized that her recent experience didn't come close to rivaling the prostitute's daily existence. In the morning, Grace's world would be a much better place. She knew the reverse wasn't the same for her new acquaintance.

Once the basin was tidied up and all hers, Grace thanked the woman and handed her all of the cash she had, sixty-five dollars. "This isn't much but I wanted to let you know how much I appreciate your kindness," Grace told her.

"Ain't this somethin'," the working girl responded, holding the folded bills up for inspection. "I saw you sitting out in that Jag, honey, but I can't take this."

"No, it's all right. Really," Grace insisted.

"You ain't got to tell me twice. Business must be real good in the hood, but if'n that trick beat on you, you deserve to keep every penny." She'd assumed the worst because Grace had been crying.

"No, I just had a very bad evening." Grace didn't have the heart to explain things to the woman whose woes ran much deeper than hers. "Take care of yourself out there," Grace said as her company tucked the money inside her bra for safekeeping.

"You too, honey. Don't let 'em get the best of you."

After Grace made up her face as best she could, she settled back into the car with Wallace. Her countenance was noticeably different. She smiled as the streetwalker waved good-bye to her from the curb. "Okay, let's go," Grace said softly.

"What was all that about?" Wallace questioned.

"Girl talk. You wouldn't understand." She nestled against the seat with a new lease on life and a definite respect for women having to do what they saw fit to survive. It felt good helping out a fellow female, even if the money ended up in her pimp's pocket. As far as Grace was concerned, at least it allowed the woman to take a pass on a few tricks if she wanted to and cool her heels in the meantime.

"Wow, talk about impressive." Wallace was surprised when Grace pointed out the cutest little house on the block as the one Skyler lived in with his grandmother.

Grace admired the new paint job, done in white, with neatly trimmed green accessories, resurfaced roof, iron fence, and rosebushes to set it off. "Yeah, I like it too," she agreed. "But we have to get our story straight, because André is going to be full of questions when he sees me with you."

"Right, right." Wallace gave Grace a brief once-over and then submitted his suggestions. "First thing, lose the panty hose."

Initially, she refused. "Excuse you. You would enjoy the show, but I'm not taking off my panty hose in this car with you sitting two feet away. Uh-uh. Not gonna do it."

"I'm just saying, André could get the wrong idea. The hose are torn. You're rolling up with me. He sees something that isn't there. I'd hate for him to lose respect for you over nothing."

"I see what you mean," Grace acquiesced begrudgingly. "Turn your head," she demanded. "I don't want *you* to go getting the wrong idea either." Wallace did as he was told, although he did sneak a peek when she slid her dress up in order to wiggle the hose past her hips. Grace caught him looking but kept it to herself. She would have had more of a problem if he hadn't copped a freebie. He was a man, after all. "Okay, now I'm ready."

"Not quite. Touch up your lipstick so it doesn't look like I've stolen a few kisses on the way over," Wallace suggested. Grace popped the vanity mirror again and nodded. That wasn't a bad idea.

"That oughta do it. Now, what's our story?"

"Don't ask me, I draw the line at lying to children," Wallace joked.

"Thanks for nothing. That's just like a man to clam up when the going gets rough," she hissed harmlessly. "I got it. I'll simply tell him that I couldn't get to my car when he called. If he doesn't buy it, I'll tell him shut up, sit down, and be still. That's worked fine up 'til now."

Grace stepped out, adjusting her dress and imagining the look on her son's face when he got a load of Wallace sitting in the driveway. That's when she hoped to avoid being forced to lie to children herself. Both antsy and tired, Grace tapped lightly at the brand new screen door.

André gushed with glee as he opened up. "Ma, me and Sky," he began to tell her until she corrected him. "Uh, Sky and I were waiting on you, but this fly Benz rolled up, and guess who was in it? Allen Foray! He said he saw us sitting in his guest seats and wondered where you were. You said not to accept rides from strangers, and everybody knows Allen, so we got him to bring us here. Please don't be mad, Ma, you said you wouldn't be mad." André gasped for air after his long dissertation and waited for Grace's approval.

"Sure, that was all right, I guess, but I do need to speak with Miss Pearl a minute."

"Ma, whose tight Jag is that out there?" André asked, looking past her.

"Don't you worry about that, just get your things so I can get you to bed," she demanded.

"Okay, okay. That's tight, huh Sky?" Skyler had joined him at the doorway and was every bit as curious until he recognized the fancy vehicle.

"Yeah, it's tight all right," Skyler answered with a calm resolve. "C'mon Dré, I got something to tell you." They departed to Skyler's bedroom, then closed the door behind them.

"Miss Pearl," Grace called out toward the woman's bedroom. "It's Gracie."

"Chile, I know who it was the minute I saw you out in that car, sliding out of your panty hose."

Grace thought she was going to die. "You saw that?"

"Girl, yeah," Miss Pearl snickered. "You think you're the first mother who went to extra measures making sure her son didn't know she was still a woman?"

"Miss Pearl, it wasn't like that," Grace argued, very embarrassed.

"I'm sure it wasn't, or you'd have had 'em put away in your purse a lot sooner. Don't fret none of that. The boys are fine. They're all a roar after riding in that ballplayer's big, expensive car. He took 'em for burgers and everything." Miss Pearl grinned as she pictured all the fun they'd had. "Probably the best night of their lives, I'd say."

"Yes, ma'am, I'd say you're right about that. Thanks again for watching Dré. See you at work bright and early Monday morning?"

"Naw, but I'll get there at ten like I'm supposed to," the old woman corrected her. "Don't go crawfishing on me now. Bright and early ain't part of the deal."

"Yes, ma'am. We did say ten o'clock, didn't we?"

"Sho' did, and tell that Mr. Peters I said hello when you get back to the car." Grace wanted to hide her befuddled expression but couldn't. Talk about all of her business being exposed for public scrutiny. "And tell him I understand what he's aiming to do with Skyler, too. He needs to know that I don't hold nothing against him."

Again Grace was confused but thought it better to play along. "I will," she agreed before hugging Miss Pearl tightly. "I'll see you on Monday."

When André met Grace at the front door, he was checking her like a grown man. She offered him an open opportunity to say what was on his mind, but he let it pass until they were out onto the cement porch. "So, you're dating Mr. Peters?" he asked like a man twice his age.

"No, he's just helping me out. I couldn't get to my car fast enough when you called me. Wallace was at the fund-raiser too, and he didn't mind bringing me. Is that okay?"

"Huh, it's works for me if it works for you. Mr. Peters is okay. All the women teachers seem to dig him, too. If you want to see what he's about, I'm with it," André added, his head cocked to the side like he had thought it over and given his blessings. "You could do a lot worse than him, I guess."

Grace was taken aback by his mature sincerity. "I'll try to

remember that if Mr. Peters decides to ask me out, now that I know it works for you." She looked at Wallace taking it all in. She thought about letting him sweat it, but felt that would have been unfair so she tossed him an expression conveying that all was well.

André sat in the backseat and spoke to his favorite teacher as if the lift home wasn't out of the ordinary in the least. He relived the basketball game, the burgers, the discussion afterward, and the chance to ride in a hundred-thousand-dollar car with chrome spinning rims. André had fallen asleep by the time they reached home. Grace woke him up and helped him stagger to the door. She waved good-bye to Wallace and spent half the night wondering why Edward had decided to reenter her child's life after such a long absence. She also lent some time to what Miss Pearl had said regarding Wallace's efforts to help Skyler, and not holding anything against him because of it. There were so many questions without the answers to make sense of them. Answers are what Grace wanted, almost as much as the good night's sleep she needed.

21

Reflections in Blue

The next morning, Grace rolled around in bed until she couldn't stand lying there any longer. She tussled with a pillow that blocked her view from the alarm clock on her nightstand. "Ten o'clock already," she moaned. Grace figured that André must have helped himself to cold cereal because he hadn't bothered to disturb her for their normal Saturday flapjacks, bacon, and cheese grits breakfast. Before she could swing both legs over the side of the bed, she heard the doorbell chime. Her cell phone began to vibrate simultaneously. "André!" she yelled. "Dré, please get the door for me!" Her caller ID flashed Linda's name. "Linda, what's up?" she said into the flip phone.

"Obviously not you," Linda answered with a rise in her voice. "Get your butt out of that bed, girl, and let me in."

"Huh? I'll call you back, Linda. Someone's at the door." Grace yawned, rubbed her hand across her face, eased into a silk robe and strolled into the den. "Dré!" she hollered a second time, stumbling across the note he'd left for her: "Mama, I'm gone to the rec center to hoop. I've got some money. See you later. André." When the doorbell chimed again, Grace remembered why she'd walked into the den in the first place. "Coming," she said, much too softly for anyone on the other side of the door to hear. She looked out of the window and saw Linda's car, a tiny yellow Volkswagen Beetle. Grace opened the door, then turned around and started off in the other direction without as much as a hello.

"Well, good morning to you too, Grinch," Linda joked, following closely behind Grace. "You got a man shacked up in here, and is he still naked?"

"No and no, although that wouldn't be such a bad idea considering how messed up my life is right now." Grace waved at the refrigerator and shuffled off toward her bedroom. "Whatever you find in there you can keep."

"Uh-uh, I'm taking you to breakfast so you can tell me *all* about last night. Then, after the juicy details, I'll drop you by the hotel to pick up your car."

"Oh, I've forgotten about being stressed and stranded. Be back in a sec."

"Hurry up, Shelia's supposed to meet us at Nookie's."

Grace stopped and slung her head around as if it weighed a ton. "Nookie's?"

"Yeah, you know, that charming little breakfast nook off the Knox-Henderson exit."

"Oh, yeah," Grace remembered. "That's the place with the fruit crepes, the good ones."

Linda was thumbing through the latest issue of *Essence* when Grace finally pulled herself together. "Whew, it's about time." Linda closed the magazine and tucked it under her arm. "I hope Nookie's serves lunch," she teased sarcastically.

"Cut me a break, I got my feelings beat on last night," Grace complained, strapping on the darkest sunshades she could find.

"That's what I'm talking about. What else of yours got beat on last night?"

Grace cut her eyes at Linda over the top of her shades.

"Believe me, that was enough," she informed her inquisitive friend.

"Well, depends on who you ask. Shelia spent all night putting in work for her new Icemaker Deluxe with a lettuce crisper."

"She went home with that guy?"

"Think she didn't? Then they went shopping this morning. Wanna guess where to?"

"Appliance World," Grace said, knowingly. "Gotta hand it to Shelia. She never loses her focus on the resources of romance."

"She always says it's better for a sistah to give when she can receive something that comes with a receipt and a warranty."

"Okayyy," Grace chuckled. "The only thing I've ever gotten for my troubles is a thirteen-year-old who's starting to look too much like his father. Edward Swenson is going to be the death of me."

Linda followed Grace out to the car, pondering each step of the way. Once they were en route to the restaurant, she had to inquire about the night before to see if it had anything to do with Grace bringing up an old name that represented nothing but old news and nonsense. "Edward Swenson," Linda sighed, as if his name was tied to her miseries as well. "That's a name I haven't heard in a long while. Does he still send checks for André?"

"Yeah, he's been paying into Dré's college fund. I haven't cashed one of those checks in thirteen years. I couldn't bring myself to, no matter how hard times were when André was little and I was working on my master's. Pride, girl, it's always been the witch I couldn't seem to ditch."

After allowing Grace's words to sink in, Linda was no closer to the story she was trying to get her hands around without coming right out and asking. She and Grace were friends, true enough but Grace was changing, into who she didn't know. "If the money is coming in on time, why are you sitting over there looking like the color blue?"

"That's funny, because that's exactly how I feel." Grace leaned her head back against the headrest to settle into the seat as well as into the conversation. "If confusion were a color, I'd be wearing that one too."

"You and me both," Linda suggested, as she still had no clue what had transpired to ruin Grace's night and left her with one heck of a heartache hangover. "It's killing me not to ask why the finest schoolteacher I've ever laid eyes on was packing you off into the darkness, and how your panty hose ended up in your purse the morning after."

Grace cocked her head at Linda. "And how would you know that?"

"I saw them when you dug out your house keys to lock up. Like I wasn't supposed to notice two feet of nylon hanging out of a three-hundred-dollar purse. What? Now, you may as well go on, and tell me all about it."

Grace nestled back into her seat again, brooding over the details she didn't mind sharing with Linda. "I wish there was a sexy scenario to paint for you, but it didn't go down like that. Not even close. I was in such a hurry to see about André that I must've walked right past Edward and didn't even notice him. But as soon as I heard his voice calling my name, I knew it was nothing but trouble."

Linda's eyes widened with surprise. "Edward was at the fundraiser last night?"

"Yeah, he was probably hiding in the bushes and waiting on a good time to strike. I shouldn't have let it get next to me, but after he started tripping about how he wanted to be a better father and questioning my decision to keep him out of my son's life, it got out of hand, I got out of hand, and the only thing that stopped me from giving him a suede sling-back enema was Wallace stepping in to calm me down." The smile that tickled at Grace's lips when she said his name caused Linda to ask more about him.

"Hmm, this Wallace you're getting all happy faced about, is he the reason you can't get yourself to trash a certain set of women's unmentionables?"

"Huh, everybody and their mama has seen my unmentionables since I took them off, but no, not really," Grace told her, with the smile intact. "I was a wreck after having it out with Edward. Ooh, I wanted to get all up in him. I snatched off my shoes and was heading back inside to get in a few good licks. He's bigger than me, but I had rage on my side. Wallace didn't want André to see me with my hose all jacked after that and get the wrong idea. He's very thoughtful, you know," Grace added, reliving the incidents she wouldn't soon forget.

"No, I didn't know that about him," Linda remarked to goad Grace on.

Grace blushed as she thought about Wallace taking over after she'd lost control. "He *rescued* me," she giggled, before realizing how adolescent it sounded. "I mean, he showed up when I needed a strong shoulder to lean on. I wished he'd have used it to knock Edward flat on his behind."

Linda picked up on something and speculated whether Grace was aware of it or not. When they were escorted to a booth near the window, she stared at Grace until she could no longer put off inquiring about it further. "Grace, do you really like this Wallace, this dashing blackjack-dealing-old-English-reciting sexy superhero?"

Grace's eyes gleamed before she turned them away from Linda's. "I don't know why you'd say that. I just met the brotha." Grace looked at Linda to see if she'd bought it. She didn't.

"If you'd have been listening to yourself on the way over, you might have a different perspective from the one you're trying to pawn off on me." Linda picked up Grace's shades from off the table and put them on her face. "Wallace is so thoughtful," she mocked, bobbing her head like a lovesick debutante. "He rescued me. I wish he'd use those big strong shoulders to knock that Edward flat on his mean old behind." Linda broke out laughing when she observed Grace's mortified expression.

"Oh, Lin, was I that bad?"

"Worse," Linda verified quickly. "I left out the cute little giggle you do whenever you mention his name."

"I do not giggle when I mention Wallace's name." Grace wanted to scream when she started giggling on cue.

Linda nodded her head and pointed across the table at Grace. "See, I told you."

"What am I going to do now?" Grace asked. A bad case of panic spread across her face. "I can't be trying to date and . . . and get down like that with my son's teacher. That's . . . that's nasty!"

"Only if y'all get down," was Linda's heady response. "You never know, Grace, it could be the best kinda nasty you ever had the pleasure of getting down with, seeing as how thoughtful and strong he is. After you're done, then you could get him to beat up Edward."

Grace choked on a sip of ice water. "Uh, now you're speaking my language."

"It sounds like music to my ears." Linda began snapping her fingers to the beat of an oldie but goodie. "Happy feelings," she crooned. "Where's Frankie Beverly when you need him?"

"I'm sayin'." Grace bobbed her head to the rhythm going on inside it. "Thanks so much Linda, you didn't have to get out of your warm bed to drag me out of mine."

"That's what you think. How else was I going to find out if you got some last night? Shelia called me twice already asking if I'd heard anything yet. Wait until she gets wind of your baby-daddy drama and Mister Super Sexy convincing you to jump out of your drawze in the front seat of his car."

"Bump that, those were not my panties," Grace objected. "Uh-uh. No."

"Did you wear panties with that dress last night?" When

Grace didn't answer Linda got what she was looking for. "All right then, the panty hose may as well have been your drawze. Either way you chalk it up, that man had you all up in his vehicle, with . . . what? Yo booty . . . out."

Both Linda and Grace were doubled over and gasping for breath when Shelia arrived and hopped into the booth with them. "Okay, what I miss?" She rattled off. It was difficult to make out Linda's abbreviated version amid the unbridled hooting and hollering going on. "Uh-huh, uh-huh," Shelia uttered, listening intently but only catching about every fourth word. "Wait, *who* had their booty out?"

22

Let's Talk About It

Grace spent the remainder of the weekend extremely confused about André's father and the strange way he'd seemed to pop up out of thin air after all these years. For the first time since her son was a toddler, Grace felt nervous about everything he did. She paid closer attention to André's metamorphosis into a young man. She remembered the joy she got watching him maneuver his way around the basketball court. She replayed each of their conversations over the past month and also noted his introduction to puberty, his flirting with cheerleaders, his increasing male bravado, and his more mature style of carrying himself than she was accustomed to. Grace lost a great deal of sleep over allowing Edward to slip back into André's life after he was already half grown. No matter how many ways she sliced it, her son would soon be facing issues best tackled by a man, but Grace had serious reservations about his father fitting that bill. Regardless, Edward had engineered a smashing comeback, and she'd have to find a way to accept it.

Throughout Monday, Grace received e-mails from associates seeking details stemming from the incident at the hotel. Rumors were swirling around, including wild tales of her alleged arrest and attempted assault. She did the best she could to squelch them at every turn, but she had herself to blame. Edward's unfounded remarks and arrogant attitude should have been addressed differently, better, she thought after sending an e-mail to Patrik, the director. Grace explained that she was just fine and that it had only been a misunderstanding blown out of proportion. What a mess!

Grace hid in her office for most of the next week, ducking phone calls and doing what she could to improve her frame of mind. Taking a break from her seclusion, she stood in her office doorway and peered out of it. Chandelle was fussing at some poor soul on the phone about her cable bill; Awkward Bob was watering the plants, this time dressed in a lime green Vera Wang jumpsuit; Ms. Pearl was making a great impression by bringing freshly baked goodies every day; and there was not one sign of Pretty Ricky manipulating female employees with his meet-me-in-back-of-my-van routine.

When Marcia happened by, Grace stopped her and decided it was time they had a chat about nothing in particular. "Marcia, pop in for a minute. Have a seat and take a load off." As Grace circled her desk, Marcia grew increasingly pensive. This wasn't like her boss to make time for idle chitchat. Because Grace had always been strictly business, it was unnerving to get invited in to roost without any apparent goal to speak of. But Grace didn't realize this when she asked, "Tell me, Marcia, how's it going?"

Marcia placed a handful of files on her lap and followed Grace around the desk with a weary eye. "Uhm, how's what going, Miss Hilliard?"

Grace realized she wasn't any good at office small talk, but she'd already committed herself. "Oh, I don't know. How's life?"

Shuddering at the thought of something bad coming out

of an impromptu discussion with senior management, Marcia began to hyperventilate. "Uhhh. Whewww. Uhhh. If you're going to fire me, just come out with it, because I think it's cruel to beat around the bush and torture me with head games."

Grace dumped a half-eaten sandwich into the trash can, then she flew around the desk waving the sandwich bag out in front. "Marcia, calm down! Marcia! Marcia! Breathe. Nobody's talking about firing you." The nervous assistant held the bag over her mouth and panted until her breathing returned to normal.

"What? You didn't pull me in here on the chill-tip to let me go?"

"On the chill-tip?" Grace repeated, noting the white girl's slick usage of street talk. "I'm not sure what you thought, but I did honestly ask you to come in so we could just . . . visit."

"Well, I don't know," Marcia answered with a hint of trepidation. "You've never wanted to just . . . visit before, so I figured this was one of those new corporate methods of catching employees off guard and sticking it to them before they had a chance to go postal."

"I can see that this is very upsetting to you, and perhaps this wasn't a good idea," Grace surmised correctly. "Let's just pretend that it never happened, and go back to the way it was, when I didn't make time for you."

"That's something I can live with as long as I'm still employed because you've been acting kinda strange since that meltdown you had outside the Grande Hotel." Marcia covered her face with her hands after letting it slip that she also knew about Grace's all-out tantrum. "I'm sorry, please don't fire me!"

Grace's face was tight enough to tear. She slammed the door and threw both hands on her hips. "Em, put your hands down," she ordered as quietly as humanly possible. "Now, tell me where you heard about my . . . meltdown."

"You called me Em, now I know I'm gonna get canned."

"Not if you tell me what I want to know." Marcia began to sniffle, but Grace refused to let her cry her way out of the situation. "Be strong, Em. Be strong."

"I knew coming in here would lead to something bad," Marcia cried. "I just knew it. If I tell you how I heard about it, I'll have to tell you who I heard it from, too."

Grace stood over her, about to lose her cool again. "That depends on what you've heard. Out with it."

Marcia peered up at Grace like a frightened squirrel about to give up her favorite nut. "Okay, but for the record, I'm not a rat. I'm telling you under duress."

"Duly noted, now spill it!"

"All right, here goes. The other day, I was minding my own business and having lunch at the mall. Then up came Ricardo from the delivery route."

"Pretty Ricky?" asked Grace.

"Yeah, that's what they call him. So, he wanted to get to know me better, and I was on my lunch break. This led to that, and before I knew it, he was telling me how he overheard this paralegal talking about you as some lawyer who's tied up in an ugly marriage gone south, child-support money, and your meltdown at a highbrow fund-raiser, which otherwise sounded very nice." Marcia held her right hand up, cautiously blocking her face in the event that Grace had another of those meltdowns she'd heard about.

"Quit that. You don't have to be afraid of me!" Grace yelled. "Relax. I'll work this out like I should have in the beginning."

Marcia wanted to retreat when Grace's eyes grew dim with resentment. "Miss Hilliard, can I go now?"

"Yeah, we're through here. Thanks for stopping in."

Marcia bolted for the door with her files in hand. Grace stopped her in midstride. "One more thing! Stay out of the back of Pretty Ricky's van. And if you didn't know, that's nasty."

Marcia hid her face with the stack of files and cowered behind it. She thought of lying about her encounter with the delivery guy, but knew that Grace had the goods on her. "Yes, ma'am." Too ashamed to continue the conversation, Marcia whined before leaving, "Is there anything else?"

"Yes, please send gifts to Mr. Allen Foray, he's in the Rolodex, and Mr. Wallace Peters over at John Quinn High. You can call there to get the address. Send something nice from me, but not too personal. And Marcia, I owe you. Thanks."

"Yes, ma'am," was all Marcia could say before scurrying off down the hall.

Grace returned to her leather chair, rocking in it slowly and contemplating what to do about this newly acquired bit of information. She wanted to assume Edward had put her business out on Front Street but she couldn't be sure that it wasn't her own bad actions that spearheaded her character assassination. Since it was impossible to rewind the tape with Edward, Grace figured it was best to revisit their discussion about André. *That is what Edward had approached her about*, she reasoned. That's what she'd grant him, a nice, quiet talk about their son.

Since Marcia was busy arranging gifts to be mailed out, she had her hands full. Grace didn't know the first thing about tracking down Edward, but she remembered him mention that he'd been in town for three years. She decided to run a Yahoo query for his name, just as if he were a prospective client. A quick search proved successful. The first article she opened discussed how Muriel Swenson, the wife of Dallas County Assistant District Attorney Edward Swenson, filed for legal separation two months before citing irreconcilable differences. Grace almost cheered his misfortune, but caught herself. Just because he wasn't man enough for her when she needed him didn't mean he hadn't given his all to make the marriage work with this Muriel person. Besides, that wasn't Grace's issue—straightening out the situation on her side of the fence was. Before signing off, something told Grace to scroll down further and see what else Edward had been up to, but she didn't. Later on, she'd wished she had.

"Dallas County Courts please," Grace requested from the directory assistance operator. "Yes, the Assistant District Attorney's office. Thanks." She jotted down the number, then promised herself not to get rattled this time around. "Take a deep breath and keep your chin up." The phone rang three times before someone answered with a down-home country twang.

"Dallas County Courts, how may I direct ya call?"

"Yes, could you forward me to ADA Edward Swenson's office?" Grace told the woman quickly before changing her mind. "Thank you." While she waited, she doodled hearts on her steno pad.

"ADA Edward Swenson's office," answered another voice, warm but more direct than the first. "Hello, this is the Assistant District Attorney's office," she announced after Grace neglected to speak up.

"Uh, yes, I'm trying to reach Edward Swenson," Grace said finally. "Is he in?"

"Miss, is this regarding a pending case?" the gatekeeper asked.

"No, it's of a personal nature."

"Personal?" A few seconds passed before the gatekeeper asked, with a more aggressive tone, "Who is this, and exactly what is this about?"

Grace was at a loss for words. The gatekeeper's warmth had suddenly evaporated altogether. "Excuse me?"

"I asked *who* you were and what you wanted with District Attorney Swenson."

Holding the phone like it was a hot curling iron, Grace took a defensive posture. "Obviously, I'm not familiar with City Hall protocol, but I don't see how who I am makes a bit of difference about whether he's in or not. Is he or isn't he available?" Another stint of silence rolled by before the questioning continued.

"If I'm going to tell Mr. Swenson that he has a call waiting, I'll need your name for the record, won't I?"

"I know one thing. All this is not necessary just to speak with a city official," Grace snarled. "Maybe I should be taking your name to report your funky attitude to Mr. Swenson." *This is harder than trying to talk with the president,* Grace thought, *although I don't know why anyone would want to talk to his sorry butt either.*

"Who should I say is calling, miss?" the gatekeeper prodded again, with the bad attitude still very much evident.

"You can tell him that Grace Hilliard would like to speak with him, if that's not asking too much."

"Did you say Hilliard? Grace Hilliard?" the woman repeated.

"That's right." Grace was feeling herself now. She was also willing to bet that after Edward heard her name, he'd jump through flaming hoops to get at the telephone. Then, Grace heard a familiar sound, a click on the other end as the gatekeeper hung up in her face. "Hey! Hello? Hello?" I know that chick did not just hang up on me! "Marcia!" Grace shouted after hitting Marcia's extension then the intercom button. "Marcia, get me the Dallas County Courts back on the line. I don't know what's going on down there. Buzz me when you have ADA Edward Swenson on the phone." Grace couldn't sit still while steam came out of her ears. "Some silly receptionist thinks she's going to get away with slamming the phone down in my face," she said aloud, seething with animosity. "I ought to take my behind up to the courthouse. Then we'll see how tough she is. Ig'nant chick."

Marcia buzzed her back within seconds. "Miss Hilliard, he's on line two."

"Who, Edward?" Grace couldn't believe how quickly Marcia had gotten to him and also how amicably he'd agreed to hold.

"Yes, ADA Swenson's on two," Marcia confirmed.

"Thanks, I'll take it. Hello, Edward?"

"Grace?" a deep voice asked, with a certain amount of concern behind it.

"Yes, Edward, this is Grace. I didn't mean to bother you during office hours but I felt that we, I uh, needed to apologize for what happened the other night."

"This doesn't sound like Grace Hilliard," he joked.

"Don't be silly Edward," she countered. "One silly city employee per day is enough to get on my last good nerve. Who was that phone checker, anyway? You know she hung up on me?"

"Well, she takes her job seriously, and says that you were being evasive and wouldn't offer any information."

"Then how did she know who to tell you I was then, huh?" Grace made some snap assumptions. "That overprotective paper pusher wouldn't be the cause of your impending separation with Morticia, now, would she? Or the same one who's been running around telling all of my business?"

"That's insane. The girl who took your call is a paralegal. She helps me out with the calls from time to time, and no, nothing is going on between us," he protested. "Regardless of what you might think, I'm a happily married man, but you wouldn't know anything about that." Grace had a chip on her shoulder the size of a small country. In not so many words, she was asking for Edward's worst, and she was getting it.

"You're right," she admitted, with a reluctant chuckle. "No I wouldn't. This is just like old times, huh, Edward?"

"Not all of our old times were like this, Grace. It was the end result, though. And listen, I can't let you get away with being the bigger person. I could have chosen my words more carefully, but *Muriel* and I have been working out a minor snag with my long hours away from the family. I shouldn't have let that get in the way when I ran into you. It's been a long couple of months."

"Now that, I understand. See, for my son André, it's been

a long lifetime of wondering if his father cares about him, cares if he grows up to be something, or if his father is worth the mental energy it takes to forget he has one." It was Edward's turn to check himself. Grace couldn't see why he refused to concede that his firstborn was part of his family, too. However, Edward's true intentions were as plain as day if she'd only paid attention to what he said.

"I guess I deserved some of that. Okay, all of it. We should have had conversations like these years ago. Maybe then, things would have been different. Why don't we get together over dinner and map out some terms? It isn't too late, you know." If Grace didn't know better, she would have thought he was hitting on her instead of trying to mend fences with his child. "By the way, I saw how chummy you were with my frat brother when he interfered."

"And?" Grace uttered, more perplexed than ever. "That's got what to do with André?"

"Just how serious is it between you and Wallace? I mean really, Grace, you could do better."

"Better than what, Edward? I know you're not insinuating that your brand of better is worth mentioning." Grace put her hand over her mouth, as she felt sick to her stomach. "Is that why you all of a sudden fell from the sky after all this time, because your dutiful wife is tired of your idea of better? Your wife is leaving you, and you want to have a pissing contest with Wallace over me? Too triflin', Edward."

"Grace, I was excited to hear that you called, and, yes, the paralegal has gotten it in her head that my marriage hitting a rough spot has given her the opportunity to step up next. I'll fix that, but come on, you and I do have unfinished business."

It was then Grace realized that Edward's intentions concerned her love life more than they did with atoning for his lack of guidance in their son's life or apologizing for shirking his fatherly duties. Grace had never felt sorrier for any man than at that very moment. More so, she was determined to shield André from ever feeling like she did then, empty to the core. "Say his name, Edward," Grace demanded calmly. "Since we've been discussing our son, you haven't once said his name. I want to hear you say your son's name. Say it! André! Say it! I want to hear you say that your name is Edward, and your son's name is André."

"I'm not playing this game of yours, Grace. I know very well what my son's name is. Let's you and I meet and talk about—"

"I'm all talked out, Edward. This is the end of the line. It's obvious that you don't know me like you think you do, so I'll make it plain. Don't ever go getting all up in my face about André the way you did last week or there may not be anyone around to stop me from doing what I will . . . do to you." Tears raced down her cheeks as she steadied her voice. "I won't let you hurt him, not like this."

"Oh, now you're threatening me?" Edward popped off indifferently. "Whatever."

"I wasn't finished," Grace answered quickly. "If you force me to hurt you in order to keep André safe from you, I will. You'd be smart to forget about our unexpected run-in, if that's what it was. *I* don't want you. And, *we* don't need you." The next sound Edward heard was a long, cold, dial tone. Grace had said her piece, and meant every single word.

23

Tossin' and Turnin'

Two days had crept by slowly since Grace told Edward where to get off, but that didn't stop him from harassing her at the office. She didn't accept his calls or read any of the lengthy messages he left with Marcia. Actually Grace ignored just about everything, including her work at the marketing firm. She had immersed herself in going backwards to avoid her present state of unrest. Closed up in her office, she played with the idea of hooking up with someone from her past until she'd had her fill of passionate memories and needed something more substantial, something real. On the way out of the parking garage, she called Greg, who was very surprised to hear from her. She asked if he had a free minute to talk. He said that he did, but only a minute because he was expecting company within the hour. Grace verified that she would have said what was on her mind and be out of his hair by then.

When she arrived at his home, she neglected to park her SUV in his garage. Greg was putting the finishing touches on a collection of cartoon animals he'd created for a top television network. Covered in an assortment of watercolors, he answered the door with paintbrush in hand. Grace pressed her chest against his, finessed the brush from his hand, and then tossed it on the floor. Greg opened his mouth to protest, but she shoved her tongue in it.

"Okay, that's different," he moaned. "Ooh, good different."

"Mmmm, shut up. I thought I'd come by for a little touch and tickle," Grace told him, ripping his T-shirt from the neck on down. She groped at the swelling in his pants with her hands, and kissed his chest with her full lips. "Can you handle that, huh? A little touch and tickle?"

"You know I can, but you said you wanted to talk," he mentioned halfheartedly.

"Yeah, about that," Grace cooed, sucking on his nipple while unfastening his blue jeans, "I decided that wasn't going to be enough for me. How about you? You'd rather talk, Greg?"

"Who me? Nah, I'm speechless. When a fine woman shoves her hand down my pants, ain't much else to say." As Greg watched Grace strip off her clothes like never before, he remembered why her hormones were boiling over. "Grace, this might be a bad time to bring it up, but what about that celibacy thing you were into?"

"We're not going all the way, just far enough to remind me what I've been missing." Grace jumped on him in the middle of his living room after he tripped over the bunched denim surrounding his ankles.

"What do I get out of this?" he asked, nearly out of breath.

"You get to wash my back," Grace answered seductively, then pulled every stitch of clothing off his body.

"That'll, that'll work for me." Greg was counting himself lucky that he had found the best kind of woman, as far as he could tell, one who was backsliding and didn't make any bones about it. He didn't want to take any chances on Grace coming to her senses, so he hurried into the bathroom. He couldn't get the water going fast enough. "It's good and hot," he panted. "Come on in."

"Whooo. It's perfect," Grace moaned, as she stepped beneath the showerhead. "Don't say another word. I'd rather you used your mouth to make me scream." Greg's face lit up after hearing Grace's command. "Just a little maintenance, and I'll be all right," she said, breathing heavily. Eager to please, Greg lowered himself to his knees. Anticipation traveled through Grace's entire body as she guided his head between her thighs and held it there. While gyrating feverishly, her legs began to tremble. "Ooh, Greg. It won't be long. It won't be long. Hmmm, it's good. You're taking me there, baby. You're gonna fool around and make me . . . make me . . . ooh-oohhh . . . ahhhhh!" she screamed endlessly. "Ahhhhhhhhh!" Her body jerked profusely, and her legs weakened.

Greg dashed from the shower soaking wet. He left Grace standing there, in the rapture of lust, just long enough to slap on a condom. Soon after returning, he bent Grace over the bathtub to give her more than she came there for. She grasped for something to hold on to but her hands found the flimsy shower curtain instead. Greg's bare feet slipped on the wet tile as Grace ripped the curtain from the rod. "Here. Greg, right here," she told him, gesturing wildly toward a puddle of water on the bathroom floor.

Moving rapidly to do as he was instructed, Greg pulled Grace down on top of him. Grace's face contorted with ecstasy. "You've been missing it too, haven't you?" she hollered. "You've been missing this! Is it good? It's good? Give it to me! Give it to me!" Greg kept on giving it to her until they both collapsed on the floor in a mound of steaming flesh, thoroughly satisfied and completely spent.

Grace climbed off of him and stumbled to the towel rack to dry off. She was fully dressed and before Greg knew it, she was on her way out of his house. "Grace, you gonna call me, right? Grace!" he yelled from the open door, wrapped in a damp towel.

As Grace backed her car out of the driveway another woman was pulling hers in. Grace sneered at the white woman in a gray soccer-mom minivan, then she slammed on the brakes. The stark expression staring back at her was one of jealously and disbelief. Grace hit the power window button. Once the window lowered, she leaned over to get a good look at the date she'd beat out for the starting rotation. "Sorry, but you might want to turn that thing around and go home," Grace suggested recklessly. She felt intoxicated, having let it all hang out merely minutes before. "Believe me, he's got nothing left."

When Grace tore out of the driveway, Greg sprinted after the minivan heading down the opposite side of the residential street. He waved furiously with one hand and held on to the towel with the other. Grace could still hear him shouting, "Come back, Muriel! Come back! What did she say to you? Come baaack! She's my cousin. Ahh, man, I'm getting too old for this." It didn't occur to Grace at the time that Greg's Muriel was also the same Muriel she'd read about from the Yahoo article outlining Edward's pending separation. Maybe now that she'd fallen out with Greg, those very public differences she had with her husband wouldn't be so gravely irreconcilable.

Three days after ruining Greg's playdate with the minivan-driving soccer mom, Grace was desperately trying to deal with breaking her solemn vow. Satan had chased her into the arms of contempt. It hadn't occurred to Grace that he had constructed a catastrophic set of circumstances by using André's wish to get to know his father against her. Meanwhile, she was growing closer to despising the woman she had become, one who allowed fear and uncertainty to derail her. Satan was busy pulling at her soul from both sides and in the middle. Fear and uncertainty rendered Grace utterly confused, twisted in the worst way and trading in her faith because of it.

The Friday afternoon call she received from Tyson was

met with a welcome grin. He said he'd been thinking about Grace and wanted to know if she'd make time for a couple of drinks to ease his yearning for her. She agreed without hesitation on a time and place, but that meant having to skip André's important basketball game. Typically, missing out on a significant event in her son's life would have been out of the question before, but Tyson's call hit Grace where it hurt. *There'd be other games*, she convinced herself after the Devil jumped into the deal and made her tragically defective logic seem perfectly rational. Tyson wanting to meet with Grace in public was a new development for him, but Grace's flawed reasoning caused her to see this as an opportunity she couldn't pass up. Other than their quiet day at the park, Tyson was adamantly opposed to being seen with any woman, citing it as a privacy issue he'd just as soon not discuss. *This could be it, the turning of the tide*, Grace foolishly convinced herself. Likewise, she tried to convince herself that it wasn't so bad hooking up with Greg because that allowed her to get everything out of her system. Anyway, all Grace would be willing to give Tyson was a chance to be heard, that's what she wanted to believe.

Grace sat out in the parking lot of Café Bleu, an upscale happy hour spot on the north side. She wore her favorite dress, a camel-colored Gucci that fit her body like a glove. Tyson had bought it for her while on one of his business trips to New York months ago. He didn't have to ask her size beforehand. He simply showed up with the gift wrapped in a Neiman's box with a satin bow. He'd even seen her in it once, complimented how nicely it accentuated her figure, and then he'd immediately begun peeling it off with his teeth. When that memory came back to Grace as crisp as a hot southern sunrise, a haunting chill rolled over her. She considered calling Tyson to cancel but couldn't muster up the power to dial his number once she'd recognized his car parked a few spaces over from hers. "What to do?" she heard herself say. "I'm here now, and so is he." Grace turned off the ignition and sat there, watching as people entered the restaurant she, at one time, frequented on a regular basis. However, it lacked the same allure that it once did. The neon sign didn't shine as brightly, nor did the anticipation of meeting someone to share her free time with. It was the same but different, and not the type of good different Greg had mentioned. Against Grace's better judgment, she was determined to meet Tyson, have a few drinks, and listen—only listen. But first, she had something to say.

God. It's me again—Grace. I sure hope you're listening because I really need you to hear me tonight. I know that you're well versed on my shortcomings concerning sins of the flesh, so I'll get right to it. Lately, my desires have gotten the best of me. This celibacy thing we've talked about isn't working out quite like I'd hoped. It seems that the harder I try to do right, the more I want to do wrong. Not that it's an excuse, it's just that I get so lonely sometimes. I've even fooled myself into thinking that sharing a man's warm embrace could somehow satisfy those urges, but it's never enough. Eventually, I find myself wanting more and more until, well, you know the rest. I guess what I'm praying for is some extra consideration this evening because that old feeling has me wanting to do the kinds of things I promised I wouldn't. You know my weakness, so I'm asking for the strength to make it through the night. Thank you, God, for hearing me out. In Jesus' name. Amen.

Grace's eyes darted up toward the sky as she climbed out of her vehicle. Although she felt uncomfortable and out of place when entering the hot spot, she needed to be sure what awaited her on the inside.

"I'll have a cranberry on the rocks," Grace told the bartender, apprehensively surveying the swarming pickup joint. Tyson appeared unexpectedly before her drink had arrived. "Hey, you," she hailed.

"Grace," Tyson replied warmly. He actually embraced her

like it had been decades since he'd done so. "That dress. There's that dress I've been dreaming about."

"I'm surprised you remember. It was thrown clear across the room the last time you laid eyes on it." Grace was happy she'd decided to stay because Tyson was the best-looking man in the entire restaurant, and he was with her. Although it wasn't a declaration of love, it wasn't a bad start.

"I saw your car outside," she said, her eyes all aglow. "When did you get here?"

"Not too long ago, but seeing you in that dress makes me wish we were alone, somewhere else, you know what I'm saying," he added with emphasis.

"I just got here, what's your hurry?" After having asked God for strength, Grace did not want to go out like that, at least not that fast. "I thought we'd hang for a minute and soak up the atmosphere and catch up," Grace suggested.

"Grace, I'd love to. Sitting here with you is real cute, but I'm not going to have all these people in my business. I'm feeling *extra* after a double shot of that Grey Goose. You know better than anyone what that does to me." Tyson planted an extremely endearing kiss on her neck. "Better than anyone." Yes, she knew all too well that expensive vodka added the extra punch Tyson had alluded to. "I'm going to step into the men's room. Please don't break my heart when I get back." The thought of getting some of Tyson's *extra* caused Grace's head to swim. She was daydreaming about it when a man she'd met recently approached her, arm in arm with a very attractive woman.

"Grace Hilliard, I knew that had to be you causing a commotion up in here," the man complimented. "Brotha's finally stopped trying to get at my woman when you came in."

"I'm sorry, you look familiar but . . ." Grace responded, unable to figure out who that incredibly charming man was.

"Kenton, Kenton Reese," he said eventually, his ego slightly bruised when Grace didn't readily recognize him.

"You have our marketing account, Dream Creams. Remember we met? The conference room?"

It did finally dawn on her that Kenton was the man she'd flipped over after Chandelle's big build-up. "Oh, yeah. I'm sorry."

"Don't apologize Grace," chuckled Kenton's pretty date. "He could stand a dose of humility every now and then. I'm Delta, Kenton's fiancée."

"Oh, I remember now," Grace said excitedly. "Kenton did tell me that he was in love with some adorable sistah he couldn't do without." Grace did fudge on Kenton's appraisal regarding his utter devotion, but she didn't see any harm in it. "You've trained him well, and I'm taking notes."

Kenton laughed. "Okay, I know when I'm outnumbered. It was good seeing you again, Grace. Our products are flying off the shelves since you took the helm on our campaign with Allen Foray. Much respect."

"Don't mention it. Dream Creams' success is doing wonders for our numbers as well." Grace winked at Kenton's fiancée with the utmost respect. "Delta, hold him close, girl, he's a keeper."

"He ain't crazy. I'd have him arrested then kill him dead if he tried to leave me. We's gon' get married and make us some babies," she joked, pulling Kenton closer while she was at it.

"I know that's right," Grace co-signed, genuinely happy for Delta despite having just met her.

"That reminds me of something we discussed at the tail end of our meeting," Kenton mentioned in parting. "The right one find you yet?"

"Not that I know of, but a wise woman told me that I should learn to look lost."

Delta's expression changed when she saw the two of them bonding in a way she wasn't all that secure with. "That sounds like great advice, Grace. Good luck."

"Thanks, Delta. Nice meeting you. And Kenton, I'll be

expecting a wedding invitation in the mail. Send it to the office, you know the address."

Tyson jingled his car keys to announce that he was back and ready to take the party to that other place he'd hinted at. Grace stood up from the bar stool and took his hand. After exiting the restaurant, she yanked on it. "Hold on Tyson, wait a minute. You know, you told me that I would want more than you were willing to give, and you were so right about that. I do want more. Unless something has changed on your end, I have no business doing what you're trying to take me some other place to do. I'm way past playing around in hotel rooms near the loudest ice machines you can find. So, if that's still your best offer?"

Tyson huffed. He shook his head and gazed up at the darkening sky. "You're about to break my heart, aren't you, Grace?"

"Your spirits, maybe, but I've never been close enough to your heart to make a dent."

Tyson appeared to be more disappointed than heartbroken over the possibility of being turned down. "So what are you saying?"

"Look at me," Grace insisted when he began pouting like a spoiled little boy. "Do you want to be my man, Tyson? Answer me. You want to be my man? Because that's the least I'm willing to settle for." Grace placed her fingertips against his thick chest. "The very least," she added to remove any doubt that she was serious.

Tyson winced as if he'd been stabbed in the heart. "Is it like that, Grace, the very least?"

"Yes indeed. See, there's this other guy I know. *He* wants to be my man. *He* wants to take care of me. And *He* is willing to love me back unconditionally. *His* name is *Jesus*, and what he's offering is a whole lot better than your sneak'n-freak'n idea of commitment. Sorry, but that's not gon' get it anymore. Not even close. Why don't you go on back inside and wave your car keys around? You're bound to catch something; brothas like you always do. I've got the second half of a freshman basketball game to make. Good-bye, Tyson." He remained there, on that same piece of cracked pavement, with his mouth hanging open as Grace hit the avenue and disappeared into the sunset.

24

A Can't-Miss Treat

Leaving Tyson in the dust was the easiest decision Grace had had to make in weeks. She had regained her inner strength, and the fears that had consumed her were all but a distant memory. Although she was sorry for her recent transgressions, her repentant spirit was emphatically opposed to allowing brief moments of weakness to prevent her from being the Christian she wanted to be. Grace's expectations were high and her mind was fixed on enjoying life as intended, diligently seeking the Kingdom, and keeping her eye on that prize. She also expected trials and tribulations to continue because the Bible teaches that following Jesus requires crosses to bear. No, it wouldn't be easy, but anything worth having never was.

After parking at the back of the high-school parking lot and noting the vast collection of cars, Grace gathered that the basketball game was more important than she had previously predicted. She didn't want to imagine how badly guilt and sorrow would have beat on her like a kettledrum had she missed it for a meaningless tryst with Tyson. Thank God for miracles, large and small.

Very appreciative that He was still in the blessing business, an affectionate smile accompanied Grace into the gymnasium. It beamed even brighter when she saw that Wallace manned the cash box at the door. "Heyyy Grace, glad you could make it," greeted the extremely happy cash-box attendant. "That son of yours is lighting up the scoreboard."

"Wow, it's packed in here," Grace hollered over the cheering fans. "Where's the other guy, the one who normally works the door?"

Wallace narrowed his eyes and pulled Grace closer to him so that he wouldn't have to shout his answer. "He was arrested last week. Got caught spying on the girls' locker room from a hole he'd drilled. They ran a story on the news and everything."

"I haven't watched TV in months, but I knew something was wrong about him," she said, while digging in her purse. "Here, this is all I have." Grace pulled out a twenty, but Wallace refused it.

"No, this one's on me. Enjoy the game."

"What?" she yelled over the noise.

"I said, enjoy the game!" Wallace repeated louder. He handed her an orange-and-blue pom-pom fastened to a thin wooden stick. "You'll need this for the game. It's a good one."

"Oh, thanks. See you later," Grace answered before stepping away to hunt for an available seat.

The second half got under way as she reached the home team's bleachers. André whizzed by her with the ball, blazing up the court. She watched him direct his teammates in the same fashion Wallace had directed his class. Players dashed in and out with precise maneuvers as André instructed. Grace was amazed at how fluently her child moved with the basketball. He was in a zone, scoring, slashing, and rebounding as if possessed. Everyone was screaming André's name and waving handmade signs to root him on. Intermittently, Grace glanced at the door where Wallace sat behind the small table. Each time she looked his way, he was looking back at her. She almost felt like a high-school kid herself, participating along with a roaring crowd and shouting names of the players she heard others chant.

There was a time-out called with ten seconds left on the clock after André had his ball stolen. He'd been careless and dribbled it away from his body. Grace remembered Skyler telling him that would happen against a better opponent. The team's coach pointed his finger in André's chest when the boy lowered his head. Grace wasn't bent out of shape over some coach getting in her son's face about feeling down on himself because she would have done the same thing had she been close enough.

"Keep your head up, boy!" Grace shouted boldly. "Don't give up, Dré, ten seconds is a long time!" Those seated near Grace applauded her optimism despite their team being behind by one point.

"You tell him, honey!" bellowed the leggy blonde Grace had met in line that night outside Wallace's classroom.

"Spartans! Spartans! Spartans!" they cheered increasingly louder as the referee whistled for play to resume.

Grace held her breath when the other team passed the ball around to run off the remaining seconds. André's expression hardened. Grace hadn't seen him so immersed in a battle since he was four years old and struggling to conquer the alphabet. With his tongue poking out of the corner of his mouth the way she remembered from back then, André chased the boy who'd taken his ball. "That's it, Dré!" Grace screeched at the top of her lungs. "Stay with it!"

As if he'd heard his mother's voice amid hundreds of others who were shouting directives while the clock ticked down to six seconds, André lunged at the ball handler and cut his eyes at the opposing player moving toward him. He doubled back and slid between them. The ball dribbled off someone's shoe. Grace's heart stopped when André scooped it up and sprinted down the hardwood toward his team's basket. The clock ticked down to one second. Grace closed her eyes and turned her head away. A resounding hush fell over the audience as André hoisted a shot from the half-court line. The buzzer sounded just as the basketball swooshed through the net. Pandemonium filled the tiny gymnasium. Grace was the last person to learn that her son's team had won the game.

"He made it?" she asked frantically. "He made it?" All she could hear was screams of jubilation that André's miraculous shot was nothing but net. Her chest swelled with pride as he was mobbed by his teammates. Pom-poms flew, and Grace thanked God again for allowing her to witness André's finest moment.

Grace was jostled and shaken while receiving thunderous congratulatory pats on the back typically awarded to the father of outstanding athletes after they had performed the unthinkable, but she was just as pleased to accept the accolades that she deserved both as mother and father.

"Dré actually made that shot," Grace said to Skyler for the umpteenth time as her son exited the locker room following a short team meeting. He had the game ball tucked beneath his arm like the old teddy bear he wouldn't be seen without until he started preschool and discovered that teddy bears weren't allowed.

"Yeah, but he shouldn't have got his ball snatched in the first place," Skyler teased him. "Ain't that right, Rookie?"

"You told me to keep it close," André replied, with a colossal dose of humility. "I got it back, though, didn't I?"

"And you knew what to do with it too," Skyler gushed approvingly.

"Atta boy," Grace squealed with delight. "Ain't no quit in him."

"I'm a Hilliard, Ma," André said as if it went without saying. He handed Grace the game ball, then threw his long arms around her neck.

"What's this for?" she asked as Wallace eased up behind the family reunion in session.

"It's for the most valuable player, Grace," Wallace informed her. She blushed when he reached out to congratulate her.

André nodded his head. "Tell her, Mr. Peters. The best player deserves the rock. We couldn't have done it without you, Ma."

"I don't understand," she said, confused by the ceremony and its sentiment. "I didn't have my behind out there fighting for every second until the time ran out."

"Maybe not, but I heard you in the stands," André explained. "I heard you telling me to stay with it."

"Yeah, we all heard her," Skyler joked, using his fingertips to plug both ears. "I probably won't be hearing anything else for a long time either."

"Go on, boy," she giggled. "If I didn't bust an eardrum every now and then, what kinda mother would I be?"

"Not mine," André chuckled. "Y'all ought to hear her yelling at me to get out of bed in the morning. That would wake the dead." He and Skyler wandered off to join a group of students loitering near the exit.

Grace held the basketball like a Mother-of-the-Year trophy. "What do I do with this?" she asked finally.

Wallace rubbed the top of it with his left hand, then hunched his shoulders. "An award such as this doesn't come every day. It's suitable for mounting."

Grace agreed. "Then that's just what I'll do. I'll have it mounted so everyone can see what my son thinks of me."

Wallace slid both hands in his trouser pockets as he was accustomed to doing when nervous. "I'm very glad that you made it here to see the big finish. Some things can't be appreciated the same way, hearing about them secondhand. It kinda makes you want to celebrate, doesn't it?"

Knowing what he was driving at, Grace batted her eyes. "Are you asking me out on a postgame victory date?"

"That depends. If you'll say yes, I am. You know how hard it is for a man to deal with rejection from a beautiful lady. I'd hate to put it out there and have it come back all beat down and stepped on." Although Wallace had made several attempts to contact Grace by phoning her, she hadn't returned a single one of his calls, so he figured his chances were slim to none.

Grace studied his pitiful expression and couldn't help but feel sorry for him. "Wallace, I would love to, let me check with Dré." Grace had another reason to be thankful for ending up in the right place at the right time. Wallace's stock was rising in the available-men market. On a real date, she'd have an opportunity to investigate his long-term yield potential before making a sizable investment. It was finally time for Corporate Grace to sit down and take notes for Grace the mother, and CEO of Team Hilliard. Regardless of the outcome, she had already begun to value Wallace's friendship immensely.

It took some doing, but Grace managed to tear André away from a particular cheerleader with a fondness for a coming-of-age Hilliard man. He was glad to hear that Grace wasn't there to drag him home. André had been working up the nerve to ask her if he could trot off for burgers with Portia. Grace wasn't in favor of him and the precocious cheerleader being alone for a solitary minute, so she struck a deal.

"Get Portia's mother on the phone," she demanded. "If she says it's okay, then Wallace and I will make it a foursome."

"Ahh man," André protested. "Ma, you're kidding right? Forget about it then. I don't like her that much."

"Suit yourself. I'll tell Wallace—Mister Peters—that we

can celebrate another time." Grace turned to walk away, hoping André would experience a change of heart.

"Okay, okay," he whined under his breath. "It doesn't matter that Portia's a sophomore, and a cheerleader captain with her own car?"

"Oh, that cinches it. Now I know that I'll need to holla at her parents. Her own car? Humph, I'll be standing over here when it's time to introduce myself to her people." Wallace had been watching the interaction between them but couldn't make heads or tails of it when Grace returned wearing an odd expression. As he asked for the verdict, she shook her head. "I'm not sure," she answered. "But I think I just brokered a double-date with my own child. Lawd have mercy."

Portia whipped out a top-of-the-line cell phone and dialed up her father, who happened to be a judge. The Honorable Howard Rosewood spoke to Grace. He vouched that his daughter was extremely trustworthy and respectful for a girl her age. Then he went further and applauded Grace for caring enough to get involved. It was set, a double date at French's Fries, a greasy spoon that offered a clog-your-heart menu. Grace hadn't eaten any high-fat, high-calorie junk in such a long time that she was really looking forward to it.

Portia led the way, Grace followed closely, André and Wallace brought up the rear. Their caravan motored into the diner's parking lot. Grace was tickled when it appeared that the cunning little cheerleader-chick made an effort to park her foreign two-seater sports car at the farthest end of the lot so that she and Dré could enjoy a long, quiet walk up, and perhaps the same after dinner. The girl had spunk, Grace conceded. She liked that, mostly because Portia reminded Grace of herself as an overly aggressive tenth grader.

Wallace met them inside the burger pit. "I've asked for a booth, if that's all right?" His comment was directed at Grace, but her son intercepted it.

"I'd rather sit over there," André answered, pointing

across the restaurant to a small table near the kitchen. "Is that cool with you, P?" he hinted to Portia.

"Huh? Oh, yeah, we'll give the grown-ups some privacy," she offered slyly. "Besides, they don't want to be bored with our juvenile conversation. Come on, Dré." *Come on, Dré?* That little hussy had probably been ordering boys around since she'd discovered how easy that was to do. Grace had to hand it to her, though, she was a fast learner.

When André started out after Portia, Grace tugged at his gym shirt. "Hey, you have any money?" she asked quietly so as not to embarrass him.

"Yeah, but she's treatin'."

"So!" Grace snapped. "You shouldn't get in the habit of letting women pay your way. Man up and handle the check when it comes. Got me?"

"Yes, ma'am," André answered, his eyes cast down toward the floor. "Anything else?"

"No. Have a good time, son. If Portia wants to drive you home, I guess that'll be okay, too." Dré's eyes widened with anticipation. "Straight home," Grace clarified when it appeared he'd gotten a bit too excited.

"Thanks, Ma. See you later." André looked in the young girl's direction. "I'll be over there if you need me." He strolled off casually with his heart pounding and ego lifted. It was the ending to a perfect evening for him: a winning shot and his first date with the prettiest girl in school.

On the other side of the burger joint, Wallace welcomed Grace back. "Is everything going to be okay? Looks like you had a bit of trouble cutting the apron strings."

"Shoot, I barely had a chance to see what the boy was up to before he snatched them off," she told him, with a concerned expression. "He's really growing up fast, Wallace."

Not sure how to respond to that, Wallace grinned instead. "I'll bet. I've seen him mature in the short time he's been in my class. You've done well."

Grace blushed nervously, then fidgeted with various

items on the table. "Sometimes I wonder how much further along he'd be if, you know, he'd had a man around."

"By *a man*, you mean Edward?" Wallace questioned for more reasons than one.

Again Grace fidgeted before she breathed life into what had been troubling her. "I don't know what I mean. Edward is the boy's father. Although it doesn't seem right, him trying to claw his way back into Dré's life like this. Maybe it's too late for him to come around trying to play the good-daddy role." Wallace leaned back in his chair. He pretended to read over the menu, but he didn't fool Grace. "What?" she asked, wide eyed and wanting to know why he opted to remain silent on the matter.

"It's none of my business, Grace. And anyway, you probably wouldn't like my answer." Wallace looked up to find her staring at him, so he had no choice but to continue. "I feel that a child, especially a young man, should have every opportunity to bond with his father, unless of course it becomes detrimental."

Grace frowned playfully, then sneered at Wallace. "Who asked you?" she joked. "Next time, mind your own business."

Wallace laughed as he threw up both hands in a defensive posture. "See, you had to ask."

"You don't even like Edward, and you're taking his side. I see how this works, men sticking together."

"It has nothing to do with what I think of Edward. If he fell off the end of the earth, that'd be fine with me." His harsh words concerned Grace because she didn't have an inkling as to what caused them. This edgy side of Wallace was one she hadn't seen.

"Was it that serious, what went down between you two?" she asked apprehensively. After the waiter took their orders, she got more of an answer than she'd bargained for.

Wallace was fidgeting now, and he had a difficult time maintaining eye contact because Grace had unknowingly opened up an old wound that had yet to heal completely. "Do you know why tonight's basketball game was so important?" Grace shook her head that she didn't. "The last time a John Quinn High School's freshman squad beat Judson Prep was eight years ago. It wasn't a big deal then, but the star of that team was Skyler's older brother, Donnell. He was a talented kid. As a senior, he was touted as a can't-miss pro prospect, the same way Skyler is now. Every college in the country wanted Donnell, and all he wanted to do was help his grandmother put food on the table so Skyler would have a decent meal. Those boys had to bury their mother a couple of years prior to that. Money was scarce, so Donnell hooked up with some rough dudes from the block. Nothing big at first, a couple of break-ins." Grace envisioned Skyler's face as Wallace traveled deeper into the story. "Eventually, Donnell got himself jammed up over a liquor store robbery. The owner told the police that the star basketball player was driving the getaway car."

As Grace listened attentively, she became a bundle of nerves. "Was it Donnell behind the wheel?" she asked pensively.

"Well, a tired grandmother showed up at my office bright and early one morning asking me to prove that it wasn't."

"Miss Pearl," Grace thought aloud. "But why you?"

"Yeah, Miss Pearl. It seems like a millions years ago. I was a young attorney, full of myself, and competent enough. She begged me to take the case, saying how Donnell had always been a good person but had a chip on his shoulder because of his mother's drug overdose. Miss Pearl convinced me that although he'd made some mistakes, he deserved another chance, a better chance for a good life. I agreed, took the case, and went up against this new hotshot Assistant District Attorney fresh off the Atlanta Circuit of Appeals courthouse steps." Grace didn't have to say Edward's name to confirm that's who Wallace was talking about. "The DA's office put on a good case, but all Edward saw was another menace to society fit for a jail cell. He wanted a conviction, and his name in the papers attached to it. I swayed the jury into believing that a man shouldn't be judged solely by the company he keeps. I argued that Donnell was in the car but had no prior knowledge of the planned robbery. Edward didn't prove otherwise, so Donnell was found innocent. He went home as if nothing had ever happened. The college recruiters were staked out at his house just as they done before, fighting for the opportunity to sign him to a four-year scholarship."

Grace was reluctant to ask the burning question. "Then, how did he get killed?"

"This is where the story gets sketchy. Within a month, Donnell was in another car outside another liquor store that was being robbed when a police cruiser happened to roll by. They got into a shootout with the thugs inside. Donnell was hit several times in the crossfire."

There was pain behind Wallace's gaze then, a pain cutting so deep that Grace couldn't fully comprehend it. "That's why Miss Pearl said to tell you that she understood what you're trying to do for Skyler?" Grace said, finally piecing it all together.

"It's the least I can do, considering how I'm partly responsible for Donnell's death. If I hadn't defended him, he'd be in prison instead of in the ground. Over one thousand days later, I'm still at war, with my love for the law on one side and Donnell's blood on my hands on the other. My penance is to see to it that Skyler makes it to college, so I took a job at his high school to look after him and others before they make life-altering or life-ending decisions."

"Oh, Wallace, it wasn't any more your fault than it was Edward's for losing the case to you," Grace asserted thoughtfully. She placed her hand on his. "You did the right thing. Sometimes events happen out of our control. You did what a good lawyer was supposed to do. You looked out for your client. God had other plans for Donnell. God took him," she added, allowing her conviction to guide her words.

"I wish I could feel the same way, Grace. True enough, I can't fault Edward. He hadn't been in town that long, and the trial embarrassed him. I was a nobody who took down one of the city's brightest legal minds. Edward holds a grudge to this day over getting his hat handed to him in court."

"That sounds like my baby-daddy all right," Grace joked to lighten the mood. "He always did take losing like a bitter pill. I remember how angry he got once when I spanked his behind in a friendly game of Scrabble. He called me a cheat and flipped the board over."

"It was that same attitude that caused a troop of officers to separate us," Wallace confessed with a wide grin. "Edward and I came to blows outside the courtroom after I'd outfoxed him. Sometimes, I wonder if he'd gotten the best of me, I would have felt any better about myself at Donnell's funeral."

Grace tilted her head back but kept her eyes locked on Wallace's. "Uh-uh, don't you let *anybody* put a mark on that face," she flirted openly. "I've gotten quite used to seeing it just the way it is, and I couldn't stand to see it any other way."

25

Diggin' You, Baby

Grace exchanged subtle glances with Wallace throughout dinner. When the bill arrived, she tried to wrestle it away from him. "No, no. I'm paying for this," she insisted. Wallace leaned in with a smooth and determined demeanor.

"Are you going to let André's date shell out money for him to stuff his face after feeding his ego?" he questioned wisely.

"Of course not. I told Dré he better not let Portia pay for his dinner," Grace contended in no uncertain terms. "I didn't raise him that way."

"Good, you just made my point," Wallace replied craftily. "My mother didn't raise me that way either." He'd finessed the bill from Grace through some pretty slick back door litigating.

"You tricked me," Grace pouted. "You knew I would expect Dré to step up, didn't you?"

"More than that, I counted on it. Any lawyer worth his salt gets the best results by asking questions he already knows the answers to. Just gotta know what to ask," Wallace threw in as a bonus. He was clever, very clever. Grace found herself admiring that quality about him, among other things. She hadn't given the date much thought before she sat down, but she found herself enjoying every bit of it and dreading the moment for it to end. In the meanwhile, she'd dig in and ride the current until it bucked her, hoping for a chance to saddle up again.

Grace pitched an awkward smile in Wallace's direction. "The first time I saw you at the gym, I wondered why you were there, who you were, and what you spent your days doing. I had no idea you were giving back to the community like most of us say we will. I didn't have a clue that meeting you would turn into something this nice. I'm sorry for ignoring the messages you left on my home number."

"Yeah, I made no bones about leaving André my work, home, and cell numbers, and then I had him read them back to me. I was pushing it when I gave him the number at *my mama's* house."

"You did not," Grace sang playfully.

"No, but I would have if I thought it would have worked. I wanted to see you again, Grace. Is that so bad?" Once again, he asked a question where he was certain of the answer.

"Truth be told, I wouldn't have minded running into you," she revealed as if it pained her to do so. "Not that I've been looking forward to it, but I thought you'd have asked me by now why I've blown you off."

Wallace crossed his arms and nodded slowly for effect. "Now that's a good question, one that undoubtedly would not benefit me. However, I suspected that you needed time to work out some kinks in your life. You couldn't do that with me hanging around. I figured you'd eventually realize what I have already."

Grace was as curious as a cat. "And what have you realized, Wallace?" she meowed, wanting to sample more of his scrumptious charm.

"That you and I should take some time and see if we are as compatible as I think we are." He observed Grace looking upside his head like it was sprouting horns.

"What? I know you're not talking about sexually compatible."

"See, that's the problem with most single people nowadays. No one wants to court anymore like folks did back in the old days, you know, take it slow and actually find out if you see things alike, manage your lives with similar beliefs, and both have an affinity for the Lord." Grace was still looking at him, although much differently now. "If you ask me," Wallace continued, "that's why the divorce rate is so incredibly high. Too many of us are trying to back into a great relationship the wrong way."

"Do you seriously intend for me to believe that a fine man like you isn't sexually active?" Grace blurted it out before she could stop herself. Wallace grinned so hard, it was embarrassing for the both of them.

"Ah, you think I'm fine? My assessment of you is mutual," he said, returning the compliment. "To answer your question, I am not currently sexually active at the moment, nor am I physically, emotionally, or mentally involved with anyone."

"Are you gay?" Grace blurted out again, kicking herself after the fact.

"No, never been, and I'm definitely not interested in getting down like that," Wallace answered emphatically. "Don't tell me you're one of those women so stuck on themselves they think a man who's not trying to hit the sheets must be gay?"

Grace sat up straight and stared down at the table in a self-reflecting manner. "I'd hate to think I was one of those women, but I find myself sitting here and doing my best to find something wrong with you for carrying on a decent conversation that hasn't been centered around somebody taking off their clothes. You're right. I owe you an apology, Wallace."

"Apology accepted, but I'm no saint, Grace. I've made my share of mistakes, too, but I'm trying to do better."

There were so many details Grace wanted to share regarding her dating downfalls but she couldn't see muddying the waters. "That's refreshing," she said, mulling it over. "I'm not quite on your level yet. This whole open dialogue up front and personal biz is new to me, refreshing but new. Would it be out of line if I asked how long it's been since you—"

"Yes, now that would be way out of line," Wallace answered with a surprised raised brow. "You don't know me like that. Let's keep our clothes on and see how this goes. I dig you. That'll do for now."

"Reeeally," Grace said in a slow and low manner, knowing good and well that he did, in fact, dig her very much.

"Yeah, really," Wallace whispered across the table. His eyes stayed locked on hers until they noticed time had slipped by like a sneaky thief. Neither of them knew how to say good night, so Wallace walked Grace to the car, shook her hand tenderly, then tore himself away. *Get behind me Satan*, he thought while fighting the urge to kiss her, *and stop pushing!*

Grace road a natural high all the way home. She basked in the afterglow of an old-fashioned, stimulating, grown-folks conversation about things that actually mattered. Unfortunately, an unexpected visitor knocked her off the cloud she'd ridden in on before she had the chance to thoroughly enjoy it.

An unfamiliar red Cadillac with a soccer-dad sticker in the back window rested against the curb in front of Grace's house. She noticed it but assumed that one of the neighbors had a guest who'd parked there by mistake. When she unlocked her car door, someone called out from the end of her driveway. It was Edward.

He stood there with his hands in the pockets of his business suit. "Grace!" he called out again, waiting for an invitation to come closer. When she neglected to offer one, he took slow, calculated steps toward her. Grace didn't know what to say as a knot formed in her throat. Edward said, "Sorry for showing up without clearing it with you, but I figured that a face-to-face would help foster a more civil discussion."

"Hello, Edward," Grace said eventually, her arms crossed and taut. "How did you know where I live? I've always had the child-support checks sent to a post-office box."

"I've always known. Friends in high places. You might want to remember that."

"And I thought you wanted this to be a civil discussion," she said to stay on an even keel.

"Okay, then let me start over." As he raised his hand to loosen his necktie, Grace recoiled. "What? Are you afraid of me? You think I'd come here to harm you?"

Grace was obviously guarded, and she had good reason. Edward had meant nothing but harm to her since abandoning his responsibilities. As far as she knew, a strange man was stalking her, and had the nerve to pop up at her front door. "Honestly, I don't know what to think, but I need for you to leave. You have not been invited, and I'm very uncomfortable with this," she maintained evenly.

"I'll bet André disagrees with you," Edward predicted arrogantly. "Let's ask him if I'm welcome or not."

"So you finally learned to say his name. Good for you. However, Dré doesn't make any decisions here, your being here is highly inappropriate, and you are trespassing. Don't make me call the boys in blue and turn your idea of a face-to-face into something more triflin' than it already is."

Edward huffed, staring up at the sky. "Huh, guess I was wrong about you. Church-goin' Christians supposed to be hospitable and all." He made the mistake of getting under Grace's skin after he'd failed miserably at his original goal, getting under her dress. "Is this what Jesus would do?" he asked, for the sole purpose of provoking her.

"I couldn't say for sure with a hundred percent certainty, but I'd have to guess that He wouldn't be so quick to invite a devil inside His home either." Two points for Grace. She'd met Edward's loaded question with a proper response befitting a Christian. "With that, I'll say good night and goodbye," she said defiantly.

Edward barked, louder than she thought necessary, "I am going to see Dré and—"

"Don't you call him that! That's a term of endearment and affection. You don't deserve to call him that. As a matter of fact, I've had about enough of your sorry *going to's* and *fixing to's* for one night. Now you can stand here until the police show up, or you can take my advice and trot on back to Muriel and *your family*." Edward acquiesced to avoid being threatened with a police arrest tacked onto his otherwise distinguished résumé and headed back the way he came with his tail tucked between his legs. He knew Texas stalking laws were severe and left no wiggle room for unwanted trespassers. Edward valued his position with the county, as well as his freedom. Whether he liked it or not, he was forced to play the cards Grace dealt if he truly wanted an opportunity to make amends with André.

For Grace, it was way past too late to salvage the love lost between them. Her heart pounded as she locked the dead bolt from the inside. She brushed the curtains aside with the back of her hand to see if Edward had heeded her advice. He was gone, but his presence lingered behind. Grace's head was swimming. She partially wanted to let him in for André's sake but didn't know how she could, especially since he continued pulling one Houdini act after another. What's she to do, she pondered. With the telephone trembling in her hand, she managed to dial Wallace's cell phone number, then closed her eyes to rest them.

"Hello, Grace," he answered on the first ring. "What's wrong?" How he knew something was bothering her didn't get called into question; she was simply glad that he did.

"He was here when I got home," she said using one slow breath.

"Edward," Wallace said. "Do you want me to come over?"

"No, I don't think so. He's gone now, and I doubt that he'll be coming back."

"Did he hurt you?"

"No, not where anyone could see," she replied softly.

"Is André all right?" asked Wallace, covering all bases.

"I don't think he's still awake. The light is off in his room," Grace added in a low, secretive tone.

Wallace rubbed his temples, deciding how deep he should get involved in another man's business. "You want to talk about it? I'll try to be objective, but I need you to know that'll be hard to do." He felt like jumping in his car and speeding to her rescue again. Wallace was falling and couldn't get out of his own way.

"I'm confused and torn over keeping Edward's wishes from Dré. That is his father and he should be allowed to—"

"Then give him what he wants, Grace," Wallace interjected, to help her along. "Let Edward meet his son and take it from there. André may never forgive you otherwise. It seems insane, if you ask me, but children often love the ones who've caused them the most pain, absentee fathers especially. Why don't you sleep on it and the answer you need won't be far behind."

"You mean pray on it," she said, knowing what he was asking her to do.

"Yes, open up your heart to all the possibilities, and expect the best, whatever that happens to be." Wallace's recommendation was impartial, sensible, and thoughtful. He was praying that Grace found it in herself to accept it. Only time would tell if she did.

"I'm calling it a night, Wallace." Grace didn't readily say how she planned on working out her dilemma going forward. In the meanwhile, "Thank you," would have to do.

"Hey Ma, who was that man at the door a minute ago?" André asked, behind a hearty yawn. His sudden appearance startled Grace. She was caught between the lie she started to tell and the truth keeping her from it.

"It was your father, Dré. For the past couple of weeks or so, he's been talking about seeing you." The whole truth came pouring out with reckless disregard to how the boy would take it.

"My dad! He was here?" André shot across the den to search through the window. "He was here, Ma, and you sent him away? How could you? Now he'll never come back," Dré sobbed. Grace rushed over to comfort him, but he withdrew from her embrace. "Mama, how could you do this to me? How could you?"

Grace tried to explain, but the words were stuck down so deep that she couldn't find them. Tears flooded her eyes as André bolted into his room and slammed the door. Her knocks went unanswered. From the other side, she heard the muffled cries of her son's heart breaking, and she knew she was the cause of it. Grace had to make it right. André meant the world to her, the whole world. It would be the last time she'd underestimate the power of a boy's love for his father, even if they had yet to meet. She'd always assumed that nothing could shred the strong bond she shared with André. On a night that began perfectly, she couldn't have been more wrong.

The following morning Grace awoke with puffy eyes and an enormous headache. She'd cried herself to sleep at about three A.M. but it felt like she'd been out for days. What could she do to fix the situation, played over and over like a bad made-for-TV movie rerun. She checked in the kitchen but found nothing disturbed. There wasn't one trace of cold cereal on the countertop, no remnants of spilt milk, and no other signs that André had ventured from his room. Grace couldn't bring herself to go through her normal Saturday ritual of whipping up flapjacks, cheese grits, and crisp bacon only to have her son refuse it in an adolescent act of rebellion.

She scribbled a short letter, notifying André that she'd be walking if he needed her, and placed it on the breakfast table. Grace was a mile away from her house when droplets of rain began falling from the sky. The immediate forecast hadn't called for precipitation, but in Texas weathermen were often more wrong than right.

After the initial scattered shower subsided, Grace pushed on. With another mile behind her, she felt larger drops landing on her face. Then she heard thunder as the clouds seemed to burst all at once. Caught in an escalating downpour, she wisely doubled back for home. By the time Grace reached the one mile marker, she was drenched. Water had already begun to wash over the curb, warning of a flash flood to come. She'd seen cars and homes washed away by instantaneous storms taking less than an hour to wreak havoc. Getting drowned by one of them crossed her mind so she opened her stride and jogged as long as she could before finding shelter beneath a group of large oak trees four blocks away from her street.

As the rising water began to stall several passing cars, Grace was shaken by a chorus of thunderous clamor in the darkened sky. A loud, blaring distress horn sounded, meaning that a thunderstorm warning was in effect. Grace wiped her face with the soaked sleeve of her sweatsuit, thinking how the horn's blasts came a little too late to do her any good. While watching an impressive display of lightning crackle across the sky, she sat under the mighty oaks until it was safe to venture out into the open. During the thirty-three minutes which had trickled by, she watched, waited and wondered. Grace watched the nasty storm roll in as it pleased, waited for it to let up, and wondered how long she'd have to deal with the personal storm God had seen fit to rain down on her personal life. She also sat amidst those trees, trying to better understand His plan for her and why Edward was playing a major part.

Grace had nearly given up trying when she stumbled onto a nugget from her childhood. She couldn't have been more than ten when an old minister preached a sermon about getting God's attention. He had lectured earnestly that everyone who goes through their roughest episodes has God's undivided attention because He put something on them serious enough to guarantee He'll get theirs in return. Grace was well aware that she had the Lord's attention, and figured on making the best of it while she did.

Once the rain eased into a light drizzle, Grace vacated her safe haven. Passersby gawked at the woman, who resembled something the cat dragged in, seemingly on a casual stroll. Not one of them comprehended the peculiar smile anchored to her face. It was one of peace and tranquility, two of the three things she'd prayed for. Her son's forgiveness was the third.

André stood barefoot in gym shorts underneath an umbrella at the corner. He'd found Grace's note, become alarmed, and struck out looking for her. "Ma, I was getting worried," he said, throwing his arms around her shoulders. There wasn't an inkling of anger from the night before.

"Oh, thank you so much, Dré, but you shouldn't have come out without any shoes on."

"Shoes can't help you in this stuff," he replied, splashing around in a deep puddle on the sidewalk. "You ever see a duck in a pair of shoes?"

"Well come on in the house, Duck," Grace teased. "We can talk about your dad over breakfast."

"For real?" André cheered, pumping a raised fist. "Yesss!"

26

Soup for the Soul

Grace spent the remainder of Saturday under the covers with a stuffy nose and fever as strange bedfellows. Even though she was in the confines of a warm home, she still felt cold. Wallace called twice to check on her but she was too sedated and woozy from a half bottle of Nyquil to hold a coherent conversation. André ran it down for him though, including his corny ducks having no need for shoes, barefoot in the rain, bit. He also informed Wallace how sick his mother was and promised to do his best in taking care of her. When a special delivery arrived from the local Chinese restaurant with three quarts of wonton, egg drop, and chicken-noodle soup, André set up a serving tray and waited on Grace hand and foot. He followed Wallace's instructions to the letter. Shelia called to brag about her new Deluxe Icemaker II refrigerator but the fanfare had to be postponed until Grace was up to hearing all about it, per Dr. André's strict orders.

The following morning, Grace came around slowly. Sitting through a three-hour church service was out of the question. Her head was clearer, although she couldn't shake an ugly cough-syrup hangover. She even managed a labored smile when she told Dré how proud he'd made her and thanked him for his attentiveness. André admitted that Wallace had coached him on his bedside manner but he couldn't read Grace's expression after he'd come clean.

"Son, let me share something with you," she said, propping up pillows against her headboard. "Sometimes people do things they're sorry for later, including me. It's all a part of living, I guess. Your father made a mistake many years ago. He never meant to leave us, but he was so young then, and so was I. Our plans didn't even up when it came down to it, but he loves you. He waited a long time to try and prove it, but he finally came around. I think he deserves to get to know a special kid like you." The enormous smile André hadn't yet grown into shone brightly on his face. "I've made some calls, and, well, if you want to, we can stop by and introduce you to him."

"Now? We can go now?" he beamed. "Ma, I'd really like that."

"Okay, get yourself together, and I'll do something to my head." Grace ran all ten fingers through her wild hair and laughed. "On second thought, I'll make do with a baseball cap. We don't have all day." André shot out of her room with the quickness of a jungle cat. Grace allowed Wallace's words to resonate through her mind as she climbed out of bed. *Then give Edward what he wants. Let him meet his son and take it from there. André may never forgive you otherwise.* Grace finally felt she was up to the task and felt good about it, as long as it was on her terms.

After traveling to a swanky neighborhood she'd only heard about, Grace circled the block twice. Eventually, she spotted the red Caddy parked outside a beautiful split-level, light-colored brick house on the corner. Then out of nowhere, she noticed a gray minivan like the one she passed when leaving Greg in nothing but a towel and on his own to sort out things with the pissed off white woman who showed up late for her sloppy seconds. Grace thought it unusual that the minivan had the same soccer-mom sticker on the back window. *I guess there're a lot of kids taking up soccer these days,* she decided.

"Okay, Dré. Are you ready for this?" she sighed, hoping deep inside that she would be as well.

"Uh-huh," he replied anxiously. "Let's go."

"Just a second," Grace stated abruptly. "No matter what happens, these people love you. It might take a little getting used to, for everyone, so soak it up and be strong."

"Yes, ma'am." André stared out of the car window as his mouth fell open. "That's a big house."

"It's not so much bigger than ours," she debated, slightly jealous that her son held praise for the other side of his gene pool. "I like my house just fine," she added in a snippy tone.

"Me, too. Let's go see this one," he urged, seconds before his feet hit the pavement.

Grace stood behind André as he rang the doorbell. She was nervous and vigilant, and she knew she should have been committed for popping up at Edward's house without giving him notice. André received a brisk elbow nudge when he pressed his face against the stained-glass cutout in the door. "Don't be acting all ghetto, like you haven't been anywhere," Grace reprimanded him.

Someone was approaching the door from the inside. Grace wanted to duck and run but it opened too fast for her to make a swift getaway. Edward appeared wearing faded jeans, athletic tube socks, and a black concert T-shirt from the 1980s. He took a long look at Grace, then a short one at André. "Hey," Grace announced cordially as if he had been expecting them. "Edward, aren't you going to invite us in?" she quipped, her voice high pitched and shaky. As Edward moved his lips to speak, a woman appeared behind him, a white woman.

"Eddie, who's this?" she asked, all June Cleaver–like

while studying André. When her eyes floated past the boy and connected with Grace's, the jig was up. She almost had a cow as her memory and recollection of seeing Grace before jarred her. The hateful look she tossed on her front porch would have gotten *Leave It to Beaver* cancelled.

Straight out of a scene from a prison courtyard, no one backed down from the standoff, so Grace slid into corporate mode and facilitated a meet-and-greet. "I'd prefer to do this inside, but it'll work just as well here. Edward Swenson, this is André Devon Hilliard, your son. Dré, shake the man's hand like I taught you."

Edward lumbered forward, uncomfortable as all get-out. "Hey, man, uh . . . André. It's a pleasure to finally meet you." He shook the boy's hand like he didn't know when to let go. "Uhhh . . . this is Muriel, your . . . my wife." The poor woman was as white as a sheet.

"Uhhh, h-hi André," Muriel stammered, stumbling forward, while uneasy about getting too close to the black woman standing behind him. "Miss," she saluted Grace, with a desperate expression pleading for Grace to keep her secret quiet.

"Muriel," Grace replied plainly, with an imagine-seeing-you-again smirk.

"Oh, let's get inside," Edward suggested finally. He peered up and down the street cautiously as if the neighbors were ready to turn him in to the homeowner's association for allowing two more black people into his home.

"Should I take off my shoes?" André asked after noting that neither Edward nor his petrified wife wore theirs over the plush white carpet.

"No-no, it's all right," muttered Muriel. She motioned toward the vast living area with high vaulted ceilings, then shot a nasty sneer in Edward's direction. "I'll get snacks," she mouthed, barely audible. "Grace, dear, do you mind helping me . . . in the kitchen . . . please?"

"That's a good idea. Why don't we leave the men alone

to get acquainted?" Grace didn't have to guess what Muriel the soccer mom was dying to discuss. "Nice home, by the way," Grace complimented during their short jaunt over sand-colored ceramic tile.

As soon as she set foot in the kitchen area, Muriel made a calculated about-face. She was pacing and wringing her hands, doubting she knew where to begin. "Look, Grace. I knew you recognized me the moment we met," she chattered nervously. "I'm not proud of my affair with Gregory." *Gregory*? "Eddie and I have been on the rocks for years, and we're working through it, but I just—" she explained, barely treading water before Grace jumped in to save her.

"Hey, hey! Muriel. I don't care what you and Gregory, or you and Eddie have going on. Believe me, I have enough business of my own to see to. Don't concern yourself with me telling your husband because that's your thing. How you get by has nothing to do with me."

Calmly considering Grace's nonthreatening attitude, Muriel nodded her appreciation. "Thank you. Does that mean you're not going to see Gregory anymore? I mean, this could get kinda sticky."

Only moments before, Grace had let the married woman off the hook and there she was chomping at it again. "You're kidding me, right? You got issues. Greg should be the least of your worries, unless your affair isn't casual—oh my God, you're in love with him." Grace knew she'd guessed correctly when Muriel turned beet red at the mere mention of it. "What's up with you? You have a thing for black men or something?"

"I don't want to talk about this anymore," Muriel backpedaled. Her self-righteous tone had Grace fuming.

"Greg isn't the first, is he? There have been others." Grace didn't await a response because her answer was written all over Muriel's face. "Yeah, you got issues."

"Mommy! Mommy!" squealed two of the cutest little tan-colored girls with long curly hair. "It's a boy in there with Daddy, he's our brand-new brother, and he's brown," one of them hooted.

"Hey, you guys," Muriel greeted them, like the perfect homemaker. "Becca, May. This is Miss Grace. She's your brand-new brother's mommy."

"She doesn't look all that brand-new to me," the younger of the two complained. That was May. Grace figured her for around four years old, and the other one at six or so.

"That's because she's not new, Silly," Becca blasted her younger sibling. "She just looks old because she's so brown."

"Okayyy," Grace said aloud. "It's nice meeting the two of you too. I'm going to check on the fellas." Muriel's eyes followed her out into the hall. She wondered how long Grace would keep her word about Gregory, if at all.

"So, how's it going in here?" Grace inquired, shrouded in fake merriment.

"Oh fine, fine," was Edward's take on it.

"Yeah, Ma. We're talking about basketball and school and stuff," André chimed in.

"Good, then I'll be back to get Dré in a couple of hours, if that's fine with you Edward." She'd picked up that trick from Wallace. There was no way in the world Edward had it in him to refuse sharing this special moment in time with his son, as least not to André's face. "By the way, nice house you got here, *Eddie*."

"Oh yeah, thanks," he said, like his mouth was full of rocks. "We'll talk, we'll talk later, Grace."

"I'm certain we will, at that," she chuckled on her way out.

Grace continued to laugh as she started her car, looking back at Edward's house. The empty expression on his face when Grace announced that their son was staying behind was a Kodak moment. Muriel, on the other hand, was a flatout head case. She had more skeletons buried in her backyard than a Civil War cemetery. One black man wasn't enough to satisfy her cravings—she had to rack them up by the shipload. Edward must have been coming up short between the sheets, Grace assumed, and she couldn't have been happier that it wasn't her having to hunt for homeboys in the minivan after years with dear ole *Eddie*.

After Grace hummed to the R&B station all the way home, she opened her freezer for an ice cream treat. Feeling free and easy, her pleasant humming continued until someone knocked at her door. She put the ice cream back and then strolled into the foyer, praying that it wasn't Edward all burnt out on the father-son time already and returning André, slightly used.

Shelia pounded at Grace's door again, with Linda shaking her head. "She might be asleep," Shelia told her while rapping on it more persistently.

Grace peeked out of the side window. She recognized Linda's car in her driveway, then playfully snatched the door open. "Why are y'all out here trying to knock a hole in my house?"

"That wasn't none of y'all," Linda replied. "That was her." Linda sold out Shelia and then barged in. "Move, Grace, we're hungry. I mean, we came to visit our sick friend, but since we don't see one, we're hungry."

"And I want to tell you all about Harold and my new icebox," Shelia offered, jutting her chest out as if the twins had something to do with the latest appliance to accessorize her overstocked showroom.

"Come on in then." Grace stepped aside before Shelia ran her over the way Linda had. "Thanks for checking on poor little ole me, but Wallace hooked me up some soup to make it all better."

"Ooh, Wallace. Schoolteachers make house calls now?" Shelia snipped, envy abounding. "Is he still here?"

Grace walked toward the kitchen, knowing that her cronies were sure to be in perfect step, tracing hers. "No, and he hasn't been here yet."

"All right, there's a story here, and I won't be denied." Linda plopped down in a chair and Shelia shoved her face in the refrigerator.

"Who has ever been so sick that they needed one, two, three quarts of soup," Shelia counted. "That man wanted you to get well soon, for real."

Once her guests' bowls were simmering hot, Grace broke everything down for them. She shared her son's spotlight in the sun at the basketball game, her impromptu date with Wallace, Wallace's advice regarding Edward's desire to meet Dré, and Grace giggled all the way through her synopsis explaining how she'd dumped André, practically on his daddy's doorstep for milk and cookies prepared by that hot-in-the-tail homemaker married to Edward.

Shelia cussed up a storm because she hadn't been there to witness any of it, but Linda was looking at Grace as if she had sprouted a second head. "Grace, Edward's situation is a trip, granted, but what about yours? I've sat here and listened to your Wallace this and Wallace that. You're really into him?"

"The question is, has *he* been getting into Grace?" Shelia jabbed distastefully.

When the phone rang, Grace hopped up to get it. "Good girls don't tell," she said, suggesting that there was something to be told. "Anyway, Wallace had to fly down to Miami on business."

"Truth be told, I can't say what good girls do," Shelia declared, "but I do know that good girls don't have three buckets of soup sent to 'em from Florida."

"Shush!" Grace hissed. "It's Wallace and he didn't send all of that stuff. He had it delivered from that Chinese restaurant over on Parker." With a schoolgirl's giggle, Grace answered the call. "Hey, you," she sang into the receiver.

"No, I'm not sick anymore, thanks to someone in particular. Huh? Nobody but Lin' and Shelia, the girlfriends I told you about."

"Nobody but?" Linda objected jokingly. "I'll say."

"Mmm. Oh, hold on, Wallace." Grace held the phone against her chest to muffle her voice. "It's time for y'all to scram. My man-friend wants to talk to me, and I don't need nobody sitting up under us. Y'all might hear something you like, and I've got enough competition already, so run along."

Shelia walked over to the refrigerator and cracked it. "See how easy a sistah's nose can get pushed wide open. Let one, ooh-wee fine black stallion get inside her head, and suddenly she ain't got no more room for her girls. I, for one, ain't mad atcha. Be like that, Grace. Linda, help me get this bucket of wonton, and we'll be out."

"Yeah, I'll take the egg drop and be on my merry way, thank you very much," Linda agreed, with a sleeve of Grace's double chocolate-chip cookies tucked inside her purse. "Give us a shout when you get sick again. We'll be right back here to look in on you."

"And your groceries," Shelia clamored honestly. "Give Wallace our love after you've given him what he's calling long distance for."

"Mind your business, and lock the door as you leave," was the best way Grace could say "hurry up and get out of my house" without hurting somebody's feelings.

Grace didn't hesitate to tell Wallace how thoughtful his gesture was, and also how much she'd missed his company over the past two days. She got around to hinting about accompanying him someday when he had another business trip. Wallace did Grace one better. He offered to take her along to help celebrate his parents' fortieth wedding anniversary in two weeks. Of course, Grace voiced her trepidations concerning what André might think about it and what to do with him while she was away. By the end of their lengthy conversation, she knew exactly how to keep her son busy for an entire fun-filled weekend. He could stay at his father's and play big brother to May and Fay or whatever Muriel had named those two little darlings of theirs. After Grace agreed to travel with Wallace on a short road trip to Austin, she found herself counting the seconds until she'd have him all to herself, one on one.

27

Lawd Have Mercy

Days after Grace had dropped the bomb on Edward Swenson's household, she was back to doing what made her tick. Corporate Grace held the reins, guiding the Pinnacle marketing firm into an extremely profitable quarter. Ted, the senior partner, seemed pleased as punch with her idea of bringing Miss Pearl aboard until he barged into her office one afternoon wearing a wicked scowl. "Grace, I'm having a big problem with that new hire of yours!" he snarled. "I know we're trying to do right by Miss Pearl, but I can't take it anymore."

Grace was upset. She'd heard nothing but great reports about the older woman's stellar cleaning skills, so this was news to her. "What's wrong with the way she's keeping up around here, Ted? The restrooms have never been cleaner, and I absolutely love the homemade desserts she's spoiling us with."

"That's the problem!" Ted argued. "Since she's been here, I've gained ten pounds, and boy, I don't have to tell you how that's becoming a big problem in the Lansford master bedroom. It's getting so that I can't *keep up* with that greedy young wife of mine."

Grace tried to hide her face but couldn't restrain the hilarity coming out of it. "Whooo, too much information. I'm sorry for laughing, but that's a visual I'd rather not have. I'll talk to Miss Pearl and convince her to cease and desist with the goodies."

"No!" he objected hurriedly. "Let's not get hasty. All I want is for her to slow down the production, not close up shop. I'm in love with those peanut butter truffles she makes, and I'm not looking to give 'em up completely. How about we ask her to scale back the snacks to once or twice a week?"

"I see. Consider it done." When Grace got a load of Ted's pot belly, she curved her lips into a smile. "Maybe you could do some sit-ups or crunches to even things out."

"I'm not a fanatic. It's taken me years to build a shed over the good stuff. It adds character."

"Once again, too much information," Grace insisted, "way too much. Now you've gone and pushed the envelope clear off the table. I'll speak to Betty Crocker, and you . . . you go on back to your office and take that shed with you." Ted stared down at his tight button-down shirt and massaged his belly all the way out of Grace's office. "Good grief," she sighed, pushing her assistant's extension on the telephone. "Marcia, please send in Miss Pearl when you see her. Thanks."

Within seconds, Skyler's grandmother stuck her head into Grace's office. "Yes, Miss Grace, you wanted to see me?" She shuffled in slowly, fearing that her work wasn't up to par, or worse.

"Miss Pearl, you don't have to be so formal with me. Gracie has been fine up 'til now and it still is," Grace said compassionately. "How is everything going?"

"Okay, I guess. The people are nice and respectful. I like the job you got me, if that's what you're asking."

"Yes, that's what I'm asking, but I'd also like to know how things are going at the house."

"Oh, me and Skyler love it so. It's a blessing. An oven that don't short out makes it a heap easier to bake all those sweets I've been bringing up to the break room."

"Funny you should mention that," Grace said, looking for the right words to soften the blow. She knew that providing afternoon treats made Miss Pearl feel very important. "It's been brought to my attention that while everyone absolutely adores your treats, we're starting to enjoy them too much for our own good."

"Huh, 'specially that head man, Mr. Lansford. Last week, I had to clean up a mess of crumbs from around his desk. He must've eaten a dozen truffles before the others had the chance to get a single whiff." Miss Pearl's lips curled into a soft grin when she thought back on the fuss Ted made over them. "If he don't watch out, that pretty little wife of his is gonna be sore at him."

"And we can't be a party to that, Miss Pearl. Why don't you cut back on the sweets to once a week, and together, you and I can save Mr. Lansford's marriage."

"I guess he don't have to know we're helping him out behind his back," she decided. "That it? Okay, I'd better get back to work then. Yesterday I caught that Bob fella, who likes wearing frilly clothes, coming out of the men's room, and I almost tore up my knee trying to get outta the way. They got a name for boys who parade around in soft getups, but I can't recollect what that is right now."

"It doesn't matter. Bob's a good employee. He's just going through a phase at the moment," was Grace's best effort at squashing that particular discussion, although Miss Pearl had another comment to get off her chest.

"That's what they calling it now, a phase? Lawd, when I was coming up they called it sissified. He might as well come on out the closet. It's a heap more room out here than it is in there. Thanks for the talk, Gracie, I love this job and would hate to lose it flapping my gums with you. Good day." She tossed Grace a grand smile as she climbed out of the chair to leave.

After having been warmed throughout, Grace listened to Miss Pearl humming a few bars of "Lift Every Voice and Sing" while she trod along, pushing a mop bucket down the hall. Long gone had been the days of fighting for equal rights for colored folk, the cleaning lady once told Grace, but the fight to maintain dignity while working the most menial of jobs would continue forever. Grace remembered the prostitute from the fast food restroom and couldn't have agreed more. Pride was a luxury that poor people couldn't afford when the lights were cut off.

Later in the day, the call Grace had been anticipating interrupted her thoughts of seeing Wallace again. "Yes, Edward, I can talk. Go ahead."

"I'll bet you don't feel bad about dragging our business in front of Muriel's face?"

"Actually, I've never felt better. My world is clicking on all cylinders now that I don't have to keep anything from our son."

"I don't like hiding anything either, Grace," Edward elucidated, not too convincingly. "It's not like she didn't already know about André, but springing him on her was kinda cruel. She's gotten over it, but I'm afraid she's not quite over you."

Grace leaned back in her chair and rocked in it before questioning the last comment. "What do you mean? Has Muriel come out and said so, or has she been hinting around to something bothering her after meeting me?"

"I can't explain it. Maybe it's petty jealousy, a woman thing. She's been up late worrying about you creeping behind her, I know that much."

"Far be it for me to help you with your wife's esteem, but she'll see that you and I have only one thing in common, a boy who enjoyed being with his father. Tell her I said she doesn't have a reason to be concerned about me, not one."

"Well, I'll see what I can do to smooth things over. Would it be all right with you if I contacted André at home?" Since Edward seemed to be on the straight and narrow, Grace told him that would be just peachy with her. "I'll try to reach him in a day or two. The girls can't stop talking about their new big brother. They think he hung the moon."

"Play your cards right with Dré and he'll begin to feel the same way about you," Grace informed him before ending the phone call. She was glad for the first time that Edward had called. Her neck wasn't sore from overwhelming tension like before, and it seemed that the wedge between them was weakening. Grace had God on her side, and He was using Wallace to help facilitate a number of changes in her life. Wallace's friendship inspired Grace to expect more from men. How to go about getting it had to be orchestrated properly if she expected things to blossom into a long-term relationship. In no time flat, something suggested what Grace's next move should be. As usual, she responded in grand fashion.

She stood up from her desk and headed over to close the office door. On her way back, she smiled and clasped her hands gently as if one of them belonged to Wallace. Her smile hadn't dissipated one iota by the time the phone began ringing on the other end.

"Hello, this is Wallace."

Grace melted as his voice hummed in her ear. "Hey you," she purred tenderly. "I hope that I'm not disturbing you."

"No, don't be silly," he answered. "The only way you could do that is if you stopped calling me."

"Ooh, you always seem to know just what to say to get a girl thinking. That's another reason I'm calling."

"Okay," he offered in a questioning tone, not sure how to respond to her loaded comment. "What's the other reason?"

"Well, like I said, I was thinking about you attending church service with me this Sunday. If you're not too busy," she added, crossing her fingers.

"Oh, a church date?" Wallace said with a slow rise in his voice. "I see."

"You see? That's not quite the answer I was shooting for," Grace admitted, somewhat disappointed.

"Then how about an emphatic *I would love to?* Will that one suit you, or should I have it written across the sky in bold print?" Wallace fully understood the implications of a church date when Grace invited him to worship with her and André. It was commonly known to be a precursor to a trip down the aisle. With that in mind, Wallace still agreed to accompany her.

"A simple yes would have sufficed," Grace replied eventually, after imagining Wallace going through the trouble of paying to have an airplane spell it out high above her office building. "It's a date then. And Wallace, thank you, for everything."

"You're very welcome, for everything. And if you don't mind, I'd rather pick you guys up and ride over together."

"Yes, that would be nice," Grace purred again, "Very nice. I'll look forward to it. Bye." She lowered the phone receiver on its cradle and sighed longingly. "Wow, what a man."

As their date officially started at the church foyer on Sunday morning, it swelled with the faithful awaiting services to begin. Grace was glowing inside, and outside, too, for that matter. The tangerine wool blend two-piece skirt set she wore, with matching pumps, was the perfect ensemble for the occasion. Fitting comfortably into a size ten, she didn't mind the short cut of the tailored jacket. After catching several brethren in the congregation stealing a glimpse, it affirmed that they didn't mind it, either. Grace was accustomed to being greeted with men's roving eyes. However, she didn't know what to make of the additional attention thrown at her by fellow sisters in the congregation. Single women who barely spoke to her before then casually struck up conversations to wrangle introductions with Wallace in the event that Grace failed to close the deal. Somehow, she'd obtained instant celebrity status, and by the end of the amens and hallelujahs, she proudly wrapped her arm in Wallace's and pulled him so close that the female wolves in nightclub clothing couldn't sink their teeth into her eye candy. Grace was beginning to understand the level of work that went into putting her brand on a fine hunk of man to discourage would-be rustlers with a mind to do the same.

"Grace, don't drag him off before I get the chance to meet him," Albert the skirthound announced. "It's good to finally see what's been keeping Grace from me after all this time." Amid Grace's cold stare, Albert didn't step off right away. "Watch your back, now," he warned Wallace. "Until y'all tie the knot, I still got a shot." Grace was looking at Albert cross-eyed like "I know you-do-not" when Sister Kolislaw tapped her on the shoulder outside the exit doors.

"Sistah Hilliard, you're looking mighty spry this afternoon. Who's the lucky man?" she questioned happily.

"Sister Kolislaw's the wife of one of the deacons, Wallace," Grace told him, while flaunting him simultaneously. "This is Wallace Peters. Sister Kolislaw here has been my personal mentor in the matters of the heart, among other things." André snickered when he overheard that comment. Grace was quick to run him off with a patented go-on-and-play-child motherly expression.

"My, my, Sistah Hilliard," uttered Grace's mentor, adorned in a light shade of pink from top to bottom. "When you set your mind to something, you go all out. He's a real looker."

"Thank you, ma'am," Wallace replied fondly. "Grace is quite the looker as well."

"Uh-huh, you have a sharp eye for detail." The gray-haired lady took her time sizing up Wallace's expensive shoes and neatly pressed black designer suit. "Do you have a church home, brotha Peters?" she asked, and then winked at Grace.

"Yes, ma'am, I do. Though I'm not in attendance with the saints as often as I should," he admitted openly.

"We can fix that lickity-split, huh, Grace?"

"If you say so," she agreed, squirming out of that one.

"Well, I didn't aim to hold y'all from supper, but I had to see for myself what the fuss was about." Sister Kolislaw squeezed both of Wallace's hands firmly. "I'm looking forward to seeing you here again, son. And, if I'm as sharp as I used to be, Grace would too. Nice to know you." She pulled Grace aside to confer quietly. "He found you all right. Now what are you going to do about staying found? You'd better get to knowing what his intentions are and where his heart is before bringing him back up in here. There were a lot of sistahs taking numbers and getting in line this morning, and not all of them had their husbands' blessings. If I hadn't invested over thirty years with the one I got, I'd have been right along with 'em."

Grace was halfway through dinner when she experienced thoughts of Wallace falling prey to another woman. She hadn't taken the time to inquire about his plans for marriage, but the fact that André was chowing down on a slab of chicken-fried steak in front of them wouldn't allow for it, although offering Wallace an innocent cup of coffee at her home just might.

Sitting on the passenger side of a moving car was a thrill in itself for Grace, after having been André's personal chauffeur from his birth. She wanted to reach across the console several times and rest her hand on Wallace's arm during the drive over. A wide-eyed man-child sitting in the backseat prevented her from moving on it, not to mention what reaction it would have drawn from the driver's side of that shiny luxury car. Sure, Grace had seen Wallace eight times now, and yes, she was counting, but how well did she really know him? Come to think of it, how well did he know her, she also considered as they approached her driveway. Getting rid of André was Grace's top priority if she expected to create an avenue to facilitate a twenty-questions session that was long overdue.

"Dré, aren't you going to hang out at the recreation center this afternoon?" she baited him once they were inside.

"No, ma'am. It's Sunday, the rec is closed on Sunday." André sat on his bed and eased off his church shoes. "Whew, I can't wait to turn on the Mav's game. Allen Foray is leading the conference in points per game. Maybe Mr. Peters can watch it with me?" *Maybe Mr. Peters has better things to do*, Grace thought to herself.

"Um, I was thinking that Wallace and I could have a chance to talk in the den. Do you mind catching the game upstairs in the study?" Grace was willing to buy André a ticket, call him a limo, and rent a chaperone if that would have gotten him out of the way momentarily.

"Na, I don't like that TV," he replied nonchalantly. "Tube's too small. I'd rather hang out in the den with y'all." André glanced up at Grace, who was biting on her bottom lip. He flashed an impish grin and chuckled. "Gotcha! Ma, I know you like Mr. Peters. I'm a kid, but I'm not stupid. He likes you too."

"Oh Dré, you ought to be ashamed, playing me like that. So, you are actually okay with me and your teacher hitting it off?"

"It's not up to me, but he's cool as teachers go. Everybody likes him. Don't sweat it. The Mav's game don't, uh doesn't, come on until six. Y'all will be finished talking by six?"

"Let's see," Grace said, noting that the current time was two-fifteen. "I don't know. That'll be cutting it kinda close. You may have to miss the first quarter."

André sprang off the bed in a panic. "Ma', I can't miss—" he started to complain, before seeing Grace's smile light up the room.

"Gotcha back!" she told him. "Never forget, I'm the one who invented gotcha. Sure, we'll be done hours before game time. And thanks for understanding that mamas need special friends, too. Portia isn't the only woman with her eye on a cutie."

"Was that a family meeting going on in there?" asked Wallace when Grace returned from André's bedroom.

"Kinda, sorta," she answered. "We had to get on the same page, mine. Coffee or tea?" she asked, approaching the pantry. "I think there is some chamomile and peppermint."

"I'd like a glass of orange juice, if that would save you some trouble."

"It wouldn't be any trouble, but I also have OJ. That boy loves the stuff. If Dré could pump it in his veins, he would."

Grace gestured toward the living area. Wallace was eager to escort her into the open room where there was a comfortable sectional to relax on. As it turned out, he was as anxious as Grace had been to discuss grown folks' business. But before they did, Wallace had her cracking up when he shared tales of his own dating disasters, especially one about meeting a particular woman affectionately referred to as Pumpkin by her professional handler, Sly the Pimp. Regardless of how many times Wallace selected various other singles' profiles on a Web site and arranged dates to talk face-to-face, Pumpkin kept showing up with Sly demanding a small sitting fee for her time.

"Oh, yeah, I've had my run-ins with Sylvester Greenberg," Grace was almost too embarrassed to say. "He's Jewish, and he says being a black man is a state of mind. Oomph, he wouldn't be so quick to say that if he actually was one, 'cause too many of y'all are property of the state, doing time. Suddenly a faint memory pushed its way to the front of Grace's. "Pumpkin? Pumpkin? Is she a thick chick, long braids, and runs real fast in high heels?"

"That's her," Wallace verified, with displeasure. "I think she showed up for our first date wearing high-heeled running shoes," he mused. Grace nearly fell off the couch because she was laughing so hard. "Sly couldn't catch her either, not in his platforms."

"You're so crazy, Wallace," Grace mused, while flirting along the way. "I should have known you'd be witty and charming. Most men are fortunate to luck up on one out of two."

"Is that what you're looking for, a charmingly witty man who has a working girl's beeper number in his Rolodex?"

"That's a start, I guess," Grace said, gazing into his eyes. "Seems that our friendly conversation finally made it here, to the good part. Yes, I would like a man who can make me laugh like there's no tomorrow. Not every day is a good one, you know."

"I concur. Sometimes a woman needs to feel she can be herself without some stiff-backed brotha viewing it as a pitfall. What else?" he asked, seeking additional attributes that might apply to him.

"Umm, I think you have a lot of what I tend to appreciate. You've shown yourself to be thoughtful, considerate, and spiritual. I could go on, but there are some essentials about you that I don't know, for instance, your views on marriage."

"I'm all for it. God made it, and I have faith that I'll be good at it," Wallace answered. "What else? This is easy. Keep 'em coming."

"Okay, Easy, how long do you think a couple should date before getting engaged?"

"Most men see an engagement as a stall tactic while deciding if their woman is worth moving forward with or not. Personally, I view an engagement as the period of time between a man discovering that he's found the woman he's meant to spend the rest of his life with, and making it a reality. Me, I don't believe in taking too long to make a decision about anything. Either it's my style, in my size, and in my price range, or it isn't." Grace was pleasantly surprised at his candor, although she had to see if Wallace could walk the walk or if he was just talking.

"Wow, impressive," she admitted. "With all of that figured out, why haven't you gotten married?"

"Give me a minute. We just met," Wallace replied seriously. "Oh, please don't clam up on me. I would have assumed another question was on deck, ready to be fired, or are you finished?"

"I'm trying to pretend that I'm not stunned after your last answer. Most men prefer a root canal to discussions like this."

"I thought you'd have caught on by now, Grace. I am not most men."

"Whoa," Grace exhaled. "You can say that again. A single man with your qualities doesn't remain single unless he wants to be. That could be construed as a sign of selfishness, a fear of commitment, or greed. Which is it? You a greedy brotha, Wallace? Huh? Or, are you the kind who's prone to run and hide when it's time to see the preacher?"

"Honestly, I've been each of those at some point or another, and then I grew up."

"One more question," Grace asked, genuinely interested in what he'd say regarding an extremely personal issue. She observed him closely to note if his eyes shifted left to retrieve a lie stored in his head for such an occasion. "Have you ever been in love before?"

"No," he responded, unfazed, with his eyes locked directly on hers. Wallace didn't have to guess that another question was burning a hole in Grace's chest, so he took it upon himself to address it nonetheless. "Why not? I've been saving it." His answer was better than Grace had anticipated. She did notice previously that Wallace knew exactly what to say to get a girl thinking, and she was right. *Lawd have mercy.*

28
Babes and Buicks

Edward was acting edgy when he picked up André for the weekend. The boy didn't catch it but Grace recognized his pained expression from the last days of her courtship with him. Edward often sulked when felt cornered or obligated to perform beyond his natural desire. With any luck, since some years had passed from the man he used to be, Grace could trust him to do right by André, at least for a couple of days.

Wallace knocked at the door about a half hour after Edward left, but it wasn't soon enough for Grace. She had been pacing the floor, counting the minutes. It required every ounce of fortitude she could muster to restrain herself from leaping into his arms and dragging him into the bedroom. Instead she pouted playfully. "Oh, Wallace, I was starting to think you'd forgotten about me."

"That would be impossible," he enlightened Grace. "I couldn't do that if I tried."

During a brief stop at a convenience store, Wallace dashed in for bottled water and snacks to share on the open road. Grace sat in the car, looking at the world from a new perspective, one which appeared so clear that she couldn't imagine viewing it without Wallace as a scenic backdrop.

"Tell me about them, your parents," Grace requested, when Wallace guided the sedan safely onto the interstate.

"The folks," he said smoothly, as if enjoying a sip of expensive champagne. Grace saw glimpses of admiration in his eyes before he began to talk about them. "They're a fine pair. My mother is a staunch believer in all things working together for the benefit of the family. She does her best to keep my dad in line while he constantly tries to prove who's boss."

"Your mom," Grace said as if she already knew.

"Yep, and Dad knows it, but that doesn't stop him from kicking up dust now and again. You'd think after being married for forty years, he'd have figured out there's no use in fighting battles a man can't win in his own home." Grace was amused. Men she'd gotten to discuss relationships with, in general, were prone to speak of women as second-class citizens after the I do's were done. Wallace's outlook was different. It was a breath of fresh air. Before meeting him, Grace had only read about men so wonderfully well rounded like him. But her Wallace was real, and she craved as much of him as she could stand.

"I'd imagine your father is busting with pride over his son, the successful lawyer-slash-educator. What line of business was he in?" Grace asked as she stared longingly at him.

"*Is* in," Wallace corrected her. "Oh yeah, he's still at the firm, lawyering he calls it, and has been since before I was born." Wallace went on to divulge how he'd always seen himself walking in his father's shoes, and how he'd pursued law to please the old man. Wallace remembered watching his father circle the courtroom and stab fear into opposing counsel with his capacity to sway undecided jurors by the conclusion of his opening statement.

"He sounds like quite a man," Grace whispered. "You had

no choice but to grow up and be somebody."

"Like you weren't meant to be a partner in one of the fastest-growing marketing firms in the southwest? Come on, Grace. Your steady rise was done so sweet it had to be a plan."

Out of nowhere, Grace became somewhat melancholy as she remembered her upbringing. "Afraid not, no structured plan, anyway, although I can understand trying to please parents. I set out to prove to my mother that I could provide for me and Dré without begging a man to contribute financially, so she took it upon herself to needle Edward for child support without my permission. Because of her wisdom and tenacity, her grandson has one-hundred-fifty-six checks deposited in a college fund. You know, I never had the chance to thank her for doing what I had too much pride to do myself." Grace's mother passed away after battling breast cancer. She would have been thrilled at how well Grace had made out on her own. Joey, Grace's only sibling, was a Cincinnati police officer who loved his work, and loved women even more. He'd visit her and André about every other Christmas, and always showed up sporting his latest trophy girlfriend. Strong family ties were a foreign entity that Grace had suddenly felt sorry for missing out on. "You know, Wallace," she continued solemnly, staring at the countryside out of the car window, "André is similar to a lot of your students. His mother has never been married, and neither was hers. Three generations of strong black women trying to prove something, I guess. To whom, I don't know. Maybe to ourselves."

Wallace stretched out his right arm and rested his hand, palm facing upward, for Grace to interlock with hers. As if it was second nature, she pressed her palm against it and allowed her fingers to fall between his. She felt comforted, cared for, and content, like a woman with the right man is supposed to.

Driving through the hill country of Texas, Grace was amazed how dissimilar it was from Dallas. The terrain displayed red dust–colored canyons and the greenest mountains imaginable. The varying landscapes were indicative of the life she'd led, not at all aware of other wondrous things to behold, although so close that she could have reached out and touched them. Meeting Wallace removed the veil from her preconceived notions concerning how a real shot at love was supposed to be. Grace stared at him for miles. She was absolutely captivated by the view.

While rolling into a gated subdivision laced with million-dollar estates, Grace turned to Wallace and looked at him over the tops of her shades. "Uh, Wallace, is this where your parents live?"

"Yeah, they sold the big house on the edge of Austin and moved inward about ten years ago," he said without an ounce of pretension. "My mother said she was tired of living in a small part of it while having to care for the entire place." Grace peered out at a collection of tall stucco fortresses, sandstone masterpieces, and other houses designed with an early European flair.

"If the *big* house was that much bigger than these mansions, I don't blame her." Extravagant homes didn't usually cause Grace to develop uneasy vibes, but her perception of Wallace's family had just changed. As they unloaded the car in the circular driveway, Grace pictured stuffy, black Republicans with very little tolerance for commoners. She was ashamed for thinking such a thing the very moment she laid eyes on them.

A beautiful light brown–skinned woman in her late thirties opened the front door, gripping a half-empty cocktail glass. Grace expected her to offer warm salutations but to the contrary, she leaned against the door frame and sneered at the new arrivals. Grace and the woman continually looked one another over until Wallace saw what was happening. His disapproving glare made the pretty woman laugh. "Yeah, it's him!" she hollered back into the house. "Y'all should come and see this. Pooter brought a woman with him. She's fully grown and everything." *Pooter? What kind of nickname is that?*

"Girl, stop tripping," Wallace heckled her. "You act like you've never seen me with a woman before."

"Not at yo momma's house," the woman teased, an air of invincibility idling beneath her white linen slacks and blouse. Grace watched the strange interaction but reserved her comments as the woman made her way down the elevated cobblestone walkway. "What you got to say to that?"

Wallace glanced at Grace, then back at Ms. Invincible. "I refuse to answer on the grounds of self-incrimination. Therefore, I plead the Fifth," he joked, almost face to face with her. "You look good, Bev, real good." When Wallace reached out to offer a loving embrace, Grace felt severely out of place. "Beverly, this is Grace Hilliard, of the Dallas Hilliards," he announced playfully. "Grace, I'm pleased to introduce Beverly Ann Peters, my sister and former world-class tattler."

"Hey, girl," Beverly said to Grace before going back to Wallace. "If I remember correctly, you were always the one running up in Daddy's face like a back stabbing rat, telling on me." Beverly parked both hands on those narrow hips of hers and stuck out her chin. "Daddy, Bev is smoking your cigarettes again," she mimicked. "Bev was with that boy again. Bev snuck out her window again. Daddy, Daddy, Daddy. I'ma tell it!"

"She's got you there, Pooter," a stately man agreed, also in linen, and leather sandals. "You were quite the little snitch at times, and proud of it too." The older man's hair was graying at the temples, but he appeared too young to be Wallace's father, so Grace assumed he was an uncle or older cousin. "So, who's the lovely lady?" the older gentleman asked. He was giving Grace a thorough once-over like Beverly had.

"Dad, this is Grace. Grace Hilliard," Wallace hailed, awaiting his father's reaction.

Grace smiled at the youngest-looking old man she'd ever

seen. "Glad to meet you, Mr. Peters," she said after he waved from atop the walkway.

"'Y'all married?" he asked, with an unlit smoking pipe hanging from his mouth.

"Watch your man fold up like a cheap suit," Beverly whispered.

"Nah," Wallace answered too quickly for Grace's taste. She was glaring at him when Beverly nudged her from the other side.

"Not married huh?" Mr. Peters restated, his wife now by his side, grinning at her adorable son as if he were still the proud little snitch that Beverly despised so much growing up. "You riding her around the countryside like you married. Son, and I want the truth, did you get this young lady into trouble?" he asked gruffly, while laughing on the inside. Beverly snickered and turned away so Grace wouldn't see her laugh. Wallace looked at his father like he'd stumbled out of the house with his pants down.

"Come on, Dad, don't do this," Wallace chuckled uneasily, feeling the pressure of a peculiar homecoming. Grace found herself enjoying this odd brand of horseplay among father and son. Seeing Wallace go up against a master of litigation proved sobering. At least now she knew he was human.

"Is she with child?" the patriarch barked, from the cusp of the porch. Wallace was about to say something. Then he looked over at Grace as if he didn't honestly know for sure. They'd never talked about it. Grace's hands were on her hips now, and she was looking at Wallace with a you'd-better-speak-up-for-me expression plastered on her face.

Wallace swallowed hard. "No, sir, she is not with child," he answered positively.

"Good, then come on in the house. Why do you have this pretty brown thing standing out in the street anyway?" Mr. Peters complained. "Mama, Pooter done showed up at the house with a woman. She must be special."

"I can see that for myself," replied the cinnamon-hued,

refined prototype of her daughter, Beverly. "Grace, I'm Wallace's mother, Olivia. Please overlook Wallace's father. He seems to have forgotten his manners in the presence of a beautiful lady. Come on in, we'll get acquainted. Leave the luggage. The boys will get it." Grace eased the bag off her shoulder and then marched up the steps to the front door, flanked between Mother Peters and Beverly.

While Wallace and his father lugged the suitcases inside, Mother Peters started reminiscing, and before Grace knew it, she'd begun schooling Grace on her son and filling her in on some of Wallace's childhood mischief, his young man's follies, and romances that went awry. "He couldn't have been more than twelve or thirteen when he said he was running away because we wouldn't let him go skating with this little white girl in his class. Pooter didn't know that her father was into some heavy drug trafficking and about to get shipped off to prison for a very long time. Of course, he thanked us for it later on."

Grace flipped through pages of a thick photo album. Wallace's face seemed to be in every frame. His formative years were undoubtedly happy ones, as he was always ready to smile for the camera. "Mrs. Peters, I've noticed that y'all refer to Wallace as Pooter," Grace chuckled. "I'm afraid to ask, why?"

"Give him a cup of milk and you wouldn't have to ask," Beverly answered on her mother's behalf.

"Ooh-ooh, we couldn't take that boy anywhere for the first three years of his life without getting shamed into leaving everywhere we went," Mrs. Peters explained. "We thought he was just being rude until we learned that he was lactose intolerant. He couldn't have diary products and then go out in public. Humph, Pooter was the nicest thing we could think to call him." Grace was doubled over, along with her new acquaintances. "I'm apologizing again for the way my dear husband is acting, but he's just as shocked as we are."

"I don't understand," Grace professed awkwardly. "Beverly, you said something about Wallace not having brought a woman here before. I thought you were just razzing him."

Beverly poured herself another drink, then sat alongside her mother at the patio cocktail table. "See, when Wallace was in college, he said he'd never marry because there were too many single women who needed his attention," replied Beverly, with a rueful expression. "He was talking globally, mind you, worldwide. Yeah, he was pretty full of himself for a while, and we had given up on him sticking with a woman long enough to see what she had to offer before moving on to the next one. He was convinced that sexing a sistah up helped him get to know the real her after her guard came down."

"Uh-huh, more like after her panties came down," quipped Mother Peters.

"Wallace?" muttered Grace, certainly not her Wallace.

"Oh, he was a handful," Beverly continued. "Wallace had it all figured out, he thought. I told him he didn't know a woman any better after sleeping with her, except for what she'd learned from other men. His relationships only served as exercises to keep him busy until he realized that he didn't have a clue how to pull off staying in one. So, you can imagine how we felt when he rolled up here . . . with you. Dad wasn't the only one fearing you must've been pregnant in order to accomplish that."

Grace was shocked. "You're serious, Beverly? You thought I'd trapped him?"

"Well, can you blame us, taking into account his past behavior?" she proposed, as a very concerned older sister.

"Wallace seems so different from the way you've painted him. He's been nothing but the perfect gentleman," Grace said, to them as much as to herself.

"Well, he has been different since he decided to teach school," Beverly reasoned. "How'd you two meet?"

"Actually my son is in his freshman-level English class,"

Grace told them without considering the implications of her statement.

Mrs. Peters smiled uncomfortably. "Oh, you're divorced?" When Grace shook her head, Mother Peters cut her eyes at Beverly, then poured herself a tall cocktail as well. "Have any other children, do you?"

The atmosphere stiffened momentarily until Grace spoke up begrudgingly. "No, ma'am, just the one."

"I'm sure he's a good kid," Beverly assumed as she stuck up for Grace. "I wonder what's keeping the men."

In the upstairs hallway, Wallace was having his own difficulties dealing with a worthy interrogator, his father. Mr. Peters sat in a wicker chair while his son hustled travel bags into the guest rooms. "This Grace, is she formally educated? And I'm not talking about one of those computer degrees you can buy off that Internet, either."

"Dad, Grace is a great girl. And yes, she's been to college, a real one with books and everything."

"Not bad, not bad. So, can I get my hopes up that someday I'll have babies bouncing off my knee and a house full of pitter-pattering little Wallaces? Sure would be nice to feel like I've led a full life before going to meet my Maker. I'm not getting any younger, you know."

"You're only sixty-three, Dad, and a healthy sixty-three at that," Wallace argued, with sweat beading up on his forehead. "What's all this talk about babies, anyway? You haven't been interested in who I might be making them with before now."

"Because you haven't popped up and sprung one of your playmates on us before this," his father fired back. "Look, why shouldn't I get excited about grandchildren? You got yourself a pretty young thing, educated, with child-bearing hips. Yeah, I saw 'em when she came in the house. And it would appear to me that you're applying for the job. So all I'm asking is, when are you gonna punch the clock?" Wallace's tired eyes begged for his father to let up, but he didn't until he'd had his final say. "Son, you caught yourself a good one by the looks of things. You're already halfway there. I like her."

"We finally agree on something, I like her, too." Wallace's grin was returned by his father's.

"Then it's settled!" Mr. Peters declared loudly. "Put a ring on her finger and a bun in her oven. Hey, Pooter, do you need your old man to hip you to a couple of things to help facilitate the postnuptial pleasantries? You know I was a wildcat back in the day."

"Hey, hey, I'm way too old for the birds-and-the-bees speech. I've figured out a few things myself to get me by." Wallace felt ridiculous posturing for his old man's approval concerning his savvy in the sack, and even more so after his father's next comment.

"Humph, sounds like you do need to hear the speech, if all you're doing is getting by." Wallace had to scratch his head over that one.

When he rejoined Grace and the girls on the luncheon patio, the mood was lukewarm. Beverly was fanning the heat away from her face with a magazine cover. Mother Peters was staring into the bottom of an empty drink glass, and Grace was as quiet as a church mouse. Wallace kissed his mother on the crown of her head, told her that he'd missed her, and then asked what they'd been up to while he was upstairs. Beverly stopped fanning and looked at Grace. "Nothing to speak of," Beverly lied believably. "We're just too hot out here to keep a good conversation going."

"Let's move the party inside then," Wallace suggested, helping Grace from her chair before he'd done the same for his mother, a gesture that didn't go unnoticed.

Grace gathered that Wallace's sister, Beverly, was around thirty-nine, a few years older than Wallace, and married to her law firm. She appeared to have no interest in putting her career on hold for a family at the moment—she stated that mommies didn't make the best litigators due to too many time constraints and conflicts to deal with, so she passed on motherhood for lawyer-hood. However, Beverly empathized with Grace, and that resulted in an instant bond between them. Also this particular homecoming provided a minor diversion from Beverly's parents' usual inquisition about her plans for a husband and children.

After dinner Beverly invited Grace into the study for evening libations, which was also the perfect place for the two of them to listen in on Wallace getting grilled by his father about the first grown woman he dared to introduce.

"Pooter, for a grown woman, Grace sure doesn't eat much," Wallace's father proclaimed. "How does she keep meat on her bones if she won't eat?"

"Something's wrong, I don't know. A bad case of nerves, I guess," Wallace surmised, unsure as to why Grace had been uncharacteristically quiet and reserved. "Since she was out on the patio earlier today, she hadn't said much at all. It's not like her."

"That Grace," Mr. Peters said, "she's a stunner, though, and it looks like she's built for speed." Wallace hid his face, knowing where this conversation was headed. "Is that it? Is that why you brought her down here with you, because she rides smooth like a showroom new Coupe de Ville?"

"Hey, Dad, keep it down," Wallace pleaded. "You know these walls have ears. Grace isn't like all the other women I've met. She's entirely a different breed. It's got nothing to do with how she rides. I'm taking it slow. It'll be worth it because she's worth it. We, uh, haven't been intimate . . . yet." When Wallace confessed, in private he thought, that he hadn't even kicked the tires, much less checked under the hood, his father wasn't sold on that being the most prudent way to go about business.

"Wallace," his father called him for the first time since he'd arrived, "I'm not about to tell you how to go about selecting a woman, but you oughta test-drive it before you make a major investment, if you know what I mean. And, for my future grandchildren's sakes, I hope you do."

Immediately after hearing her husband, Mother Peters stepped out of the kitchen where she has been putting away the flatware and holding her tongue. "Slow down a minute," she objected. "I know that wasn't Harvey Peters I just overheard trying to get his son to rush a young lady into bed, and for what? That insidious checking-under-the-hood logic makes perfect sense only if Wallace was in the market to buy a Buick, as opposed to settling down with a good woman." Then, she quickly reminded her husband of something he may have forgotten. "You should be the one to talk, Harvey. In case it has danced out of your memory, I'll tell it like it used to be. Wallace, your daddy chased me down the aisle after courting me for five months. I cut him off at intense handholding," Mother Peters recounted. "An older woman, a friend of my aunt's, explained to me that the key to a short engagement is a virtuous woman refusing to give in to married folks' affairs before taking the vows. That's right! He was on his knees outside my window begging for me to give in, but I wouldn't. He even got rained on a couple of times and I felt sorry for him when he did, but I held strong. I wasn't gonna let any fellow play me cheap, and Grace should do likewise." After the cat got out of the bag, Harvey Peters was hiding his face.

Beverly and Grace were overheard laughing uncontrollably after catching this time-tested marital strategy, which Mother Peters had employed to perfection. Her short engagement had led to a wonderful marriage, forty years of blissful misunderstandings and joyous disagreements, each of which helped to make their friendship stronger.

Before allowing Grace to depart from her home after two days of enjoyment and fellowship, Mother Peters apologized for her reaction upon hearing about André. Then she embraced Grace compassionately and told her to leave married folks' affairs to married folks if she seriously intended on becoming one herself. Sister Kolislaw's similar instructions came to mind as Grace said her good-byes, thinking "the more things changed, the more they stayed the same."

29

Revelations

The slow ride back on Sunday afternoon proved to be a premonition of things to come. Grace felt as if she belonged to Wallace somehow. She couldn't deny being more emotionally tied to him than she had been to any man since she'd shielded her heart behind Edward taking an extended leave of absence. But she and Wallace weren't two college kids trying to figure out how life worked while jacking it up in the process. This was *it*, two adults discovering how much they admired and adored one another. The stage was set to chase the very illusive *it*, which the Bible detailed plainly in Proverbs eighteen, stating that "A man who finds a wife, finds a good thing and obtains favor from the Lord." That's what Grace had in mind while wondering how serious Wallace was about settling down and saving his love for the woman he could build a forty-year relationship with. *Slow down, Grace*, she told herself repeatedly, *slow down. This might feel like the end-all be-all, but it's still brand new.*

During the next two hours on the road, Grace and Wallace traded glances as their fingers danced the way both of them wanted to, closely, skin on skin and without inhibition. "Thank you for sharing your family with me, *Pooter*," Grace teased.

"Oh, not you, too. It's bad enough I have to hear that from them."

"Okay, okay. I'll leave the name-calling to those who knew you when," she apologized. "Now I see why you're such a good catch. You had good home training." When Wallace looked over at Grace, there was another thought idling there behind her steely gaze.

"A penny for your thoughts," he asked.

"They're worth a lot more than that, but I'm in a charitable mood. I must say that I never thought I would . . ." Grace said, hesitating, and taking a deep breath.

"What? That you would be falling for a schoolteacher, charmingly referred to by his unrelenting family as Pooter?"

Grace laughed then lowered her head. "No, it's just that I never thought I'd be falling in love at all."

Wallace squeezed her hand, signifying that he felt the same way. "Grace, do you believe in Greek mythology?" She shrugged her shoulders, not having given it much thought. "Well, there's an old tale that makes a lot of sense. See, Plato wrote of these androgynous people, perfectly round and asexual in nature. They spent all of their time trying to roll up Mount Olympus because they desperately wanted to be among the gods. The story goes that Zeus became annoyed with their efforts, so he cut each of them in half. Ever since, they've been relegated to scooting across the earth in search of their other half, their soul mates. All these centuries later, we're still at it and stumbling over ourselves."

Grace nodded her head slowly. "Hmm, do you think Plato was suggesting we shouldn't spend so much time looking for that perfect love, our soul mate?"

"I think that those androgynous people were made complete in themselves but didn't know it. They were whole and complete as is, like you and me. I've had the chance to examine who I am and what I need in a woman, not one who will complete me, but one who will adequately complement me, and me the same for her." Chills ran down Grace's spine, and her fingers tingled. Either she was having a heart attack or she was actively experiencing the aftershock of love in its purest form, void of fear or remorse.

After taking time to reflect on Wallace's philosophy of what his needs entailed, Grace had one last question begging to be submitted. She calmed herself and came out with it from the bottom of her heart. "How will you know when you've found her?"

Wallace grinned, peered in his rearview mirror, and pulled onto the shoulder of a desolate stretch of farm road. "I already have, Grace, and I just took her to meet my parents," he answered sincerely. Grace raised her hand in a cautious and deliberate motion to remove her sunshades. They slid off her nose and fell into her lap. She was speechless for several moments. Her lips moved but nothing came out until she forced it.

"This is crazy, Wallace. No man meets a woman and within a couple of months knows she's it for him."

"That's not quite the response I had in mind, but I do understand your apprehension. Most women think they have to pull teeth to get a man to commit. Well, I happen to have grown fond of my teeth and plan on keeping all of them."

"Wallace, this is so sudden," said Grace, with her eyes fixed on his. "Can I think about it?"

"Sure. You don't have to decide today. I'm not going anywhere."

"Okay, but are you sure?" she asked, not believing those words actually came out of her mouth.

"Wanna know how sure? I've already picked out the ring." With his hand, Wallace motioned toward the glove box Grace slammed her foot against on the night she had had it out with Edward. "Go on. Open it," he urged her.

Grace gawked at Wallace, then at the latch on the glove box as her hands shook. When she tugged at it, the door fell open. A small powder-blue box sat inside. *Tiffany blue*, she recognized right off. "Oh my God, you are crazy."

"Crazy about us, and ready to prove it," he said, with a soft kiss on her lips.

"Breathe, Grace, before you make a fool of yourself in front of this wonderful man," she said aloud before realizing that she had. "Did I just say that?"

"Uh-huh, I heard it," Wallace replied, smiling awkwardly.

Caught up in her surprise, Grace closed the small door with the blue box remaining inside. "I might be sorry later, but I'm not ready. We haven't even . . . yet."

"We could work backwards, have sex on this lonely highway, and then get married if you want to risk it, but I'll have to warn you, many have subscribed to that way of thinking and later wished they hadn't." Wallace saw that Grace's mind was trying to process his proposal but couldn't. She was in a foggy state of confusion, and he saw that too. "It's like I said before, you don't have to give me your answer today. I'm yours until you tell me otherwise. Unless, of course, you don't want me."

"Oh, wait a minute now. Let's not get out of hand," she objected hurriedly, tears misting up her eyes. "I just need a little while to get used to the idea of you and me. I want to be sure that I'm as crazy as you are, if that makes any sense." Grace took a tissue from her purse, wiped her eyes, exhaled deeply, and spent the next seventy miles trying to keep her hand out of that glove box.

Wallace set Grace's bags down on her doorstep. After he whispered in her ear how much he loved her she cooed like a giddy schoolgirl with a major crush. "I'll call you later," she whispered back. "We'll talk about it, okay?"

"You know, we could go on in the house, sleep together, and get it over with?" Wallace offered in jest.

"Man, don't make me jump you right here on my driveway. Humph, you don't know me. I'd have my way with you," Grace said suggestively.

"Yeah, I know you well enough, and I still want you for myself," he said, kissing her again.

Grace opened the door, wanting to pull Wallace inside. Instead, she playfully pushed him away before accepting his proposition.

As Grace stepped inside, André startled her. He was sitting on the sofa with the lights off. Since he wasn't supposed to have returned home from his father-son weekend until later that evening, Grace's expression, sprinkled with grave concern, had Wallace feeling like an outsider. He determined it was best he leave them alone to hammer out whatever it was that put such a worrisome look on Grace's face. "Call me. I'll be there," he mouthed, pulling the door closed from the outside.

As soon as Wallace drove away, hoping that he was doing the right thing, Grace wasted no time getting to the bottom of André's distress. "Hey, Dré," she greeted, taking a seat beside him, "I didn't know you'd be back so soon." Her son appeared to be locked in a catatonic trance. "Dré, I need for you to tell me why you're sitting here like this. If something went wrong between you and your dad, I want to know about it." He looked up for the first time to acknowledge her presence, but he remained reluctant to speak. "At least you can tell me what y'all talked about, what you did together." She hoped that Muriel wasn't the cause of her son's downtrodden disposition.

"Nothing," André answered matter-of-factly. "We went to Footlocker, then for some eats. That was it, a bunch of nothing." He went on to explain casually how he played with the girls and hung out at the house mostly. Eventually, he divulged that his father took him shopping for sports gear, then took him to a sports bar where they watched an entire basketball game on the big screen before their outing took a turn for the worse. "It was a real trip, Ma, every single time I started talking about me and school and the stuff *he* missed by not being there when I was little, *he* changed the subject. All *he* wanted to know was how long you've been seeing Wallace . . . uh, Mr. Peters, and how serious it is between y'all. Just before we left the restaurant, he got a phone call and argued with some man on the phone about Miss Muriel, but I couldn't tell what for because he sent me away to the car when he got mad. After all this time, Mama, *that man* still don't want anything to do with me." André looked at Grace with sad, piercing eyes. "Are you sure he's my real daddy?" Heartbroken, all Grace could do was listen. "Well, if you ask me," he continued, "you could've done better than him. If that man ever shows up here again, tell him I don't want to spend any more time with him; that'll make us even. I don't know how I expected a father to act. Guess I thought maybe he'd be a lot more like Mr. Peters. Humph, my daddy wasn't even close. Whew, good thing you didn't let him marry you when I was a baby. Now I see why. I'm tired, Mama, I'm going to bed."

Although André was visibly disappointed, he dealt with everything much better than Grace did. She beat herself up over Edward's behavior for hours while trying to get Edward on the phone so she could tell him just what she thought of him but he wouldn't answer. For that, she owed Edward a stern tongue-lashing and she was going to get at him but good, despite what Muriel had to say about it. Grace had warned Edward she was willing to hurt him, if that was the only way to stop him from destroying her child. He should have believed her.

Grace left word with André where she was going and how she planned on having it out with his father once she'd gotten there. André pleaded with her not to go, but she was determined to strike back. Considering the way Grace tore out of the garage, André had reason to be fearful. He called Wallace and explained everything, including the gun she'd taken from her nightstand, the one she'd purchased years ago when they lived in the old neighborhood.

Wallace took down the address and told André to sit by the phone and wait. He hopped in his car and sped across town thinking of how much he'd shared with Grace, how much he loved her, and how serious he was about being there for her and for Dré as well. Grace was beside herself and driven by anger. Wallace couldn't protect her if she made it to Edward's home before he did. Luckily, he found the address just as Grace marched angrily up the walkway. She was cradling a black handbag and telling herself that it had to be done. None of the wonderful things she'd accomplished in her career entered her mind. Neither did helping Miss Pearl, Skyler, or being there for André. Blinded by guilt and raw emotion, Grace couldn't see anything past retribution.

"Grace! Stop!" Wallace yelled, leaving his car parked in the middle of the street. She turned and looked through him as if he didn't exist, then quickly resumed her ascent toward the house. "Grace! Baby, please don't!" Wallace begged while sprinting up the lawn.

Suddenly, the front door flew wide open. Muriel emerged from it, running barefoot, with patches of hair torn from her head and blood streaming from several different places. "Someone has to stop it!" she screamed. "Eddic's going to kill him! The girls' father! Eddie's got him!"

Neither Wallace nor Grace understood her hysterical rants, but they did understand something had to be done. Pushing past Grace to get inside, Wallace told her to call 911. Grace clutched at his shirt to keep him from going further.

"No, Wallace! Wait for the police!" she wailed. "Wait!" Although Grace had a pistol in her bag, she didn't dream of getting Wallace involved in her personal calamity. Pensively, she stood in the doorway as Wallace raced toward a room on the first floor, where they'd overheard two men shouting ferociously. "Wallace!" she shouted while searching for the telephone. Muriel beat it up the stairs leading to the upper level when she heard her daughters crying for their daddy.

"Hello, police!" Grace yelled into the cordless phone as a thunderous gunshot sounded off the walls. She cowered to the floor, shuddering. Two additional shots exploded. Without regard to the 911 operator, Grace dropped the telephone when Wallace staggered into the hallway with his hands and shirt covered in blood.

"No, Wallace," she cried sorrowfully, rushing to help him. "No, no, no! I'm sorry. I'm sorry. It's all my fault." Grace was distraught, so Wallace grabbed her by the shoulders and shook her hard.

"Don't say that, and don't touch anything," Wallace commanded. "When the police come, don't say a word."

Grace didn't comprehend what he said but agreed merely to appease him. "Okay, okay," she muttered, touching his chest with her outstretched fingers. Wallace didn't appear to be physically injured, but he collapsed on the nearby love seat with his head in his hands.

Muriel locked the girls in an upstairs bedroom, then stormed into the downstairs study, where the shots had been fired. Her bloodcurdling scream shook Grace down to her core as she started toward the study to see if there was anything she could do to help. She anticipated the horrifying remnants of one man raging against another. Unfortunately, it was far more gruesome than she was prepared to handle.

Splatters of deep crimson spotted two of the walls inside that room. Edward's body lay still in a widening pool of blood, his life draining from it. A silver automatic pistol rested at his feet as Muriel crouched over another man, caressing his hair. At his side, a smudged 8 x10 picture frame with a photograph of Edward serving cake at a child's birthday party.

"Damn you, Albert! He didn't know," Muriel blubbered uncontrollably while gently coddling the dead man's remains. "Eddie didn't know!" she cried.

In spite of missing half of his face, his skull blown apart, Grace recognized the man laying in Muriel's arms immediately. She stared at him endlessly, sorry for the times she'd snapped at him for making indecent proposals and lewd advancements at the church. Albert Jenkins, the minister's son and the congregation's skirt-chasing baby-making machine, was dead.

Amid Muriel's excruciating moans and police sirens blaring in the background, Grace couldn't hear another sound. The next thing she remembered was regaining consciousness to the smell of a pungent odor being waved in front of her face by an emergency paramedic. She'd become overwhelmed by the ghastly scene of two dead men and the bewildered woman who'd brought about both deaths.

Child protective services had arrived and taken the girls away after packing a suitcase full of their clothing. Crime-scene investigators photographed every inch of the room and the lower portion of the house. Television news crews reported the double homicide from Edward's front lawn, just on the other side of yellow crime scene tape and much to their dismay. As the coroner's office tagged and bagged the bodies, police detectives paraded throughout the house, collecting evidence and gathering what information they could by interrogating Wallace, Grace, and Muriel separately.

They didn't get much from Grace, still shaken and pitiful. Through teary eyes, she scanned the den fearing the discovery of her black leather handbag, the one with her gun inside. After fainting, she was out cold when Wallace took the time to hide it in his car before police cruisers littered the block. If they had found it on the premises, they would have devised a way to connect Grace to the murders, and Wallace wasn't about to let that happen. He invoked his right to remain silent when learning he had become a prime suspect in both killings. Muriel was the key, they thought, although she had no idea what happened after the three men were in that hellish room alone.

Muriel, wrapped in a blanket, was ghostly white, rattled, and sedated. After a criminal psychologist arrived to get inside her head, she tried to explain how Albert ended up in the Assistant District Attorney's home on a warm Sunday evening. She told the lead detective that while living in Atlanta, she met and married Edward. After they began having problems, she sought her first legal separation. During that time, she conceived a child with Albert Jenkins, Edward's racquetball partner and family friend, and then she later conceived another child with him despite reconciling with her husband. Muriel went on to say Edward had no prior knowledge that the girls weren't fathered by him until he began receiving unsettling messages on his cell phone by a man threatening to seek joint custody of his daughters. Albert had exchanged words with Edward earlier in the day on his cell phone, Muriel chronicled. Then at about four-thirty, someone called the house several times but wouldn't say who they were or what they wanted. At five Albert showed up, drunk and hostile toward Muriel. When Edward intervened, Albert whipped out birth records and medical documents proving that Edward's blood type showed he couldn't be the father to the daughters he was raising. Subsequently, both men argued, terrifying the children, so they took the heated discussion into the study. Edward didn't want to believe Albert, his long-time friend. It was too far-fetched to be true, he thought, until Muriel made the mistake of admitting to an affair. Edward became furious. He'd backhanded her hard across the face and then proceeded to drag her out of the house by her hair. Muriel darted back in soon after she'd been tossed on the lawn like garbage. After overhearing Edward threaten to have Albert arrested, she stormed back outside for help. That's when Grace and Wallace showed up. The detectives realized Muriel had told them all she knew.

She was taken to the hospital for observation and placed under a strict suicide watch.

When the police learned that Wallace was a lawyer with no apparent ties to either of the two dead men, as Muriel corroborated before she was taken away, Edward's boss, the city's DA, signed a typed document barring Wallace or Grace from prosecution. For the record, they needed to know what went down after Muriel was assaulted by her husband.

Wallace read over the document twice, looking for loopholes that could have come back to haunt him after giving his side of the story. A court stenographer was called in because Wallace refused to be carted downtown in a patrol car. Even then, he was concerned about his students and having to explain why their teacher was escorted away from a widely publicized crime scene by uniformed police officers.

The stenographer typed continuously as Wallace described the sequence of events with Grace listening on silently. "I came here to speak with Edward regarding an old case we litigated years ago," Wallace lied smoothly, to keep Grace and André out of the official report. "As I neared the house from the walkway, Muriel, the wife, came tearing out of it, beaten and in hysterics. She screamed that someone had to stop something from happening inside the house. Of course I didn't know what she meant until she insinuated Edward was going to kill a man. 'Eddie's got him', she screamed." Wallace saw that Grace was reliving the horrible scene hours later, just as he was forced to do. "I ran into the house, heard men shouting, and I tried to get it resolved without anybody getting hurt. Obviously, it didn't turn out the way I'd planned. Edward was backed against the desk with his hands up. He was demanding that the other guy, Albert, leave or he'd make him. Albert said he wasn't leaving without his kids or a special writ of joint custody, signed by both biological parents of record."

Grace suspected Albert's intrusion had more to do with extorting money from Edward to leave his family alone, seeing as how Albert was notorious for the shirking responsibilities for the children he'd seen regularly. Somehow, it felt awful thinking bad of the dead, so Grace huddled up in the blanket provided to her and speculated how such a terrible thing could have happened in the first place.

When asked how the discussion escalated to bullets flying, Wallace's eyes closed momentarily. "Albert held the weapon on Edward, then he pointed it at me for butting in." Wallace omitted having met Albert a couple of weeks before when he attended church with Grace because it would have drawn red flags from the investigators. "I tried to explain that I was Edward's lawyer in such matters and prayed he would give up his weapon. While he was going off on me, Edward grabbed something from the desk and flung it at him. A shot fired and struck Ed in the chest, but it didn't stop him from charging. He must've wrestled the gun away because the next two shots killed Albert, one in the side, and the other in the head, just above the right temple." Wallace was grilled about his own miraculous escape from the perilous barrage of bullets in the small room. He glanced up toward the ceiling before answering. "It wasn't my time to go," he told them, in a subdued tone. "However, the time has come for me to leave here." Without asking for permission to go his own way, Wallace got up from the kitchen table and took Grace by the arm. "Come on, I'll see to it that you get home." Once again, he had rescued her, although this time it was from an unthinkable fate.

Grace knew how close she came to being killed that day, so very close. Thankfully, it wasn't her time to go either, she concluded after it was over with, said and done. There was so much to be thankful for and an abundant life to live. Grace knew that as well, and she was grateful.

Once ushered past the camera crews and pushy reporters, Wallace walked Grace to his car and buckled her in safely. Neither of them had much to say until they traveled miles from the subdivision. "You need me to stop for anything on the way home?" Wallace asked softly, not taking his eyes off the white lines on the freeway.

"No, I just need to get home and see about André. No doubt he's been watching everything on TV. I thought about calling him, but I didn't have the words. Maybe if I hold tight, long enough, they'll come."

"You're the one who's been through a lot," Wallace said, reaching for her hand to hold his. "Don't be surprised if André is holding it together like a champ. All he's ever had was you, and you're still here for him, to love him and care for him. You're all he needs, Grace."

"What about me?" she asked, not having thought about what she'd do with the life God spared until that precise moment. "Can we talk about what I need?" As Wallace exited the off ramp, Grace cleared her throat. Suddenly, she leaned toward the glove box and then opened it. "Imagine that," she sighed, pleasantly surprised that the tiny blue box was in the same place she'd left it. Grace lifted the box top and unsuccessfully fought back tears when marveling at the three-carat princess-cut diamond resting atop a custom designed band of platinum. "This is what I need. Well, not this, exactly, although it's very beautiful. I . . . I need to know that you will continue to love me in the end the way you have from the beginning. Oh, who am I fooling? I can't wait to be your wife, Wallace." She took her eyes off the ring and cast her gaze toward him, but he didn't answer immediately. All choked up, Grace swallowed hard to clear her throat again. "That's if you still want me."

Wallace stopped the car in Grace's driveway, then shut off the ignition. "Remember when I saw you coming in from the rain? I knew then I would always want you in my life, nothing could or ever will change that. Yes, Grace, I would be honored to spend the rest of my life with you."

Grace lunged over the console and hugged Wallace until she began to cry. André wandered outside and stood beside the car after he'd grown tired of watching them from the window. He was holding up as well as Wallace had predicted. When Grace climbed out to meet him, he looked past her with his curious gaze trained on Wallace.

"Is Wallace okay, Ma?" asked André, surveying the dry, dark stains on his teacher's shirt.

"Yes, he's all right. Not a scratch on him."

"Good, 'cause I've gotten used to him just the way he is."

"You and me both, son," agreed Grace. "You and me both."

Epilogue

It had been several weeks since the fatal shootings. The city of Dallas continued buzzing with gossipy tales of betrayal, interracial lust, and murder. André didn't shed a single tear when he attended Edward's funeral with Miss Pearl, Skyler, Grace, Wallace, and a who's-who of important city officials. By then, the word had gotten out about Edward's illegitimate teenage son, who was awarded a two-million-dollar insurance settlement as his only surviving heir. Grace, as her son's guardian, endorsed the check and deposited it along with the other child-support assistance Edward had provided over the years. Muriel's children had no claim to the money because, after all, they were fathered by Albert, who left behind seven kids but not one life-insurance policy. Grace promised to set up college funds for May and Becca because that's what Edward would have wanted. Muriel had to make it on her own, the best way she could, Grace decided.

As mourners dissipated from the burial site, André stared at them from the backseat of Wallace's car. He started to ask

Grace why so many people showed up to his daddy's funeral but instead mulled it over until he came to a conclusion that made sense in his young mind. Like him, André reasoned, scores of people had come because someone else made them.

Five months after the most tumultuous storm of Grace's life had blown through, she'd found herself in the women's lounge of another church on another Saturday afternoon. The same grunt of a wedding planner that barked orders to bridesmaids at Chandelle's wedding was at it again. Grace was forced to hold back a few choice words as she tarried through her normal prewedding ritual of mixing makeup foundation with traces of an exotic eye shadow to create a perfectly blended shade. This time, though, that perfect tone was fashioned for her.

Awkward Bob threw a hissy fit until Grace agreed to let him do her face. Actually he wasn't half bad, for a man who did his own face only half the time. Linda fussed over her hair. Shelia flirted with every available man who looked at her twice, but all she needed was one who seemed interested in treating the twins to a lingerie shopping spree. Her tiny condo couldn't stand another appliance of any kind.

Chandelle popped her head in to announce that the show could now officially get under way, since she'd arrived. Immediately afterward, she embraced Grace and kissed her on the cheek, much to Awkward Bob's dismay because he had applied her makeup perfectly moments before. "Grace, you're beautiful," Chandelle said, beaming from ear to ear. She rolled her eyes when Grace and Awkward Bob both said "Thank you" simultaneously. "Whut-ever, Bob," Chandelle hissed. "Grace, I can't believe you're finally settling down and letting someone make an honest woman out of you. It seems like yesterday that I was sitting in the chair with people fussing over me. Huh, enjoy it, girl 'cause it don't last," she chuckled, holding back her postwedding woes as not to diminish Grace's day in the sun.

"Thank you for everything, Chandelle. You inspired me and had me re-examining my life with a husband in the picture. That was the family portrait I always wanted to hang over my fireplace, but I didn't know how to go about getting it done. Now I'm sitting here, nervous as all get-out, and heating up too, if you know what I mean."

"Oh, do I," Chandelle sang fondly. "If I were you, I'd skip the panties. Getting out of them wastes three to four seconds, you'd better recognize."

Grace's mouth fell open. "Chandelle, you need to hush. You're in a church."

"And I'm talking married folks' business to a woman who's gonna be married in about thirty minutes."

"It's bad enough that I'm having second thoughts about wearing this white gown. My son is out there ushering. It's not like I'm going to fool anybody."

Chandelle took a seat next to Grace and shooed Awkward Bob away so she could have a heart-to-heart. "Grace, listen to me. There's a lot of things I don't know. I've proven that beyond a shadow of a doubt. Now, there are two things that haven't gotten by me. One, is that nobody is fooled by a thirty-six-year-old sistah as lovely as you, and the other is that every woman deserves to wear white. A wise lady once told me that, and she couldn't have been more right. Good luck out there, and don't forget, they all came here to see you. Gotta run, Marvin isn't used to being alone in public without me, and I aim to keep it that way. There are already way too many single hoochies sitting in the back."

"Places everyone," chirped the tightly wound wedding planner. "I said, let's do this!" Every one of the attendants leapt up and scattered like ants at a barbecue. "That's more like it," she boasted proudly. "What about you two?" She was speaking to Linda and Shelia, but she had no idea who she was talking to.

"Uh-uh, Miss Likes-to-Shout," Shelia spat loudly, "you

might run your mouth, but you don't run this. See, Grace is our best friend."

"That's right," Linda co-signed.

"Bridesmaids are the next best thing to getting married, ain't that right, Linda?"

"You know it is," Linda agreed wholeheartedly. "The next best thing."

"So, look here, if you plan on being able to get around without that clipboard broke off in yo—"

"Whoa-oh!" blurted Bob. "I think she's got it."

Shelia sucked her teeth and let it go. "I'm just sayin' we need a little time to be alone with our best friend before we have to share her with a man who might not let her come out and play when we want her to. Is that too much to ask from the next best things? I didn't think so. Poof, wedding planner be gone, and take Bewildered Bob with you." Grace laughed at two of the sweetest friends a woman could wish for as they did the best they knew how to engineer some private time. Shelia handed Grace the snapshot taken by the waiter at the restaurant who was working for a larger tip. "Friendship personified," she said, with a heavy sigh. "Remember this?"

"Of course I do," Grace cooed lovingly. "I didn't know you kept it. And don't worry, both of you will always be my girls. Always."

Linda slammed the door and locked it after Bob finally agreed to leave, following a terrible tantrum. Shelia primped Grace's hair while admiring how angelic she looked in the mirror. "You've been through a lot, Grace," Linda said sympathetically, also peering at her reflection. "If anyone could have come out of it on top, it had to be you."

"Yes, Lawd," Shelia chimed in. "We bet each other a car note over that vow of celibacy you were so serious about before meeting Wallace."

"And who won?" Grace asked them. "Who bet that I'd hold out all the way?"

"Uh, actually, we both bet that you wouldn't," Linda admitted reluctantly. "Shelia gave you sixty days, tops, before you fell on your face, and on some man's, too, while you were at it."

"Uh-uh, neither one of you heffas had faith in me," Grace chuckled. "It was hard, real hard at times."

"We know, we know. But you made it through unscathed," Linda assumed incorrectly.

"Not quite, I did fall on my face, but I repented, asked forgiveness, got my head together, and got back on the right track."

Shelia smirked at her reflection. "So, was Wallace one of the faces you fell on, Sister Grace? Huh, inquiring minds want to know."

"Sho' do, real bad." Linda cocked her head to the side.

"Y'all know I usually don't do this, but I'll tell you. I showed my tail before Wallace and I became an item. A minor hiccup, but that's it. Since then, I've been exclusive and waiting until tonight. I do expect to pull a few muscles though, making up for lost time."

Someone had to voice what Grace's closest friends were thinking. Shelia stepped up and laid it on the line. "Grace, honey? I know that Wallace is a real sweetheart and everything but . . . What if he can't do what you need him to do, when y'all doing it? And what happens if he's not *real tall*?"

"That is a valid question, Grace. It would be wonderful if Wallace could keep up in the bedroom," Linda stated suggestively.

Grace had considered that, of course. Successful marriages weren't all dependent on good sex, but deep inside she prayed for Wallace's health, width, and length during their journey together. "Ladies, thanks for your concern, but I am hopelessly intrigued, utterly devoted, and positively in love with this man. That's what's important. But if by chance there is a glitch in the program, I'll just have to tutor him day and night until he can catch on and keep up. I've spent a lot of time on my knees to get this far. And now that I'm here,

I'm looking forward to spending a lot more time down there, with my husband."

After spending a few days locked in the wedding suite at a remote island resort, Grace was certain that her vow of celibacy, although she'd fallen short, provided an avenue for God to work out things in her life that she couldn't see coming on the horizon. Once the rhetoric had been put aside, Grace was also certain that Wallace could do more than merely keep up. The blushing bride sent out a stack of postcards, when she came up for air, on the fourth day. The messages she addressed to Linda and Shelia were written in code. "Dear ladies, We're having a great time. The room is very nice. Hallelujah, Wallace *is tall, reeal tall*. Grace."

Want more Victor McGlothin?

Turn the page for previews of

SLEEP DON'T COME EASY

MS. ETTA'S FAST HOUSE

BORROW TROUBLE

and

SINFUL

Available now wherever books are sold!

SLEEP DON'T COME EASY

1

The night before lightning struck, Vera Miles witnessed one thing she never thought possible. When she came up empty after trailing a client's husband over a week, it appeared out of nowhere like a flash. It had to be the first time in history a black woman became fighting mad because her man was *not* sneaking around. Most of them, still in the market for a good man, would never have considered the thought of dismissing a good man, so Vera knew right off that something about Sylvia Everhart didn't fit. The hired snoop stood in her client's plush office, which was excessively decorated with finc furniture and extravagant original artwork, wondering why the woman glared at her with clenched teeth after hearing that her husband Devin had not cheated nor displayed any evidence to suggest he was the philandering type. Even after Devin Everhart babysat a few drinks at an upscale, happy hour mix-and-mingle joint, he kept to himself, despite several women offering a menu of after-hours innuendo they assumed he was there to get.

For seven days, Vera followed Devin from his office

building to a residential hotel a few blocks away, where he rented a room on the first floor. During that week, he ordered fast food and stepped out for quick bites, then returned to his single room with double beds, but always alone. Having been a private investigator for more than three years, Vera found it easy to make rational assumptions when shadowing a person for any length of time. She rarely had to guess whether there was a weakness for gambling, a predilection for sexual deviance or struggles with the bottle, because habits, especially bad ones, always had a way of showing themselves, like a stubborn pimple dabbled over with several layers of makeup. Before too long, it was bound to rear its ugly head.

During the previous week, Vera grew to appreciate the kind of man Mrs. Everhart's husband was, probably more than she'd care to admit. Not only was he nice to look at, he had proven to be a conscientious worker who believed in being on time for the nine-to-five grind and back on the clock after lunch at exactly an hour on the dot, with no deviations. Most women would have been smart enough to admire his dependable and responsible work ethic. While contemplating the drastic measures other women would have gone through to snag a quality mate like Devin, Vera found herself staring at a family of college degrees on her client's wall. Coincidentally, she tried to figure out how a woman with so much book sense suffered miserably when it came down to the good old-fashioned common sense necessary to cherish a fine man like hers.

Maybe Vera had tipped her hand by allowing myriad unprofessional thoughts to slow dance around that notion in her head too long. Perhaps Mrs. Everhart read those thoughts clearly enough to recognize Vera's lustful deliberations with her husband in mind. Whichever the case, Mrs. Everhart was mad as hell and didn't have any qualms about letting Vera know it when she finally switched her gaze from the client's accomplishments to the client's strained expression. That was the first time the private eye noticed how the woman's head seemed too big for her frail body. It had a lot to do with her outdated Mary-Tyler-Moore-flipped-up hairdo nesting above her shoulders and the fact that Sylvia Everhart was swelling with a rising tide of contempt. Seeing as how being hit with contemptible behavior from clients typically came with the territory, Vera shrugged off Mrs. Everhart's evil eye like water down a duck's back. After all, her client wasn't necessarily a bad person despite her soured disposition. Actually, under other circumstances, she might have even been tolerable. The woman's complexion was a shade lighter than Vera's, more of a toffee-brown hue. However, her spindly legs and slight build packaged into a perfect size four was enough to make Vera dislike her from the beginning. In fact, Vera considered all skinny women to be evil until proven otherwise. So far, not a single one of them had been given the benefit of the doubt. Not one.

After another long bout of silence, which was attached to that lingering glare Mrs. Everhart had propped up with a healthy dose of attitude, she decided to work her strategy from another angle. "I see," she said, looking Vera over as if she wasn't close to being satisfied with her abilities as a PI and just as displeased with the snug fit of the navy colored corduroy slacks hugging her curvy hips. Vera, whose figure floated between sizes ten and twelve depending on the cut, was partly to blame. At the time, she was an everyday twelve, hoping to get by with half a wardrobe that should have been given up, let out, or traded in. And Vera should have given it a great deal more thought before leaving the house with that particular pair of dress slacks wrangled over all her womanly goodness. True, it was an error in judgment to think that no one would have noticed, but that was beside the point. Mrs. Everhart's disapproving sneer overshadowed Vera's first mistake of the day. She'd graded Vera with her narrowed, condescending eyes, which pushed Vera farther away from observing professional courtesy and much closer to opening her mouth with something she had been dying to say.

"Perhaps," Mrs. Everhart continued, after a pinch of silence skirted by, "perhaps you didn't adequately apply yourself on my behalf, Ms. Miles."

"Vera," the PI whispered uncomfortably, after having been chastised.

"Excuse me?"

"I said Vera. Call me Vera."

"Like I was saying, *Ms. Miles*, I've paid you good money and I expect good results." That inflated head of hers begun to bobble slightly from side to side as she pressed hard with an ink pen against her checkbook. "Why don't I sweeten the pot? Some people need more inspiration than others to try harder." Mrs. Sylvia Everhart reached out her hand, accessorized with a host of diamond trinkets. "Here is a check for two thousand dollars. Perhaps doubling your weekly fee will entice you to get out there and bring me something I can use," she spat irritably.

A prideful disposition kept Vera from taking the check which dangled from the tips of the rich woman's skinny fingers like a doggie treat offered from a doting master. The only thing missing was the customary pat on the head that generally followed such an gift. Pride that Vera's grandparents instilled during her upbringing wouldn't allow her to bow and shuffle. It made her feel like a pooch presented with scraps from the eccentric woman's table, one with far more money than couth. That's when Vera sized her up for another reason. She figured Sylvia to be about five-five, a few inches shorter than herself, and guessed that she was at least thirty pounds lighter. Before Vera realized it, she'd imagined how silly Mrs. Everhart would look face down on the mean streets of Dallas after tossing insults then immediately being introduced to the concrete on the heels of it. But, they weren't on the mean streets and there was no real reason for Vera to get all worked up behind some stuck-up rich chick, black woman or not. Besides, no one would have known about the stack of situational ethics Vera kept tucked deep down in the bottom corner of her purse had she taken the money, added two-thousand digits to her bank register, and then sat at home on her butt watching *Tru TV* for a week. There were a number of ways to get even with the stick figure of a woman whom she couldn't stand but violence was the first one that came to mind. No one would have been the wiser, except Vera and that stubborn pride of hers. The same pride that made her strong some times played her like a fool. This was one of those foolish times.

"On second thought, Mrs. Everhart," Vera said, declining the money, "why don't you keep that money to buy yourself a clue? And if you happened to smarten up, you'd use it on a gang of marriage counselors to help you keep that good man of yours. I've had the pleasure of watching him for a solid week and he was a model husband, even when presented with some pretty nice can't-miss opportunities, if you know what I mean. Now here's something else you probably didn't know. Most men are generally as honest as their options but not Devin—he appeared to be a man who was missing his wife and wishing he was home." Sylvia put Vera in the mind of a toy poodle when she marched her child-like frame toward her in an angered rant.

"That shows just how little you do know, Ms. Miles. *Mr. Everhart* left home on his own accord, so I know he's out there running behind some tramp willing to degrade herself by doing the things men fascinate themselves with. I'm not into greasing his ego or anything else for that matter. I don't have to and I won't."

Vera couldn't believe her ears or her reaction. "Well, maybe you should have. Then your man might've stayed home." Those eleven little dirty words just slipped right out of her mouth before she could tell them to go sit down and mind their own business.

"How dare you!" Mrs. Everhart yelled, from somewhere above the top of her lungs. "Get out!"

Vera swore that all three of the wall mirrors in that office were going to shatter against the woman's loud screeching pitch. Laughing in her client's face behind a teenaged-style tantrum was Vera's next thought commingled with one that served the situation a tad bit better, so she went with the latter. "OK, I'll leave, but not before I tell you what I think the problem with you really is. Uh-huh, it seems to me that you were hoping your breakup was brought on by what some other woman was doing, but then you looked at me like I had on two different colored shoes when I showed up and informed you that Devin had not taken up with anyone else. That's disturbing, because it forces you to look at yourself and open to other folks' questions as to why your man ran off. I might be wrong but I doubt it. The way I see it, *Sylvia*, this is a big mess you've gotten yourself into and there isn't anyone else around to blame it on."

Suddenly, Mrs. Everhart's top lip began to quiver. She was so mad that Vera nearly giggled at the mere thought of that swollen head of Sylvia's popping off at the neck.

"Are . . . you . . . finished now or should I call the police to have you removed from my building?" Sylvia threatened.

"Yeah, I'm through but don't think about stopping payment on the check for the work I've already put in, or I'll be back and not as pleasant as I've been today."

Vera was well aware that people didn't like paying for bad news, unless it was wrapped around some want ads and grocery store coupons, so she raced to the nearest Wells Fargo branch to tender the check that was burning a hole in her pocket. She might have played a fool for the occasion, but she'd never once been mistaken for stupid.

It was just Vera's luck that the windows at the in-store

branch were closed, so she cussed the bank's employees under her breath for closing down on time as she headed up the aisles to shop for a few female necessities. Getting over her last client's upsetting idea of what a marriage was supposed to be still troubled Vera, so she cussed Sylvia Everhart's silly ideologies altogether. Several shoppers threw strange glances her way and each of them was extremely close to getting cussed out too. That's what usually happened when CRUMBS (Clients, Reasonably Upset and Meaning to Bust Somebody) didn't get what they wanted via Vera's investigation services. They'd smart off to her face and she'd cuss them out later, behind their backs.

That night, Vera applied all five of her bedtime beauty secrets then slid beneath the covers to rest her troubled mind. She closed her eyes, repeating her personal PI Anthem while trying to feel good about the money she had made, until the sandman climbed into bed right along with her. *Once the case is closed and the money is made, don't matter win or lose. Some bills have been paid.*

MS. ETTA'S FAST HOUSE

1

Penny Worth o' Blues

Three months deep into 1947, a disturbing calm rolled over St. Louis, Missouri. It was unimaginable to foresee the hope and heartache that one enigmatic season saw fit to unleash, mere inches from winter's edge. One unforgettable story changed the city for ever. This is that story.

Watkins Emporium was the only black-owned dry goods store for seven square blocks and the pride of "The Ville," the city's famous black neighborhood. Talbot Watkins had opened it when the local Woolworth's fired him five years earlier. He allowed black customers to try on hats before purchasing them, which was in direct opposition to store policy. The department store manager had warned him several times before that apparel wasn't fit for sale after having been worn by Negroes. Subsequently, Mr. Watkins used his life savings to start a successful business of his own with his daughter, Chozelle, a hot-natured twenty-year-old who had a propensity for older fast-talking men with even faster hands.

Chozelle's scandalous ways became undeniably apparent to her father the third time he'd caught a man running from the backdoor of his storeroom, half-dressed and hell-bent on eluding his wrath. Mr. Watkins clapped an iron padlock on the rear door after realizing he'd have to protect his daughter's virtue, whether she liked it or not. It was a hard pill to swallow, admitting to himself that canned meat wasn't the only thing getting dusted and polished in that backroom. However, his relationship with Chozelle was just about perfect, compared to that of his meanest customer.

"Penny! Git your bony tail away from that there dress!" Halstead King grunted from the checkout counter. "I done told you once, you're too damned simple for something that fine." When Halstead's lanky daughter snatched her hand away from the red satin cocktail gown displayed in the front window as if a rabid dog had snapped at it, he went right on back to running his mouth and running his eyes up and down Chozelle's full hips and ample everything else. Halstead stuffed the hem of his shirttail into his tattered work pants and then shoved his stubby thumbs beneath the tight suspenders holding them up. After licking his lips and twisting the ends of his thick gray handlebar mustache, he slid a five dollar bill across the wooden countertop, eyeing Chozelle suggestively. "Now, like I was saying, How 'bout I come by later on when your daddy's away and help you arrange thangs in the storeroom?" His plump belly spread between the worn leather suspender straps like one of the heavy grain sacks he'd loaded on the back of his pickup truck just minutes before.

Chozelle had a live one on the hook, but old man Halstead didn't stand a chance of getting at what had his zipper about to burst. Although his appearance reminded her of a rusty old walrus, she strung him along. Chozelle was certain that five dollars was all she'd get from the tight-fisted miser, unless of course she agreed to give him something worth a lot more. After deciding to leave the lustful old man's offer on the counter top, she turned her back toward him and then pretended to adjust a line of canned peaches behind the counter. "Like what you see, Mr. Halstead?" Chozelle flirted. She didn't have to guess whether his mouth watered, because it always did when he imagined pressing his body against up hers. "It'll cost you a heap more than five dollars to catch a peek at the rest of it," she informed him.

"A peek at what, Chozelle?" hissed Mr. Watkins suspiciously, as he stepped out of the side office.

Chozelle stammered while Halstead choked down a pound of culpability. "Oh, nothing, Papa. Mr. Halstead's just thinking about buying something nice for Penny over yonder." Her father tossed a quick glance at the nervous seventeen-year-old obediently standing an arm's length away from the dress she'd been dreaming about for weeks. "I was telling him how we'd be getting in another shipment of ladies garments next Thursday," Chozelle added, hoping that the lie sounded more plausible then. When Halstead's eyes fell to the floor, there was no doubting what he'd had in mind. It was common knowledge that Halstead King, the local moonshiner, treated his only daughter like an unwanted pet and that he never shelled out one thin dime toward her happiness.

"All right then," said Mr. Watkins, in a cool calculated manner. "We'll put that there five on a new dress for Penny. Next weekend she can come back and get that red one in the window she's been fancying." Halstead started to argue as the store owner lifted the money from the counter and folded it into his shirt pocket but it was gone for good, just like Penny's hopes of getting anything close to that red dress if her father had anything to say about it. "She's getting to be a grown woman and it'd make a right nice coming-out gift. Good day, Halstead," Mr. Watkins offered, sealing the agreement.

"Papa, you know I've had my heart set on that satin number since it came in," Chozelle whined, as if the whole world revolved around her.

Directly outside of the store, Halstead slapped Penny down onto the dirty sidewalk in front of the display window. "You done cost me more money than you're worth," he spat. "I have half a mind to take it out of your hide."

"Not unless you want worse coming to you," a velvety smooth voice threatened from the driver's seat of a new Ford convertible with Maryland plates.

Halstead glared at the stranger then at the man's shiny beige Roadster. Penny was staring up at her handsome hero, with the buttery complexion, for another reason all together. She turned her head briefly, holding her sore eye then glanced back at the dress in the window. She managed a smile when the man in the convertible was the only thing she'd ever seen prettier than that red dress. Suddenly, her swollen face didn't sting nearly as much.

"You ain't got no business here, mistah!" Halstead exclaimed harshly. "People known to get hurt messin' where they don't belong."

"Uh-uh, see, you went and made it my business by putting your hands on that girl. If she was half the man you pretend to be, she'd put a hole in your head as sure as you're standing there." The handsome stranger unfastened the buttons on his expensive tweed sports coat to reveal a long black revolver cradled in a shoulder holster. When Halstead took that as a premonition of things to come, he backed down, like most bullies do when confronted by someone who didn't bluff so easily. "Uh-huh, that's what I thought," he said, stepping out of his automobile idled at the curb. "Miss, you all right?" he asked Penny, helping her off the hard cement. He noticed that one of the buckles was broken on her run over shoes. "If not, I could fix that for you. Then, we can go get your shoe looked after." Penny swooned as if she'd seen her first sunrise. Her eyes were opened almost as wide as Chozelle's, who was gawking from the other side of the large framed window. "They call me Baltimore, Baltimore Floyd. It's nice to make your acquaintance, miss. Sorry it had to be under such unfavorable circumstances."

Penny thought she was going to faint right there on the very sidewalk she'd climbed up from. No man had taken the time to notice her, much less talk to her in such a flattering manner. If it were up to Penny, she was willing to get knocked down all over again for the sake of reliving that moment in time.

"Naw, suh, Halstead's right," Penny sighed after giving it some thought. "This here be family business." She dusted herself off, primped her pigtails, a hairstyle more appropriate for much younger girls, then she batted her eyes like she'd done it all of her life. "Thank you kindly, though," Penny mumbled, noting the contempt mounting in her father's expression. Halstead wished he'd brought along his gun and his daughter was wishing the same thing, so that Baltimore could make him eat it. She understood all too well that as soon as they returned to their shanty farmhouse on the outskirts of town, there would be hell to pay.

"Come on, Penny," she heard Halstead gurgle softer than she'd imagined he could. "We ought to be getting on," he added as if asking permission to leave.

"I'll be seeing you again, Penny," Baltimore offered. "And next time, there bet' not be one scratch on your face," he said, looking directly at Halstead. "It's hard enough on women folk as it is. They shouldn't have to go about wearing reminders of a man's shortcomings."

Halstead hurried to the other side of the secondhand pickup truck and cranked it. "Penny," he summoned, when her feet hadn't moved an inch. Perhaps she was waiting on permission to leave too. Baltimore tossed Penny a wink as he helped her up onto the tattered bench seat.

"Go on now. It'll be all right or else I'll fix it," he assured her, nodding his head in a kind fashion and smiling brightly.

As the old pickup truck jerked forward, Penny stole a

glance at the tall silky stranger then held the hand Baltimore had clasped inside his up to her nose. The fragrance of his store-bought cologne resonated through her nostrils for miles until the smell of farm animals whipped her back into a stale reality, her own.

It wasn't long before Halstead mustered up enough courage to revert back to the mean tyrant he'd always been. His unforgiving black heart and vivid memories of the woman who ran off with a traveling salesman fueled Halstead's hatred for Penny, the girl his wife left behind. Halstead was determined to destroy Penny's spirit since he couldn't do the same to her mother.

"Git those mason jar crates off'n the truck while I fire up the still!" he hollered. "And you might as well forgit that man in town and ever meeting him again. His meddling can't help you way out here. He's probably on his way back east already." When Penny moved too casually for Halstead's taste, he jumped up and popped her across the mouth. Blood squirted from her bottom lip. "Don't make me tell you again," he cursed. "Ms. Etta's havin' her spring jig this weekend and I promised two more cases before sundown. Now git!"

Penny's injured lip quivered. "Yeah, suh," she whispered, her head bowed.

As Halstead waddled to the rear of their orange brick and oak, weather-beaten house, cussing and complaining about wayward women, traveling salesmen, and slick strangers, he shouted additional chores. "Stack them crates up straight this time so's they don't tip over. Fetch a heap of water in that barrel, bring it around yonder and put my store receipts on top of the bureau in my room. Don't touch nothin' while you in there neither, useless heifer," he grumbled.

"Yeah, suh, I will. I mean, I won't," she whimpered. Penny allowed a long strand of blood to dangle from her angular chin before she took the hem of her faded dress and wiped it away. Feeling inadequate, Penny became confused as to in which order her chores were to have been performed. She reached inside the cab of the truck, collected the store receipts and crossed the pebble covered yard. She sighed deeply over how unfair it felt, having to do chores on such a beautiful spring day, and then she pushed open the front door and wandered into Halstead's room. She overlooked the assortment of loose coins scattered on the nightstand next to his disheveled queen-sized bed with filthy sheets she'd be expected to scrub clean before the day was through.

On the corner of the bed frame hung a silver-plated Colt revolver. Sunlight poured through the half-drawn window shade, glinting off the pistol. While mesmerized by the opportunity to take matters into her own hands, Penny palmed the forty-five carefully. She contemplated how easily she could have ended it all with one bullet to the head, hers. Something deep inside wouldn't allow Penny to hurt another human, something good and decent, something she didn't inherit from Halstead.

"Penny!" he yelled, from outside. "You got three seconds to git outta that house and back to work!" Startled, Penny dropped the gun onto the uneven floor and froze, praying it wouldn't go off. Halstead pressed his round face against the dusty window to look inside. "Goddamnit! Gal, you've got to be the slowest somebody. Git back to work before I have to beat some speed into you."

The puddle of warm urine Penny stood in confirmed that she was still alive. It could have just as easily been a pool of warm blood instead. Thoughts of ending her misery after her life had been spared fleeted quickly. She unbuttoned her thin cotton dress, used it to mop the floor then tossed it on the dirty clothes heap in her bedroom. Within minutes, she'd changed into an undershirt and denim overalls. Her pace was noticeably revitalized as she wrestled the crates off the truck as instructed. "Stack them crates," Penny mumbled to herself. “Stack ’em straight so’s they don’t tip over. Then fetch the water.” The week before, she’d stacked the crates too high and a strong gust of wind toppled them over. Halstead was furious. He dragged Penny into the barn, tied her to a tractor wheel and left her there for three days without food or water. She was determined not to spend another three days warding off field mice and garden snakes.

Once the shipment had been situated on the front porch, Penny rolled the ten-gallon water barrel over to the well pump beside the cobblestone walkway. Halstead was busy behind the house, boiling sour mash and corn syrup in a copper pot with measures of grain. He’d made a small fortune distilling alcohol and peddling it to bars, juke joints and roadhouses. “Hurr’up, with that water!” he shouted. “This still’s plenty hot. Coils try’n’a bunch.”

Penny clutched the well handle with both hands and went to work. She had seen an illegal still explode when it reached the boiling point too quickly, causing the copper coils to clog when they didn’t hold up to the rapidly increasing temperatures. Ironically, just as it came to Penny that someone had tampered with the neighbor’s still on the morning it blew up, a thunderous blast shook her where she stood. Penny cringed. Her eyes grew wide when Halstead staggered from the backyard screaming and cussing, with every inch of his body covered in vibrant yellow flames. Stumbling to his knees, he cried out for Penny to help him.

“Water! Throw the damned . . . water!” he demanded.

She watched in amazement as Halstead writhed on the ground in unbridled torment, his skin melting, separating from bone and cartilage. In a desperate attempt, Halstead reached out to her, expecting to be doused with water just beyond his reach, as it gushed from the well spout like blood had poured from Penny’s busted lip.

Penny raced past a water pail on her way toward the front porch. When she couldn’t reach the top crate fast enough, she shoved the entire stack of them onto the ground. After getting what she went there for, she covered her nose with a rag as she inched closer to Halstead's charred body. While life evaporated from his smoldering remains, Penny held a mason jar beneath the spout until water spilled over onto her hand. She kicked the ten gallon barrel on its side then sat down on it. She was surprised at how fast all the hate she'd known in the world was suddenly gone and how nice it was to finally enjoy a cool, uninterrupted, glass of water.

At her leisure, Penny sipped until she'd had her fill. "Ain't no man supposed to treat his own blood like you treated me," she heckled, rocking back and forth slowly on the rise of that barrel. "Maybe that's 'cause you wasn't no man at all. You just mean old Halstead. Mean old Halstead." Penny looked up the road when something in the wind called out to her. A car was headed her way. By the looks of it, she had less than two minutes to map out her future, so she dashed into the house, collected what she could, and threw it all into a croaker sack. Somehow, it didn't seem fitting to keep the back door to her shameful past opened, so she snatched the full pail off the ground, filled it from the last batch of moonshine Halstead had brewed. If her mother had ever planned on returning, Penny reasoned that she'd taken too long as she tossed the pail full of white lightning into the house. As she lit a full box of stick matches, her hands shook erratically until the time had come to walk away from her bitter yesterdays and give up on living out the childhood that wasn't intended for her. "No reason to come back here, Momma," she whispered, for the gentle breeze to hear and carry away. "I got to make it on my own now."

Penny stood by the roadside and stared at the rising inferno, ablaze from pillar to post. Halstead's fried corpse smoldered on the lawn when the approaching vehicle ambled to a stop in the middle of the road. A young man, long, lean, and not much older than Penny took his sweet time stepping out of the late model Plymouth sedan. He sauntered over to the hump of roasted flesh and studied it. "Hey, Penny," the familiar passerby said routinely.

"Afternoon, Jinxy," she replied, her gaze still locked on the thick black clouds of smoke billowing toward the sky.

Sam "Jinx" Dearborn, Jr., was the youngest son of a neighbor, whose moonshine still went up in flames two months earlier. Jinx surveyed the yard, the smashed mason jars and the overturned water barrel.

"That there Halstead?" Jinx alleged knowingly.

Penny nodded that it was, without a hint of reservation. "What's left of 'im," she answered casually.

"I guess you'll be moving on then," Jinx concluded stoically.

"Yeah, I reckon I will at that," she concluded as well, using the same even pitch he had. "Haven't seen much of you since yo' daddy passed. How you been?"

Jinx hoisted Penny's large cloth sack into the back seat of his car. "Waitin' mostly," he said, hunching his shoulders, "to get even."

"Yeah, I figured as much when I saw it was you in the road." Penny was one of two people who were all but certain that Halstead had killed Jinx's father by rigging his still to malfunction so he could eliminate the competition. The night before it happened, Halstead had quarreled with him over money. By the next afternoon, Jinx was making burial arrangements for his daddy.

"Halstead got what he had coming to him," Jinx reasoned as he walked Penny to the passenger door.

"Now, I'll get what's coming to me," Penny declared somberly, with a pocket full of folding money. "I'd be thankful, Jinxy, if you'd run me into town. I need to see a man about a dress."

BORROW TROUBLE

1

Night Train

A tortuous evening of bowing and shuffling had gotten the best of Baltimore Floyd, just like a one-armed boxer's desire to climb back into the ring got him knocked out every time. Flashing that cheesy grin he hated had left the smooth tan-colored drifter with a mean streak thicker than train smoke. Smiling back at countless blank faces of discouragement while serving a host of ungrateful, high-brow travelers in the last two dining cars on the Transcontinental Steamer had him wishing for better days and easy money. In the winter of 1946, times were hard. That meant tips didn't come easily, and come to think of it, "please" or "thank you" didn't, either. Hearing the train's whistle blow when it crept slowly across the Missouri state line put an awkward expression on Baltimore's face, one that almost slighted his charmingly handsome good looks. Agreeing to sign on at the railroad company as a waiter for an endless collection of snooty voyagers, with nasty table manners and even worse dispositions toward the Negro help, was simply another in a string of poor decisions plaguing Baltimore, who was a professional baseball player hopeful mostly, and a man with troubles certainly.

He'd seen nothing but rotten luck during the past month. The worst of it had happened when the gambling debt he couldn't pay off came haunting around his rented room to collect at about three o'clock in the morning. Two pistol-toting "go-getters" is what Baltimore called the hired thugs who broke down the door at Madame Ambrose's boarding-house, aiming to make him pay the devil his due or else send him straight to hell if he couldn't. It was a good thing the lady with the room directly across the hall from his didn't like sleeping alone, or he'd have been faced with meeting the devil firsthand that night. With three dollars in his pocket, every cent of it borrowed from the gracious neighbor lady, Baltimore had lit out of Harlem when the sun came up. He'd hitchhiked south, with a change of luck in mind and a bounty on his head.

Unfortunately, the change he'd hoped for was slow in coming, and his patience was wearing as thin as the sole on his broken-in leather work shoes. That awkward expression that welcomed Baltimore into Missouri melted into a labored grin when his best friend, Henry Taylor, a sturdy, brown-skinned sack of muscle, popped into the flatware storage room, balancing two hot plates weighed down with porter-house steaks, mashed potatoes, and green beans. Henry, just as tall as Baltimore and substantially brawnier, presented the dinner he'd undoubtedly lied to get his hands on or outright stole, while maintaining his professional, "on the time clock" persona. His black slacks held their creases, the starched white serving jacket was still buttoned up to the neck, and his plastic Cheshire cat grin, which the customers always expected, made a dazzling appearance.

"Dinner is served boss and not a moment too soon," Henry announced, once the door was latched behind him.

"You ole rascal, I don't care what you had to do to come up with this meal fit for a king, but I hope your eyes was closed when you did it," Baltimore teased, salivating over a dinner much too expensive for the likes of them. "I can't wait to get my hands on—," he started to say before hearing a light rap against the other side of the storage room door. "Here. Put the plates in the bread box, Henry," whispered Baltimore, fearing another waiter wanted to share in their late-night treasure. Some of them were unscrupulous enough to make waves by reporting thefts to the crew supervisor if they didn't get a cut.

"Shut that cupboard door all the way so's they can't smell the taters," Henry mouthed quietly as the light tapping grew into more insistent knocks.

When Henry opened the storage room door slowly, he was surprised to see a white face staring back at his. The man, who appeared to be nearing fifty, was fair-haired, with pale, blotchy skin. He was thinking something behind those steely blue eyes of his, Baltimore thought as he leaned his head over to see who was disturbing the first decent meal he'd had in a week. "Sorry, mistuh, but the dinner car's been closed for hours now," uttered Henry, guessing that was what the man wanted. "We's just putting the dishes away."

"Either one of you boys interested in making a few dollars, fetching ice and fresh drinking glasses for me and some sporting friends of mine?" the intruder asked, fashioning his remarks more in the manner of a request than a question.

"Naw, suh, I'm . . . I'm really whooped," offered Henry in a pleading tone.

"Hell, naw," was Baltimore's answer. "We's retired for the evening, done been retired, and besides, you don't see no *boys* in here." Venom was dripping from his lips after slaving deep into the evening only to incur some middle-aged white man getting between him and a four-dollar plate of food, with an off-the-cuff insult. "You best get on back to those sporting friends of yours," Baltimore added when the man didn't seem too interested in budging.

Henry swallowed hard, like always, when Baltimore got it

in his head to sass a white man to his face. He swallowed hard again when this particular white man brushed back his green gabardine jacket just enough to reveal a forty-four-caliber revolver.

"Yeah. You'll do rather nicely," answered the man in the doorway. He was leering at Baltimore now and threatening to take his bluff a step further if necessary. "Now then, I'd hate for us to have a misunderstanding. The head conductor might not like that, especially if he's awakened to terrible news."

Baltimore squinted at the situation, which was brewing into a hot mess he'd have to clean up later. He was in deep because he'd already decided just that fast to lighten the train's load and teach the passenger a lesson about respect he would take to his grave. Considering that the train wasn't due to arrive at the Kansas City station until eight a.m., only a fool would have put his money on that particular white man's chances of breathing anywhere near 7:59. "Well, suh, if'n you put it that way, I guess I'm your man . . . uh, your boy," Baltimore told him, flashing the manufactured beaming smile he was accustomed to exhibiting when bringing customers their dinner bill. "Just let me grab a bite to eat, and I'll be along directly."

"You'll come now," growled the uninvited guest. "And button your clothes. You look a ruffled sight," he added, gesturing at Baltimore's relaxed uniform. "I'll be right out here waiting."

"And he'll be right out, suh, right out," promised Henry, pulling the door closed. "Baltimo', what's gotten into you? That's a white man, and he's got six friends in that pistol, waiting to do whatever he tells 'em to."

"He ain't gonna shoot nobody," Baltimore reasoned as he fastened his serving jacket, huffing beneath his breath. "A stone killer does the doin' and don't waste time on the showin'. I'll be back tonight. You go on and have at my supper, too. Ain't no use in letting it get cold. Be too tough to chew then, anyway."

Henry put his face very close to Baltimore's in order to get his undivided attention. "Ahh, man, I know that look in your eyes, and I hate it. You got trouble in mind, but you told me you was through with that sort of thing."

Baltimore sighed as he eased a steak knife into the waistband of his black work slacks and pulled the white jacket down over it. "Don't appear that sort of thing is through with me, though, does it? Think of me when you eat my share. It'll make me feel better knowing you did."

Waiting impatiently in the aisle, the insistent passenger raised his eyes from the silver coin he'd been flipping over his knuckles when Baltimore came out of the tiny closet, holding a stack of glasses on a round tray. "Good. I was starting to get concerned about the two of you." The man was fond of the joke he'd told, so he chuckled over it, but neither of the black men found it amusing in the least. Both of them saw a dead man pacing in the other direction, wearing an expensive suit and a brown felt hat, and playing an odd little game where the stakes were dreadfully high. It was a skins game, Baltimore's favorite. Killing the white man on their way to the smoking car crossed his mind, but he suspected there'd be money to be had at the end of the night, maybe a lot of it. Before he chased those demons away, he told them to come back later, when he'd have need for them.

"I'm going to say this only once, so pay attention," the man grumbled. "When we get inside, I don't want you to speak, cough, or break wind. There are some very important people in there, and they won't stand for an uppity nigger interrupting their entertainment," he warned Baltimore. "I'll give you ten bucks for your time, when I'm convinced you've earned it." When Baltimore's gaze drifted toward the floor, the white man viewed it as a sign of weakened consent. He had no idea just how close he came to having his chest carved up like the porterhouse left behind in the flatware cabin. "Good," he continued. "Don't make me sorry for this."

"I'm already sorry," Baltimore wanted to tell him but didn't. Instead, he played along to get along, but soon enough he found himself wishing for a seat at that poker table. As the night drew in, and the smoke from those fancy cigars rose higher, so did the piles of money. Baltimore had learned most of the gamblers were businessmen heading to Kansas City for an annual automobile convention. He'd also discovered that the man who'd coerced him into servitude went by the name of Darby Kent, and for all of his gun-toting rough talk, he was the sorriest poker player this side of the Mississippi and spitting out money like a busted vending machine. Darby often folded when he should have stayed in, and then he often contributed to someone else's wealth when everyone reading his facial expressions knew he had a losing hand. After three hours of fetching and frowning, Baltimore was really disgusted. The way he looked at it, Darby was shoveling over his money, the money Baltimore had planned on relieving him of after the fellows were finished matching wits.

"Darby, looks like a bad run of luck," one of the other men suggested incorrectly. It was a run of overgrown stupidity.

"I'll say," another of them quipped. "Gotta know when to say when." After watching Darby toss back another shot of gin, he shook his head disapprovingly. "On the other hand, if you don't mind fattening my wallet, I won't, either." That comment brought a wealth of laughter from other players sitting around the musty room, smelling of liquor, sweat, and stale tobacco.

"I'll agree that the cards haven't exactly fallen in my favor up 'til now," Darby said as he grimaced. "Perhaps I could use a break." He laid the cards on the table, next to a mountain of money Baltimore guessed had to be close to ten thousand dollars. "Come on, you," Darby ordered his reluctant flunky, while motioning for Baltimore to collect his serving tray and an extra ice bucket.

Leaving all of that loot behind was like pulling teeth, but Baltimore forced himself to walk away. Had he not been confined to a moving train, there would have been a golden chance to stick up the card game and make a fast getaway. Unfortunately, there wasn't a hideout to dash off to afterwards, so the idea passed just as quickly as it had entered Baltimore's head. Baltimore fumed every step of the way he followed behind Darby, staggering and sullen. He was mad at himself for not going with his first mind to end their arrangement before Darby had all but opened his billfold and shook out a big stack of money for the better-suited players to divide amongst themselves.

When they reached a nearly depleted icebox inside the abandoned dinner car, Baltimore began filling one of the wooden buckets. Darby steadied his shoulder against the door frame to light up a cigar. He huffed and cussed that he should have been more conservative with his wagers.

"I'm beginning to think, maybe I've taken those other fellows too lightly," Darby opined openly, as if Baltimore gave a damn what he thought. Tired and angrier now, Baltimore sought to put that silly notion to rest.

"Say, Darby, lemme ask you something," Baltimore said, seemingly out of nowhere. He was facing the man while holding the bucket firmly at his side with his left hand, keeping his right one free. "Do you always lose your ass after showing it? I mean, you have got to be the dumbest mark I've ever seen." Baltimore watched Darby's eyes narrow disbelievingly after hearing a much cleaner diction roll off the black man's tongue. "See, the way I figure it, you resort to pattin' that pistol of yours when men like me don't step lively fast enough. I'll also bet the ten dollars you owe me that you're all bark and no bite. Ain't that right, suh?" Baltimore added, showing him how black men were skilled at adapting their speech to fit the occasion. When Darby stopped puffing on the stinky cigar poking out of his mouth, Baltimore smiled at him. "Ahh-ahh, not yet. I'll also bet you a nickel to a bottle of piss, if you go pulling that heater on me, you'll be dead before your body drops."

Darby spat the cigar onto the floor as he reared back and went for the revolver. Baltimore slammed the heavy ice bucket against his gun, snatched him by the throat, and then punched the steak knife into Darby's gut so hard, the handle broke off. Darby's mouth flew open as he anguished in pain. Baltimore watched intently as the white man gasped for breath like a fish out of water and clutched at the opening in his stomach. When Darby fell onto his knees, pain shooting through his body, he began to whimper softly. Baltimore was quick to stuff a bar towel in his mouth to shut him up. "Uh-huh, I knew you were all bark," Baltimore teased as he removed the pistol from Darby's shoulder holster and began riffling through his pockets. "Let's see how much you still have, you sorry bastard. Seventy-two dollars?" he ranted. "I knew I should have stuck you sooner." Suddenly, Baltimore heard someone coming, but there was nowhere to hide, so he raised the dying man's gun.

"Baltimo', that you?" someone uttered from the shadows. "Baltimo', it's me. Henry."

"Whewww, man, I almost blew a hole in you, thinking it was one of them white boys coming to see about the ice," Baltimore cautioned his closest friend. "Here. Hurrup. Help me get his jacket and pants off him."

Henry's eyes grew as wide as saucers. "Why you want to go and do that?" he asked apprehensively.

"'Cause he's just about my size, this here is a damn nice suit, and I don't want to get no blood on it," Baltimore told him flatly. When Darby's upper body started convulsing, Henry was ordered to stop it. "Come on now. Hold his head still."

Struggling to hold the man down, Henry was forced to

snap his neck when the groaning grew too loud to bear. After realizing what he'd done, Henry fell over on his behind like a repentant sinner. "Now you done got me involved," he fussed.

"Being my friend is what got you involved, Henry," Baltimore corrected him. "And you came through for me. I won't forget that. Now, let's get him off this train before somebody comes."

Reluctantly, Henry climbed to his feet and helped wrestle off the dead man's suit. He spied the fancy wing-tipped shoes on Darby's feet, but he could see right away, it wasn't any use to take those. Darby's feet were nearly four inches shorter than his. Then, he caught a glimpse of a shiny gold ring on the man's finger as they opened a dining car window to ease his body out onto the countryside. "Hold up, Balt. I'ma take this here ring for my troubles."

Baltimore pulled Darby's legs up to the sliding window and pushed against the cold January winds. "Naw, don't take the ring. It's the same kind the other fellas had on. That could come back to haunt you. Leave it on him. Hell, let the coyotes get it." Henry considered what his partner in crime had told him, pretended to agree, but then decided to swipe it, anyway. He eased the ring off and slipped it into his pocket behind Baltimore's back. As the train whipped around a bend, the wind howled. Henry closed the window while Baltimore neatly folded Darby's suit under his loose jacket.

"Where're you going now?" Henry asked, as he rolled out a mop bucket to clean up the mess they had made doing away with the corpse.

"To sleep so's I can get to dreaming about that steak that's been calling my name," Baltimore answered, slapping thirty dollars in his accomplice's palm. "Send somebody to wake me when we pull into Kaycee. Boy, I sho' am tired." He patted Henry on the back and started off, with a carefree saunter, as if he hadn't moments before goaded a man into a fight and ended his life as a result. Baltimore's ice-cold veneer aided him in sending Darby to another world altogether, but it didn't do a thing in the way of shaking off that bad luck shadow dogging him from town to town.

SINFUL

Chandelle stood in the kitchen of her small apartment, wrapping flatware in old newspaper. She was so excited when their mortgage loan for the house on Brass Spoon was approved two weeks before. Marvin had been sulking, been uncharacteristically unemotional, and been lacking what Chandelle needed in the bedroom. Although she tried to overlook it, his increasingly long hours at his job had only intensified an issue, and so did the anemic paychecks he'd been bringing home despite pulling double shifts. After being married for three years, she thought she knew her husband. In short order, Chandelle had to learn the hard way how little she knew herself.

"Marvin, do we have any more old papers?" she yelled, standing over a stack of china plates yet to be wrapped. "Marvin!" she shouted when he didn't answer.

"Yeah, I'm watching the game. Cowboys about to get that touchdown," he answered finally.

Chandelle rolled her eyes, then pretended she wasn't bothered that he didn't jump into action the way he used to when they first married three years ago. Then, he was all about her, and she missed that. To make matters worse, lately it seemed he'd been all about him, and that was unacceptable. "Marvin! I need you to get some more newspaper. I'm out already, and I haven't even done the china from our wedding yet. Marvin!" When Chandelle stepped around the corner into the tiny den, Marvin's eyes were fastened to the expensive flat screen as if he were sitting in the stadium on the fifty-yard line. "Ah-hmm," Chandelle uttered, clearing her throat. "Forget it, I'll run to the corner store myself," she said, pretending to collect her purse and coat.

"Good, now I can finish watching the boys put it on them rusty-butt Redskins," Marvin said, louder than he should have.

Chandelle cocked her head to the side, smirked her displeasure, and began to fume over the way her husband had blown her off for a stupid football game. "So, you really are gonna let me go out into the cold while you sit on your behind watching those scrubs lose another game?"

"What? Chandelle, don't trip," Marvin barked, dismissing her.

"Don't trip?"

"Hey, didn't you say you were going? Who am I to stop you?" Marvin answered. "Wait 'til halftime, and then I'll go. Otherwise, pick me up some pork skins, and I'll see you when you get back."

Yes, something had definitely changed. There was a time, not so long ago, when Marvin wouldn't have thought of sending his wife out into the elements. Chandelle didn't understand how it happened or when exactly, but she felt compelled to get at the root of the problem without waiting another minute. "Marvin, I want to talk," she announced, while standing directly in front of the television. "So you need to turn that off."

"Move, Chandelle," he fussed, trying to shoo her away. "Move girl, quit playing now."

Defiantly, she refused to relinquish her position. Instead, she crossed her arms and flashed Marvin a hardened stare. She said, "I'm not moving, so you can either watch the TV through me or you can talk to me. It's up to you. He leapt off the sofa, gently scooped her up, and moved her from blocking the tube. "Oh, it's like that now, huh?" Chandelle ranted, "You just gon' resort to putting your hands on me. Uh-huh, that's the way it always starts, with playful nonaggressive manhandling but before long the pushing, shoving, and slapping starts! Is that what you want to do, Marvin? You want to beat me?" Although Chandelle wasn't serious about Marvin hurting her, she was willing to say just about anything to get a rise out of him, since it had been awhile since he'd orchestrated one in the sack.

Marvin frowned at her, vehemently objecting to her unwarranted outburst. "Whutever, Chandelle. If that's what you call me putting my hands on you, you're slippin'." When her bothered expression didn't change in the least, Marvin huffed and marched past her. He snatched up a thin jacket off the wooden coatrack near the door. He wrestled it on quickly and felt in his pants pocket for the car keys. "Okay, since you want to put on a show, I'ma go watch the rest of the game at Chubby's where ain't nobody gonna be silly enough to jump up in front of the TV."

"Oh, I'm silly!" she sassed. "So how long have you had that opinion of me? You didn't used to think I was so silly when you begged me to marry you. Chandelle, I love you, I need you," she mocked. "Now look at you. All I wanted to do was talk, but you'd rather send me out into the cold so you can watch some stupid team who ain't worth a bent nickel anyway."

"Everybody's entitled to their own opinion," Marvin said casually as he searched around in the den for his keys. When Chandelle spotted them first, she dashed over to the end table and grabbed them. He said, "Cool, give 'em to me and I'll head back after the game."

"Ain't giving you nothing until you tell me what's wrong with you. Lately, you been hanging out with the boys, and that's not like you, Marvin. We hardly say two words to each other when you do come home, and that's not like us."

"Chandelle, we can talk about this when I get back from Chubby's. Now give me the keys," he demanded, getting more annoyed by his overdramatic wife.

"Uh-uh, not until you tell me what's so important out there that you can't seem to stay away from it. What's at the club that you don't have here? Drink, we got that. Music?" Chandelle asked, turning up the stereo system louder than she meant to. "What? Sounds like music to me. Oh, is it sex you're out there hunting for? Nah, I know it can't be that, because you don't even want the good stuff going to waste up in here." Chandelle was exasperated. She'd used everything she knew to make Marvin argue with her, but still he refused. He simply stood there with an annoyed look on his face that made her want to fight even more.

"Are you through now?" he asked finally. "Can I go, or are you not finished with the theatrics?"

"Why not, it's obvious that you don't care about us anymore. I don't know why we're moving on Friday. What we have now isn't much of a home. Three thousand square feet won't change that," Chandelle concluded loudly.

"Now you're talking," said Marvin, with a noticeably more excited demeanor. "I'm still not sold on buying that big of a house to begin with."

"Negro, please! The way you were running behind that real estate agent, you'd have said yes to every house she showed us if I wasn't there to stop you."

"Well, she was a hard worker, and I appreciate that," he answered and not too convincingly. "It's hard dealing with people who don't know what they want. I ought to know. Down at Appliance World, I spend most of my time breaking down my extensive product knowledge, per the salesman handbook, and explaining the differences between products.

Then the customers either go with the cheapest appliance or the one that matches what they already have. I'm just saying Bernie was a hard worker, is all."

"Yeah, I see she did a job on you. Since when did you start calling her Bernie, Marvin? Have you been talking to her when I'm not around? Y'all got a little thing going on?" Chandelle interrogated.

"Now I know I need to bounce. Give me the keys, Chandelle," he asked, sticking out his hand to receive them. "Chandelle, quit playing now and give 'em to me!" Instead of complying, she grabbed her sweatpants at the waist and dropped the keys down inside them.

"How bad do you want them?" she goaded. "Bad enough to take them from me?" As soon as she smarted off, Marvin lunged toward her. Chandelle shrieked at the top of her lungs, laughing as she ran around the small room to avoid capture. Marvin chased and Chandelle shrieked until he'd caught up to her. Unfortunately, Marvin stumbled over the sofa ottoman and came crashing down on the coatrack, knocking Chandelle against his prized flat screen. She tried to brace herself but couldn't. Chandelle and the television slammed hard against the floor. Both she and Marvin watched as a big puff of smoke rose from the expensive TV.

"It's ruined!" he shouted. "Twenty-five hundred dollars gone because you wanted some attention! I'm tired of how you act when you don't get your way. Now look at what you made me do!" Marvin was hot. Admittedly, he hadn't been as thoughtful as when they initially married, nor did he fully understand why. He still loved Chandelle, but she always demanded more than he had to give. He sometimes wondered if she should have married one of the ballplayers she'd dated before meeting him. Maybe then, she'd be happy now. And then too, maybe so would Marvin. After brooding over the television, smashed beyond repair, he went over to check on Chandelle when it appears she was actually injured. "You okay baby?" he asked, sincerely concerned.

"No, I'm not okay, and why did you check on that stupid thing before coming to see about me?" she replied, more salty than hurt. "Maybe now we can talk like I wanted to in the beginning."

Before Marvin had the time to process Chandelle's complaints, there were three hard knocks at the door. When they weren't answered quickly enough for someone's satisfaction, someone beat on it again.

"What?" Marvin yelled as he opened the door to find two police officers, one black and the other as white as a snowy day, and neither of them appeared too happy about being shouted at. "Well, what y'all want?" Marvin asked rudely. "Ain't nobody selling drugs here, so you might want to go and harass somebody else."

They took one look inside the apartment, discovering a knocked-over television set, a hole in the wall caused by Marvin flying into the coatrack that stood next to it, and Chandelle limping over to rest on the sofa. Both cops stepped inside the house then, and backed Marvin against the wall. "Miss, we're answering a public-disturbance call. One of your neighbors reported loud screaming and fighting," the taller, white officer stated, as if asking for Chandelle's side of the story.

The black cop had positioned himself between Marvin and the very attractive woman who was adequately filling out those sweatpants in a way that he appreciated. "Sistah," the black one called out to get her attention. "This your husband?"

Chandelle winced while rubbing her hip. "Yeah, we're married," she said softly.

"That don't give him the right to get physical with you, though," he told her, in a comforting voice that Marvin found offensive.

"Say, man! What do you think you're doing?" Marvin heaved, objecting to the officer using the situation to flirt with his wife.

"Shut up!" the black officer asserted. "I bet that's one of your problems, you don't want to listen." Again, he eyed Chandelle for her approval. Again Marvin objected harshly.

"Man, this ain't even right," he barked. "Y'all just can't run up in here like this and talk to me like I don't have any rights."

"And you can't go slapping your wife around any time you feel like it," replied the white cop.

"Sistah, did he hit you?" the black officer asked Chandelle.

"No, he didn't," she answered. "It wasn't even like that. Besides, it was partially my fault."

"Yeah, that's what all battered women say," the black office contended. "And I guess that flat screen just tossed itself on the ground 'cause it got tired of working?" His countenance had quickly undergone a sudden shift when Chandelle seemed to be protecting Marvin.

"Look, officers, this is a misunderstanding—" Marvin tried to explain before the black cop shut him up by placing his hand on his holstered department-issued revolver.

"Nah, I understand real good how this sorta thing goes," he assumed incorrectly. "Miss, you say he didn't hit you but it's obvious you're shook up and mishandled. Now, how do you expect us to believe he didn't put his hands on you?"

"Well, yeah he did but it wasn't . . ." Chandelle began to say before she realized those were the magic words the cops were waiting for. "Hey, hold on."

"It's too late now, ma'am," argued the white one as his partner took great pleasure in doing the honors.

"Homeboy, you picked the wrong day to jump on your girl, and as fine as she is, you deserve to go down," the other whispered to Marvin, while tightening the cuffs behind his back. "You have the right to remain silent."

"Ahhh, man. Y'all taking me to jail?" asked Marvin, as he dug his heels into the carpet. "This ain't right. Chandelle, please tell them I didn't mean to hurt you."

"She already told us all we needed to hear to lock you up for spousal abuse. Anything you or your wife says can be used in the court of law," he continued sarcastically as he gave Chandelle the evil eye like a jerk who had just been rejected at a nightclub. "That means you oughtta shut up, and ole girl should have kept her trap closed too." He shoved Marvin in the small of the back with his nightstick to prod him along when he saw that there might be a struggle in the making.

"Man, you ain't got to be pushing that thing in my back," Marvin snapped, as he exited the apartment. "Y'all know this ain't right!"

Chandelle was mortified. It was all happening too fast for her to grasp. One minute they were horseplaying, and the next, he was in the midst of being hauled off. "I told y'all he wasn't trying to hurt me. I told you that. Hey! Where are you taking him?" She chased down the stairs behind them, barefoot and beside herself. "Wait. Marvin, I didn't mean for this to happen."

"Go back in the house, Chandelle. You've said enough already," he answered, as they shoved him into the back of the police squad car. She backed up onto the curb and watched as they drove away, wondering how something so innocent turned out to be so bad. Tears streamed down her face as she climbed the stairs to the apartment. The look on Marvin's face, as if he'd been betrayed and heartbroken, was indelibly stamped on Chandelle's mind. She was afraid he wouldn't be able to get past it. However, Chandelle had no idea how much she'd be faced with letting go and getting past, once she learned that another woman had paid Marvin's bail and taken him in to help soothe his pains, and hers.